Danielle Steel has been hailed as one of the world's most popular authors, with over 530 million copies of her novels sold. Her many international bestsellers include *Loving, Star, Family Album, The Ring, Summer's End, Season of Passion* and other highly acclaimed novels.

Visit the Danielle Steel website at www.daniellesteel.com

By Danielle Steel

* published outside the UK under the title PASSION'S PROMISE

DANIELLE STEEL

Wanderlust

sphere

SPHERE

First published in Great Britain in 1986 by Michael Joseph Ltd
Published by Sphere Books Ltd in 1986
Reprinted by Warner Books in 1994
Reprinted by Time Warner Paperbacks in 2002
Reprinted by Time Warner Books in 2005
Reissued by Sphere in 2010
Reprinted by Sphere 2011, 2012

A CIP catalogue record for this book
is available from the British Library.

ISBN 978-0-7515-4388-9

Typeset in New Baskerville by Hewer Text UK Ltd, Edinburgh
Printed and bound in Great Britain by
Clays Ltd, St Ives plc

Papers used by Sphere are from well-managed forests
and other responsible sources.

MIX
Paper from
responsible sources
FSC
www.fsc.org FSC® C104740

Sphere
An imprint of
Little, Brown Book Group
100 Victoria Embankment
London EC4Y 0DY

An Hachette UK Company
www.hachette.co.uk

www.littlebrown.co.uk

To my most beloved wanderers,
both of whom would infinitely prefer
the Amazon, or Manchuria,
and certainly the Orient Express,
to a stroll in Central Park . . .
Both of whom began my life,
in different ways . . .
the one to whom I gave
the very beginning of my life . . .
and the other all the rest:
My father, John,
and my husband, John . . .

And to a very, very special little girl,
Victoria, precious, precious child.
May you not wander too far away from me
as times goes on,
but just far enough to satisfy your soul.

With all my love,
d.s.

Wanderlust

wander, wander
wandering,
meandering,
the urge to roam,
to dance,
to fly,
to be,
the search for
free,
the need to see
to go
to find
to search
to do,
my thirsts
so easily quenched
so close to home
and yours so grand,
so elegant,
so marvellous,
climbing mountaintops
and elephants
and tiger hunts
and dancing bears
and far off stars
and trips to mars
and all of it
so wild,

so vast,
so free,
as you go wander,
wander,
wandering,
and then the best
part of all
when, satisfied,
complete,
and happy now,
you wander
slowly
home
to me.

Everything in the house shone as the sun streamed in through the long French windows. The carved mahogany mantelpiece in one of the two front parlours had been polished until it sparkled, its carved rosettes and female busts oiled to perfection. The long marquetry table in the centre of the room was equally handsome and had been equally well tended, although it was almost impossible to see it beneath the neat stacks of treasures that had been gathering there for weeks. Carved jades, enormous silver platters, lace tablecloths, two dozen magnificently carved crystal bowls, and at least three dozen silver salt and pepper shakers, and fourteen silver candelabra. The wedding gifts were lined up on the table, as though waiting for inspection and at the end of the table a pad and black fountain pen, where each name could be inscribed, the donor and the gift, to be thanked when the bride had time. One of the pantry maids dusted the offerings daily, and the butler had seen to it that the silver was polished, just as everything in the Driscoll mansion was. There was an aura of restrained opulence here, of enormous wealth that was clearly apparent but never flaunted. The heavy velvet drapes and lace curtains in the front parlour kept out curious eyes, as did the heavy gate surrounding the house, the well-tended hedge, the trees beyond. The Driscoll home was something of a fortress.

A female voice called out from the main hall just past the sweeping staircase. The voice was barely raised but one could hear it clearly, as a tall young woman with small hips, long legs, and deliberately carved shoulders stepped into the front parlour. She was in a pink satin dressing gown, wore her reddish hair in a chignon, and looked to be barely more than in her early twenties. There was a softness to the drape of the satin gown, yet there was nothing soft about her. She stood erect, looking directly at the table laden with gifts, her eyes moving slowly across the treasures, nodding slowly, and then stepping closer to the table to read the names she had written down . . . Astor . . . Tudor . . . Van Camp . . . Sterling . . . Flood . . . Watson . . . Crocker . . . Tobin . . . They were the cream of San Francisco, of California . . . of the country. Fine names, fine people, handsome gifts. Yet she did not look excited as she took a quick step to the window and stood looking out at the gardens. They were immaculately kept, just as they had been ever since her childhood. She had always loved the tulips her grandmother planted each spring, a riot of colour, and so different from the flowers in Honolulu . . . she had always loved this garden. She exhaled slowly, thinking of all she had to do that day, and then wheeled slowly on a pink satin heel, squinting dark blue eyes at the richly burdened table. The gifts certainly were pretty . . . and the bride would be too . . . if she ever went for a fitting. Audrey Driscoll glanced at her slender wrist and the narrow diamond watch that had been her mother's. It had a small ruby clasp and she loved it.

There were two pantry maids on the main floor, a butler, an upstairs maid to tend to their bedrooms, and a cook belowstairs with a maid and an assistant of her own . . . two gardeners . . . a chauffeur . . . in all a staff of ten that kept Audrey very busy. And yet she was used to all this. She had been running the house for fourteen years now, since she had come to the house from Hawaii. She had been eleven then, and Annabelle seven, when her parents had died in Honolulu. There had been nowhere to come but here. Her mind drifted back to the foggy morning they'd arrived, as Annabelle clutched her hand and sobbed loudly, terrified. Her grandfather had sent his housekeeper to bring them back from the Islands, and she and Annabelle had been seasick all the way home. But not Audrey, never Audrey. It was she who nursed old Mrs Miller, the housekeeper, when she died of influenza four years later. But it was Mrs Miller who had taught Audrey everything there was to know about running a fine old house like this one. She had also taught her exactly what her grandfather expected. And Audrey had learned her lessons well. She ran his house to perfection.

The whisper of her pink satin dressing gown was the only sound in the empty room as she hurried into the dining room, took her place at the empty table and pressed the discreet ruby and jade bell push beside her seat. She took her breakfast here every morning, unlike her sister, who ate breakfast upstairs, on a tray covered with impeccably starched linen.

A maid in a grey uniform with stiff white apron, cuffs, and cap immediately appeared, glancing nervously at the tall young woman sitting so erect in the Queen Anne chair she always occupied at the foot of the table.

'Yes, Miss Driscoll?'

'Only coffee for me this morning, thank you, Mary.'

'Yes, Miss Driscoll.' Her eyes like blue glass, there was no smile as Audrey watched her. They were afraid of her, most of them, except those who knew her well . . . who remembered the little girl careering around the lawn . . . the childhood games . . . the bicycle . . . the time she fell out of the Australian pine tree . . . but this Mary knew none of that. She was a girl of Audrey's years, and she knew only the woman with a firm hand and strong ideas and only secretly a splendid sense of humour. It was hidden there in the dark blue eyes . . . it was there . . . if one knew how to find it. But too few did . . . she was only . . . Miss Driscoll . . . the spinster . . .

They called her the spinster sister. Annabelle was the beauty. It was no secret between them. And Edward Driscoll had always said it openly. Annabelle had the frail blonde look of an angel, that look of total fragility that was so popular in the thirties . . . and the twenties . . . and decades and centuries before that . . . Annabelle the little princess . . . the baby . . . Audrey could still remember holding her in her arms and crooning to her after their parents had died on the way home from Bora-Bora. Their father had never been able to resist an adventure, and their mother had followed him everywhere he went, for fear that he would leave her if she didn't. In the end, she had even followed him to the bottom of the ocean. The wreckage was never found. The ship went down in a storm two days out of Papeete, and the girls were left alone in the world, with only their grandfather ... poor Annabelle had been terrified when she saw him, and Audrey had held her hand so tightly their fingers were white as he watched them. ... Audrey smiled to herself as she thought of it. He had terrified them even then. Or tried to ... especially poor little Annie.

Her coffee was poured from a silver pot with an ivory handle. It had come home with her from Honolulu, along with other treasures that had belonged to her parents. Her father had cared little for all of that, and most of what her mother had brought from the mainland had remained in crates. He was far more interested in jauntering around the world, far more in love with the albums he put together after his travels. Audrey had them still, on bookshelves in her room. Her grandfather hated seeing them, they only served to remind him of his loss ... his only son ... The Fool, he always called him. A wasted life ... two wasted lives ... and two little girls foisted on him. He pretended to hate the inconvenience at the time, and insisted they would have to make themselves useful. He had demanded that Annabelle learn to embroider and sew, and she had, but his demands of Audrey had been fruitless. She enjoyed neither sewing nor drawing, nor gardening, nor baking. She was hopeless at watercolours, wrote no poetry at all, hated museums, and the symphony even more ... but she liked photography, and adventure books, and tales of distant, far-off places. She went to lectures given by absurd, remote scholars, and often stood out at land's end, her eyes closed, sniffing the sea, thinking of the distant shores reached by the fingertips of the Pacific Ocean. And she ran a fine house for him, had a good hand with the servants, checked over the books for him each week, kept the house well stocked, and saw to it that no one cheated him of a penny. She would have been good at running any business, except that there was none to run. Only the home of Edward Driscoll.

'The tea is ready, Mary?' Without looking at her watch, she knew that it was eight fifteen and she knew that her

4

grandfather would be down at any moment, dressed as he was each morning, as though he still had an office to go to. He would harrumph, look at Audrey angrily as he always did, refuse stolidly to speak to her, glare once or twice, sip his tea, read the newspaper, eat two soft-boiled eggs, one slice of toast, drink one more cup of English tea, and then bid her good morning. His morning ritual did not unnerve Audrey, who barely seemed to take notice of him. She had begun reading his newspaper when she was twelve, and had discussed it with him seriously whenever she had a chance. At first, he had been amused, and then eventually he had realised how much of it she absorbed and how well formed her opinions were. They had had their first major political disagreement on her thirteenth birthday and she hadn't spoken to him for a week, much to his delight. He had been terribly proud of her then, and still was. It was a great source of pleasure when shortly afterwards she found her own paper at her place in the morning. Since then she read her paper every morning, and when he finally wished to speak to her, she was more than happy to discuss with him any items that had caught his interest. They would then proceed to argue horribly about everything they read, from world political to local news, even to stories about dinner parties given by their friends. They rarely agreed on anything, which was why Annabelle hated having breakfast with them.

'Yes, miss. The tea is ready.' The maid in the grey uniform said it as though gritting her teeth, bracing herself for an enemy attack, and a moment later it came. His careful step in the hall, as his impeccably shined shoes left the Persian rug for a moment before meeting another in the dining room, his growling harrumph as he pulled back his chair, sat down, and stared only for a fraction of an instant at Audrey, and then carefully unfolded his newspaper. The maid poured tea while he glared at her, and then cautiously he sipped it. By then, Audrey was engrossed in the news, totally unaware of how the summer sunlight shone on her copper hair and her long delicate hands holding the newspaper. For an instant, he watched her, caught as he often was by her beauty, though she didn't know it. It was that which made her even more lovely, the fact that she never gave it any thought. Unlike her sister who thought about nothing else.

'Good morning.' It was a full thirty minutes later before the words erupted from him, his immaculate white beard barely moving as he spoke, his blue eyes a blaze of summer sky that belied his eighty summers. The maid jumped as he spoke, as she did each morning. She hated serving him breakfast, just as Annabelle hated eating with him. Only Audrey seemed impervious to the gruffness of his manner. She acted no differently than she would have if he had smiled and kissed her hand and called her pretty names each morning.

There were no pretty names on Edward Driscoll's tongue. There never were. Never had been, except for his wife, but she had been dead for twenty years, and he had pretended to be hardened ever since then, and in many ways he was. He was a handsome, beautifully groomed man, once tall and still erect with snowy white hair, a full beard and handsome, broad shoulders. He walked with a careful but determined step, a silver-tipped ebony cane held in one powerful hand, as he gesticulated forcefully with the other. As he did now, glancing over at Audrey.

'I suppose you read the news. They nominated him, the fools. Damn fools, all of them.' His voice boomed in the wood-panelled dining room as the young maid quaked and Audrey unsuccessfully concealed a smile. She met his eyes squarely with her own blue eyes, and there was a hint of similarity between them.

'I thought you'd be interested in reading that.'

'Interested!' he shouted at her. 'He doesn't have a chance, thank God. Hoover will get in again. But they should have gone with Smith instead of that idiot.' He had been reading of Franklin Roosevelt's nomination at the Democratic Convention in Chicago, in Lippmann's column. And Audrey had easily anticipated his reaction. He was a staunch supporter of Herbert Hoover, in spite of the fact that this had been the worst year of the Depression thus far. But her grandfather had refused to acknowledge that. He still thought Hoover a fine man, despite the armies of starving unemployed across the nation. The Depression had not touched them, and so he found it impossible to fathom the extent to which it had touched others.

But Hoover's politics had caused Audrey's 'defection,' as Edward Driscoll called it. She was going to vote for the Democrats this time, and she was very pleased with Franklin Roosevelt's nomination.

'He won't get in, you know, so don't waste your time looking so pleased for him.' Edward Driscoll looked irate as he set down the paper.

'He might. He really should.' Her face sobered, thinking of the economic condition the country was in. It was terrifying, and it always upset her. Her grandfather didn't like talking about it, because doing so implied that it was Hoover's fault. Annabelle didn't seem to care what he said, but Audrey was very, very different. 'Grandfather,' she eyed him carefully now, fully aware of what she was doing and the reaction she would get from him, 'how can you pretend that nothing is happening out there? This is 1932, scores of banks just went under in Chicago, right before the Democratic Convention; our whole country is out of work, starving in the streets. How the devil can you ignore that?'

'It's not his fault!' He banged a fist on the table and his eyes blazed.

'The hell it's not!' Audrey spoke heatedly but with an undertone of ironic candour.

'Audrey! Your language!' She did not apologise to him, she didn't feel she had to. He knew her well and she knew him. And she loved him dearly, whatever his politics were.

She smiled at him now as he glared ominously at her. 'I'll make you a bet right now that Franklin Roosevelt gets in.'

'Nonsense!' He brushed away the thought with a hand that had been only Republican for a lifetime.

'Five dollars says he does.'

7

He narrowed his eyes at her. 'You know, despite all my efforts, you have the manners of a truck driver.'

Audrey Driscoll laughed and stood up, looking anything but that in the pink satin dressing gown with slippers to match, and there were tiny diamonds clipped to her ears. Like the watch, they had been her mother's and she always wore them. 'What are you doing today, Grandfather?' He didn't do a great deal any more. He saw his friends, went to lunch at his club, the Pacific Union, and when he returned he took a nap every afternoon. In his eightieth year, he was entitled. Once, he had been one of San Francisco's foremost bankers. But having retired ten years before, his life was quiet now, except for his two granddaughters living with him, soon to be reduced to one. But as he had admitted to a friend only the day before, as long as it was only Annabelle, he wouldn't miss her. She was the acknowledged beauty, but Audrey had the spine and spirit. He needed her. But he and Annabelle had never really become friends. Audrey always stood between them, more than anything to protect her little sister. Annie was the baby she had inherited from her mother, and she had never let her down, and wouldn't now. She was planning a magnificent wedding for her.

Edward Driscoll's eyes met Audrey's now. 'I'm going to my club, and I suppose you and your sister are going to Ransohoff's to spend all my money.' He pretended to be distressed, but in spite of the Depression, he wasn't. All of his money was so carefully invested that the bad times had barely made a ripple on his private waters.

'We'll do our best.' Audrey smiled matter-of-factly at him. She bought very little for herself, as was always the case, but Annabelle still needed a number of things for her trousseau. And there were to be seven bridesmaids in her wedding. Audrey was to be maid of honour. J. Magrien had done the wedding gown, of antique French lace, encrusted with tiny pearls, with a high, high neck, which would frame Annabelle's delicate face, with a veil of the same antique lace and French tulle to set on her spun gold hair. Audrey was extremely pleased with the effect of the beautiful veil and gown, as was Annie. The only problem was getting her to go to fittings. The wedding was in three more weeks at Saint Luke's Episcopal Church, and there were a thousand details to attend to.

'And by the way, Harcourt will be here for dinner.' She always tried to warn him in the morning. Now and then he forgot, and he would be furious to find some strange face, or even a familiar one, at his dinner table with no warning. And now he stared at her, as he always did at the mention of his future grandson-in-law. He was never quite convinced that Audrey wasn't jealous. It was difficult to imagine that she wasn't. Annabelle was only twenty-one, and Audrey was twenty-five after all, and in most people's eyes, not the family beauty. She had a tendency to make herself plain, to wear her hair pulled back too tightly, no rouge on her ivory cheeks to give them some colour, no mascara to darken her auburn lashes, no lipstick to accentuate the full lips that would have been sensuous if she'd let them. But she seemed to want none of that. She had had no serious beaux. There had been several suitors over the years, but her grandfather had always scared them off. And Audrey didn't seem to care. To her, they all seemed so sedentary and very boring. She sometimes dreamed of a man like her father with adventure in his soul, and a passion for exotic places, but she had never met anyone even remotely like him. And Harcourt didn't fit the bill either, though he was perfect for her sister.

'He's a handsome lad, isn't he?' Her grandfather's eyes combed hers, as they always did, expecting to see something that wasn't there and never had been, even if she had met Harcourt first, even if he had taken her dancing once or twice. But she had relinquished him happily to her sister, and in spite of what people might think, she did not pine for him or regret it. He would never have fed the hunger in Audrey's soul – she doubted if anyone could. What she longed for she found in the photographs she took, and the tattered albums left to her by her father. There was something deep within her so like him. Even their photographs were much the same, their eye, their perception, their hunger for the rare and faraway. . . . 'Harcourt will make a good husband to Annabelle.' Her grandfather always said it as though taunting her, or pressing her to see her reaction. He still thought she had made a mistake in giving him up, to her younger sister. He still didn't understand what was within her. Few people did. No one in fact. But it didn't matter to her. For years, Audrey had been used to keeping her own counsel about her private dreams. She couldn't indulge them anyway. Her place was here, running her grandfather's home and being there for him. And now she smiled at her grandfather, with the slow smile that began in her eyes and moved cautiously to her lips and made her look as though she were restraining gales of laughter. It always made one wonder what the rest of the joke was, as though she knew something one didn't . . . as though there was more . . . and there was . . . there was a lot more of Audrey Driscoll, but no one knew it. Even her grandfather didn't suspect just how far her dreams went, or how great her hunger to follow in her father's footsteps. She was not cut out for the life destined for the women of her times, as she knew only too well. She would rather have died than settle down and marry Harcourt.

'What makes you think he'll be such a good husband?' She smiled mischievously at her grandfather. 'Just because he's a Republican like you?' Audrey teased him and he took the bait.

Edward Driscoll's eyes darkened and he was about to answer her as they heard a sigh behind them. It was Annabelle in a cloud of blue silk and cream-coloured lace, her hair cascading over her shoulders as she looked at Audrey in despair. She stood almost a foot shorter than her older sister, and she seemed extremely nervous, as her hands fluttered like tiny birds. To Audrey she always seemed so graceful. She was unlike Audrey in so many ways, and she relied completely on her calm, capable older sister.

'Are you two already talking politics at this hour of the morning?' She cast a hand over her eyes as though she were in pain and Audrey laughed. They talked politics much of the time, mostly because they enjoyed it. They even enjoyed their fights, which invigorated them both, though horrified Annabelle, who found the subject of politics boring, and their arguments completely unnerving.

'Franklin D. Roosevelt won the nomination at the Democratic Convention in Chicago last night. You might like to know that.' Audrey always thought it important to keep her informed, although she never cared and Annabelle looked up at her blankly.

'Why?'

'Because he beat Al Smith and John Garner.' Audrey spoke matter-of-factly and Annabelle shook her head, looking petulant and annoyed, but very pretty.

'No . . . I mean why would I like to know that?'

'Because it's important!' Audrey's eyes blazed at her as they did at no one else. She wouldn't tolerate that nonsense from her, although she herself had known for years that it was hopeless. Annabelle didn't give a damn about anything except her face and her wardrobe. 'He may be the next president of our country, Annie. You have to pay attention to things like that.' She tried to be gentle with her, but there was an edge to her voice. She had always wanted her to be more interested in the world, and yet she wasn't. It was amazing to realise how different they were. Sometimes it was hard to believe they came from the same parents. Even their grandfather had said as much.

'Harcourt says that an interest in politics is vulgar in a woman.' She shook her golden curls and looked defiantly at them both as Edward Driscoll stared at her in fascination. She was an amazing little creature, and pretty certainly. And she was actually a great deal like her mother . . . but Audrey . . . Audrey was so like the son he had loved . . . if only he hadn't . . . but there was no point thinking that now . . . damn crazy places . . . he had been everywhere from Samoa to Manchuria over the years, and what good had it done him? 'Besides,' Annabelle went on, 'I think it's disagreeable of you to be talking politics at breakfast. And bad for your digestion.'

11

Edward Driscoll looked truly stunned and Audrey had to turn away to conceal her smile. When she turned back again their eyes met over Annie's head. There was a hidden caress there for her, not that he would ever have known the words to put to it. 'I'll see you both at dinner tonight. And Harcourt.' He made good his escape into his library as Audrey watched his retreating back. He was a little more bent than he had been the year before, but barely. He was a proud, strong man, and Audrey felt she owed him a great deal. The rest of her life perhaps . . . or at least herself for the rest of his. He needed her to run his house. And as she thought of it, she looked down at her younger sister. She had a great deal to learn about running a home, and she had staunchly refused to learn any of it from her older sister insisting that Harcourt said all she had to do was look pretty and have a good time and he'd take care of the rest for her. Harcourt thought it was 'vulgar' for a woman to take too much responsibility, Annie said whenever she could, unaware of the barbs she was casting at her sister, who remained steadfastly amused, and unaffected by Harcourt's views of what was 'vulgar'.

'Don't forget you have a fitting for your wedding dress today,' she reminded Annabelle as they drifted from the room, just as the library door slammed firmly closed. Audrey knew that he had gone in there to smoke a cigar and sit by himself for a while, before being driven to the Pacific Union Club. He would sit staring into the distance, dreaming of old times, reading letters from friends, composing responses in his head before writing them out that afternoon. There was little left for him to do, unlike Audrey who had a wedding for five hundred guests to plan, and a sister who relied on her completely.

'I don't want to go downtown today, Aud. It was too hot yesterday afternoon, and I still have a headache.'

'Too bad. Take an aspirin before you go. You only have three weeks until the wedding. And did you check the gifts that came in yesterday?' She took her firmly by the arm and shoved her gently into the front parlour. The long table was hourly more laden with offerings from their friends and Harcourt's.

'Oh, God . . .' She started to whine, which always made Audrey want to shake her. '. . . look at all the thank-you notes I'll have to write! . . .'

'Look at all the pretty gifts you got! Be grateful, don't complain.' Audrey was more like Annabelle's mother than her older sister. She had had Audrey's undivided attention for fourteen years, to a far greater extent than she would ever have had their mother's. Audrey had even gone to college nearby at Mills, so she could be close to her sister, who had not gone on to college after Miss Hamlin's. But no one had expected her to, since everyone said that Audrey had the brains and Annabelle the beauty.

'Do I really have to go downtown today?' She looked imploringly up at Audrey, who marched her upstairs, made her get dressed, and sat her down to write half a dozen thank-you notes while she got dressed herself, and at ten-thirty they were both ready when the chauffeur drove up in the dark blue Packard their grandfather kept for their use. It was a beautiful summer day, the first week of July, and the sky was as blue as it had been in Hawaii.

'Do you still remember it, Annie?' Audrey asked her as they drove downtown, but the pretty blonde in the white linen dress and big picture hat only shook her head. The memories had all faded when she was a little girl, unlike the photographs in their father's treasured albums. They were the only thing that Audrey still clung to from the past, but Annabelle didn't really care about them. She had always thought them uninteresting and strange and terribly foreign, and more than a little scary, which was precisely what Audrey loved about them. You could almost smell the faraway places in them as you looked at the pictures of mountains in China and rivers in Japan . . . people wearing kimonos pushing funny little carts, fishing by the side of streams and staring out at you, as though they were about to speak to you in their own tongue. . . . Sometimes, as a little girl, Audrey had fallen asleep with the albums in her lap, dreaming that she was in one of those exotic places . . . and now her own photographs captured something unusual and exotic, even in ordinary surroundings.

'Aud?' Annabelle was staring at her, as the car drove up to J. Magrien's. Audrey gave a start and smiled at her; she had been letting her mind drift, which was unusual for her. She was always so busy, particularly now with so much to do for Annie's wedding. 'What were you thinking just then?'

'I don't know.' Audrey averted her eyes. She had been thinking of a photograph of their father in China twenty years before. It was a photograph Audrey had always especially loved, one of him laughing as he rode a little donkey.

'You looked so happy.' Annabelle was all innocence. Audrey smiled and glanced out the window, and then looked at her sister.

'I must have been thinking of you . . . and the wedding . . .' She followed Annabelle out of the car, and a few people on the sidewalk stared. It was rare to see a Packard these days. Most people who owned them had had to sell them. Audrey followed Annabelle to the store feeling suddenly strange, as though she had been pulled back from a great distance from the photograph she'd been thinking of in the car to this terribly worldly self-indulgent place, and the transition seemed very strange as a symphony of French perfumes drifted through the air and hats and silk blouses and gloves seemed to dance before their eyes, all of them pretty and all of them very expensive. Audrey suddenly found herself thinking how foolish it all was, how pointless . . . how wrong. There were other things in life that mattered more . . . other people who couldn't afford food or warm clothes for their children in winter . . . there were shantytowns all over the country filled with people who no longer had homes, and yet here she was with her little sister buying expensive clothes, and a wedding gown that cost more than a college education.

'Are you all right?' Annabelle looked at her for a minute in the dressing room where she was trying on her gown.

For an instant, she had thought that Audrey looked green, which she had. She had felt almost ill from the contrast of what she'd been thinking.

'I'm fine. It was just a little warm here, that's all.' Two of the saleswomen rushed off to get her a glass of water, and by the water fountain as one of them poured and the other one held the glass they whispered to each other.

'Poor thing . . . she's so jealous of her sister she's green . . . poor thing . . . she's The Spinster.' Audrey never heard the words but she had heard them often enough before. She was used to them by now, and didn't really care, not even as she sat in their drawing room that night, making conversation with Harcourt Westerbrook IV, waiting for Annabelle to come downstairs, and her grandfather to return from his club. He was late, which was unusual for him, and Annabelle was too, which in her case, was to be expected. She was always late, always flustered, except with Audrey calmly taking charge of everything for her.

'Is the honeymoon all set?' There seemed to be nothing to talk to him about except the wedding. With any other man she would have discussed the Democratic nomination but she knew Harcourt's views only too well on the subject of women discussing politics with men, or with anyone for that matter. Audrey found herself wondering what they had ever talked about when they went dancing. Perhaps the music, or did he think the conversations about that were vulgar too? She started to laugh at the thought and then had to sober herself immediately. He was describing their honeymoon plans at great length. They were taking the train to New York, then the *Ile de France* to Le Havre, on to Paris by train, and from there to Cannes for a few days, followed by the Italian Riviera, eventually Rome, then London, and then back on the ship and home. They planned to be gone for two months and it sounded like a very nice trip, although not quite what Audrey would have planned. She would have travelled to Venice, and from there taken the Orient Express as far as Istanbul . . . the very thought made her eyes dance but Harcourt's voice droned on, talking about a cousin of his in London who had promised to arrange an audience with the King. Audrey was pretending to be enormously impressed as her grandfather walked in, and stared ferociously at Harcourt. He was about to comment that no one had warned him they were having guests when Audrey walked over to him, squeezed his arm and led him towards Harcourt with a pleasant smile. 'Do you remember my telling you Harcourt was coming tonight?'

He stared at her malevolently for a moment as he narrowed his eyes, and then, distantly, he remembered something she might have said to him that morning. 'Was that before or after you made all those damn fool remarks about Roosevelt?' He looked annoyed but not totally displeased and she laughed as Harcourt looked shocked.

'Unfortunate, isn't it, sir?'

'It won't matter a damn. Hoover will get in again.'

'I certainly hope so.' Another ardent Republican – Audrey looked disgusted by both of them.

'He'll destroy this country for good if he does.'

'Don't start on your theories about that!' He let out a roar but instantly lost his audience as Annabelle arrived on the scene wearing a gown of pale blue watered silk and looking like something in a painting. She was absolutely exquisite with her huge blue eyes, delicate features, and halo of blonde hair. Understandably, Harcourt looked completely bowled over by her and his eyes were riveted to her. He only took his eyes off her long enough to cast a disapproving glance at Audrey on their way into the dining room.

'I hope you weren't serious about Roosevelt.'

'I certainly was. This is the worst year this country has ever known and we have Hoover to thank for that.' She spoke calmly and with a certainty that was difficult to deny, but Annabelle looked at her imploringly as she tucked a hand into Harcourt's arm.

'You're not going to talk politics tonight, are you?' The big blue eyes looked trusting and almost childlike. Harcourt patted her hand.

'Of course we're not.'

Audrey laughed and there was a twinkle in their grandfather's eye as well. She was dying to hear what everyone had been saying at his club, even though most of them were Republicans, of course, but she always thought men's conversations so much more interesting than ladies'. She always had. Except men like Harcourt, who refused to discuss serious subjects with women. She found it exhausting to chat and prattle and smile as Annabelle did all evening long. And Audrey was exhausted by the time he left, while Annabelle sailed happily up the stairs like a little angel. Audrey came up more slowly on her grandfather's arm, giving him time to climb the stairs with his cane. As always, he looked handsome and dignified. She almost wished that one day she might find a man like him. She knew from his early photographs that he had had elegance and style, and he had a bright mind and strong ideas. She could have lived easily with someone like him. And if not easily, then happily at least. Audrey and the elderly gentleman were alone in the hall as he looked down at her. She was almost as tall as he was, but even bent as he was by his years, he stood half a head taller than she.

'You have no regrets do you, Audrey?' It was a funny question for him, and his voice was gentle for once. The gruffness and bluster and bravado had vanished. He wanted to know what was in her heart. He wanted to be sure, for his own peace of mind, that she had no second thoughts about Harcourt.

'Regrets about what, Gramp?' She hadn't called him that since she was a child, but the name came easily to her lips now.

'About him . . . young Westerbrook. You could have had him yourself.' He spoke in an undertone, afraid that someone might hear him. 'He took you out first. And you're older than Annabelle . . . you'll make a better wife one day . . . not that she's a bad girl . . . she's just young . . .' He didn't understand her.

Audrey smiled gently at him, touched by his concern. 'I'm

not ready to get married yet. And he wasn't the right man for me anyway.' She smiled as she looked at her grandfather.

'*Why* aren't you ready yet?' He leaned heavily on his cane as they stood face-to-face in the dark hall. He was tired, but this was important to him, and she sighed as she thought about his question.

'I don't know . . . but I know there are other things I have to do first.' But how could she explain it to him? She wanted to travel . . . and take photographs . . . make wonderful albums of her own . . . like her father's. . . .

'Like what?' He looked concerned by her words. They rang an old chord of memory . . . that had cost him his son . . . 'You don't have anything foolish in mind, do you?'

'No, Gramp.' If nothing else, she wanted to reassure him. She owed him that much. And he was an old man after all. 'I don't even know what I want. But I know Harcourt Westerbrook isn't it. Of that I am absolutely certain.'

He nodded his head, satisfied, and looked deep into her eyes. 'Then it's all right.' And if it hadn't been? If she had wanted him? She wondered about that as she kissed him goodnight, and turned as she heard his door close a moment later. She stood outside her own door, thinking of what she had said. She wasn't even sure why she had said the words, except she knew that they were true . . . there *was* something she wanted to do . . . something . . . places she had to go . . . people she had to see . . . and mountains and rivers . . . and smells . . . and perfumes . . . and exotic foods. . . . She knew as she softly closed her door that she could never have settled down with Harcourt, or maybe anyone at all. There was something much greater she needed to feed her soul, and perhaps one day soon she would go . . . following her father's footsteps taking pictures as she went . . . going back on the same mysterious journeys, and magical trains, like a trip back in time, into the albums . . . with him.

2

On the morning of July twenty-first, Audrey stood downstairs in the front hall, looking at her watch and almost instinctively waiting for the chimes of the dining room clock to begin telling them the hour. The car was waiting for them outside, and she assumed that the guests were already at the church waiting for them. Her grandfather was tapping his cane as he stood nearby, and she could feel the servants' eyes peeking at them from everywhere in the house, anxious to see Annabelle as she came downstairs. And it was well worth the wait when she floated slowly downstairs in a cloud of white, like a vision. She looked like a fairy princess or a very young queen, as she seemed to float just above the ground, her tiny feet in creamy satin slippers, her hair like spun gold in the crown of antique lace and tiny pearls, her tiny waist seemingly carved out of one slender piece of ivory, and her eyes dancing with delight. She was the most beautiful girl Audrey had ever seen, and she smiled with tenderness and pride as she watched her.

'You look so lovely, Annie.' The words were much too small, but they were all Audrey could think of. The endless fittings had been worth the trouble. The dress fitted her to perfection. Audrey was wearing peach silk trimmed in antique beige lace, and the bridesmaids were wearing the same colours, but in a paler shade, and Audrey looked unusually beautiful in the warm colour with her deep copper hair. It brought out the creamy colour of her skin, and her blue eyes seemed to dance as Annabelle smiled back at her sister.

'You look beautiful, you know, Aud ...' Somehow, she never thought of her that way, but she was ... she really was. It actually surprised her. It wasn't often she really thought about Audrey. She was always there, just as she always had been.

Audrey looked at her happily, satisfied with her months of work, her years of love. Annabelle had grown up to be just what she should have been, and now she would be Harcourt's wife, and live happily ever after, in Burlingame. It was what she was suited for, what she wanted to do. She would be a pretty little wife to him and she would settle down now . . . settle down . . . the words echoed in Audrey's head and she could almost feel a chill. She had always hated those words . . . settle down. To her, it sounded like dying.

'Are you happy, Annie?' She searched her younger sister's eyes. For so many years now she had cared for her . . . making sure she went out warmly dressed . . . that she had her favourite dolly when she went to bed at night . . . and didn't have nightmares any more . . . that she was never alone . . . that her friends were always nice to her . . . that she went to a school she liked . . . Audrey had fought Grandfather tooth and nail about that. She hadn't wanted to board at Katherine Branson's across the bay, she had wanted to go to Miss Hamlin's, and she got what she wanted . . . Audrey had seen to everything, right down to today, to the last detail of the magnificent dress. And she wanted her to be happy now. She had always wanted that for her . . . too much perhaps . . . she had spoiled her over the years, probably more than their parents would have, but she always seemed like such a little girl. She still did, even now. Audrey's eyes searched her face, wanting to be sure that Annie felt she was doing the right thing. 'You love him, don't you?'

Annabelle's laughter rang out like a little silver bell in the front hall, as she stood surrounded by her white veil, and caught a glimpse of herself in the mirror that hung there. She was fascinated by what she saw . . . she had never seen anything more beautiful than her gown, and her voice sounded vague now as she answered her sister. 'Of course I love him, Aud . . . more than anything. . . .'

'You're sure?' It seemed like such an enormous step to Audrey, which it was. But Annie didn't even seem frightened, just excited.

'Hmm . . .' She was adjusting her veil, and her grandfather made his way down the stairs to the car on the butler's arm.

'Annie? . . .' Audrey felt a nervous flutter in her stomach as she watched her. What if . . . if she weren't doing the right thing? Had she pushed Annabelle into this? Had anyone else, by insisting it was the right match for her? And what did that matter? She wouldn't have been swayed by that herself, but Annabelle . . .

Her younger sister turned to her with a dazzling smile, and for an instant, Audrey felt relieved. 'You worry too much, Aud . . . this is the happiest day of my life.' For an instant their eyes met and held. She did look happy, Audrey had to admit to herself. But happy enough? And then suddenly she smiled. Annabelle was right. She did worry too much. It just seemed such an incredibly big step to take. She wondered why Annabelle wasn't afraid, but it was clear she was not, as she reached out and took her sister's hand in her own, tightly bound in the creamy kid glove. Her eyes were serious now. 'I'll miss you, Aud. . . .' Audrey had thought of it, too. It was going to be so strange having her gone. For fourteen years she had taken care of her as though she were her own child, and now she would be gone. She felt more like the mother of the bride than the maid of honour when they stood for one last moment in the front hall, as the cable car rumbled by outside.

'Burlingame isn't very far, you know.' But her eyes filled with tears anyway, and she reached out and gave Annabelle a gentle hug, not wanting to crush her veil. 'I love you, Annie . . . I hope you'll be happy with Harcourt.'

Annabelle only smiled again as she pulled away and started out of the front door, whispering over her shoulder, 'Of course I will.'

The horn of their grandfather's Rolls-Royce sounded, and he was fuming as Annabelle settled her voluminous dress in the car around them. It enveloped them all and there was hardly enough room for all three of them.

'Expect them to wait all day in the church, do you?' her grandfather barked at her, squeezing the head of his cane in his hands. But it was clear from the look in his eyes that he was moved by how lovely she looked. She reminded him far too much of a bride he had seen twenty-six years before. She had been even prettier than this child . . . the girl who had married his son Roland . . . it was eerie how much Annabelle looked like her. He felt as though he had travelled back in time as he stood in the church beside Audrey watching Annabelle say her vows and look happily up at Harcourt.

There were tears sliding slowly down Audrey's cheeks as she watched her younger sister getting married, and she felt her eyes swim again as she watched her grandfather lead her out in a slow, graceful waltz a little while later at the reception. It was difficult to remember that he normally walked with a cane and he seemed to have forgotten it too as he moved her elegantly around the floor and then deposited her at last with her husband. He stood looking lost for only a moment and then moved slowly away, suddenly looking very old again as Audrey touched his arm.

'May I have this dance, Mr Driscoll?' Audrey stood almost as tall as he – their eyes met and he smiled. The love they shared was obvious in the look they exchanged. There was a strange poignant feeling to this day, as though Annabelle's leaving was binding them closer together, almost like a marriage of their own, and they both felt it.

And after a few turns on the dance floor, she led him gently to a chair, without making him feel old and infirm. She insisted that she had to check up on a few things behind the scenes, and as usual, she did a fine job. Everyone commented on how lovely the reception was, and when Annabelle left at last in a shower of rose petals and rice in a white wool suit, Audrey looked pleased at the way it had gone. They shook hands with the remaining guests and she went home with her grandfather in the Rolls.

It seemed years since they had left the house that morning,

and Audrey herself was exhausted. They sat in front of the fireplace in the library as the fog rolled inexorably in, and they listened to the foghorns in the distance.

'It was pretty, wasn't it, Grampa?' She barely managed to stifle a yawn and she sipped the little glass of sherry he had poured her. The rest of the guests had consumed gallons of champagne from his private stock, which had been discreetly brought to the hotel, but she had actually drunk very little and the sherry relaxed her now as she stared into space and thought of her sister's wedding . . . the little girl she had cared for, for all those years, and now suddenly she was gone. She and Harcourt were staying in a suite at the Mark Hopkins tonight and in the morning they were taking the train to New York, where they would board the *Ile de France* on their way to Europe. Audrey had promised to see them off at the train, and as she thought of it, she felt a shaft of envy slice through her, not for what they would share with each other, but for the trip they would take. It wasn't an itinerary she would have planned, but she suddenly realised that she envied them the escape. And with a feeling of sudden guilt, she glanced at her grandfather, as though fearing that he might have read her mind. It seemed unfair to be so anxious to get away, but there were times when her desire to see something new almost overwhelmed her. There were times when dreamy nights spent turning the pages of her father's albums just weren't enough . . . she wanted more . . . she wanted to be one of those people in the pictures on those fading pages.

'We ought to take a trip together one of these days.' The words blurted out of her mouth before she could stop them, and her grandfather looked at her, startled.

'A trip? To where?' They had been planning to go to Lake Tahoe in August. They always did. But he instantly suspected she meant something more, and something about the way she said it reminded him far too much of Roland.

'To Europe maybe, like we did in '25 . . . or back to

Hawaii. . . .' And the Orient from there, she wanted to add, but she didn't dare to say it.

'Why would we want to do that?' He looked annoyed, but it wasn't annoyance he was feeling, it was fear. He didn't mind losing Annabelle, but he was terrified of losing Audrey. Life wouldn't have been the same without her, without her competent hand, sharp mind, her way of perceiving things, and the wonderful battles they had shared for almost two decades now. 'I'm too old to go travelling halfway around the world.'

'Then let's go to New York.' Her eyes lit up, and for a moment, he almost felt sorry for her. There wasn't much she could do on her own, and most of the girls she had gone to school with had long since been married. Most of them had two or three children already, and husbands who could take them wherever they wanted to go. Audrey was still waiting in the wings for a man who it seemed was not destined to appear, and in some ways Edward Driscoll felt guilty. It was no wonder she had never found a man. She was too busy running his home and taking care of her sister. But now at least she was gone . . . he felt no regrets at all, as he looked at Audrey's pretty face, the peach silk hat cast aside now, and her thick brandy-coloured hair cascading to her shoulders. She was a damn pretty girl . . . a fine-looking woman, he added silently to himself. 'Well, why not?' She was looking at him expectantly, and he had forgotten what she'd said, but she seemed to expect an answer.

'Why not what?' He looked both confused and annoyed, and Audrey realised that he was tired after the long day, and he'd probably had a little too much champagne, not that it would do him any harm, and he was drinking a cognac now. But he was by no means drunk, and she looked at him hopefully.

'Why not go to New York, Grandpa? We could go in September when we come back from the lake.'

'Why would we want to do that?' But he knew why. He had been young once . . . he had had a wife . . . though she

24

hadn't been all that fond of tramping about. It was Roland who had had that bug, their only son, and God only knew where he'd got his hunger for travel and adventure. It was probably in Audrey's blood, Edward Driscoll mourned silently to himself, but it had killed his son and he wasn't about to let Audrey indulge in it. 'New York's a damn unhealthy place, too crowded, and too far away. You'll feel better after you get to the lake, Audrey. You always do.' Edward Driscoll glanced at his watch then, and stood up with only a slight wobble in his knees. It had been a big day for him, not that he was likely to admit it. 'I'm going up to bed, and you'd best do the same, my dear. You've had a long day, getting that child married off.' He patted her arm on their way upstairs, which was an unusual gesture for him, and that night he stood at his bedroom window watching the lights shine in hers, wondering what she was doing, and what she was thinking. He would have been startled had he seen her sitting at her dressing table, staring into space, her pearls in her hand, thinking of the trip she wanted to take, halfway around the world and of the pictures she longed to take when she got there. Her grandfather, this house, her sister, the wedding, all were forgotten as Audrey sat and dreamed, and then at last she shook herself back to the present, stood up, stretched, and went to her dressing room to get undressed. It was only a few minutes later when she slid between the cool sheets and closed her eyes trying not to think of all she had to do the next day. She had promised to take care of everything for Annabelle while she was away . . . overseeing the new house . . . the painters . . . the furniture due to arrive . . . the wedding gifts to put away . . . as always, she would do it all . . . as always . . . faithful Audrey . . . she drifted off to sleep dreaming of Annabelle and Harcourt . . . and a house on a tropical island as her grandfather shouted to her from the distance . . . 'Come back . . . come back' – but she wouldn't.

3

Typically, in spite of the three weeks she spent at Lake Tahoe at the Driscoll summer home, Audrey managed to have everything in order for Annabelle and Harcourt when they returned in late September. There was a small but adequate staff in the pretty little stone house that Harcourt had bought for them. The rooms were painted in the colours Annabelle had wanted, the furniture was in place, their car had even been serviced and Audrey had seen to it herself that it was started regularly so that the battery didn't die in their absence.

'Your sister certainly does know how to run a house, doesn't she?' Harcourt commented at breakfast after their first night back, and Annabelle smiled at him. She was happy he was pleased. She had been afraid that he would be angry with her for letting Audrey do it all, but she did it all so well, why not let her? Harcourt appeared to agree. Although on California Street at that exact moment no one was praising her domestic skills. Her grandfather was ranting about his eggs being overcooked and his tea not being made properly, and what was more, he hadn't had a decent breakfast in weeks, he roared. They had a new cook and he was harassing Audrey that she wasn't as good as the last one.

'Can't you find a decent cook for this house? Am I expected to eat food like this for the rest of my days, or is it that you're trying to kill me?' Audrey repressed a smile at the tirade, he had been saying the same thing for days and she was already looking for someone else to replace the new cook he didn't like. She was used to it and this morning she was more preoccupied with what she had read in the papers. The average weekly wage was down to less than seventeen dollars from twenty-eight dollars only three years before, and there were breadlines everywhere. Some five thousand banks had failed, more than eighty thousand businesses had gone bust, and so many people had committed suicide. The state of the nation was becoming more and more disastrous. And the statistics in the morning paper were frightening. The gross national product had fallen to half its level of three years before. It was really an impossible situation, and her brow was furrowed as she drank her coffee.

'I don't know how you can continue to ignore what's going on, Grandfather.' She only called him that when she was angry with him, and she was angry at what was happening to the country and his continued defence of Herbert Hoover.

'If you spent more time paying attention to what goes on in this house and less time noticing what goes on in the world, we'd have a better cook, and I would have a decent breakfast.'

'Most people have no breakfast at all. Have you thought of that?' She was on one of her rampages, he knew. But he didn't mind – secretly, he enjoyed them. 'The country's going all to hell.'

'Has been for years, Audrey. That's nothing new. And it isn't exclusive to this country either.' He poked a finger at the newspaper. 'Says here that Germany is crawling with unemployed, and so is England. They have it too. So what? You expect me to sit home and cry about it?'

That was the frustrating thing, there was so little one could do. 'At least you could vote intelligently.'

'I don't like what you call intelligence.' He glared at her, but he was raving mad when the election results came in and Roosevelt beat Hoover by taking sixty percent of the vote. Audrey was delighted and they had a rousing row. They were still fighting about it that night when Annabelle and Harcourt came to dinner. They left early, Annie saying that political conversations gave her a headache, but she managed to confide her secret to Audrey nonetheless. She was expecting a baby in May. Audrey was delighted for her. She was going to be an aunt. It was an odd thought as she walked her grandfather upstairs that night, still muttering about Hoover's defeat. But she wasn't listening to him now, she was thinking about Annabelle and her baby. Annie would be twenty-one when the baby was born . . . twenty-one . . . and she had everything she always wanted. Audrey was twenty-five and had accomplished nothing at all. It began to depress her as the rainy season set in, and even the books she read seemed gloomy. But as Annabelle's pregnancy advanced, she was too busy to be gloomy. There was so much to do, the layette to buy, the nursery to set up, the baby nurse to hire, and Annie was too tired to do much of it herself. As usual, Audrey did it all for her. Just after their grandfather's eighty-first birthday the baby was born, a big, healthy boy who didn't seem to have caused his mother too much trouble. Audrey was the first to see them both, after Harcourt, of course, and she saw to it that everything was in order at the house before Annie and the baby came home from the hospital two weeks later.

Audrey was standing in the nursery folding a little pile of blue blankets and taking a quick inventory of little Winston's new world when Harcourt stopped in the doorway. 'I thought I'd find you here.' His eyes bored into hers as though he had something to say to her, and Audrey turned, surprised. They seldom had much to say to each other. Most of Audrey's dealings were with her sister. 'Don't you ever get tired of doing things for her?' He walked slowly into the room and Audrey set down the little pile of blue blankets as she shook her head, and smiled.

'Not really. I've been doing it for a long time.'

'And you're going to go on doing it forever?' It seemed an odd question and there was something strange in his voice as he advanced towards her and she suddenly wondered if he had been drinking.

'I've never given it much thought. I enjoy taking care of things for Annie.'

'Oh?' He raised an eyebrow and stood so close to her in the sunny little nursery that Audrey could almost feel his breath on her face, and then suddenly he reached out and touched her. His hand was gentle on her cheek, as he drifted a finger lazily to her lips, and then tried to pull her towards him. For an instant, shocked at what he was doing, she didn't resist, and then, just as quickly, she pulled away, avoiding his lips, which brushed her silky hair. He reached out and grabbed her waist with two powerful hands as she tried to escape him.

'Harcourt, stop it!'

'Don't be such a prude . . . you're twenty-six years old for chrissake, are you going to play spinster virgin forever?' It was an unkind thing to say and his words hurt her more than his hands as he pulled on her hair, and tilted her mouth up to his so he could kiss her. Her protests were garbled as he did, and she pushed him away with more force now, beginning to look very angry.

'Harcourt, dammit, *stop!*' She wrenched herself away from him, breathless, and moved instinctively to the other side of the room, the baby's crib between them. 'Are you crazy?'

'Is it crazy to want you? I could have married you, you know.' And he thought now that he probably should have, no matter how difficult she was, with her damn political ideas, all the books she read, and her fancy education. He would have given her something else to think about, and at least she had more spirit than his wife. He was already tired of Annabelle's helplessness and constant childlike whining. What Harcourt wanted was a woman. A real one. Like Audrey.

'You seem to be a little confused.' Audrey was eyeing him sharply now. 'You're married to my sister, and you could never have married me.'

'Why not? You think you're too good for me, Miss High and Mighty? Too smart?' He looked angry at the thought. The truth was that she was smarter than most of the people she knew, women or men, but he didn't like that idea. 'You're a hot little number waiting for the right man, and you made a big mistake bowing out on me, Audrey Driscoll.'

'Maybe so.' She repressed a smile. He was ridiculous really, and undoubtedly harmless. She felt sorry for Annie, having to deal with him, and she suddenly wondered if he had been assaulting all their female friends of late. She hoped not, because if so the word would get around. 'But in any case, Harcourt, you're married to Annabelle now, and you have a beautiful son. I suggest you behave like the head of a family, and not a damn fool or a masher.'

His eyes blazed as he stood across the crib from her, and grabbed her arm. 'You're the damn fool. . . .' His voice was very measured when he spoke again. 'Do you know that we're alone in the house, Audrey? All of the servants are out.'

For an instant she felt a shiver of fear run up her spine. But she wouldn't allow herself to be afraid of him. He was a damn fool and a spoiled boy and he was not going to hurt her or do anything he'd regret. She wouldn't let him. And she said as much in a blast that made him relinquish his grip on her arm, and she straightened the jacket of her dark blue suit, and picked her handbag and gloves off the changing table where she had left them.

'Don't ever do this again, Harcourt. To anyone. But definitely not to me.' She narrowed her eyes as she looked at him. 'Because if you do, I'll have your wife and your son back in my house so fast your head will spin. You don't deserve to have them here if you're behaving like this. Pull yourself together *fast*.' She looked ominous as she stood in the doorway, still furious at him for the stupid thing he'd done.

His eyes were empty as he looked at Audrey and she could see now that he was slightly drunk, although not very. Not drunk enough to excuse his boorish behaviour. 'She doesn't know how to love anyone.' And the truth was that he wasn't sure he knew how either, but he had instinctively sensed that this woman did, that there was more buried in his wife's older sister than anyone would ever know, and it was all wasted, locked up, and probably always would be. 'She's spoiled and selfish and helpless and you know it. It's your damn fault for treating her like a baby all her life.'

Audrey shook her head, loyal to the end. 'Maybe if you were kinder to her, she'd grow up now.'

He shrugged, leaning against the dresser then, staring at his sister-in-law, wondering if she'd tell his wife what he'd done, though he wasn't even sure he cared. Somebody would tell her eventually, and there had been others. He'd been playing that game for a while. He'd been tired of Annie for months. All she ever did was talk about the baby. And she even moved into her own bedroom to protect the baby ... maybe now things would be different ... but he had learned to like the variety in the past few months. Also the intrigue of having little affairs with their friends, or his friends' wives, which made life more interesting. He looked at Audrey and something oddly perceptive spoke up in him, something he knew Audrey wouldn't want to hear. 'You know why she's childish, Aud? Because you made her that way. You did everything for her. Everything. And you still do. She can't even blow her nose by herself. All she does is expect someone else to do everything for her. She wants to be taken care of all the time, because you took care of her all her life and now she expects me to pick up where you left off, and no one can live up to what you've done for her. You're not even human. You're some kind of a machine that runs houses, and orders curtains and hires servants.' The words were unkind, but some of them were true. She had babied Annabelle ever since their parents died, and maybe she *had* done too much for her. She had worried about it herself more than once. But what else was she to do? Let her fend for herself? She couldn't have ... the poor helpless little thing. ... Audrey's eyes filled with tears at the thought, and the memory of how Annabelle had sobbed when their parents died when she was seven still pained her ... it had been so awful, for both of them. ...

'She was very young when our mother died.' Audrey straightened her back and fought back the tears. She felt she had to justify her actions to him now – what if he was right? What if she had crippled Annie for life? He had called Audrey a machine ... a machine to order curtains and hire servants ... was it true? ... was there no more humanity to her than that? ... was that how people saw her? In her anguish she instantly forgot how differently he had seen her only moments before. How human and desirable. The word *machine* had hurt her to the core.

'Your mother has been dead for more than fourteen

years, and you're still doing it all for her. Look at you' – he waved at the neat stacks of blankets and booties and sweaters – 'you're still doing it, Aud. She doesn't do anything for me or herself, or even her baby. *You* do it all. I might as well have married you.' He leered at her again, and she walked swiftly down the hall before he could approach her. She wasn't going to wrestle with him again, nor would she answer him as she ran down the stairs to the front door. He called after her, standing on the landing looking down at her as she yanked the front door open. 'One day you'll come to your senses, Audrey. One day you'll get tired of mothering her, and taking care of your grandfather and running everyone's house but your own, and when that happens, give me a call. I'll be waiting.' His words were answered by the door slamming behind her. She ran all the way to her car, a sob caught in her throat, which exploded as she started the car and drove towards El Camino Real.

But what if he was right? . . . what if that was all her life consisted of? . . . taking care of Grandfather and Annabelle forever . . . she was twenty-six years old and had no real life of her own. She didn't really mind it. She was always so busy . . . and then she felt gnawing despair as she remembered his words again . . . she was busy ordering curtains and hiring servants . . . and folding baby blankets for someone else . . . she had no real life of her own. She didn't even have time to take photographs these days. She hadn't touched her camera in months, and all the dreams she had once had of adventure and travel had waited . . . but for what? What was she waiting for? For Grandfather to die? What if he lived for another fifteen years, or even twenty . . . he could live to be a hundred and one. His own grandfather had lived to a hundred and two, and his parents were well into their nineties when they died . . . and then what? . . . how old would she be? She would be in her forties then with half a lifetime wasted . . . little Winston would be grown. . . . For the first time in her life, she suddenly felt as though life had passed her by, and she had a feeling of mounting panic all the way home, which almost exploded in her as she walked into the front hall and found her grandfather in a rage, waving his cane at two maids and the butler. The chauffeur had smashed up his car that afternoon when he'd hit the cable car as he came around the corner. Her grandfather had fired him on the spot, ordered him out of the car, and driven the Rolls home himself. It was parked somewhat erratically outside, and he looked flushed and irate as he waved his cane now at Audrey.

'And what's the matter with *you*? Can't you even hire me a decent chauffeur!' He had had the same man for seven years, and had been extremely pleased with him until now. Suddenly Audrey was looking at them all with wild eyes, and exploding in incoherent sobs as she mounted the stairs to her room two at a time, thinking that Harcourt had been right. That was all she was good for . . . worse still, it was all anyone cared about, the only light in which people saw her . . . hiring and firing servants and running their homes . . . her dreams had been all but forsaken. She lay on her bed and sobbed, and it was in total amazement that her grandfather knocked on her door a little while later. He had never seen her like that and he was terrified. Something had to have happened to her. It had, but it was nothing she could explain to him. She had no intention of betraying Harcourt to him, and he wasn't really what mattered in all this. What mattered was how she felt, and the realisation she had come to all at once. She knew just as surely that she had to do something about it now. Before it was too late.

'Audrey? . . . Audrey . . . my dear . . .' Her grandfather moved cautiously into the room and she sat up, her face red and streaked with tears like a child, the navy suit all askew. She was still wearing her navy and white spectator pumps as she lay on the bed. 'My dear, what's wrong? . . .' She only shook her head, crying still and trying to regain her composure. How was she going to tell him? How was she going to leave? But she knew she had to now. She couldn't wait any longer. It was time to get away from the maids and the butler and the soft-boiled eggs at breakfast, the rituals, and Annabelle, and even her new baby. She had to get away from all of them, before it was too late for her.

'Grandfather . . .' Her eyes sought his, and from some hidden pocket within her she felt a small surge of courage. He sat carefully on the edge of her bed, sensing that what he was about to hear was something portentous. Perhaps she was getting married, although he didn't see how. She was always at home with him, except on the rare occasions when she dined with one of her friends from Miss Hamlin's, or went down to Burlingame to dine with Harcourt and Annabelle. 'Grandfather . . .' She almost choked on the words, but she had to say them. She plunged ahead fearing the pain she would cause him. But he had survived other things . . . the loss of his son . . . his wife before that. . . . 'Grandfather, I'm leaving.'

He seemed not to understand at first. Then he spoke in measured tones. He *had* understood her. He had had this same exchange once before, a long, long time before, in the same room . . . with Roland. . . . 'To go where?'

'I don't know yet . . . I have to think it out. But I know I have to go . . . to Europe . . . just for a few months. . . .' Her voice was barely more than a whisper, and for an instant he closed his eyes. For an instant, just that, he thought that her words would kill him. But he couldn't let them do that . . . couldn't . . . he had lived too long, and they all did that to you in the end . . . they hurt you until you could bear it no more. It didn't pay to love anyone as much as he loved her. It didn't . . . but he couldn't help it, and then with almost a groan of pain he held out a hand to her and she came into his arms and he held her tight, wishing he could keep her there forever. But she wanted just as desperately to leave him.

'I'm so sorry, Grandfather . . . I know how you must feel. But I promise I'll come back . . . I swear. . . . It won't be like Father.' She knew what he was thinking, and as two lone tears rolled slowly down his cheeks, he only nodded.

4

The train to Chicago left from Oakland and Annabelle, Harcourt and her grandfather had insisted on coming to the station with her. She had decided not to fly but to savour each moment of the trip east by taking the train. Annabelle chatted all the way across the bay on the ferry, and Harcourt kept looking meaningfully into Audrey's eyes over her head, as though he were about to sweep her into his arms and give her a long passionate kiss goodbye in front of his wife. Audrey would have laughed at the look in his eyes, except for her concern for her grandfather, who had been strangely quiet for days and spoke not at all on this final morning. He had said not a single word over his tea, had not touched his egg, despite the excellent new cook Audrey had hired for him, and he never even opened his newspaper. It was obvious that he had a heavy heart and Audrey had been deeply worried about him as she closed the last of her bags, and stood glancing around her room for a last time. She was terrified that her going might precipitate a heart attack or a stroke, or that, worse, he might just give up on life once she was gone. But for once in their lives, they all had to stand on their own two feet without her. Just for a few months . . . just long enough for her to see a little piece of the world and get some of this wandering out of her system. She had promised him a thousand times that she would be home in no time at all. But he never seemed to believe her. 'I'll be home by September, most likely, or October at the very latest, Grampa . . . I swear.' He had looked bleakly at her and shaken his head, insisting that he had heard those words before, too long ago, and Roland had never come home from his wanderings at all . . . never. . . .

'This is different, Grampa. . . .'

'Is it? Why? What will make you come back, Audrey? A

sense of obligation to me? A sense of duty? Will that bring you back?' He spoke almost bitterly, and yet when, finally, she offered not to go, he wouldn't let her cancel the trip after all. He knew how much it meant to her, and he knew also that, for her sake, he had to let her go, no matter how painful it was for him. And indeed it was. He felt suddenly ancient, and as though something he had silently kept at bay for years had finally beaten him. He had always feared that one day she would leave him . . . that one day she would follow in her father's footsteps. She was so like him, and she had always loved those damnable albums. She was leaving them in her room, abandoned now, while she went to relive her father's adventures with her own camera on her shoulder, a Leica that she treasured.

She clung to her grandfather at the station, suddenly feeling how frail he was, and holding him close to her, regretting her wild flight and suddenly hating Harcourt for making her question her whole life. What right had he to do that? . . . except that he had been right to push her. She had to do what she needed to do now. She had to . . . she had to . . . for her own sake. She had to do something for herself now . . . not Grandfather or Annie. She kept reminding herself of that as she held tightly to her grandfather's hands and then she could not restrain the tears as she clung to him. The others were a few feet away and she looked into his eyes as the tears rolled down her cheeks. She felt like a child leaving home for the first time, and she suddenly remembered the pain of leaving Hawaii for the last time after her parents died.

'I love you, Grampa . . . I'll be home soon. I promise.' He took her face gently in his hands and silently kissed the tear-stained cheeks. All his gruffness was gone now. And the raw surface of his love for her was exposed to the pain of her departure.

'Take care of yourself, child. Come home when you're ready. We'll all be waiting.' He spoke quietly and it was his way of saying he would be all right without her. He wasn't quite convinced of it himself, but he felt that he owed her her freedom. She had given him so much in the last fifteen years, and it was her turn now, although he wasn't enamoured of the idea of her travelling alone, but she kept insisting that this was 1933, and modern times, and there was no reason for her not to travel alone. And she was only going to Europe. There were friends of her father's she intended to look up in Paris and London, Milan and Geneva, if she got there. There were people everywhere she could turn to, but she had eyes now only for her grandfather as she watched him slowly step down from the train, his cane in his hand, his hat on his head, his frame tall and spare and his eyes piercing hers as he stood proudly on the platform. And then, finally as the train began to pull away, he smiled at her. It was his farewell gift to her, the gift of letting her go off on her adventures. Harcourt had held her too tightly when he kissed her goodbye, and Annabelle hadn't stopped talking, terrified of what she would do if little Winston's nurse quit, or the upstairs maid left. ... Harcourt had been right ... she had done too much for them all. And it was Audrey's turn now. She waved as long as she could, and then the train went around a bend, and they were gone, like mirages.

It took two days and two nights to reach Chicago and Audrey spent the entire time reading the novels she had brought with her. She had her own compartment with a drawing room and a sofa berth, and on the first day she finished *Death in the Afternoon* by Ernest Hemingway, and felt filled with his spirit of adventure as she read of the bullfights he was so intrigued by. Immediately after that she read *Brave New World* by Aldous Huxley. Each seemed appropriate to her mood of discovery and adventure. She spoke barely a word to a soul all the way across the country. She would only get out of the train from time to time to stretch her legs, or eat an indigestible meal in one of the stations, reading a book as she ate, and afterwards she would munch the candy bars she had bought there. She had a passion for 3 Musketeers Bars, and bought them to eat while she stayed up late at night reading. She was having a wonderful self-indulgent journey, and for the first time in years, she had no one to think about except herself. She didn't have to worry about planning meals or approving menus, or scolding maids, or dressing for dinner on time. She wore a grey flannel skirt for the entire trip, and she had brought along several blouses. She had started out with a pink crêpe de chine tied demurely at the neck, and the pearl necklace her grandfather had given her for her twenty-first birthday. On the second day she wore grey silk, and on the last night white crêpe de chine. She wore a fox jacket in the evening chill when they stopped at Denver, but after that it grew warmer and warmer as they crossed the country. It was mid-June, and by the time they reached Chicago, Audrey donned a white linen suit and the new white shoes she had bought for the trip with a navy heel and a navy strap across the instep. They were the latest fashion, and she felt very chic as she stepped off the train with a big hat tilted to one side, her coppery hair cascading around her face as she hailed a porter. She took all of her things to the La Salle Hotel, where she spent the night before boarding the train again the next morning for the brief trip to New York. And suddenly the excitement of what she had done overwhelmed her. She almost wanted to stand in the street and laugh she was so pleased with herself, and even the pain of leaving her family seemed to dim now.

It was only when she spoke to her grandfather that the pain revived again. And even then, only briefly. He sounded gruff when she called, but the gruffness barely concealed the loneliness that was so evident in his voice.

'Who?' he had barked into the phone when she had called him, and she smiled in her hotel room, staring unseeing out the window as she held the phone.

'It's me, Grampa. Audrey,' she repeated. 'You can't have forgotten me already.'

'I was listening to Walter Winchell.' She quickly calculated the time difference, and knew he was lying to her. He didn't want her to know he'd been sitting by the phone, praying she would call him. 'Where the devil are you anyway?'

'In Chicago. At the La Salle Hotel.' She had given him her itinerary before she left, at least as much of it as she knew, but the La Salle was on it.

'What is that? Some cheap hotel?'

'Of course not!' She laughed, suddenly missing him terribly. She felt far, far from home, and very lonely for him. 'It's near the Loop. And you've stayed here, too. You told me so yourself.'

'I don't remember.' But she knew he did. He was just being difficult, to ease the loneliness he felt without her. 'When do you go to New York?'

'In the morning, Grampa.'

'Well, see to it that you stay in your compartment. There's no telling what trash will be on that train. You have your own compartment, don't you?' He sounded nervous and she was touched.

'Of course, Grampa.'

'Good. Then stay in it.' And then suddenly, he sounded meek, and almost pleading. It was so uncharacteristic that it brought tears to her eyes. 'Will you call me from New York?'

'The moment I arrive.' Her voice was gentle in his ears, and silently, at his end, he nodded. He wanted to thank her, but he didn't know how. He was even grateful for the call from Chicago.

'Where are you staying in New York?'

'The Plaza, Gramp.'

'That's right.' And then a silence. 'Take care of yourself, Audrey.'

'I will, Grampa. I promise. And you too. Don't stay up too late tonight.'

'Be careful on that train!' He sounded worried again. 'Stay in your compartment!'

Of course, she did not heed his words on the Broadway Limited the next day. The lounge car was too intriguing

39

with its well-populated bar patronised by happy, chattering people. The restaurant was equally plush, and the meal was superb, served by a waiter in tails. She shared a table with a couple on their honeymoon, and a very respectable-looking attorney from Cleveland, with a wife and four kids at home. But he asked if he could see her in New York anyway, and even offered her a ride in his cab from Penn Station to her hotel. She declined, and sped away from the station in a taxi of her own, and she began taking pictures. She leaned forward in her seat in the enormous cab, braced herself and began snapping photographs of skyscrapers, and passersby, catching odd angles, funny hats, and the expressions on faces. She had a real genius for what she saw in the camera's eye, and she was totally engrossed as they pulled up to her hotel. There were hansom cabs parked outside, and the driver glanced at her curiously as she paid him.

'You a tourist or a pro?' He couldn't figure her out. She was attractive and well dressed, and yet she looked like she really knew what she was doing with her camera.

She smiled at him as the doorman took her bags. 'A little bit of both.'

'You wanna tour of New York?' He looked hopeful.

'Sure.' She glanced at her watch. 'Give me an hour. I'll meet you here.' It was a beautiful, sunny afternoon, and she had nothing but time on her hands, and a city to discover all by herself.

The driver promised to return, and he was as good as his word. An hour later, she was back in the cab, whizzing past landmarks she had never seen during any of her trips to New York: The Empire State Building, Saint John the Divine. She even got him to drive her through Harlem, where her camera worked overtime, and she bought ice-cream cones for two little girls after taking their pictures.

It was a heavenly day, a heavenly trip, a heavenly moment in a lifetime. And when she got back to her hotel, she felt as though she had seen it all. She had taken six rolls of film, of buildings, of people, of Harlem, of Central Park, the East

River, the Hudson, the George Washington Bridge, Wall Street, Saint Patrick's. She bubbled over when she called her grandfather that night, and she was still feeling exhilarated when she took herself to '21' for dinner. It was the most famous speakeasy in New York, and one of the few where they'd let her in alone. She went in a pretty black cocktail dress, and two men approached her the moment she sat down, but the head waiter quickly asked them to return to the bar from whence they had come. Audrey returned to the Plaza, as she had left it, without an escort.

She had three days to spend in New York before boarding the ship, and she used them well. She visited all the sights she had wanted to see and even went to two films, both of them starring Joan Crawford, whom Audrey loved, *Grand Hotel*, which also starred Greta Garbo, and *Rain* with Crawford and Walter Huston. Both had come out the year before, but Audrey had never had the time to see them. Now she had nothing but time. She came out of the cinemas feeling decadent and pleased, so much so that the next day she went to a matinee of *A Bill of Divorcement* with Katharine Hepburn.

She walked endlessly looking into the shops, and her only real regret was not being able to go to the El Morocco, which had opened a year and a half before; Audrey had heard entrancing stories about it from Annie. They had gone on their honeymoon and apparently the decor was done in zebra stripes, and all the café society types hung out there, drinking and dancing until the small hours, beautiful women in fabulous clothes and handsome men looking extremely sexy and romantic. It was a scene Audrey would have liked to see, although there was no decent way for her to do so. She didn't know a soul in New York and she wouldn't have dreamed of going alone, even if she could have.

She was fascinated, though, as she wandered the streets – the women looked so chic and the men so well dressed. Somehow it made San Francisco seem very sleepy, and she tried to describe it all to Annabelle when she called her.

41

'You're so lucky, Aud . . . I'd give anything to be there with you.'

'Everyone is wearing the most exquisite little hats, and the prettiest dresses.' They both knew that 'funny little hats' were the rage that year, but seeing dozens of them perched on heads everywhere suddenly brought it all to life. Everything was so much bigger and brighter and more exciting than it was in California. Suddenly San Francisco seemed so staid and sedate, and in fact it was. Audrey was thrilled to have escaped, even if only briefly.

'Did you go to El Morocco?'

Audrey laughed and shook her head as she stared out the window of her hotel room and talked to her sister. 'Of course not. How could I? I don't know anyone here to take me.'

'I hear that they let people in free if they're good-looking and beautifully dressed. . . .' Her voice trailed off hopefully and Audrey laughed again. She had heard that too, it was the only way they could keep full and looking successful during the Depression. They let beautiful people in to make the place look busy and then their regulars would come, and no one would be the wiser.

'I don't think that would get me very far, without an escort.' She said it without regret, and at her end Annabelle shrugged. It was stupid of Audrey to go travelling alone like some old woman. But she sighed, then said, 'Maybe you're better off that way, Aud.' She didn't want to say more. There was a catch in her voice that made Audrey wonder what Harcourt had been up to.

'Is everything all right?' Her heart went out to her little sister as she asked. In her eyes, Annabelle was still a baby. 'Is anything wrong?' She sounded like a tigress ready to defend her young, but Annabelle denied that anything was amiss, and Audrey wanted to believe her.

'We're fine. It's just . . . so difficult without you. I don't know how you do everything just right, and . . .' There were tears in her eyes, but fortunately Audrey couldn't see them.

42

'You do just fine. Just have patience. You can't learn everything overnight.'

'Harcourt thinks I can.' She sounded woebegone now, and Audrey smiled.

'Men don't understand things like that. Look at Grandfather.' Annabelle smiled through her tears. 'You're doing just fine.' It was the same encouragement she had given her for a lifetime. 'You do a beautiful job with little Winston.' Actually it was true. She was like a little girl playing with her dolly.

'I'm so afraid I'll do something wrong. . . .' She started to worry and Audrey cut her off.

'You won't. You're his mother. *You* know what's best.' She was now thinking of how expensive the call was going to be. She had only brought five thousand dollars of the money her parents left her when they died, and it had to last for the whole trip. 'I'd better go now, love. I'll call you before I sail.'

'When's that?'

'In two days.' She knew Annabelle didn't envy her that. She had always been desperately seasick on their trips back and forth to Hawaii. Harcourt said that she hadn't come out of her cabin on the *Ile de France* once during the whole trip on their honeymoon. But she had recovered very quickly once in Paris. Chanel, Patou, Vionnet. She had made the rounds, and had spent a fortune. 'Take care of yourself, and give Grandfather my love.'

'He never calls me,' she wailed.

'Call him, for heaven's sake!' Audrey sounded annoyed. Annie never thought of reaching out to anyone. She waited for everyone to come to her. 'He needs you now.'

'All right . . . I'll call him. And call me if you get to El Morocco!' Audrey laughed to herself as she hung up the phone. How different they were, it was funny to think about it sometimes, and how Annabelle would have hated the trip she had planned for herself once she reached Europe. Chanel and Patou were nowhere on Audrey's itinerary. She

43

had other fish to fry, and as soon as she reached the ship the next day, she felt her heart race. She stood looking up at the four smokestacks of the *Mauretania*, and suddenly it was like a dream come true. Even her father's albums faded from her mind, all she could think of were her own travels, her own adventures, her own plans, as she settled into her cabin on A deck. There was no one to see her off of course, but she wandered upstairs when they set sail, and watched the ship pulling slowly away from the dock as passengers threw streamers and confetti and called out to friends on shore. The boat's horn sounded, drowning out all other sounds, and beside her she saw a couple arm in arm, she in a beautiful pink silk suit with one of the exquisite little hats that Annabelle would have so loved. She had raven black hair and huge blue eyes and creamy skin, and she wore pink linen T-strap shoes edged in gold, and as she waved to a friend on the shore Audrey was aware of a very large diamond bracelet. Then as the boat horn faded, she heard the sound of her laughter, and saw her kissing the man who was with her. He was wearing white linen trousers and a navy blue blazer, a hat pulled low over one eye, and together they looked extremely dashing as they strolled off arm in arm, still laughing and stopping to kiss from time to time. Audrey found herself wondering if they were on their honeymoon, and she was almost sure of it later when she saw them sipping champagne in the lounge before dinner. She saw them eyeing her then, and she watched them from across the dining room that night. The woman was wearing a spectacular white evening gown with a plunging neckline, her husband was in black tie, and Audrey herself had worn a grey satin evening dress that suddenly looked a great deal less sophisticated than it had only a few months before in San Francisco. But she didn't really care. She was having a marvellous time watching everyone else, and she put her silver fox jacket around her shoulders as she went out on deck after dinner. And there she saw them again, kissing in the moonlight and holding hands. She sat down in a deck chair and looked out at the moon, and smiled as they walked past her again, and then suddenly she was startled when they stopped near her chair and the woman smiled at her.

'Are you travelling alone?' She spoke directly to Audrey and she was even more beautiful when one looked into the incredible sapphire eyes, in fact they looked more like blue diamonds.

'Yes, I am.' She felt suddenly shy. It was one thing to dream about having adventures, and quite another to embark on a trip all alone, and have to meet new people and explain it all to them. She felt suddenly awkward and young as the exquisitely dressed young woman walked towards her.

'My name is Violet Hawthorne, and this is my husband, James.' She casually waved the same hand that, earlier, had worn a diamond bracelet, only now it was wearing a very, very large emerald ring with a bracelet to match, what she had failed to mention to Audrey was that 'James' was actually 'The' Lord James Hawthorne, and she was Lady Violet, a marchioness by birth. But there was nothing haughty or snobbish in her eyes as she smiled at Audrey, and her husband wandered over to shake her hand, chiding his wife for being rude, but there was laughter in his voice, and he looked as though he could hardly keep his hands off his spectacular-looking wife as he put an arm around her shoulders.

'Are you on your honeymoon?' Audrey couldn't resist asking and they both laughed.

'Do we look like that?' Violet laughed at the thought. 'How shocking . . . that terrific anxious look that tells everyone you can't wait to get to bed. Darling, really, how awful. . . .' Audrey blushed at the frank words, but all three of them laughed and Violet was quick to correct her. 'I'm afraid we've been married for six years and have two children waiting for us at home . . . no, we've just been off on holiday. Actually, James has a cousin in Boston, and I wanted to come to New York. It's absolutely marvellous this time of year. Are you from New York?' She smiled as she

45

asked, seemingly oblivious of the staggeringly handsome portrait she made, standing there in her white evening dress, trailing an ermine wrap, with the emeralds flashing in the ship's lights. Audrey was quite overwhelmed and felt absolutely like a bumpkin.

'Actually, I'm from San Francisco.' Lady Violet's eyebrows shot up in interest. She had the most expressive face and seemed hardly older than Audrey.

'Are you? Were you born there?' She loved to ask questions, and her husband was quick to intervene, chiding her laughingly.

'Will you stop interrogating people, Vi. Really you must stop that!' But Americans had been extremely tolerant of her, in fact very few seemed to object, if any, and they were quite happy to answer all of her questions.

'I don't mind,' Audrey was quick to interject and Lady Violet apologised.

'I'm so sorry. James is right. I have a frightful habit of asking too many questions. In England, everyone thinks me terribly rude. Americans seem to be better sports about it.' She smiled ingenuously and Audrey laughed.

'How very interesting.' She sounded genuinely fascinated and Audrey laughed, realising that she hadn't introduced herself to them yet. She held out a hand, and they completed the formal introduction and then James invited her to join them for champagne. He was an incredibly handsome man with shiny black hair, broad shoulders, and impeccable, aristocratic hands. Audrey had to fight herself not to stare at him, but he was so good-looking that one found oneself mesmerised by him as he talked, and to watch them together was like watching a film. They embodied all that was glamour. They had it all, they were beautiful people in beautiful clothes, with witty things to say, incredible jewels, and an air of ease about them that anybody would have envied.

'Do you come to Europe often?' It was Violet, asking questions again, but this time James didn't try to stop her.

'I've only been once,' Audrey confessed. 'When I was eighteen. I went with my grandfather. We went to London and Paris, and a week at some spa on the Lake of Geneva. And then we went home to San Francisco.'

'Evian probably. Terribly dull, isn't it?' Violet and Audrey both laughed, James sat back watching his wife. He was obviously crazy about her, and as Audrey watched them she felt sorry for her sister. That was what marriage should have been like, two people who care about each other, who enjoy the same things, not strangers who only cared about how they looked to others. She would rather remain single for her entire life if she couldn't wait until she found a man just like this one. But she found that she didn't envy Violet at all. She enjoyed watching the two of them together, as Violet went on chatting. 'My grandmother used to have this funny old house in Bath. She used to go there for the "waters", and every year they would send me with her. I cannot begin to tell you how much I hated it . . . except,' she looked up at James with a broad smile, 'there was one summer that wasn't quite as awful.'

'I broke my leg shooting in Scotland, and went to stay with my great aunt, much against my will and better judgement, but . . . there were a few benefits. Little Lady Vi here was one of them . . .' His voice trailed off enticingly and she took the bait good-humouredly.

'You mean there were others?'

'. . . Oh, a pretty little thing at the bakery, as I recall, and . . .'

'James, how could you!' He was teasing her and she loved it. Audrey spent a delightful evening with them, laughing and teasing and talking about California and the places she wanted to see in Europe.

'How long are you planning to stay, Audrey?' James asked her pleasantly as he poured the last of their second bottle of champagne into their glasses.

'More or less until the end of the summer. I've promised my grandfather I would get home then. You see, I . . .

it's rather complicated, I'm afraid. I live with him, and he's eighty-one years old.'

'Must be rather dreary for you, my dear. . . .' James sounded solicitous but she was quick to shake her head, out of love and loyalty, and the fact that she had always loved living with him. It was just that now, for a little while, she needed to do something different.

'He's a wonderful man, and actually we get along very well.' She smiled. 'Not that you would believe that if you saw us together. We fight about politics constantly.'

'That's good for one's health. I always argue with Vi's father. We enjoy it very much.' They all smiled – in one night they had become the best of friends. 'Now, tell us your plans.'

'Well, London first, and then Paris, and then I thought I might drive down to the South of France. . . .'

'Drive?' He looked surprised and she nodded. 'By yourself, or with a driver?'

She smiled at him. 'You sound just like my grandfather. You'd be surprised, I'm a very good driver.'

'Still . . .' James wasn't at all sure he approved and Violet waved the enormous emerald ring at him.

'Don't be so old-fashioned. I'm sure she'll do very well. And then where?' She turned interested eyes to Audrey.

'I'm not sure. I thought I'd spend a little bit of time on the Riviera, and then drive or take the train into Italy. I want to go to Rome . . . Florence . . . Milan . . .' She hesitated for only a fraction of a second, and neither of the other two noticed. '. . . and if I have time, I might spend a few days in Venice, and then I'll take the train back to Paris, and from there home.'

'And you plan to do all that by September?'

'What I can . . . there are other things I'd like to do too, but I know there won't be time. I would have liked to go into Spain, perhaps Switzerland . . . Austria . . . Germany . . .' India, Japan . . . China . . . she almost laughed at herself. The entire world was so appealing to her, it was like a giant apple that she wanted to bite and bite and bite until she devoured the whole thing right to the core, seeds and all.

'I don't think you'll have time for half of that.' James looked doubtful and Violet looked intrigued.

'And you're doing all that alone?' Audrey nodded. 'You're very brave, you know.'

'I don't really think I am. It's just . . .' She looked honestly up at them and she seemed very young. '. . . I've always wanted to do something like this . . . my father was that way. He travelled all over the world, and then finally he wound up in Hawaii, but he was travelling to Fiji and Samoa and Bora-Bora . . . I think it's something in my blood. All my life I've dreamed of travelling like this . . . alone . . . meeting people, doing things . . . and now, suddenly, here I am. . . .' She looked as though she were about to explode with joy and Lady Violet threw her arms about her and gave her a hug.

'You're a funny girl, you know. And terribly brave. I'm not sure I'd have the courage to do anything like that, without James.' He smiled benevolently at her. He was beginning to think of bedding down with her for the night, and in a little while Audrey and her adventures would be distinctly *de trop*. He had eyes only for his wife. 'Are you enjoying yourself so far?' As usual, Violet was curious.

'I am.' Audrey smiled at them, and she had correctly sensed James's heightening interest in his wife. It was late anyway, and it had been a long day for all of them. She stood up, smiling at them, and shook hands with them both again. 'I've had a wonderful evening. Thank you both. And thank you very much for the champagne.'

'Shall we do something wonderful tomorrow then? Let's have lunch, shall we?' Violet smiled and Audrey nodded.

'I'd love that. See you tomorrow then.' She left them chatting happily and went to her own cabin on the A deck. It had been a wonderful evening with them, and they were not at all the kind of people she had expected to meet. She had learned from Violet in the course of the evening that she

49

was twenty-eight, and James was thirty-three, they had a five-year-old son, also called James, and a little girl, Alexandra, who was three. They lived in London throughout the year, and had a house in the country, and in the summers they went to Cap d'Antibes. They led an indolent life of luxury and yet they weren't tiresome or snobbish. They were marvellous, and great fun to be with, and Audrey was looking forward to her lunch with them the next day. As it turned out, she spent most of the crossing with them. They became an inseparable threesome, laughing and dancing and telling tales, drinking champagne until they could barely stop laughing any more, making fun of the other passengers, and inviting them to join them now and then. But on the whole, the threesome was a huge success, and Audrey and the Hawthornes became fast friends. So much so that it was a mournful night as they faced the prospect of disembarking the next day.

'Will you come to Cap d'Antibes with us?' It was Violet's suggestion but James seemed anxious to second it. 'You'd have such a good time. We always do. There are such marvellous people, there.' Their favourites among them were the Murphys, of course, Gerald and Sara, with their endless parties, funny costumes, and intriguing friends. Hemingway had been there with them for a time, Fitzgerald always was, Picasso, Dos Passos . . . but more than that it was the Murphys themselves who were so amusing. The Hawthornes were mad about them, and counted themselves lucky to be among their friends. 'Do come.' Violet's eyes pleaded with her and Audrey was tempted to say yes. 'You're coming to the South of France anyway. Just plan to spend a little more time there.'

'Yes,' James laughed, 'rather more like two months. Good God, Audrey, Violet's brother stayed with us for seven weeks last year he had such a good time.' He pretended to frown then as he looked at his wife. 'He's not coming back again this year, is he, Lady Vi?'

'Now, don't start that again, James, you know he only

stayed for two weeks in July. And this year, he can only stay for a few days.' She turned her attention to Audrey again. 'We're counting on you. We'll be there by July second or third, and you just come.'

'I will,' she promised, and suddenly the summer looked even more exciting.

There was a whole new world to discover, with the cast of characters they described in Antibes, and all the adventures they would share. They held out excitement like a handful of gems, and their promises danced in her head like little elves, as she lay in her bunk that night and ran it all through her head again . . . a weekend in Saint-Tropez . . . gambling in Monte Carl', as Vi called it in flawless but irreverent French . . . Cannes . . . Nice . . . Villefranche . . . the very words filled her with excitement, and her heart pounded as she lay there late into the night, thanking her lucky stars that she had met them.

5

The days in London flew by much too quickly. Audrey was delivered to Claridge's by James and Vi, with a special introduction to the manager. Her reservation had been at the Connaught, but James had insisted that she change, because he preferred it. There was absolutely no reason why, and she would have been happy in either place, although James' introduction guaranteed her treatment the likes of which she'd never experienced anywhere. She attempted to explain it in a letter to Annabelle, but then finally tore it up for fear that her younger sister would be overwhelmed with envy. There were rivers of champagne, endless baskets of fruit, little silver trays of impeccable chocolates, and afternoons of shopping with Lady Vi, driven everywhere in their Rolls, taken to parties and plays. And Vi and James even gave a party for her. They introduced her to their closest friends, she fell in love with their children, and was in awe of their home. It was enormous and elegant, and looked more like a small palace than a house. Even in San Francisco, with all its grand homes, she had never seen anything like it. She almost hated to move on to Paris at the week's end, and the only thing that consoled her was the fact that she'd be meeting them in Antibes in a few weeks – she could hardly wait to see them.

Paris almost seemed dull in comparison without Violet and James. Audrey bought a wonderful little hat for Vi at Patou, and an even more wonderful one for Annabelle, which she sent home. Almost everything she saw in Paris seemed to have a jungle motif that year. She bought a wild evening gown, striped like a zebra skin, and planned to wear it in Antibes when she visited Violet and James, perhaps even to one of the fabulous parties that the Murphys gave, if they invited her. But it was the first time in Audrey's life that she felt totally independent and grown up. She didn't have to answer to anyone, or be responsible for anything. It didn't matter what time she ate, or when she got up. She combed Montmartre at night, and drank red wine at noon. She went wandering along the Left Bank, and after two weeks of glorious liberty, she took the train to the South of France.

She had decided not to drive down after all, not because she was afraid of it as James thought she should be, but more because she was feeling indolent now, and it was easier to go down on the train. She was wearing a long, narrow, pale blue skirt, a pair of espadrilles she had bought, and a big straw picture hat when she got off the train in Nice and saw Violet and James standing there, in costumes similar to hers. Violet was wearing a white sundress with a big straw hat with a red rose, and little red shoes, and James was wearing espadrilles just like Aud's. They were already tanned, and the children were waiting for them with the nurse in the car. Audrey plopped Alexandra onto her knees as they drove away, and James and Violet began singing a French song. Everyone laughed and they drove too fast with the top down. It was a summer for happiness and excitement, and their whole life was devoid of fear or any kind of worry.

Audrey fell instantly in love with their house, and with the people who came there to visit them that night. There were artists and aristocrats, Frenchmen, and women from Rome, half a dozen Americans, and the most beautiful girl Audrey had ever seen who insisted on swimming in the pool nude. Hemingway was supposed to come by but he had gone fishing on some exhausting expedition he had organised in the Caribbean instead. It was magical, and precisely what she had always dreamed. It was impossible to believe that only a month or so before she had been sedately at home, making sure that her grandfather's soft-boiled eggs weren't being undercooked.

And now she even understood her obsession with world news. It was a way of hanging on to something more, a world outside, a life beyond, only now she was part of it, night and day, with all these people she had never met before and would never see again, and the extraordinary people whom they knew and introduced her to daily. They took it all in their stride, they were all so used to it. Everyone they knew had either written a book or put on a play, created a famous piece of art, or had been born into a titled family. They weren't just people there, they were more, they were the sculptors of a magical time in history, and Audrey could feel the moments being carved, the gold dust in her hair as she watched them.

Each day when she awoke, she had the feeling that something remarkable was happening, and in truth it was, and now she understood what her father had lived and died for, the excitement he couldn't have existed without. The albums had come alive for her, except this was better still. It was her life, not his, and these were her friends now . . . and like her father, she was constantly taking pictures.

'What were you thinking of, Audrey?' Violet had been watching her, as they sat on the little lip of sand at Antibes. 'You know, you were smiling just then, and staring into space. What were you thinking?'

'How happy I am. And how far from home this is.' She looked at her friend with a smile. She already knew how sad she would be to go back in the autumn. She didn't even like thinking about it. She wanted to stay here forever, with the magic going on, but of course it wouldn't. Eventually they would all have to go home. She hated the thought, though.

'You love it here, don't you?'

'I do.' Audrey lay back on the sand, her black French bathing suit moulding her body to perfection in the sand. Beside her, Violet wore white which went well with her black hair. Together, they made quite a pair. It was a photograph Audrey would have loved to have taken. She was taking photographs constantly. And when she had them developed at a laboratory in Nice, the others commented on how good she was. Even Picasso said so one day, glancing at the prints she was sifting through. He had eyed them with interest and then looked at her with his piercing eyes. 'You have talent, you know. You shouldn't waste it.' He spoke severely and it had startled her. Photography was something she enjoyed. She had never thought of it as something not to be 'wasted'. But she had been impressed by his tone. She was impressed by everything happening around her, and she loved it.

'Why don't you stay?' Violet asked as they lay on the beach.

'In Antibes?'

'In Europe, I mean. This seems like just the right place for you.' She was watching Audrey's eyes, they looked so wistful now, as she thought of leaving.

'I'd love that, Violet. But it wouldn't be fair.'

'To whom?'

'My grandfather mainly ... he needs me there ... perhaps one day.' She didn't want to say when, but perhaps when he was no more. This had given her a taste of her life's dream. She could always come back. One day. If she was lucky.

'It doesn't seem fair, you know, to have to give up your life like that.'

Audrey looked quietly at her. 'I love him, Vi. It's all right.'

'But what about you? You can't live like that forever, Audrey.' And then she looked at her curiously. 'Don't you want to get married and have a life of your own one day?' It seemed so strange to her not to have that. She had loved James for so long. She couldn't begin to imagine life without him.

'Maybe. I don't really give it much thought. This is my life. Maybe I'm not meant to be married ... maybe that's not in The Plan for me.' They exchanged a smile and lay back on the sand. For the first time she felt that even if she never married at all, it would no longer be such an evil fate. It was pleasant being free, especially here, in the summer of 1933, in Cap d'Antibes on the Riviera.

They went to a party later that night, at the Murphys'

again, a costume party this time, and as always Gerald Murphy himself was the most marvellous of all. He was handsome and meticulous, yet he was so much more than that. He was elegant as few men ever were, elegant and imaginative, and so perfect in every detail that one wanted to sit in a corner and stare at him all night. He was one of those rare, rare people whose plumage was so fine, so delectable, that everyone admired him. He had been voted Best Dressed by his class at Yale in 1912, and they didn't even know the half of it then. Twenty years later, he was much, much more wonderful, and his wife Sara was divine. She used to wear her pearls on the beach at Antibes, and insisted it was 'good for them', as she sat chatting with Picasso in his eternal black hat.

It was a glorious summer for all of them, although less so for the Murphys than years before. They were still battling their son Patrick's TB, but at least they were all there, and there was something special and golden about each day. Audrey felt the magic spell too, as she and Violet strolled along on the beach day after day, watching the children, squinting into the sun, and feeling the sand on their legs as they lay lazily and shared a lifetime of stories and laughter and confidences. Lady Vi was the sister Audrey had never had before, the responsible one, the good friend, older by only two years, and twins in their souls. It was almost like coming home finding her, and something warm and solid was built between them that Audrey had never experienced before. And she valued it more each day. James was happy to have her around, they were a comfortable threesome, always, and he never showed the least inappropriate interest in his wife's friend. He was a gentleman and a brother and that was all.

'What are you really going to do when you go home, Aud?' Violet was watching the long, lanky girl with the dark red hair. She worried about her sometimes. She knew what an empty life she led at home, and she would have liked to see her stay in London with them, although Audrey continued to insist that it wasn't possible. She had to go back to California.

'I don't know. The same as before, I guess.' She looked over her shoulder at Violet with a smile. 'That's not so bad.' But she was trying to convince herself more than her friend. 'I did it before . . . running Grandfather's house, I mean. . . .' But nothing would ever be quite the same. Never. Not after these golden days with people one only dreamed about, in a place reserved for a magical few. And now, for these brief moments, she was one of them. But for how long? Sooner or later it would all have to end. Audrey never lost sight of that. It only served to make it all more precious to her as July drifted on.

'I so wish you could stay on for a while. . . .'

Regretfully, Audrey shook her head. 'In fact,' she sighed, and squinted up at the sun, 'I should be moving on next week if I'm going to complete my trip. I was going to drive over to the Italian Riviera and move on from there.'

'Do you really want to do that?' Violet looked crushed and Audrey laughed at her.

'Honestly? No. I want to sit right here for the rest of my life. But that isn't very realistic, I suppose. So I might as well make my way slowly back to the real world. And God only knows when I'll get back to Europe again.' Her grandfather wasn't getting any younger, and Lord only knew when she would be able to tear herself away again. Annabelle's last letter had informed her that she was terrified that she might be pregnant again. She didn't want another baby so soon and Harcourt was furious with her. Apparently, she hadn't used any precautions. Her grandfather's only letter had sounded just like him; she could almost hear him growl as she turned each page. He was complaining about Roosevelt, and assorted local events. He insisted that Roosevelt was doing nothing to help the economy in spite of all his promises of a 'new deal', and he always referred to him in his letters to Audrey as 'your friend FDR', and usually underlined the *your*, which made her laugh. Thinking about him

57

made her sigh again. How faraway it all seemed now. She glanced down the beach at James as she thought of it. He was walking slowly towards them with a tall, thin man, with hair even darker than his own, gesticulating animatedly as James laughed and pointed down the beach at them. Violet waved and glanced at Audrey with a broad smile, looking immensely pleased.

'Do you know who that is, Aud?' Audrey shook her head, amused at her friend's excitement over him. He was certainly a very attractive young man, but no more so than the countless others who came and went out of their lives. Violet had begun waving as they came down the beach, brandishing her big floppy hat as Audrey laughed. 'It's Charles Parker-Scott, the travel writer, and explorer. Don't you know him? He publishes a lot in the States. His mother was American, you know.' Audrey suddenly looked startled as she smiled. She certainly knew the name, and he was indeed famous; she had just always assumed that he was a great deal older than this handsome young man strolling down the beach next to James. But she had no time for further thought as Vi hurled herself into his arms.

'Behave yourself, old girl. That's no way for a married woman to greet a man.' James chided her with a swat on her behind but she didn't look dismayed. And Charles was obviously enchanted with the greeting.

'Oh to hell with you, James.' Vi beamed as the new arrival swept her off her feet and into his arms. 'Charlie's not a man for God's sake.' And as she said the words, he feigned chagrin, and dropped her unceremoniously into the sand at his feet, and stared down at her.

'What do you mean, I'm "not a man"?' His accent was decidedly more American than British and Audrey remembered hearing that he had gone to Yale, and he later explained that he had spent all his summers in Maine as a child, at Bar Harbor with his mother's family. And he had a strong penchant for everything from the States.

'I meant, Charles Parker-Scott, that you are practically

58

family.' Vi lay contentedly in the sand, looking up at him as he laughed, and then sat down next to her to give her a warm hug. But his eyes kept straying to Audrey. There was genuine interest there, but he forced himself to be attentive to Violet.

'How've you been, Lady Vi?'

'Extremely well, Charlie. And it will be a much better summer now that you're here. How long can you stay?'

'A few days . . . a week. . . .' He knew how their summer revels were. He had visited them before and he always had a good time. He was a strikingly handsome man, Audrey realised as she stood looking down at him, wondering why she had ever thought he was an older man. Perhaps because he had accomplished so much . . . perhaps because his extensive travels and exotic looks reminded her of her father in some ways.

He had shiny black hair that was so dark it was almost blue, and a smooth olive complexion, huge dark brown eyes, and a smile that lit up his face in an incredible way. He was long and lanky and aristocratic, and he didn't look English at all, Audrey decided as she watched. He looked Spanish or French, or Italian perhaps . . . like an Italian prince actually, and he was wearing a navy blue knit bathing suit, and it was easy to see that he had long powerful legs, graceful arms, and shoulders even broader than James'. They had gone to Eton together years before, and the two men had been like brothers for most of their youth. It was James who grabbed his shoulder now and shook him a little bit.

'If my wife will be quiet for long enough, I'll introduce you to our friend. This is Audrey Driscoll, from California.' Charles cast his huge eyes up at her, with a smile that would have made any woman melt, and Audrey felt its effect on her too as she shook his hand. It was difficult not to be affected by the way he looked, but she was more intrigued about his books, and she was hoping to talk to him about them later. They talked at length that afternoon before he went off on a drive with James, leaving Audrey and Violet alone again.

'Incredibly handsome, isn't he?' Vi smiled, proud of their friend.

'You might say that.' Audrey laughed. She had been trying desperately not to feel awkward around him all afternoon, yet he was so unassuming and relaxed that eventually one forgot his good looks. But it was certainly difficult at first. It was the most striking thing about him.

'You know, he's totally unaware of how he looks,' Violet confided over champagne on the veranda as they waited for James. They were both wearing white silk gowns looking beautiful with their deep tans, and Audrey's hair was turning a bright burnished red from the sun. 'I talked to him about it once, and I promise you, he has absolutely no idea how he affects people. None at all. Actually . . .' She stuffed some baked mushrooms into her mouth and grinned like a little girl as she gobbled them before she could speak again. 'It's amazing, isn't it, Aud? I mean you'd think he'd be used to women swooning wherever he walks. But he's so preoccupied with his books that I don't really think he cares.' Audrey liked that about him. More than that, she liked his mind. She had read two of his books and had been totally enthralled. The other author of his genre whom she enjoyed was Nicol Smith, the explorer and writer, and Charles said he was crazy about him too. They had had a long conversation about him that afternoon. Audrey had found Charles fascinating, as they talked of Java, Nepal, and India. 'All the places you'd never want to go,' Audrey teased Vi as she groaned at them.

'I can't imagine what you find intriguing about places like that. They sound wretched to me.' Audrey's eyes danced as she laughed at her friend and James arrived on the scene in a white linen suit that looked extremely tropical, with his deep tan, dark hair, and green eyes.

'Was she saying something rude again, Aud?' He helped himself to the champagne and hors d'oeuvres and turned to admire his wife. 'My, you look pretty tonight, Lady Vi. You should always wear white, my dear.' He kissed her lightly on the lips, ate another stuffed mushroom, and turned to smile at Audrey again. It was nice having her there with them, and now that Charles had arrived, they were really going to have some good times. And by later that evening that seemed an extremely likely prospect. The foursome went to dinner at a small restaurant in Cannes. They drank a great deal too much wine, and laughed themselves silly all the way to Juan-les-Pins, where they went to a party someone had told James about which they didn't leave until two, after which they moved on, and stopped at another party at Cap d'Antibes, until they finally got home at four, less drunk than they'd been in several hours, and determined to stay up and watch the dawn. James opened another bottle of champagne when they got home and drank most of it himself, Lady Vi fell asleep on the couch, and eventually, singing a rather inappropriate song, James carried her upstairs, which left only Audrey and Charles still on the veranda two hours later when the sun slowly peeked over the horizon and began to come up. As it did, Charles was watching her, with a serious look in his eyes.

'What really brings you here?' They had been chatting aimlessly for the past two hours, enjoying each other's company, and speaking of the subjects they both loved, travel to the distant corners of the world . . . the summer in Cap d'Antibes . . . their friends Vi and James . . . but now Charles was looking intently at her, wondering who she really was, as she pondered similar questions about him. It was odd to wonder what quirk of fate had brought them both here, at the same time.

She decided to be honest with him. As honest as she could be. 'I needed to get away.'

'From what?' His voice was a caress in the golden light from the rising sun. But he assumed that she had wanted to get away from a man. She was old not to be married, by the standards of their times. 'Or should I say from whom?' He smiled, and her eyes were candid as she shook her head.

'No . . . not that . . . or maybe I just needed to get away from myself, and the responsibilities I impose on myself.'

'That sounds serious.' His eyes never left hers, and he had an insatiable desire to touch her lips with his own, to run his fingertips along her graceful neck, but he forced himself to listen to her and quell the rising desire he felt for her, at least for the moment.

'Sometimes it is serious.' She leaned back with a sigh. 'I have a grandfather I love with all my heart . . . and a sister who needs me desperately.'

'Is she ill?' He knit his brows and Audrey looked at him in surprise.

'No . . . what made you say that?'

'The way you stressed "desperately".'

She shook her head looking out to sea, thinking of Annabelle, and finally allowing herself to think again of all that Harcourt had said to her. 'She's just very young. . . .' She looked back at him again. 'And I've spoiled her, I suppose. It's hard not to. We lost our parents when we were very young, and I brought her up.'

'How strange.' There was something haunted in Charles's face as he spoke.

'Why do you say that?'

'How old were you when your parents died? . . . did they die at the same time?'

She nodded, wondering why he looked so intense suddenly. 'I was eleven, my sister was only seven then . . . in Hawaii . . . and yes, they died together in an accident at sea. . . .' It still pained her to speak of it. 'We went back to the mainland then, to live with my grandfather. I've been running his house ever since, and mothering my sister . . . too much perhaps . . . at least that's what her husband says.' She looked honestly into Charles's eyes. 'He seems to think I've crippled her, that she can't do anything for herself without my help. And perhaps he's right. He said,' she tried to look amused but it was obvious that she was not, 'that all I ever do is order new curtains and hire and fire maids. And when I thought about it,' her eyes suddenly filled with tears and she was horrified, 'I couldn't really disagree with him . . . so I left . . . for a while . . . and came here. . . .' She looked away again, but Charles reached out and took her hand.

'I understand.'

'Do you?' Her eyes met his again, and her lashes were damp. 'How could you understand?'

'Because my life hasn't been so different from yours, except that there was no grandfather. An aunt and uncle for a while, but they're gone now too. My parents died in an accident when I was seventeen, my brother was twelve. We lived with my aunt and uncle in America for a year, and we hated it. They meant well,' he sighed, and his grip on Audrey's hand tightened almost imperceptibly, 'but they didn't really understand either of us. They thought me far too adventurous for my age, too independent, and much too outspoken about it, and my brother not independent enough. He was completely traumatised by my parents' death and he had never been a very healthy child.

'When I turned eighteen, we left. We came back to England and I did what I could. . . .' There was a catch in his throat, as Audrey's heart went out to him. 'He only lived another year. He died of tuberculosis at fourteen.' He looked at her emptily, with heartbroken eyes. 'I always wondered if that wouldn't have happened if we'd stayed in the States . . . he might not have . . . he could be here now if . . .'

'Don't say that, Charles.' She reached out without thinking and gently touched his cheek. 'You can't control things like that. I always felt responsible somehow for my parents' death. But that's foolish and useless. We can't control life.' He nodded. It was the first time he had ever opened up to someone as he had to her, someone he barely knew, but there was something so warm and sympathetic about her. He had been drawn to her from the first moment they met, and he was even more so now. Suddenly he wanted to tell her everything, about himself, about his life, about Sean, the brother he had lost. . . .

63

'I began travelling after that. I tried to go to university afterwards, but I couldn't concentrate after Sean died. Everything reminded me of him . . . everyone had a younger brother his age . . . or I would see children in the street who looked too much like him . . . I wanted to go somewhere I wouldn't be reminded of anyone I'd ever known . . . so I went to Nepal . . . and India after that . . . and then Japan for a year . . . and when I was twenty-one, I wrote the first book,' he smiled for the first time in an hour, 'and then it became a way of life, and I fell in love with it.' Audrey smiled into his eyes.

'You're very good at what you do.' She felt touched that he had confided in her, and she felt for his pain. It suddenly made her think of what losing Annabelle would have been like. She couldn't bear the thought, tears filled her eyes just thinking about it.

'Travelling is my whole life now,' he confessed almost guiltily, looking boyish again.

'There's no sin in that. In fact,' she sighed with a smile, as the early morning sun shone down on them, 'I envy you. My father travelled all over the world, and I've always wanted to do just that.'

'Why don't you then?'

'And Annabelle? . . . and Grandfather? What happens to them?'

'They'd probably do very well.'

'We'll see, I guess. That's what this trip is all about.'

'Antibes is hardly an exotic place, my friend.'

'I know.' They both laughed. 'But perhaps if they survive my being here, then maybe one day I can go somewhere more adventurous.'

'You should go now. One day, you'll be married and you won't have the chance.'

She smiled. She was in no imminent danger of that. 'I don't think there's any great risk of that.'

'Is there something I don't know yet? A curse on the family? Some hideous trait you've concealed?'

She laughed as he teased, and as she shook her head, the copper mane swung free. 'No. I just don't think I'm the type to get married.'

'But you've just told me that you've been running your grandfather's house for fifteen years. Isn't that training enough?'

'Yes, but I'm not married to him. To be honest with you,' and she was, totally, 'most of the men I've met don't appeal to me very much.'

'Why not?' He was fascinated by her, fascinated by everything she did and said and thought. He had never met a woman quite like her.

'They bore me to death. Like my brother-in-law. They have preconceived ideas about what women should and shouldn't do. Women should not discuss politics, or even think about such things. They should pour tea, should work for the Red Cross, should go out to lunch with their friends. And the things that really interest me are absolutely taboo. Politics, travel . . . roaming halfway around the world, with my camera preferably.'

'You take photographs, do you?' She nodded enthusiastically. 'And I'll bet you're good.' He spoke with absolute confidence in her and she was surprised.

'What makes you say that?'

'You're sensitive, perceptive probably . . . it takes a certain kind of mind to be a good photographer . . . a sharp eye, an ordered mind.'

'And I'm guilty of all that?' She laughed, surprised at his analysis of her. 'At home they just call me an old maid.' It hurt him just hearing it, and he looked angry suddenly.

'How stupid of them. The trouble is that no one understands if you don't fit in the right mould. In some ways, I have the same problem as you. I don't want to settle down with just anyone . . . never have . . . not after . . .' She knew he was thinking of Sean. 'Life is too short . . . too ephemeral . . . I don't want to waste it pretending to be something I'm not.'

65

'And what aren't you?' It was her turn to ask him questions now, and she was curious about him as well.

'I'm not a man who could ever settle down easily. Adventuring is in my blood. I love what I do. And there aren't too many women who are willing to understand that. They pretend to, at first, and then they want you to settle down. It's like putting a lion in a cage. Everyone wants to try, but then they don't know what to do with him. I was born to live in the wild. I love it there. I don't domesticate very well, I'm afraid.' He smiled charmingly and her heart gave a little tug. He was the most endearing man, and what he said next touched her too, and she understood it perfectly. 'I'm not sure I'd ever want children either . . . and that's something of a handicap. Most women want two or three.' She didn't dare ask him why, but he told her anyway. 'After Sean . . . I felt I didn't ever want to love anyone that much again . . . it was as though he were my child, and not my brother any more . . . and I couldn't bear losing him.' Charles's eyes filled with tears but he went on without shame or embarrassment, pouring his heart out to her. 'I couldn't stand loving my own children like that, and then perhaps losing one of them. It seems safer somehow to stay like this. And I'm perfectly happy, I must say.' He brushed a tear from his cheek, and smiled at her in a bittersweet way. 'It drives one's friends mad of course. Violet can never resist the urge to introduce me to every woman they know. At least it keeps things lively when I'm on this side of the world.' He hesitated, and gently stroked her hand resting in his own. 'And you, my friend? Don't you think you'll settle down one day?' She had almost given up on that, and she didn't really care any more.

'You have to give up so much . . . nothing I want fits in with marriage, in the conventional sense.'

'And children?'

She took a deep breath and looked into his eyes. 'I have Annabelle.' It was how she really felt. She had had a child, even if she hadn't borne her herself, 'and now her son . . . and Grandfather . . . I don't need children of my own.'

'You can't live a life like that though, living other people's lives. You're too good for that. There's too much of you.'

'How do you know that?' It was as though he sensed instinctively exactly who she was, and so far he hadn't been wrong. 'You're happy as you are. Why can't I be too?'

'Because I'm doing exactly what I want to do. And you're not . . . are you?' His voice was so soft, and his hand so strong as he held hers. And she couldn't deny what he said. Slowly, she shook her head. She was doing what she ought and what she must and what she should, for people she loved . . . but it was not what she wanted to do.

She smiled philosophically at him, knowing that she had made a friend she would keep for a long, long time. 'You're right, but there's nothing I can do about it . . . not now, anyway. All I can do is look at this summer like a gift, and go back when it's time.'

'And then? . . . and after that? . . . how much of your life are you willing to give up?'

She almost gulped as she said the words. 'All of it, I suppose. You can't give halfway.' He had learned that with Sean, and that was what frightened him about giving again . . . about loving someone *à tout jamais* as the French said . . . to the bottom of your soul. He hadn't in fifteen years, and now suddenly here she was, a woman who seemed to understand the very workings of his soul, just as he understood hers. It was odd finding her now. He hadn't been looking for her, and he wasn't sure he wanted to find her yet. But there she was, her hair shooting copper lights at him as the sun rose in the sky and he sat staring at her.

'You know, I don't know why we met when we did . . . but I think I'm falling in love with you . . .' She wasn't prepared for what he said to her, and her heart almost seemed to give a lurch and leap out of her chest to fly at his feet.

'I . . . I don't . . . I'm . . .' And then, not finding the words, she only nodded at him. He understood everything . . . Harcourt . . . Annabelle . . . Grandfather . . . her hunger to see the world . . . to be alive . . . to be free . . . to take

67

photographs . . . and the distant dream she had long since given up, of sharing it with someone, of finding someone who would do it all with her . . . and now suddenly here he was, their paths crossing for only hours or days . . . 'I think I am too.' She looked stunned, feeling helpless for the first time in her life. And as she reached out to him, he took her in his arms and held her so tight it took her breath away. There was no doubt in her mind that the same arrow had struck her too, and his lips brushed her hair as his hands held her close to him.

She looked up at him then and he smiled at her, and then gently at first, he kissed her as he had kissed no other woman before, and she felt her heart soar to the skies as his lips pressed down hard on hers.

It was madness really. They had been strangers only the night before. And now suddenly, she knew she was falling in love with him. And as they walked slowly back inside the house, he put an arm around her and she felt his fingers brush her neck. She felt as though she had come to a turning point in her life that night, and her life would never be quite the same again.

'Audrey . . .' He looked down at her as they stood outside her bedroom door, and he smiled gently at her again. 'We're a great deal alike, you know, you and I.' He had never thought he would meet anyone like her, and he never had before.

'It's amazing, isn't it?' It seemed wonderful and at the same time unfair. She saw everything she wanted in him, and in a few days she would never see him again. 'How long will you be in Antibes?' She barely dared to whisper the words.

'As long as I can.' Their eyes met for a last lingering look, and with a silent nod, she slipped into her room.

6

Another idyllic week had slid by, and Charles was still staying with Vi and James. They were still cavorting like children in Antibes, and the four of them went everywhere, although Audrey and Charles managed some time off by themselves every day. She usually went somewhere to take photographs, and Charles saw to it that he accompanied her. It seemed as though since he had arrived they had done nothing but explore each other's lives and it was difficult to believe that they hadn't known each other for years.

She was focusing on an ancient house in the little mountain town of Eze, as he looked at her with admiration in his eyes. He had seen her work developed now, and he knew just how good she was with the little Leica she took everywhere, and used so frequently.

'I'd like to work on a book with you one day, Aud. Would you like that?' She snapped two more shots and then turned to smile at him, and took a photograph of him with a look of surprise on his face.

'Are you serious, Charles?' She had blossomed in the days since he'd arrived. She looked more womanly suddenly, more relaxed, and there was a different look in her eyes. Vi talked about it constantly, whenever she and James were alone, and she was wondering if anything would come of it, though James insisted nothing would. Charles wasn't the marrying kind. He had said so for years, and marriage would never have fit in with his career. But it was obvious even to James, that Charles was madly infatuated with the girl. Or 'head over heels in love with her', as Vi said.

'Of course I'm serious. Your photographs are damn good. Better than what I write.'

'Hardly.' She laughed at his modesty and came to stand next to him. 'Are you ready for lunch?' They had packed Vi and

James' enormous picnic basket in the car, and they unpacked it on the mountainside, surrounded by wild flowers with the walls of Eze behind their backs, and the Mediterranean far beneath their feet. It was a view so picturesque that Audrey wondered if even her faithful Leica could capture the beauty of it. She stretched out in the grass, propped on one elbow, looking up at him, with an apple in her hand, and a smile in her eyes. 'I'm so happy here, Charles.'

'Are you, now?' He looked pleased. 'And why is that, do you suppose?' He leaned over then kissed the tip of her nose. 'Has it occurred to you that I'm happy too? Happier than I've ever been in my entire life.'

She beamed as he leaned over and kissed her full on the lips. 'What are we going to do when it's time to go back?' She had begun worrying about that. Sooner or later the idyll had to end, and she dreaded that. They both did.

'Who determines that, Cinderella? How do we know when it's time to go home?'

'I sail on September fourteenth.' Back the way she had come . . . to responsibility . . . and duty . . . and Annabelle, who was already feeling unwell with her pregnancy. Her last letter had actually been blurred by the tears that fell on the paper as she wrote, and Audrey felt guilty even staying as long as she'd planned.

'Is that written in stone?'

'No.' She sighed. 'But you know I have to go back.'

'Why?'

'You know why.'

'No, I don't.' He was teasing her, but he wanted to test how strongly she felt about it. He had had an idea that had been haunting him for days, and he was almost afraid to share it with her, for fear of what she'd say. But he knew that if he could talk her into it, her life would never be quite the same again . . nor would his.

'Charles . . .' She was looking imploringly at him, with a sorrow in her eyes he had never seen there before. Most of the time they laughed and drank champagne and went to parties with Violet and James, but it was on these little jaunts together that they had the chance to open their souls to each other, as they so often did.

'Why do you look so sad, my love?' He lay down beside her on the grass, and the warmth of his body near hers almost drove her mad. She felt things for Charles that she had never dreamed of in her entire life, but he didn't press her in any awkward ways. And now he just looked at her tenderly, tickling her ear with a bright purple flower that grew near where they lay.

'. . . Don't press me about not going home. I can't delay my return.'

'Why not?'

'It wouldn't be fair.'

'To whom?' He was pressing her, and it was very hard on her.

'To Grandfather. I know what he thought when I left, and I want to prove to him that he was wrong.'

'About what?' Charles looked suddenly mystified, until she explained.

'I think he had a kind of *déjà vu* when I left. He was terrified that I would do what my father did . . . and I promised him I wouldn't do that . . . I just can't do that to him.'

'I don't understand.' He brushed her lips with his own and she had to fight to concentrate on what she was telling him.

'My father left and never really came back. Not for any length of time anyway. He promised to, but it was stronger than he . . . he couldn't come back. He was too in love with the places he went, the people he met, the adventures he found. . . .' Her voice drifted off, remembering him. He had been the most dashing, romantic man. And then as she thought of him, she looked up at Charles again . . . they were so much alike . . . it startled her sometimes. . . .

'Is that so terrible?' It was something he understood so well. He had lived in precisely that way for the past fifteen years. The only difference was that there was no one waiting for him, anywhere. No one who gave a damn where he was

71

at any given time, except friends like Violet and James. But no one cried when he left, and no one counted the hours until he returned. In a way, he envied her that. He would have liked that about having a wife, though not much else.

'I just can't do that to him.' Her voice was as soft as the breeze that rippled through her hair.

'And to yourself? Can you give up your dreams, Aud?'

'This is my dream.' She smiled at him. 'More than my dream in fact.'

'That's not what you told me when we met.'

'Yes, it is!' She blushed, wondering what she had said, on that first night, when they'd stayed up until the sunrise and told each other about their dreams and their lives and who they really were.

'You said you wanted to see exotic places. . . .'

She stretched out her arms to take in the grandiose beauty of the mountainside where they lay in the heart of the Alpes-Maritimes. 'Well?'

'This is hardly what you had in mind . . . I think we were talking about Nepal at the time, weren't we?' He was teasing her, and pushing her, making her just a little uncomfortable without pushing too hard. He was good at it, but she was a fair match for him.

'This will do. For now.'

And then suddenly, he looked sad. 'I have to leave in a few days, you know, Aud.' It was the first she had heard of it, and she felt her heart stop at his words. She sat staring at him with wide-open eyes. It was coming to an end. She had known it would . . . she just hadn't known it would happen so soon. 'I have a story to write, for the London *Times*.'

'Now?' It was a tiny frightened word.

'Soon.'

'Where?'

'Nanking, Shanghai, Peking . . .'

'My God.' She was shocked, but she tried to be a good sport as she smiled, feeling all the air and happiness seem to leave her at once. 'That's certainly exotic, isn't it?'

72

He nodded quietly. 'I wish you could come along.'

'So do I.' She said the words honestly. It sounded magical to her. Just the names were extraordinary, but they were not destined to be part of her life. At least not now.

'You could take fabulous photographs on a trip like that.' He would lure her with anything he could, and she laughed ruefully.

'Among other things.'

'When do you go?' She reached out a hand to him instinctively and they held hands quietly under the summer sky, feeling the closeness they had built in the short time since they'd met.

'I don't know. I have some work to do in Italy first, and I thought I'd catch the Orient Express in Venice after that.'

She closed her eyes, emotions flowing, just hearing about it. He watched her face, and then saw two tears trickle down her cheek, as she looked up at him again. 'You're a lucky man.'

He shook his head, as unhappy as she was. 'No, I'm not. The woman I love is going to be halfway around the world . . . isn't she?' He pressed her hand and she sat up. She was going to have to be an adult about this. There was no point crying about what she couldn't have, and she couldn't have him. Not for long anyway. There was no point fooling herself about that.

'Why don't you come to San Francisco afterwards?' She smiled and he laughed.

'Just like that, eh? You certainly make it sound easy enough.'

'Isn't it?' She was teasing him now and he kissed her again.

'Maybe I will. And maybe I'll carry you off on a white horse, with a rose between your teeth.'

'That sounds wonderful, Charles.'

'Yes . . . doesn't it . . .' He pulled her down beside him in the grass again, and they lay in each other's arms for a time, until their embraces grew too heated to be restrained, and she wisely pulled away, as he looked regretfully at her. He respected her a great deal, but he had never wanted a woman as desperately as he wanted her, and they had so little time left.

It added a forced gaiety to the time they spent together with Vi and James. The nights became later and later each day, and filled with more champagne. And it became more and more difficult to tear herself away from him at night and go back to her own room, but she didn't want to do anything foolish before she went home. She would have had to live with the consequences for a lifetime afterwards. And Charles didn't want to take any chances with her, no matter how badly he wanted her. He loved her too much for that.

'I think I ought to start taking cold showers, or midnight baths in the sea, not that the Mediterranean is chilly enough. I'm afraid it won't do,' he teased one night as they strolled home from a party farther down the beach at Antibes. 'You're driving me mad, you know.' She felt guilty about that, and she didn't mean to tease.

'I'm so sorry, Charles. . . .' She looked up at him adoringly and he put an arm around her and brought her close to him again.

'You shouldn't be. These have been the best weeks of my life, thanks to you. I'll carry the memories with me to the end of the world.' He smiled down at her and kissed the froth of copper hair that danced around her head. He didn't know it yet, but she had a surprise waiting for him. She had been putting together an album of their days in Antibes, filled with photographs she had taken, duplicating the ones she was keeping for herself. She was going to put it all together for him before he left. He could look at it on the way to Nanking. She didn't even like to think about it now. But she had to. He was leaving in a few days.

And on their last night, they sat and watched the sun come up, just as they had on the night they met, only a few weeks before. 'It's hard to believe, isn't it?' He looked serious as he sat holding her hand. Vi and James had long since given up and gone to bed, but Charles and Audrey were in no hurry to leave each other that night. 'It seems as though I've known you all my life.'

'It's going to be so strange when you're gone again . . . so empty suddenly. . . .' She was totally honest with him. He was someone she could have said anything to, and she often did, and now he looked down at her, unable to give up the dream of keeping her with him.

'I want to ask you something, Aud. And I want you to think about it before you say no.' He stopped and took a deep breath before going on. 'Will you come with me?' Her heart stopped and it must have showed in her eyes. 'Just as far as Istanbul. You can still get back to London on time. I have to leave Venice on September third. You'll make your sailing on the fourteenth.' And then his eyes lit up as he looked at her. 'Audrey . . .' She was already shaking her head.

'I can't do that, Charles.'

'Why not? God only knows when we'll see each other again. Can you really give this up so easily, waste everything we've had?' He looked suddenly angry at her as he stood up and paced the terrace where they waited for the sun to come up. 'How can you just say no like that? Dammit, Audrey, just this once . . . think of yourself . . . think of us . . . please! . . .' He turned to her with a look that tore at her heart. 'At least give it some thought.' She promised to, but this time it wasn't her obligations that were stopping her. It was something else. She was afraid to go to Venice with him. She knew what would happen there . . . what she would do if she were all alone with him . . . she would throw convention to the winds. She was almost ready to do that in Antibes, but she didn't want to do that . . . it was a crazy thing to do. And going to Venice was like throwing herself off a cliff. All night she searched his eyes, thinking of what he had asked, and when the sun came up, she turned to him, prepared to tell him that she couldn't go with him, but he silenced her with a kiss, and then suddenly began speaking of Sean . . . and how short life was . . . how infinitely precious . . . how dear . . . and she suddenly realised just what his life was like. He was going to China to interview Chiang Kai-shek and to write about Shanghai now that it was threatened by the Japanese. What if he were killed? . . . if she never saw him again? . . . it was a horrifying thought, and as he kissed her again, and she felt his hands move slowly up her thighs, her breath caught and she almost moaned at his touch.

'Please Audrey . . . please . . . come to Italy with me. . . .' And when she looked into his eyes, she knew how desperately she wanted to. She couldn't say no to him . . . or to herself . . . not any more.

She whispered the words as he kissed her neck and fondled her breasts. 'I'll meet you in Venice before you leave.' She was shocked at her own words, but as he took her in his arms again and held her there, she didn't regret her promise to him.

It was what she wanted to do too. And she would just have to be reasonable, and not do anything too insane . . . but what could happen after all? It was only for two days before he caught the train.

They agreed not to tell Vi and James, and when he left the next day, he gave her a lingering kiss for all to see, and she waved until his car was out of sight. And Lady Vi was deeply solicitous after he was gone.

'Are you all right, Aud?' She brought her a stiff drink, and looked as though she were prepared to see Audrey collapse in a fit of tears. But she seemed satisfied when Audrey took a sip of the drink and then quietly went to her room to lie down. And when she did, she lay thinking of him, and what she had agreed to do . . . she had promised him . . . promised him . . . It was totally mad, and yet she didn't regret a bit of it . . . The Piazza San Marco at six o'clock on September first. And then, God only knew what would happen after that. But Audrey knew one thing for sure. She had to be there with him.

7

The next week sped by all too fast. Charles left, and James' brother arrived, and a few days later, Lady Vi's, and as August got under way, one had the feeling that soon it would all end. Audrey decided that it was time to begin her drive. She never mentioned to Violet or James what Charles had suggested before he left. She still wondered if she should back out, if she were doing something too totally mad, but she couldn't bear the thought of going back to the States without seeing him again. She had to meet him in Venice, even if only to say one last goodbye, and give him the album she had made for him.

It was another tearful farewell when she left Violet and James at last, and leaving the children was even worse. She had bought Alexandra a huge beautiful doll in Cannes at *Le Rêve d'Enfants*, and she bought little James a wonderful sailor suit, and a model sailboat he could sail in the park at home. She gave Violet a handsome crystal and onyx brooch, and James a case of Dom Pérignon champagne. But better than that she gave them a stack of the photographs she had taken of them. There were marvellous ones of Violet in various costumes and fabulous hats, James fooling around on the beach, and walking quietly with Charles, and another of him at sunset looking into Lady Vi's eyes with a look of tenderness that had brought tears to Audrey's eyes when she saw the photograph all blown up. They were a beautiful souvenir of a summer that none of them would ever forget, and Audrey tried to put it into words as they stood beside the car she had hired, but it was impossible to tell them what she felt. She felt far too much. For all of them.

'Thank you seems such a ridiculously small thing to say in exchange for so much. . . .' She gave Lady Vi a warm hug, and they were both crying when Violet stepped back again.

'You must write! You promised me!'

'I will! I promise you. . . .' And then she hugged James. They wouldn't be back in London yet when she left on the *Mauretania*. And he was like an older brother as he kissed her fondly on both cheeks. She couldn't help wishing that Annabelle had married a man like him instead of the one she had. She kissed the children one last time, and Violet again, and then crying openly she got into the car and slid behind the wheel as Violet shook her head again and wiped her eyes with a lace handkerchief.

She tried to smile through her tears. 'I haven't felt this awful since Aunt Hattie died last year.' She laughed and blew her nose, and Audrey did the same in the car as Lady Vi chided her. 'You shouldn't be driving by yourself. It's dangerous.'

'I'll be fine.'

'You're too independent by far!' She was sorry that nothing serious had come of it with Charles. He should have stayed and driven her to Italy, but he had been in such a hurry to rush off and do his articles. Perhaps James was right, she decided, as they waved to Audrey as she drove slowly away from them. Charles really wasn't the marrying kind. 'It's such a damn shame!' she shouted at James as Audrey disappeared.

'Well, I didn't send her away, darling. Don't shout at me.' He squeezed her shoulders and she blew her nose again and shook her head.

'I didn't mean that. I meant Charles.'

'What about Charles?' James looked confused.

'It's a damn shame he's not sensible enough to know the perfect wife for him when he sees her.'

'I told you. He's not the marrying kind.'

'That's what I mean!' She looked severely annoyed and he laughed.

'Oh, that's what you meant . . . well, he's not . . . so don't torture yourself, or poor Aud. There's no room for a woman in his life, for heaven's sake. What woman wants to put up

78

with a man racing around the world like that, living with Bedouin tribes and camels and God knows what else, except maybe a Bedouin girl.' But Violet was not amused as she glared at him.

'He's a damn fool.'

'Perhaps. Or perhaps he knows himself very well, my dear.' And then suddenly he looked troubled as he glanced at his wife. 'Do you suppose Audrey expected something to come of it? Nothing ever will, you know.'

'I think she knows that better than we do. And she's as stubborn as he is anyway. All she thinks about is her grand-father and that troublesome sister of hers. Every time that girl wrote to her, Audrey was depressed all day. The girl must cry all the time. Difficult to imagine, isn't it, Audrey is so totally opposite. And no, I don't think she expected anything of Charles, but I think it ran deeper for both of them than either of us thought.'

'What makes you think that?' James was always impressed by how perceptive his wife was. She often saw things he had no inkling of, and he wondered what she had seen or sensed about them. Charles was still his very dearest friend, and he had grown fond of Audrey during her stay with them. 'Did she say something to you before she left?'

'No.' Lady Vi shook her head. 'And neither did he, which is what makes me think that it's more serious than we think. They both made such a point about not saying anything at all.'

James looked at her as though she were quite mad. 'Sometimes you really don't make any sense.' He leaned over and kissed her gently on the lips. 'But I love you anyway.'

'Thank you, James.' She smiled and lay back in her favourite chair as they soaked up the last of the summer's rays.

Audrey drove to San Remo, Rapallo, Portofino, and Viareggio along the coast, finally abandoning the seaside there to make her way inland to Pisa and Empoli, and then south to Siena, Perugia, Spoleto, Viterbo, and then at last to Rome. But once there, she found she could barely think of what she was supposed to be seeing there. All she could think of were Violet and James, the children, their friends, and of course Charles. But she felt like a lost soul, wandering through churches and museums, the Coliseum, the Catacombs, and the Vatican. Somehow, she felt numb as she wandered through Rome alone, and it no longer seemed like such a good idea to have come. She was relieved when she took the train to Florence and gave up the hired car, but it was much the same there. Her mind wasn't on the beauty of what she was seeing, and all the churches and museums began to look the same to her. All she could think of now was getting to Venice to see Charles again. And when she boarded the train to Venice at last, she felt as though she wanted to get out and run herself. The train stopped a thousand times, or so it seemed. There were floods of people getting on and off, and at each stop, the train was more and more delayed, and by late afternoon, she was panicking. It was obvious that they weren't going to get there in time, and she suddenly realised the insanity of having made an appointment with him in a public square. It had seemed so romantic at the time, and it hadn't occurred to either of them that it was impractical, that this was Italy and nothing happened on time. The train reached the station shortly after eight o'clock, as the sun set with brilliant orange streamers flaming across the sky and tears brimming in Audrey's eyes. She was more than two hours late, and God only knew where Charles would be. By then, he would have come and gone. They hadn't even thought to agree on a hotel, although she herself had made a reservation at the Gritti, from Rome, but she had no idea where Charles would go, or if they would meet again. She had never felt as bereft in her life as when she watched the *gondoliere* pile her luggage into his gondola and she gave him the name of her hotel. And then suddenly, she decided to try anyway.

'Can we stop at the Piazza San Marco on the way?'

'Piazza San Marco?' She nodded, still in despair. '*Si signorina*.' He smiled at her with warm eyes and half of his teeth gone, the classic *gondoliere*'s hat on his head, and his powerful legs braced as he steered the graceful boat and she looked around, at the others travelling the canals in gondolas, and the sunset shimmering on the gold mosaics of various domes. It was the most beautiful place she had ever seen, and she had never felt as alone in her life as when she got out of the boat, and ran towards the square. Her eyes swept the vast expanse, taking in the Campanile and the crowds of people wandering to and from the cafés. She glanced at everyone, and ran hurriedly from one café to the next, and then suddenly she saw the dark hair, a British raincoat, the back of a familiar head, and she flew to his side, looking up at him as though she had been reprieved ... only to find that it was someone else, and she backed away in dismay and shame. Half an hour later, she was forced to admit defeat. He was nowhere in sight. Perhaps he hadn't even come, or if he had, he had left, convinced that she had stood him up. She had to fight back tears all the way to her hotel, and when the porters and *gondoliere* unloaded her bags, she walked quietly into the hotel, defeat in her heart, and heartbreak in her eyes. It was obvious to anyone that something terrible had happened to her.

The suite that had been reserved for her was far grander than any she had reserved anywhere. There was a huge canopied Renaissance bed, there were lovely antiques in the room, marble tables, tapestries. It was a grandiose scene, and she felt foolish sitting there alone. But there was nothing else to do. It was after nine o'clock by then, and there was no point combing the streets for him. She had asked the concierge if Mr Parker-Scott had a reservation there too, and she was told that he did not. There was absolutely nothing she could do to find him now. All she could do was make a tour of the better hotels the next day and hope to find him somewhere, and if nothing else, she could

81

look for him at the train station on September third, hoping to find him before he boarded the train that would hook up with the Orient Express in Austria the next day. It seemed a shame to waste two days in Venice, but as she picked at the dinner she had sent up to her room, she wondered if it was her punishment . . . if it had been wrong to agree to meet him here. She knew it was, but hadn't been able to refuse, and now all was lost. The tears began to flow as she sat thinking of him, and she only heard the second knock at the door, and muttered darkly, 'Come in,' as she blew her nose, and assumed it was room service returning for the elaborate tray they had left with her. She barely looked up as the door opened, and suddenly she gasped and stood up. It had been unlocked, and he had walked right into her room.

'My God . . . how did you . . .' Her heart was pounding as she flew into his arms, more grateful than she had ever been to see anyone, and he held her to him like a lost child . . . as he once had his brother, Sean . . . he held her so close and so tight that she could barely breathe. 'Oh Charles,' she was crying like a little girl, which was very unlike her, 'I thought I'd never see you again.'

He cooed softly to her and rocked her in his arms. 'You won't get rid of me that easily, my love. I had a bit of a fright when you didn't show up, and then I checked with the hotels and found you had a reservation here.' She looked up at him adoringly and he smiled down at her.

'I was terrified . . . I thought . . .'

'That I was dead at the very least?' He noticed the red eyes and hugged her again, smoothing down the rumpled red hair with a look of love. 'I'm a sturdy sort, Aud. Are you all right?' He looked around at the elaborate suite. 'My, my . . .' She giggled then for the first time. And she suddenly looked like a young girl to him.

'It's very grand, isn't it?'

'It certainly is.' He stood back to admire her, enormously relieved to have found her so soon. Like Audrey, he had visions of wasted days, and futile attempts to find her everywhere. 'I'm sorry you had such a fright over this, my love. I should have met you in Rome, but I had so damn much work to do.' He tossed his coat over a chair and sat down next to her, looking at her seriously as she attempted to regain her composure again. 'I want you to know that I wouldn't have left for Istanbul without seeing you.'

She smiled through fresh tears, and her voice broke when she spoke. She was so relieved to see him. 'I was thinking the same thing . . . I was already trying to figure out when the next sailing was . . . I was trying to remember if I got the day wrong . . . if I heard the wrong thing. . . .' She laughed through her tears and threw her arms around his neck. 'Oh Charles . . . I love you so much. . . .' She had to say the words, had to tell him how she felt. He meant so much to her. And he held her close to him and found her lips with his own, and now there was nothing stopping them, no conventions as houseguests, no concern about their friends, and they forgot everything as he held her in his arms and ran his hands over her. He had never been as hungry for her as he was now, and she was just as hungry for him. 'Oh Charles . . .' He looked at her carefully at last, as they both caught their breath, and gently he pulled away.

'Perhaps I should go now, Aud. . . .' His eyes searched hers for his cue, but unlike all the other times in Antibes, this time she shook her head at him, and he held his breath as he looked at her. 'I don't want to do anything you'll regret.' It had been an emotional evening for them both, a difficult day waiting to meet again. In fact, neither of them had been able to think straight since Charles had left Antibes. And Audrey had been waiting for this, and only she knew how much as she looked at him again. She knew why she had come. She had been afraid to admit it to herself at first, but she had had to do this, and she knew there would never be any regrets. From this day forth, she was his.

'I don't want you to go.' Her voice was deep and calm and sensuous as he took her hand and kissed her fingertips.

Just that made her entire body sing with desire for him. 'I love you, Charles.' It was as simple as that in the end, as simple as those words and the volumes that she felt for him.

'I've never loved anyone more,' he whispered to her, and then he stood up and picked her up in his arms and walked quietly into the next room. There were soft lights filtering in, and when he closed the door, only the moonlight swept across the floor. He could see her face and her eyes and her lips and he kissed her gently and undressed her in the dark, admiring the silver of her flesh, as he ran his hands carefully over her. She knew without any doubt that she belonged to him, and she shivered as she slid between the cool sheets and watched him undress with his back to her. He got into the bed on the other side, and met her halfway, reaching out his arms to her as she came to him, and gave herself to him in every way. Her body thrilled to his touch, and he taught her gently and well, taking her only when she was ready for him, and then when she wanted him again. He let her set the pace, and he gave her all he had, from his body, his mind, his soul, and his heart. And from that moment on, their hearts seemed forever intertwined, as she lay in his arms and slept, and this time they did not see the sunrise, as the Campanile tolled the hour, and they slept on like two children, spent by their love.

8

Their two days in Venice were like something in a dream. He took her to see all the appropriate sights, the Doge's Palace with its magnificent doors, the Rialto Bridge, Santa Maria della Salute, and the Customs House with its gold weather vane ... and even more importantly, the Bridge of Sighs, where he made her hold her breath, and they kissed, as the *gondoliere* sang to them as they passed beneath. Charles assured her that their wishes would come true as a result, and she giggled at him. But most of their time, they spent in her room. He rented a smaller room on the same floor, for appearances' sake, but he didn't even leave his bags in there. They lived together as man and wife for two days and two nights, and Audrey found herself panicking as the hour approached for him to leave. She had reservations on the train to London that same night. But the train he was taking was going to Austria, and meeting up with the Orient Express there.

She was so depressed about leaving him that as they dressed for the last time, lingering in the enormous marble bathroom that they shared, having just made love in the bath before they dressed, she could barely speak, thinking of what it would be like saying goodbye to him. And then suddenly, as she thought of it, the dam suddenly broke, and she began sobbing as she looked at him.

'Darling, don't ... don't do this. ...' He was beyond pressing her any more. He had begged her to come with him, and she had remained firm in insisting she could not. It would have been cruel to continue pushing her, and he had promised not to do it again. 'I'll come to San Francisco as soon as I can. As soon as I finish in Peking. I'll come directly by ship.' He was holding her in his arms, and she was sobbing uncontrollably. She had given herself to this man, and now she couldn't bear to leave him again. She belonged with him. Every fibre of her being shrieked at the thought of leaving him, and yet she knew she must. She had absolutely no choice. Her arms were around his neck and it was a long time before she regained control again.

Charles helped her into her dress, and watched her fasten her pearls, and her earrings and put on her big straw hat, and he wanted to stop time as he looked at her. It was the dearest moment of his life, and he noticed that Audrey hadn't touched her camera in two days. This wasn't something one could record, it was a time filled with feelings, and aching desires fulfilled at last. It was a time neither of them would ever forget, and they were both sombre as they checked out of the hotel, and watched their things being put in the gondola outside. She turned back to look up at the hotel once and then she looked sadly at him.

'I never want to come back here again, Charles.'

'Why not?' He looked shocked. Had he misinterpreted how she felt? He couldn't have. . . .

'It could never be as beautiful as this again. I want to remember it just as it is now . . . in my mind' – her eyes filled with tears and he took her hand – 'in my heart. . . .' She looked up at him with her eyes swimming in tears and he held her close and helped her into the gondola. He dreaded what it would be like saying goodbye to her. He doubted if he could stem his own tears. It choked him just thinking of it. They sat huddled together like two lost souls on their way to the station, and he took her to the train, as she was scheduled to leave first by half an hour. He watched the porter settle her things, and he stood in her private compartment with her. There was nothing left to say, except promises that neither of them could keep. He had his work and she had her family, and they loved each other in a way that few people did. They each knew that as the time finally came, and he stood holding her, tears rolling slowly down their cheeks and their eyes closed as they kissed.

He was the first to pull away. He couldn't bear it any

more. 'I love you, Aud. I always, always will.' He wanted to ask her again to come to Istanbul with him, but he didn't dare ask her again. It wasn't fair to either of them to push any more. It was time to say goodbye. It had to be faced. But it was the most painful thing that had happened to him since the loss of Sean, and he wasn't sure he would be able to bear losing her, except that he had no choice.

'I love you with all my heart,' she whispered to him. 'Take care of yourself . . . keep safe. . . .' She clung to him for a last moment, and then he hurried from the compartment and down the corridor, down the few steps and ran back to her window again. She opened it and leaned down, and he kissed her again, and they both smiled. 'See you after Peking. . . .' But she didn't even like to think of it . . . by his own admission it would be several months . . . maybe even six . . . he had no idea how long he would be tied up in China. His deadline was at year end, but with the hostilities with the Japanese he had no idea what he would find once he was there.

'I'll write to you, Aud.' It was a promise he had never made to anyone else, and he intended to keep it with her. But he stood looking at her then, wanting to ask her just once more, to go to Istanbul with him. But he didn't say the words. He kissed her once more, and then turned and hurried away before he no longer could. He couldn't have borne one of those painful scenes, standing on the platform as she pulled away. He went to his own train to wait, and twenty minutes later, he heard her train grinding slowly away, as he closed his eyes and winced, like a man facing a firing squad. He put his hand over his eyes, and lay back against the seat, thinking about her. And the images he saw in his mind's eye were so real that he could almost feel her in the compartment with him, smell her perfume, hear her voice. . . .

'You can open your eyes now, Charles.' He almost jumped out of his skin, as he dropped his hand and opened his eyes to look at her. She was standing only two feet away, smiling at him, as a porter stood juggling her bags with a look of dismay.

'What . . . my . . . for chrissake, Audrey! You almost gave me a heart attack!' He was shouting as he jumped to his feet but he swept her off her feet and into his arms, giving an alarming whoop as he did, and kissing her so hard she thought he would push her teeth down her throat. 'What in hell are you doing here?'

'I thought I'd come to Istanbul with you.' She had made up her mind as he walked away. She knew she couldn't leave him yet. It wasn't time. And she could make it back to London in time to sail on the *Mauretania* on the fourteenth, if there were no major delays. And if there were, she would catch the next ship home after that. All she knew was that she had to be with him, no matter what. 'Does the invitation still stand?' She was beaming at him now, and he desperately wanted a drink to soothe his frayed nerves.

'I think it might.' He looked down at her ruefully, and then pulled her close to him again as the porter closed the door and left them alone. 'I never want to be without you again, Aud . . . or at least not for a long, long time . . . like the rest of my life.' He smiled.

'Is that a proposal?' She looked stunned.

'Of a sort. I can't imagine living without you again, Aud.'

She felt the same way about him. But one of them would have had to give up everything. She her family, or he his career. And she couldn't imagine either of them giving up what they loved. 'I don't think it's time to worry about that yet. Maybe we should just enjoy what we have.' She was a wise woman, and she had made up her mind. She knew she had to be with him. And she intended to be. To Istanbul, certainly. And perhaps beyond. That remained to be seen.

9

They spent the night making love on their way to Austria, and when Audrey awoke the next morning, she had tousled hair and wide eyes. For a moment she had forgotten where she was going with him, and then suddenly it all came back to her, as they ground to a slow halt and she peeked out the window over Charles's shoulder, and saw the sleek blue and gold train on the other side of the platform waiting for them. The marking on the side said COMPAGNIE INTERNATIONALE DES WAGONS-LITS ET DES GRANDS EXPRESS EUROPÉENS, and suddenly Audrey was wide-eyed as she looked at it. This was the train she had read so much about, for so many years. Her grandfather had even told her about it. He had taken it years before. And there were photographs of it in her father's albums too, and now suddenly here she was, staring out at it, in all its splendour, waiting to discover its mysteries.

'Charles . . . look. . . .' She poked him like a child and he stirred sleepily and looked up at her with a lazy smile.

'Good morning, love.' He ran a hand caressingly over her behind and she smiled at him, but she was far more interested in the scene outside. Even at that hour, there were fascinating people boarding the train. Men who looked like bankers and women who looked like concubines or movie stars or presidents' wives. There was a woman draped in silver fox, and another carrying an armload of sables despite the warm September air. There were men in pinstriped suits and homburgs, with heavy gold watch chains stretched across their stomachs, as though holding them in. She was fascinated, and she reached across Charlie distractedly, groping for something just beyond him, as he looked at her, amused at her excitement over what he jokingly referred to as a 'mere' train.

'Are you crazy?' she intoned, outraged, as she found what she had been looking for. It was her Leica, and she focused it immediately on the scene outside. 'That's the Orient Express out there, not just a train for heaven's sake.' He laughed at her, took the camera out of her hands when she had had a chance to take at least half a roll of film, and set it down gingerly before pinning her down beneath his long graceful limbs and looking down at her hungrily.

'Is this why you came with me? Just to take photographs?' He was teasing her and she was laughing up at him.

'Damn right. What did you think I came here for?' He was kissing her by then, and they were both laughing, as he kissed her again and again, and then slowly the laughter faded and gently at first, and then passionately after a time, he made love to her, and she arched her back with pleasure as he teased and taunted her and then brought her to the place she instinctively sought in his arms, and when they lay peacefully in each other's arms again, she looked up at him happily. 'I'm glad I'm here with you, Charles.'

'So am I, my love.'

And she was even more so when she saw the train. The interior of the parlour and dining cars was all in inlaid wood. There were glass reliefs and shining bits of brass. The compartment they shared had a drawing room with velvet curtains and more magnificent inlaid woods. It looked more like someone's living room than a train, and Audrey continued to be awestruck as they ate lunch, still waiting for the rest of the passengers to board. It was a six-course meal, smaller than dinner of course, and there were strolling gypsy violinists to keep them amused while they are. The waiter brought them a plate of little hors d'oeuvres with steak tartare and slices of smoked salmon on dark bread before they began the meal, and Audrey was embarrassed to discover how hungry she was. They also devoured the generous helpings of caviar, and Charles commented that they were obviously showing off how excellent their refrigeration was. With their new refrigerated cars, they could serve their patrons almost anything, and they did. The rest of the repast was equally extraordinary . . . asparagus hollandaise . . . rack of lamb . . . perfect tiny shrimp . . . profiteroles. . . . Audrey felt as though she could barely stand up by the time they finished their excellent Viennese coffee, and Charles lit a cigar, which was rare for him, but after a meal as fine as that, it seemed a suitable indulgence for him.

Audrey sat back in her chair, enjoying the haze of blue smoke from Charlie's cigar, and watching their fellow travellers arrive one by one. There was a woman draped in mink over a grey wool suit, turning to speak to a man in a homburg with a monocle as they both laughed and two tiny white Pekingese barked at their heels, and in the distance two maids carrying what looked like an armful of fur coats for her. There was another woman in a red silk dress, she had incredible skin and her hair tightly pulled in a knot with two huge rubies in her ears. She looked like a demi-mondaine, and she exposed a suitable expanse of leg as she boarded the train, and there were countless matched suit-cases and steamer trunks being put on with her. And once ensconced in the huge velvet chairs in their suite, Audrey sat back comfortably, talking to Charles, telling him what her father's photographs had been like, and chatting easily with him. Travelling with Charlie was like travelling with her dearest friend. They seemed to laugh at the same things, to find the same people amusing or unbearable or ridiculous and, together, they laughed at everything. He was enchanted by how delighted she was with all of it, and he was in heaven over the idea that she had come along with him. He could hardly wait to show her Istanbul, when they arrived there, and share a night with her in his favourite hotel, before putting her back on the train again. But he couldn't think about that now. The trip was just beginning for them. It was no time to think of saying goodbye. Not yet. Not now. The fun had just begun.

That afternoon, before they left, she showered and changed for him, and she emerged from the bedroom of their suite, wearing a dress that enchanted him, it was a pink wool dress with a bias-cut drape and a little pink hat by Rose Descat that Lady Vi had insisted she buy in Cannes. It seemed perfect for this extraordinary train filled with equally extraordinary people, and for the occasion she had worn her grandmother's very large pearls, with matching pearls in her ears. Grandfather had given them to her when she turned twenty-one, and like the hat, she was glad to have them with her now. She felt very chic as they strolled the platform arm in arm, and she was surprised to see some uniforms she hadn't noticed before, as a group of men arrived and seemed to hover near the entrance to their car, conferring quietly, and looking as though they were waiting for someone, as indeed they were.

'Who are they?' She looked intrigued, and Charles off-handedly glanced at their lapels. The uniforms weren't identical, but they were similar to others he had seen in Germany.

'I think they're some of Hitler's men.'

'Here?' She seemed surprised. He had been named Chancellor of Germany seven months before, but this was Austria after all.

'There are Austrian Nazis too. I saw some in Vienna when I was there in June. Even though here I think it's fairly rare to see them in uniform. Dollfuss, the Austrian Chancellor, banned Nazi uniforms here this year, and Hitler got so mad he imposed a tax on any German visiting Austria. It kicked the hell out of their tourist business here, and I think some Nazis here just ignored the ban. Maybe these guys are here on official business of some kind.'

Audrey glanced at them again, even more intrigued. She had read a great deal about Hitler before she left the States. And Vi and James had had quite a lot to say about him. They seemed to think he was dangerous, even though in America no one appeared to be worried about that. She noticed then that the men in uniform were speaking to a man and his wife who were travelling with another man. All three of them were well dressed and in their middle years. The taller man of the two seemed quite composed as he explained something to the two Nazis, both of whom were frowning menacingly. They made a curt demand, and the shorter, older man produced two passports, obviously his and his wife's, as Audrey stared at them.

'What do you suppose they want from them, Charles?'

'Just their papers probably.' He made little of it and refilled her glass. 'Don't worry about it. They're terribly officious with each other in these countries, but they won't bother us.' He didn't want anything spoiling her trip, and he had begun to hear things earlier that year that concerned him about the Nazi regime. There was no doubt that it was good for Germany, and they were starting to build some really beautiful roads, but their violent anti-Semitism was something that didn't sit well with him. He glanced out the window as Audrey watched, and suddenly one of the men in uniform grabbed the smaller older man by the throat. Everyone on the platform seemed totally startled by it, and the woman who must have been his wife let out a frightened scream. They slapped her husband across the face, their passports disappeared, a few curt words were said to the wife and the other man, and without ceremony the two men in uniform led the smaller man away, protesting, attempting to explain something to them unsuccessfully and gesticulating and calling to his friend and his wife.

'What's he saying? . . . what did he say?' Audrey was standing nervously, frightened by what she had seen, and anguished for the poor woman who was now crying in the other man's arms.

'It's all right, Aud.' Charles put an arm around her. 'He told them not to worry about him, that he'll get it straightened out.' But now they saw all their luggage being taken off the train, and the woman was still sobbing in the other man's arms as they walked out of sight.

'My God, what happened?' Distractedly, Audrey hurried outside, and met the conductor almost at once. 'What happened to that man?' She was only slightly embarrassed for making a fuss about it. Everyone else had observed what went on, said nothing at all, and then gone on their way.

'It's nothing, mademoiselle.' He was quick to reassure her with a smile, and a glance over her head at Charles, as though he would understand. 'Only a petty criminal attempting to board the train.' But he didn't look like a criminal. He looked more like a banker, or a businessman. He had worn a fine hat, a well-tailored suit, and a thick gold watch chain across his vest, and his wife had been expensively dressed too. 'There is no problem.' He walked past her, and in an undertone told the porter to bring them another bottle of champagne, but a few moments later as someone else boarded the train she heard the whispered words, only one of which came clear to her and she looked up at Charles in dismay.

'That woman said "*Juden*", and she was talking about him, wasn't she?'

'I don't know, Aud.' He looked troubled, but he didn't want her to get even more upset than she was.

'They were Jews. Or he was anyway. My God . . . then it's true, isn't it, the things people are starting to say? My God, Charles . . . how terrible. . . .'

He gently grabbed her arm, as though to bring her back, and he looked deep into her eyes. 'There's nothing you can do about it, Aud. Don't let it spoil your trip.' He wanted that more than anything. And what he said was true. They were helpless to assist the man, so why torture themselves, and more than likely he'd be all right.

Audrey's eyes blazed at his words. 'It spoiled his trip, didn't it? And his wife's . . . and their friend's.' She glared at Charles. 'What if it were James and Violet? If they took James away, would you just let them take him, or would you do something?'

'Look, dammit,' he glared right back at her, more than a little displeased with her argument, 'that's not the same thing. Of course I wouldn't let it happen to James. But I

94

don't even know this man, and there's nothing we can do to help. Just put it out of your mind.' But it had an unsettling effect on them both, until at last the train got under way, and Charlie came to sit beside her on the small velvet settee and took her hands in his.

'Aud, there's absolutely nothing we can do about it.' He put an arm around her shoulders and she began to cry.

'I felt so terrible, Charlie . . . why couldn't we have done something for them?'

'Because you can't always. You can't stop the tides. There are ugly things happening here right now. And maybe it's important that we don't get involved.'

'Do you really believe that?' She was shocked at him.

'For myself, no. But I would never do anything to jeopardise you. If I had made a scene out there today, I might have wound up in jail, and then what would happen to you? These are powerful people here, Hitler's men. We're in no position to do anything about it, and we have to recognise that. This isn't London or New York. You're a long way from home.' She felt that now, for the first time in this ominous way, and it was difficult not to think about the man they had led away.

'It makes you feel so helpless, doesn't it?' He nodded his head silently. It had haunted him too. And what she had said to him had hit home. What if it had been James? . . . or Aud . . . it was a hideous thought as he held her close to him, and they sought comfort in each other's arms, and a while later, desire overtook them again, and he made love to her on the settee, as the countryside slid by, and they both felt more peaceful again as they dressed for dinner that night. It was more like being in a hotel than on a train, and Charles followed her quietly to the dining car, admiring the plunging neckline of her backless white satin dress that showed off the remains of her Riviera tan admirably, and made Charlie ache with desire for her again.

But they spoke of the incident on the platform again at dinner, and talking about it seemed to relieve them both.

'Is that common here in Austria? Are they arresting all the Jews?' She looked desperately concerned as the waiter served the fourth of their wines.

'I'm not sure. I heard something about it in Vienna in June, and in Berlin a few months ago. It may just be random attacks. They claim they're only after enemies of the Reich, but I don't trust Hitler somehow, and the definition leaves the interpretation rather vague. Doesn't it?' She looked unnerved and agreed with him.

'James said the same thing in Antibes when we talked about it one night. It's frightening, the way Hitler wants to militarise the country. You know, it can only lead to war. Why aren't more people frightened by that?'

'Because not very many people agree with us, I'm afraid. The Americans certainly don't. They seem to think he's marvellous, from what I can judge.'

'That makes me sick.' Audrey was thinking of the man in the station again. And Charles looked terribly serious when he lit his cigar this time. 'It's a luxury to enjoy the freedom we do.' They were reminded of it all the more as they rolled into Czechoslovakia, Hungary, and Rumania, and at the few stops they made, uniformed officials would get on. But even then, one never saw all of the passengers. It was amazing how many travelled secluded in their compartments, giving private parties for the group they travelled with, or simply being alone to watch the countryside or drink champagne with their mistresses or wives. Audrey and Charles got out to stretch once or twice, and as they rapidly approached Istanbul, she began to look sad, and it was on their last walk the night before they were to arrive that she turned her eyes sorrowfully up to his. The days in Venice and on the Orient Express had been like a honeymoon, and neither of them wanted to see it end.

'I can't believe we're almost there . . . a dream of a lifetime, and it's over in two days. Somehow,' she sighed, 'it should take longer than that, don't you think?'

Charles smiled and squeezed her hand a little tighter as

they walked along. They seemed to talk for hours about politics and books, his travels, her father's adventures so long ago, the brother he had lost, Annabelle, even Harcourt . . . her photographs. . . . There always seemed to be more to say, something more they wanted to do. It was difficult to believe that they would be in Istanbul the next day, and she would be leaving for London again the day after that, and God only knew when he would see her again.

When they boarded the train again, they sat watching the countryside roll by in the early dusk, the shepherds wandering the hills with their flocks on their way home through the woods. It looked almost biblical as night fell and Audrey held out a hand to him.

'I keep thinking about that man, wondering what happened to him.'

Charles looked at her soberly. 'They probably let him go, and he caught the next train. You can't torment yourself over something like that. This isn't the States, Aud. Strange things happen here. You can't get involved in what they do.' It was one of the reasons for his success in writing about remote parts of the world. He was a professional observer and never got involved. He had been there when the Japanese attacked Shanghai in '32, and he had been allowed to leave and had been back several times since, but part of that freedom stemmed from the fact that he never interfered with what he saw, no matter how troubling it was, and he tried to explain that to her now. 'It's the price we pay for the privilege of being there, Aud. You have to pretend it's not happening . . . or at least not to you.'

'That's awfully difficult, isn't it?'

'Sometimes. But you'll get hurt otherwise.' He sighed and sat back again. He was thinking of other things. Their last moments on the Orient Express, and then they had only one more day before she headed west again and he began his interminable journey to the East. He would have loved to take a trip like that with her one day, but he didn't even mention it to her now. Instead, he looked out into the night, thinking of the exotic pleasures of Istanbul. 'You're going to love it, Audrey. It's an incredible place. Different from anything you've ever seen.' There was something wondrous about showing it to her, like a whole new world, a new life, and she newly born into it with him. It was a heady experience for them both, and he talked about his experiences all through dinner that night, as she listened, fascinated, wishing, as he had, that there would be opportunities for them to travel together again. And after another enormous meal, they went back to their rooms, and there was a sadness in the air which they both felt, as she tried to tell him how happy she was she'd come.

But there was more they didn't know how to say. Somehow, speaking of Istanbul kept reality away, as though she would be there forever with him, and not just for one day before leaving again, to go in separate directions, back to their separate lives. It was Audrey who had the courage to say the words first, as he looked unhappily at her.

'I can't imagine a life without you any more, Charles.' Her voice was sad and soft as she looked at him. 'Isn't that strange, after such a short time?' It was almost as though they had got married somewhere along the way and hadn't noticed it, or as though the act of making love had created an unseverable bond between them. And yet that wasn't what Harcourt and Annabelle felt . . . it was more like what James shared with Lady Vi. Was it that they had been endowed with a rare gift then . . . and what would happen to it now?

'I can't imagine leaving you.' He was worried about her trip back, and her life after that. It seemed so unfair that they couldn't stay like this, travelling together, for a long, long time. 'But I don't suppose this would be much of a life for you.' He watched her eyes to see what she thought, as though testing her. He sat back in his chair with a sigh. 'Could you be happy with a rootless life like this one day?' He wasn't ready yet, but perhaps soon. He had been toying with the idea ever since leaving Antibes, and especially in the past few days on the train.

But she was always honest with him. 'I could be,' she smiled sadly at him from where she sat, 'if I didn't have my family to think about.'

'Haven't you got a right to a life of your own?' It annoyed him to hear her talk that way. He could have understood if she had told him she would detest travelling with him, but he didn't want to hear about her responsibilities any more.

'I don't have that right yet, Charles.' She never lost sight of that. 'Maybe I will one day.'

'When? When you're forty-five years old, and you've brought up all of your sister's kids? When do you think they'll let you go? Next week? Next year? In ten years? . . . five? . . . you're kidding yourself, Audrey, they'll never let you go. Why should they? You're the best thing they've got.' He was angry about it. Why should they have her if he could not. And it was their fault that she wouldn't stay with him. It didn't dawn on him that she couldn't have travelled forever with him anyway, with no formal bond, just their love to carry them along.

'What difference does it make?' She was growing angry too. They were both unhappy that their time together was almost at an end, and there was no one to be angry at except each other as they rode the last miles on the train they had enjoyed so much. 'Do you really want to be married one day, Charles?' She wasn't convinced of that, but he wouldn't admit it to her.

'Why not?'

'That's hardly the right way to look at it. "Why not?"'

'And you're the authority on marriage, I suppose. You, who consider yourself an old maid and is perfectly content to give it all up.'

'What difference does it make? Would you prefer if I were hounding you to marry me, Charles? Is that what you want? I don't really think it is.' She was shouting at him, and hadn't realised it, until he strode across the elegant drawing room and pulled her to her feet, glaring at her, with both hands on her shoulders, as though he might shake her if she didn't listen to him now.

'Do you know what I want? I want you to stay with me. I don't want you to leave Istanbul and go back to catch your damn ship. That's what I want.' There were no promises, no proposals, and no vows, but she didn't give a damn. That had never been what she wanted from him. There had been no forethought about his marrying her, no plot, no plan. She just loved the man, and she wanted to be with him too. She didn't want to go back to England to catch the ship either, but she couldn't do otherwise, and she tried to explain that to him again. 'You're twenty-six years old. You're grown up. Do what you want to do.'

'You don't understand anything.' She pulled herself from his grasp and sat down again, and he sat beside her on the settee and held her hand. Their anger was beginning to fade. It wouldn't solve anything, and they both knew that. 'Charlie, my love, if you weren't quite so free, you couldn't do exactly what you wanted either. Life just doesn't work that way. In most cases anyway.'

He looked sadly at her. He did understand. He just didn't want to. 'I suppose I forget sometimes that the rest of the world isn't quite as unencumbered as I am.' A knife pierced his heart as he thought of Sean. 'It isn't the ideal state it's cracked up to be. Maybe you're better off.' It was what made him want children now and then, the hunger to have someone tied to him and to whom he in turn was tied. But then he thought of losing Sean, and it frightened him again. And yet, in an odd way, he *was* tied to her. He felt that way, and he looked at her now with something pleading in his eyes. 'Audrey . . . what if you came to China with me?'

She gasped at his words, and looked with shock. 'Are you crazy? Can you imagine what my family would say? I'm not even going to tell them I came this far. I'd never hear the end of it. Istanbul! They would think I had lost my mind.' All except Grandfather, of course, who knew only too well what motivated her . . . that urge to roam that was bred into her . . . the demons he hated so much. But China? 'Charles, you're mad.'

'Am I? Am I so mad to want to be with the woman I love?' He sat staring at her and she couldn't answer him. She didn't know what to say to him. It was the loveliest offer she had ever had, but there was no way she could go with him. 'We could sail back to the States from Yokohama by year end.'

'And how would I explain it to them? . . . Charlie, I gave my grandfather my word. He's an old man. The shock could be too great for him.'

'I can't compete with that, can I, Aud? Men my age don't die of "shock".' He looked at her almost bitterly. He was suddenly violently jealous of an eighty-one-year-old man. 'Or even grief. I envy him your loyalty.'

'You have my loyalty too.' She spoke very gently to him. 'And my heart.'

'Then think about it. You can tell me in Istanbul.'

'Charlie . . .' She only looked at him. There was no point torturing themselves over what they couldn't have. And she couldn't have a trip to China with him. She reminded herself of that a dozen times when she went to sleep that night. She could have a brief moment in Istanbul . . . two days . . . one night . . . and then she had to head home again . . . had to . . . had to, she told herself forcefully, as she drifted off to sleep . . . but she dreamed of Charles all night long. She dreamed that she was looking for him, and she couldn't find him anywhere. She awoke in the middle of the night in tears, panicking, and she clung to him as she cried, afraid to explain how desperate she felt to be leaving him, for fear that if she told him, he would never let her go. And there was no doubt in her mind. She *had* to leave.

10

Their entrance to Istanbul was extraordinary, and he woke her early the next morning to make sure that she did not miss a moment of it. There were beaches running parallel to the train when she awoke, and the water seemed to be touched with gold as birds flew low overhead. Istanbul itself was surrounded by the Sea of Marmara on one side and the Golden Horn on the other, and Audrey thought she had never seen anything quite as magnificent as the mosques appearing with their golden domes and minarets, and then, finally as they rounded Seraglio Point, Topkapi Palace came into view, bringing with it visions of sultans and harems and extraordinary fantasies and fairy tales. It was a city that inspired fantasies of every kind, and as they pulled slowly into Sirkeci Station, Audrey felt suddenly overwhelmed by the distinctly Eastern influence she felt here. It was a place like no other she had ever known, and she was fascinated as Charles pointed out the sights to her on the way to their hotel. The Blue Mosque and Hagia Sophia, Istanbul's most famous mosque, the Column of Constantine overlooking the public square, the Grand Bazaar, and the countless other mosques and bazaars that fascinated her. Finally, her grief at the prospect of leaving him was dimmed by the excitement she felt to be here with him, for however little time. Her camera worked overtime, and he took her directly to their hotel, which was an amazing place.

He had reserved rooms at the Pera Palas, one of his favourite hotels around the world, and a dozen porters unloaded their bags as she and Charlie went inside. He had requested two rooms that were connected by a mammoth living room. And there were ten-foot mirrors with gilt frames, black panelling, rococo carving, and golden cupids everywhere. Even the lobby of the hotel had been replete with the same decor, and somehow it seemed suitable to the exotic ambience, although anywhere else, it would have seemed hideous to her. But nothing was hideous here. It was all fascinating and exotic, as she followed Charles to the Grand Bazaar and took roll after roll of photographs, fascinated by the insights and smells and meandering paths and merchants determined to sell her everything they could. Charlie watched her with delight as she took it all in, and seemed to thrive on the atmosphere. He took her to a tiny restaurant for lunch, and even the Turkish food didn't intimidate her. She loved everything. She seemed to be born to lead a life like this. 'The life of a vagabond' she described to him with dancing eyes as they walked on the beach, looking at the entrance to the city and holding hands.

And it was only when they went back to their hotel that she appeared to be sad again, and even making love didn't cheer either of them this time. There was no hiding from the realities any more. She was leaving the next morning on the train, and their brief romantic interlude, however passionate, would be over for them, forever perhaps, if life was not kind to them. She lay quietly in bed beside him after they had made love, and traced lazy circles on his chest with one delicate fingertip, as he tried not to feel all that he felt for her, at least not quite so acutely.

'When do you leave for China?' There was no point not talking about it any more. It had to be faced sooner or later. And it was already later for them.

'Tomorrow night.' He looked at her with unhappy eyes.

'How long will it take you to get there?'

'A few weeks. It will depend on my connections.'

She smiled at him. 'It sounds like fun.'

But he laughed at that. 'Only you could say that. Most women would shudder at the thought . . . most men in fact. It's a very rough trip.' In some ways, he was glad she wasn't coming. Although, selfishly, he would have loved it. 'Just think, when you're comfortably on the *Mauretania* again, drinking champagne, and dancing with some dashing man' – he felt his stomach tighten at the thought – 'I'll be crawling along some mountaintop in Tibet, freezing my ass off.'

She looked at him, but this time she didn't smile. 'I won't be dancing with anyone, Charles.'

'Yes you will.' His voice was a whisper and his eyes were sad. 'I have no right to expect you not to.'

'You forget one thing.'

'What's that?'

'I wouldn't want to. I'm in love with you, Charles.' And then she looked at him strangely. 'We might as well be married. In my heart, we are.' She wondered if he would be frightened by what she said, but she had to say it anyway.

'We are.' He said it so solemnly that she was startled, and she was even more so, when he looked down at his hands and slipped his gold signet ring from his little finger. It was engraved with his crest, and he put it on her left hand, on the finger where she would have worn a wedding ring. 'I want you to keep that, Audrey. Always.'

There were no words for what she felt, and the tears spilled from her eyes as he held her, and when they made love again, it was bittersweet, and she kept the ring on her finger and her hand tightly closed. She knew she would never take the ring off again. It was a trifle big, but not so big that she would lose it easily.

And when they got up at dusk, Charles suggested that they go out to dinner, but she only shook her head and turned back to face him. 'I'm not hungry.'

'You should eat.' She shook her head. She had too much on her mind, and she stood for a long time with her back to him, staring out the window at the minarets and the bazaars and the mosques. She seemed to be fascinated by Istanbul, but in fact she wasn't seeing anything. She was looking into her own heart and making an enormous decision about them.

He left her alone for a long time, and then he came to

her and gently touched her shoulder, and he was shocked at the ravaged face he saw when she turned to face him again.

'Oh darling . . .' He reached out to her and she stood very still. There was no choice for her any more. She should have known it in Venice. Everything was decided for her then. Or perhaps even before that.

'I'm not leaving.' She said it as though she were pronouncing a life sentence, and in fact she was. Her own. But she was not condemned to that life. She had chosen it. She regretted only the pain that she would cause others with her decision.

Charles stood very still, not sure he had understood her correctly. 'What do you mean?'

'I mean I'm going with you.' She suddenly looked much smaller, as though she had shrunk in the last hour.

'To China?' He looked shocked as she nodded. 'Are you sure, Aud?' He was suddenly afraid she would regret it. Once they began the trip, there would be no turning back. She would have to go all the way to Shanghai with him, and it wouldn't be easy, as he had already told her more than once.

'I'm quite sure.'

'What about your grandfather?' She suddenly wondered if he didn't want her along after all, and he saw hurt in her eyes and immediately reached out to hold her again. 'I just don't want you to change your mind halfway there.'

'You mean on a mountaintop in Tibet?' She smiled through her tears, and he smiled back at her as she nodded.

'Exactly.'

'I won't change my mind. I'll cable Grandfather that I'll be home by Christmas. Is there anywhere he can write to me?' Charles thought about it and shook his head.

'Not until Nanking anyway. He can write to you there. Or Shanghai. I'll give you the names of the hotels where I stay. He can write to you in care of me.' And then he realised that that would hardly be wise. And then he grinned at an idea. 'Just tell him I'm a woman you met on the trip.'

105

She smiled sheepishly at the man she loved. 'Don't laugh. I may have to.'

But he took her hands in his own then and looked into her eyes. 'Audrey, are you really sure? Is this what you want? I'd go to the ends of the earth with you, but I have nothing to lose. You do. I know what your responsibilities mean to you . . . your family . . . your grandfather . . . Annabelle. . . .'

'Maybe it's my turn now. Just this once. Maybe I can do it and they won't hate me forever.'

He hesitated for a moment and then went on. 'And after that? What happens to us then?' If she couldn't leave him now, what would it be like after China?

'I can't answer that. I don't know. I'll have to go back to them sooner or later.'

He smiled ruefully. 'It's like being in love with a married woman sometimes.' She smiled at the analogy, but she couldn't disagree.

'As you pointed out a while back, I'm not as blissfully unencumbered as you are.'

'Maybe that's why I love you. Maybe I wouldn't love you as much if you were just a loose bird like me.' He smiled down at her and stroked her hair, and she held him close, feeling the ring on her finger. She had made a commitment to him now, and yet at the same time, she felt free, freer than she ever had in her life and she was surprised at how happy it made her.

11

The telephone rang just as Edward Driscoll was settling down to listen to Walter Winchell. The maid came to knock at the library door, and she almost trembled as she approached him. He was far more querulous than he had been only a month or two before, and she knew how much he hated being disturbed.

'Excuse me, sir. . . .' Her knees almost knocked, and she could feel the lace cap she wore every evening begin to slide slowly over her ear. He hated her cap being crooked almost as much as he hated interruptions. In fact, he hated almost everything and everyone these days. He prowled the house like a policeman, hoping to make an arrest before nightfall. 'Excuse me, sir. . . .' She tried again. He hadn't responded the first time.

'Yes? What is it?' he barked at the girl and she jumped visibly. 'Don't jump like that, dammit, you make me nervous.'

'It's the telephone for you, sir.'

'Take a message. I don't want to talk to anyone at this time of night. It's almost dinnertime. Can't be important anyway. No one ever calls me.'

'The operator said it was long distance.'

His face grew instantly taut. Maybe something had happened to her, and he eyed the girl sharply again. 'Where's it from?'

'Istanbul, Turkey, sir.'

'*Turkey?*' He almost threw the word in her face. 'I don't know anyone there. Must be a mistake . . . or a prank. Hang up. Don't waste your time talking to pranksters.' If she had said France, he would have run to the phone. Or even Italy or England. He had got a postcard from her from Rome. But Turkey . . . and then suddenly, he got an uneasy feeling, and slowly he rose and signalled to the girl just before she left the room. 'Find out who it's from before you hang up.'

'Yes, sir.' She was back less than a minute later. Her eyes wide, her cap even more askew than before, but this time he didn't notice. 'It's Miss Driscoll, sir. From Turkey.'

Forgetting his cane, he almost ran to the phone, in the little room where they kept it. It was a small, echoing chamber with a narrow, uncomfortable chair. But he never could see why one had to be comfortable while one talked on the phone. The telephone was for quick business, as far as he was concerned, not all-day gabbing. He had told Annabelle that often enough, not that she ever listened to him. 'Yes?' he shouted into the phone. 'Yes?' There was so much static he could barely hear, and he was so excited he forgot to sit down, as the young maid hovered nearby, afraid he would get too excited.

'Mr Driscoll?'

'Yes! Yes!'

'We have a long-distance call for you from Turkey.'

'I know that, you fool, now where is she?' But almost as he said the words, he heard her voice, and his knees felt weak as he heard her.

'Gramps? . . . can you hear me?'

'Barely. Audrey, where the hell are you?'

'I'm in Istanbul. I took the Orient Express with friends.'

'Dammit, that's no place for you to be. When are you coming home?'

As she listened to him, he sounded so frail suddenly, and so terribly far away, and at her end, she almost gave up her plan to go to China with Charlie. But she wasn't ready to do that either. She had to tell him. 'I won't be home until Christmas.' There was a deafening silence, and she was afraid they had been disconnected. 'Grampa? Grampa? . . .'

He sat down heavily on the uncomfortable chair, and the maid ran to get him a glass of water. His face was grey, and she only hoped it wasn't terrible news. He was too old to take it. 'What the hell are you doing over there? And who are you travelling with?'

'I met a charming couple on the ship. They're English. I was with them in the South of France.' And she was hoping he would assume that she was with them in Turkey.

'Why the hell don't they take you back to England?'

'They might, eventually. But I'm going to China first.'

'You're *what*?' The girl pushed the glass of water towards him and he pushed her arm away just as quickly. 'Are you crazy? The Japanese have already invaded Manchuria. You come home at once!'

'Grandfather, I promise you I'll be safe. I'm going to Shanghai and Peking.' She thought it best not to tell him that she was going to Nanking to see Chiang Kai-shek, lest he worry even more. 'And I can come home directly from there.'

'You could also take the Orient Express back to Paris now, and get on a ship from there, and you could be home in two weeks. That makes a lot more sense to me.' Damn fool, he muttered to himself, but not loud enough to reach Audrey's ears in Turkey. She was just like her father.

'Grampa, please . . . I just want to do this. And then I'll come home. I swear it.'

In spite of himself tears filled his eyes. 'You're just like your damn father. You have no sense under that red hair of yours, do you? China is no place for a woman! Or for anyone for that matter, except the Chinese. How are you getting there anyway?' The whole scheme sounded mad to him, but it was just exactly what Roland would have done, damn him. . . .

'We're going by train.'

'From Istanbul all the way to China? Do you have any idea how far that is?'

'Yes . . . I'll be fine.'

'Are these people that you're travelling with decent? Are you safe with them?'

'Very. I promise.'

'Keep your damn promises to yourself.' He was furious with her, but it was difficult to express it with all the static on the line, and the incredible distance. It had taken eight hours for her to place the call.

'Are you all right?'

'I'm fine, if it's any business of yours.'

'How's Annie?'

'She's having another baby. In March.'

'I know. I'll be home long before that.'

'You'd better be, or don't bother.'

'Grampa . . . I'm sorry. . . .'

'No, you're not. You're just like your father. I know you're a fool, now don't be a liar. You're not sorry at all. You're crazy is what you are.'

'I love you.' She was crying now, but he couldn't tell. And so was he, but she couldn't hear it.

'What?'

'I love you!'

'I can't hear you.'

She knew his game too well. 'Yes you can. I said, *I love you!* And I'll be home soon. I've got to go now, Grampa. I'm writing to you with my addresses in China.'

'Don't expect me to write you.'

'I just want you to know where I am.'

He growled unintelligibly into the phone and then said, 'Fine.'

'Give Annie my love too.'

'Be careful, Audrey! Tell those people to be careful too.'

'I will. Take care of yourself, Grampa.'

'I have to. No one else does.' She smiled through her tears at his words, and said goodbye to him a moment later. Charles had been standing by while she called and he took her in his arms and held her while she cried after she hung up. She felt so guilty for hurting her grandfather, and she would have felt even worse had she seen his face after he hung up the phone. He sat staring at the wall in the little room with the phone, and then finally struggled to his feet, looking twenty years older than he had twenty minutes before, and just as he got back to his chair in the library, shaking from head to foot, the doorbell rang, and he almost jumped out of his skin, and shouted at the maid, 'Now what the devil is that?' He looked as though he had seen a ghost, he was so white, and the butler hurried to the door to let Annabelle and Harcourt in. They had been invited for dinner. 'What are you doing here?' he barked at them and Annabelle looked extremely annoyed. She had been feeling terrible all summer, and he made her nervous when he shouted at her.

'Don't shout at me, Grampa. You invited us to dinner tonight. Don't you remember?'

'No, I don't. Are you sure you didn't make it up to get a free dinner out of me?' He glared at her and she looked as though she were about to turn on her heel and walk out, but Harcourt was quick to calm her, murmuring something about '. . . Doesn't mean what he says . . . know how he is . . . at his age . . .' 'Don't talk behind my back. It's damn rude! Annabelle,' he barked, 'I just spoke to your sister. She's not coming home until Christmas.' He said it as they headed towards the dining room and then refused to continue the conversation until they were seated.

'But she was supposed to be home in a few weeks . . . what happened?' Annabelle was suddenly terrified that Audrey had met a man and was getting married. She had been counting on her coming home. Her household was in terrible shape, and she and Harcourt had been counting on taking a holiday. She needed Audrey to come home and stay with little Winston, not to mention to hire a new nurse, and a new cook, and a new chauffeur. Annie could never find anyone decent at all, and when she did they didn't stay. It was definitely time for Audrey to come home. 'What's she doing over there? Where is she? In Paris or London?'

For an instant, he wore a mask of doom, but he actually enjoyed unnerving Annabelle with the news. 'No. She's in Turkey.'

Harcourt looked shocked. 'What on earth is she doing there?'

'She took the Orient Express with some friends, and now she's going to China.'

'She's *what?*' Annabelle almost squealed, and Harcourt all but gaped at her grandfather, and was quick to add his opinion. Too quick, in the eyes of Edward Driscoll.

'That girl is much, much too independent for her own good. Imagine what people will think, a girl of her age going to China alone. That's the most unsuitable thing I've heard in years!'

'No, it is not.' Edward Driscoll's fist came down on the table. 'Your talking about my granddaughter in that way under this roof is a great deal more *unsuitable*, if you ask me. And in future, I'll thank you to keep your opinions to yourself. That girl has more spirit in her big toe than you have in your whole body. And Annabelle here has no spirit at all, never has had, and never will. She's got the guts of a dead mouse, even if she is my grandchild. So don't tell me about Audrey. Matter of fact, don't bother eating dinner with me either. Looking at the long face of yours, and listening to her whine,' he gestured at Annabelle, who was staring at him openmouthed, 'gives me indigestion.' He rose from the table himself then, grabbed his cane, stalked into the library and slammed the door, as Annabelle began to cry and rushed from the table to gather her things and hurl herself out the front door almost before Harcourt could catch up with her. She cried all the way home to Burlingame, accusing Harcourt of being a weakling for not defending her against her grandfather, and berating Audrey for not coming home to help her.

'That selfish bitch, staying over there like that . . . and China? . . . China! . . . she knows damn well I need help when I'm pregnant . . . she's doing it on purpose . . . she has nothing else to do . . . she's just trying to shirk responsibility . . . she's been jealous of me for years, tall ugly stick. . . .' Harcourt got an earful all the way home. But he didn't give a damn. As soon as he'd got her home, he'd go out and visit his friend in Palo Alto. He had a little cutie stashed away there, a real hot number. He'd been seeing her all summer, and Annabelle had no idea what he was up to.

Nor did Edward Driscoll, though he wouldn't have cared. He was still sitting alone in his library by the time Harcourt and Annabelle got home. In fact, he was still sitting there several hours later, thinking of Audrey ... and somehow getting her confused with Roland in his mind ... she was in China ... he remembered that ... China ... but was she there with Roland or alone? ... suddenly he couldn't remember the details. All he could remember was how much he missed her.

12

The distance from Istanbul to Shanghai was more than five thousand miles, and if the trip went absolutely splendidly Charles estimated it would take them somewhere in the vicinity of fourteen days. The articles he had been commissioned to write centred around Chiang Kai-shek's government, seated in Nanking. There was also a piece about Shanghai as a demilitarised zone, another about Peking, and they were hoping he would get some material on the Communist revolutionaries who had taken to the hills in 1928. He already had copious notes, and his credentials were certainly very good, but it was difficult to say how accessible his subjects were. The Communist 'bandits' certainly were not, and it was unlikely Charles would even be able to contact them, but hopefully Chiang Kai-shek would be willing to see Charles once he contacted him. And of course, any random ideas Charles had along the way could be spun into articles later on. He took careful notes and always had a briefcase full of notebooks and papers with him. He explained his system to Audrey as they took the train to Ankara late that night. She felt as though she had embarked on a whole new life with this man, and in many ways she had. She was even more sure of it when they changed trains in Ankara, and she suddenly began to laugh remembering the Orient Express. It seemed totally incongruous now, as she boarded another train behind two women carrying two live chickens and a small goat.

The mail train they took in Ankara took them past Lake Van, and Lake Urmia on the Persian border and across the mountains until they reached Tehran. There, the station was busy and crowded and people were chattering everywhere, as Audrey stared in fascination at them and used the Leica nonstop, while Charlie bought them tickets on the night mail to Mashhad in the northeast corner of the country, about a hundred miles from the Afghanistan border. Mashhad was a holy city and almost everyone who travelled on the train did so on their knees, in posture of devotion.

The women in the Tehran station were interesting-looking and some were beautiful, and all of them were fascinated with her, even in the simple clothes she had worn. They stared at her, and two young girls had even touched her red hair and then run away, giggling behind their veils. It was a whole new world to her, and she was suddenly the object of fascination and obvious disapproval because she did not wear a veil like the local women.

They travelled all night to Mashhad and then south into Afghanistan, and it seemed to take forever before they reached Kabul. They had travelled more than two thousand miles by then and had been on the road for a week, and Audrey thought she would go mad if she ever saw another train, and yet, somehow, as she looked around and saw the tranquil beauty around her as the sun went down, and the peasants who had travelled with them left the station with their goatskin pouches full of the little they owned, she thought that she had never been happier. She stood in the sunset for a moment looking at Charles, and saw that he was smiling at her. They were both grimy and tired, and they hadn't been able to bathe for four days, but somehow neither of them seemed to care. He put an arm around her and carried one of her three bags for her, laughing as she juggled the elegant vanity case she hadn't touched in over a week now.

'I imagine it's not quite what you thought, is it, love?' He worried now and then that it would be too much for her, but she seemed to be having a wonderful time and she was a very good sport, even when the train had derailed in the Nanga Parbat Pass and they had to walk some ten miles, she never complained. There wasn't another woman alive he could imagine travelling like this with. 'Do you have many regrets?'

'Not one,' she beamed up at him. It was exactly what she had hoped it would be, wild and uncomfortable and beautiful, and a world the way God had intended it to be, without a skyscraper in sight, or a paved street or a horn to be heard. It was beautiful, all of it, and that night as they lay on the crooked little bed in the hotel that Charles knew, she ran a hand gently along Charles's inner thigh and he sighed happily as he turned over and made love to her.

'What are you doing here, crazy girl?' He smiled sleepily afterwards. They were a long way from the rococo luxuries of even the Pera Palas in Istanbul, and Cap d'Antibes and the Hawthornes and their friends seemed to be part of another lifetime, but Audrey wanted nothing more than this, a narrow bed in an empty room and a strange world outside, discovering it all as she lay beside the man she loved night after night.

'Charles? . . .' They were both half asleep as she cuddled up to him, feeling as though she had done this all her life.

'Mmm? . . .'

'I've never been happier in my life.' She had told him a thousand times by now, but she had to tell him once more, and he smiled as he drifted off to sleep, whispering to her.

'Crazy girl . . . now get some sleep. . . .' They had to get up at six o'clock the next day, and when they did, they were given goat's milk and a piece of cheese before they hurried down the street to catch yet another train. This time they travelled to Islamabad and then straight into Kashmir. They arrived at noon, and for once the journey wasn't bad, although the train looked very old. It took them all the way to Ladakh Pass, and it was four in the morning when they arrived at last. Audrey was asleep in Charlie's arms and he looked up at the stars with a feeling of peace. The train had stalled twice, but they hadn't been asked to get out, and it had made it all the way to eighteen thousand feet and now it was slowly making the descent again. They were finally in Tibet and they had another eight hundred miles to go before they were to reach Lhasa and could rest for a day. Charlie knew the trip well. He estimated that from Ladakh Pass to Lhasa would take them roughly two days. As it turned out, it took three, and they were both exhausted when they finally reached Lhasa. They had been on the road for ten days and they were two-thirds of the way to Shanghai, but at this point in the trip it always felt as though one would never get there. Charlie took her to the inn where he always stayed, perched on a mountaintop, with orange-robed monks visible everywhere, walking slowly along side by side, chanting or in silence. One felt closer to God here, and it was so remote that it was impossible to imagine that there was another world beyond this. It was almost a mystical experience just being there. Audrey stood by the window for a long, long time, thinking of her father, and wondering if he had ever been there. She mentioned it to Charles later on, as they ate a simple dinner of rice and bean soup by candlelight. She wasn't hungry afterwards. She had been too hungry to care what they ate, which was just as well because she learned later that the tiny slivers of meat in her soup had actually been snake. She made a horrible face at Charles and he laughed at her as she collapsed into bed, and then she looked at him pensively.

'I find myself wondering sometimes, if there had been pictures of this place or that in the albums I love so much. Suddenly all of that is a blur, and this is so much more real.' She had written to her grandfather the day before, trying to explain her travels to him, and the reason why she'd come. But there seemed to be nothing to say now. This was so much more real and that seemed so terribly far away. She was also conscious of the fact that this was the first time she had ever let them down, and she was worried about that. She had in her mind that Annabelle's baby was due in March, and she would be home long before then to take care of everything for her. She still felt guilty at times, but she would make it all up to them when she went back. And Charles was probably right too, they would punish her a little bit for a while. But they could do anything they wanted to her

117

now. She had had it all, as far as she was concerned. And she felt tears sting her eyes as they left Lhasa on muleback to get to the train. They had a long way to go this time. They were going a thousand miles across the Tahsueh Mountains to Chungking. The trip took more than thirty hours on an ancient little train, and they only had time to change trains once. Suddenly Audrey was aware of a change. The weather was much cooler here, and the people looked and acted and dressed differently. She was surprised to see so many men smoking cigarettes, and even some women too, little old gnarled people smoking butts and squinting at her and Charles through their smoke as they exhaled. There seemed to be more of them suddenly, and they weren't as friendly as some of the other people they had met on their trip. She noticed it particularly as she took roll after roll of film. They stared at her endlessly, and as they boarded the train for Wuhan, a group of children ran up to her and touched her sleeve as she focused her Leica. But when she turned to smile at them, they ran away with shrieks. Charles was juggling their bags, and they were both exhausted by the previous night's train ride, and he fell asleep almost the moment they settled into the new train, his head on her shoulder, and snoring softly, as the other five people in the compartment stared openly at her. Everything seemed to be so much more crowded here, and much busier. There was an entirely different feeling than there had been in Turkey and Tibet. That had been more rugged, more primitive, more natural, and this was more populous, more foreign in some ways. They were much more interested in her than they had been almost anywhere, and she was dying to ask Charles all about it when he finally woke up. He yawned and stretched as best he could, although there was almost no room for his legs, and he was grateful for each station where they stopped. He would get out with Audrey for a few minutes to stretch.

It was an all-day journey from Chungking to Wuhan and they passed a huge reservoir on the way, but this time

Audrey was asleep and Charlie was busily writing in one of his notebooks. They had one more day's journey before they were to reach Nanking, and he was hoping to see Chiang Kai-shek there. He had a lot to think about now, the questions he wanted to ask, the tack he would take. He would be very lucky if he could see him at all. Or perhaps they would let him cool his heels for three weeks. Maybe not if the credentials Charles carried from his publisher impressed someone, or they had heard of one of his books, but Charlie's hopes weren't high, and he was only willing to wait around for a week before moving on to Shanghai. He had a lot to do there as well, and he always loved going there.

When they reached Wuhan, they went to a small hotel. It only had three rooms, but Charlie had stayed there once before. They only offered the travellers some rice and green tea. Audrey looked into the bowl ruefully and then grinned at him and shrugged. It was the first time she had really desperately missed Western food, and she would have given her right arm for a steak or a hamburger. She found herself dreaming of a chocolate milk shake as her stomach growled when they went to bed.

'Do you have any candy bars left?' She turned to Charlie hopefully. Her passion for 3 Musketeers Bars had had no indulgence in months, but Charlie had discovered some old candy bars somewhere before they'd left Italy and he had dragged them along for at least part of the trip, but he shook his head now.

'I'm afraid not, my love. Do you want some more rice? I can try. I can tell him you're pregnant or something.' He grinned and she threw up her hands.

'Good Lord, don't do anything as desperate as that, Mr Parker-Scott. I'll live. But I'm hungry as hell.' She looked ruefully at him again and he gently ran his fingers tantalisingly from her neck to her breasts, and she forgot all of her hunger except that which was for him. They lay in the dark for a long time that night, talking and whispering, as he told her tales and bits of history about the cities they were going to see. He wasn't nearly as fond of Nanking as he was of Shanghai and Peking.

'Shanghai is so incredible, Aud. There are British and French and Russians and now Japanese. It's a truly international place, and at the same time truly Chinese. I think it must be the most cosmopolitan city I know.' And the Japanese hadn't affected it unduly. They had attacked and occupied it briefly almost two years before, early in '32 and now a demilitarised zone was fragilely in effect. Chiang Kai-shek had long before retreated to Nanking, and the 19th Route Army had resisted vigorously before being forced to give up. Chiang Kai-shek had lessened his war on the Communists now that he had the Japanese to worry about and Mao Tse-tung had all but disappeared from the immediate area. There were fewer allegedly Communist heads being speared on poles in the outer regions now. The Japanese presence had created an uneasy alliance between the Communists and the Nationalists. People had other things to think about now, particularly in Manchuria.

The next day as they boarded the train to Nanking, she felt a wave of excitement sweep over her. They were almost there. Their goal had been Nanking, Shanghai, and Peking, and they were only hours away now. She could hardly wait, and that night they slept at a hotel in Nanking, and earlier in the evening Charlie had gone to Chiang Kai-shek's residence to leave his credentials and his card and a very polite letter, begging for an audience with him. They learned at the hotel that George Bernard Shaw had been there earlier that spring on the way to Shanghai, and suddenly Audrey felt the same ripple of excitement again. She was loving what she saw: the crowds of people everywhere, the costumes, the food, the smells. They had eaten a royal repast at their hotel, it wasn't just rice and green tea here. Charlie noticed that she had lost weight. They had been travelling for more than two weeks and they had come five thousand miles, for his work and her dream, and she thought she had never been as close to another human being and probably never would be again as they quietly strolled the street in front of the hotel that night watching rickshaws and a few stray cars. Audrey was ecstatic as they wandered some of the back streets, and inadvertently came upon a little house with dim lights inside, and a strange smell. She stopped, intrigued by the perfume that hung heavy in the air, and questioned Charlie who laughed when she suggested they go inside.

'I think not, old girl.' He smiled at her.

'Why not?' She was disappointed by his lack of enthusiasm and he laughed again at her naiveté.

'That's an opium den, Aud.'

'It is?' Her eyes grew wide in amazement; she was fascinated, and now she was even more interested in going in.

'You can't go in there, Aud. They'll throw us both out. Me probably, and you for sure.'

'For heaven's sake, why? Can't we just watch?' She imagined it like a bar and he shook his head.

'They're usually just for men.'

'How stupid of them.' She looked annoyed and they continued their walk as he shared some of what he knew of Chinese history with her. It was a history more extraordinary in terms of its art and its accomplishments than any other he knew. They talked for hours as they wandered back to the hotel and sat quietly in their room.

It was a full week before Charles was able to see Chiang Kai-shek, but it gave them time to rest and relax. They went for long walks and drove out into the countryside, and in the end it was worth the wait. Charles got exactly the interview he wanted with him, and he felt certain that the article would be an enormous success. He borrowed a typewriter at the hotel and began working on it immediately that afternoon when he got back, and Audrey found him hard at work and even unaware that she was there as she quietly took a seat in the corner of the room, and began writing a letter to Annabelle, trying to explain to her what she had done and seen. But she had the discouraging feeling as she wrote that her sister really wouldn't care. She wondered if anyone would. She wrote to her grandfather instead, but was afraid that even that was a wasted effort.

It was an hour before Charles looked up and noticed that she was there, and when he did, he beckoned her with a smile. 'I didn't hear you come in.'

She smiled and walked to where he sat, bending to kiss his neck as he put an arm around her waist. 'I know. You were hard at work. How did the interview go?'

'Fascinating. It's a lost cause for him, you know. Although I don't think he sees it yet. The Soviets are anxious to back Mao and support the Red Army here. Chiang Kai-shek thinks he can win, but I don't think he can. He's mounting a major attack against Mao's forces now, in fact.'

'Is that what you're going to say in the piece? That it's a lost cause?'

'More or less, though not quite as bluntly as that. It's only my opinion after all. I want to bring out what he said, in all fairness to him. He's an interesting man, though ruthless certainly. And I wish you had met his wife. She's beautiful and thoroughly charming.'

Audrey had the opportunity to meet Sun Yat-sen's widow instead when Charlie interviewed her, and she allowed Audrey to take a few pictures, which Charlie promised to submit to *The Times*.

'Do you mean it?' She was thrilled.

'Of course I do. You're damn good. As good as any professional I've worked with. Better than most, in fact.'

She looked at him pensively then. 'Were you serious about working with me one day?'

And then suddenly he laughed. 'I think I already am.' She had taken the photos of Sun Yat-sen's widow just that afternoon and they exchanged a smile. She loved working with him and hoped to have the opportunity to do so again in Shanghai.

They got ready to leave the next day and Audrey could hardly wait to see Shanghai after all he had told her. It sounded like a city teeming with people and excitement and commerce and gambling and prostitutes and exotic smells. It sounded like the Oriental equivalent of a Turkish bazaar and she was dying to see it.

She packed her things for the trip, and Charlie smiled at her as she juggled her bags and stared at her vanity case again and made a face.

'You know, I really ought to throw the damn thing out, or give it to someone. Maybe we can trade it somewhere for a goat or a pig.'

He roared at the thought and shook his head. 'Then what will you do on the ship on the way home?' She squinted her eyes, thinking about it. That seemed so remote now and it was extraordinary to think how far they'd come. 'You'd better hang onto it, Aud.'

'I don't know why. I haven't looked in a mirror in such a long time, and I'm not sure I ever will again.' Make-up seemed so ridiculous here. She had stopped wearing nail polish when they left Istanbul, and her little T-strap shoes were abandoned in the bottom of her suitcase. She had only worn oxfords since their journey to China began, and blouses and skirts, and a jacket now. She was sorry she hadn't brought more sensible things. Most of the clothes she had seemed totally inappropriate here, silk and linen suits, slinky dresses she had worn in the South of France, bathing suits, and evening gowns she had worn on the ship and would wear again on the way home. She felt even more ridiculous dragging along her fur. Although Madame Chiang Kai-shek herself was beautifully dressed and Nanking was a big city, the people didn't dress with any particular flair or interest. They wore the drab uniforms of the Chinese lower class, although Charles insisted that there were wonderful things to buy in Shanghai. She might even have a few things made. And above all, she needed a few warm things. There was a chill in the air. It was well into autumn now, and the weather would be getting cold before they got home again.

They spent the night in their room after eating an

enormous dinner at a restaurant recommended by the concierge, and Audrey snuggled in beside Charles. Once again, they had a narrow rickety bed, and everyone called her Mrs Parker-Scott now. The man at the desk had saved face for them, insisting that they must be on their honeymoon and she hadn't had time to have her passport changed. And she had been so amused that she hadn't said a thing to him.

'Do you mind, Charles? Having me pose as your wife, I mean . . .'

'Not at all.' In actuality, he looked pleased at the thought, as though he had put one over on her, and she was amused too. Everyone assumed they were married, and they were beginning to feel like it. He had even mentioned her to Chiang Kai-shek and referred to her unthinkingly as his wife. And perhaps in an important sense she was. She had pledged herself to him and come here because she trusted him. She couldn't have come farther than this with any man, or been happier that she had come, and as she kissed him again before she fell asleep, she smiled at him. They had made love when they got home, and now they were sated and content as they cuddled in the cool night.

'I love you, Charles . . . more than anything.' He smiled at the whispered words, and touched her red hair with his hand.

'So do I, Aud . . . so do I.'

13

Charles and Audrey sat on the crowded train from Nanking for seven hours, and she thought they would never arrive. He jotted down some thoughts in one of his notebooks for part of the time, and she read a book he had brought along, but she was far too interested in the passengers on the train to concentrate on much else, and she kept glancing out at the countryside as they approached Shanghai and taking pictures. But nothing had prepared her for what they saw once they arrived there, as the train pulled into the station, and Audrey stared at the mobs crowding the platform. People going somewhere, others who had just arrived, beggars, street urchins, prostitutes, foreigners, all of them jostling each other, and shouting above the din. There were children begging and tugging at her skirts, a child with leprosy with stumps where arms had been, prostitutes shouting in French to Charles, as half a dozen English travellers hastened by. She could barely hear Charles speak as she fought against the pushing of the crowd, and clung to her vanity case and the briefcase he had entrusted her with while he struggled with their valises.

'What?' He had said something she couldn't hear and she struggled to get closer to him. 'What did you say, Charles?'

'I said welcome to Shanghai!' he shouted back at her with a grin, and finally, mercifully, they found a porter anxious to take their bags. He hurried them outside to a line of waiting cabs, and the driver took them to the Hotel Shanghai, where Charlie usually stayed. The clientele was generally English and American, and the service was excellent. 'Almost like home,' he teased as the porter set their bags down in the room. They had registered as Mr and Mrs Charles Parker-Scott here, and Audrey was quite used to the name by now. She smiled at him from across the room.

'It will be very strange to be just plain Audrey Driscoll again, you know.' But that seemed a lifetime away now. Audrey Driscoll was part of another world, another life, as were Annabelle and her grandfather, and everything in San Francisco. This was the only thing that was real. The fascination of Shanghai, and the people in the swarming streets as she glanced at the window to look outside. She turned to look back at Charles again and he was watching her. He could no longer imagine a life without her at his side. They had come halfway around the world, and eventually they would go back again. And then what? He couldn't quite imagine it. He couldn't imagine settling down with anyone, and yet he couldn't bear the thought of her leaving him. But none of that had to be resolved now.

He wanted to take her to visit Shanghai a little bit before they settled down for the night, and when she had bathed and changed they went downstairs and hired a taxi again to take them to the Bund where all the European stores and buildings were, and then back into the crowded streets of Shanghai, as she stared in fascination at the armies of prostitutes roaming everywhere, the children still in the street late at night, the beggars, the foreigners. It wasn't uncommon at all to see Western faces here and there seemed to be hundreds of them; Italian, French, English, American, and of course now there were Japanese too. There were brightly lit signs, restaurants, gambling halls, opium dens. There were no secrets here, and nothing that someone wasn't willing to provide for a price. It had none of the quiet dignity of ancient Chinese history, and was in no way what Audrey had expected, but it moved at a tempo that made one's blood race and Audrey had never seen anything like it. They had an excellent French meal in a restaurant run entirely by Chinese and patronised by an interesting conglomeration of the international set, many of them accompanied by Chinese girls, and afterwards Charlie walked her back to their hotel. She gaped at the people in the streets and he teased her about her innocence. This was certainly not an innocent town. There was nothing one couldn't do or have or get, for a price.

'It's quite something, isn't it?'

'It's amazing, Charles. Is it always like this?' It seemed hard to believe that they could maintain that kind of energy all the time. And there were so many people here. The city was teeming night and day and Charlie was laughing at her.

'Yes, it's always like this, Aud. Sometimes I forget just how decadent it is, and then I come back and it takes me by surprise for a day or two.' It was in such sharp contrast to the sleepy villages one came through on the way in Tibet and Afghanistan and the rest of China. Nothing prepared one for Shanghai, and he had in no way prepared her.

'I wonder if it was like this in my father's day?'

'Probably. I think it's always been like this. If anything, it might be a little quieter now, though not much, since the Japanese attacked it. That should keep everyone on their toes.' But it didn't seem to have changed things very much.

They reached their hotel and walked slowly into the lobby, holding hands as they chatted about being there. So much so that she didn't notice the couple standing near the staircase, talking quietly, and then staring at her as she and Charles walked past.

The man was in his early seventies, the woman fifty-five or so, elegantly dressed, discreetly but expensively bejewelled and well coiffed with a smooth, perfectly done chignon, and diamond earrings in her ears. She stared at Audrey for a moment or two, and then said something to the man who wore an English suit and horn-rimmed spectacles. He looked over them at Audrey as she began climbing the stairs, nodded at his wife and was about to say something to her quietly, as she called out.

'Miss Driscoll?' Almost as though by reflex, without thinking twice, Audrey turned around with a look of surprise and looked down from whence the voice had come, to see them standing there, looking up at her and then at Charles.

'I . . . my goodness . . . I had no idea you were here. . . .'

She blushed to the roots of her hair, while attempting to appear casual, and came quickly down the few steps, still holding Charlie's hand. She gestured to him and introduced him as her friend Charles Parker-Scott.

'Of course.' The woman looked impressed. 'I've read all your books.'

'Parker-Scott you said?' The man nodded, looking with increased interest at him. 'Damn fine book you wrote on Nepal. You lived there for a while, didn't you?'

'I did. For over three years at one time. It was the first book I wrote.'

'Very, very fine.'

But his wife was concentrating on Audrey now, glancing from her to Charles with questions in her eyes. They were friends of her grandfather's, Phillip and Muriel Browne. She was something of a busybody, and was head of the volunteers at the Red Cross. She had been decorated by the French for her work with them during the First World War, and she had been married once before, and widowed of course. Phillip Browne had married her for her immense fortune, some people said. But few people had much to say about them. They were respectable certainly. He belonged to the Pacific Union Club, like her grandfather, and was the president of the Boston Bank. They travelled to the Orient almost every year, and would have been Audrey's last choice of people to run into. There was no doubt that her grandfather would hear about Charlie now, and she decided to do whatever she could to cover her tracks.

'Grandfather didn't tell me that you were over here.'

'We've been in Japan for six weeks, but we always like visiting Shanghai and Hong Kong.' She looked sweetly from Audrey to Charles, thinking to herself how handsome he was, and wondering if this were an old flame. Perhaps this was why she had never married anyone. She had always wondered about that, although she had never thought Audrey a particularly attractive girl. She seemed much prettier now, much softer as she stood with her hair in waves, framing her face, and her eyes dancing in a way they never had before. At least not when the Brownes saw her with her grandfather. It was the younger sister who was the pretty one ... married to Westerbrook, as Muriel recalled. ... 'Are you here with friends?' Muriel Browne looked directly into Audrey's eyes, and Audrey prayed she wouldn't blush as she played the drama out for her benefit.

'I am. From London. But they were busy tonight. Mr Parker-Scott was kind enough to show me around instead. It's a fascinating place, isn't it?' She attempted to sound innocent and not too bright, but she didn't think Muriel was fooled and she was right.

'And where are you staying, Mr Parker-Scott?' It was a question that took him totally by surprise, and he didn't realise quite how anxious Audrey was to throw them off.

'I always stay here. I'm very fond of the place.'

'So am I,' Phillip Browne intoned, pleased that an authority like Charles would back him up. He was going to remind Muriel of that. She had been complaining to him about the hotel only that afternoon. And this proved he was right. Best hotel in town. Had to be if a man like Parker-Scott stayed there. 'I was just telling my wife today—'

Muriel was quick to cut him off. 'We'll have to get together again before we leave. Perhaps for lunch, Audrey? And of course we'd love to see you as well, Mr Parker-Scott.'

'I'm afraid we won't have time ... we're leaving for Peking in a day or two ... and I think,' she smiled benignly at Charles, trying to get the message to him with her eyes, 'Mr Parker-Scott is working on an article. ...'

'Well, perhaps if you have time before you leave ...' Muriel looked at him, nonplussed. 'Are you going to Peking, too?' This would make some tidbit to take home with her. Stuffy Edward Driscoll's granddaughter shacking up with a writer in Shanghai ... she could hardly wait to tell her friends at home! And Charles walked right into her trap as Audrey almost groaned.

'Yes, I am. I'm working on an article for *The Times*.'

'How interesting!' Muriel cooed and clapped her hands and Audrey wanted to strangle her, knowing full well what she found interesting was the fact that she had caught her with Charles, going up the steps to their room, in a hotel. She knew full well what Muriel suspected them of, and of course she was right. The problem was how to keep her from telling her grandfather and everyone else in San Francisco.

'Mr Parker-Scott just interviewed Chiang Kai-shek in Nanking.' Audrey knew that she was embarrassing him, but she was hoping to distract the old bitch, at least temporarily, and Phillip Browne was of course enormously impressed by that. With that, Audrey turned and smiled at Charles again. 'You know, you really don't have to walk me upstairs' – she beamed at Muriel again – 'everyone is so afraid of bandits here. My friends entrusted me to Charles like a five-year-old.' She smiled at him and held out her hand. 'I'll be fine with the Brownes, and I know you wanted to go on to meet your friends.' She tried to make it sound as though there were twenty women on a street corner waiting for him, and he looked startled by her words, and then completely understood, realising how stupid he had been. He leapt right into the play with her, shook her hand, and the Brownes', made a great show of picking up his messages at the desk, waved at them, and then left, as Muriel stood staring after him, looking disappointed. Maybe she had made the wrong assumption after all. She glanced quickly back at Audrey, who was chatting with Mr Browne as they wandered towards the stairs. Their rooms were on different floors, but they deposited her in front of her door, and she shook hands with them, let herself into her room, and heaved a huge sigh of relief as they went on upstairs. She wasn't sure if they had believed her or not, but at least she'd done what she could to salvage her reputation before it was too late. She wondered what would get back to her grandfather, if anything.

She would have been considerably less relieved if she could have heard Muriel whispering to her husband as they walked upstairs. 'I don't believe a word of it. . . .'

'Of what? His interviewing Chiang Kai-shek? Are you crazy, he's the biggest travel writer there is. . . .' He looked outraged and she looked irritated with him, as usual.

'No, no, that nonsense about his going out with friends, and just taking her out to dinner tonight while her friends were otherwise occupied . . . she's sleeping with him, Phillip. I can tell.' Her beady eyes narrowed as he let her into their room with an expression of pain on his face. She was always ferreting out gossip about everyone, even here halfway around the world in a place like Shanghai.

'You can't tell anything. She's a decent girl. She wouldn't do a thing like that.' He felt an obligation to defend her, if only for the sake of his old friend, Edward Driscoll.

'Nonsense. She's an old maid. She'd have married Harcourt Westerbrook, if she could, but her younger sister walked off with him. You never see her anywhere. All she does is play nursemaid to that old man . . . and then she comes over here and kicks up her heels, where no one will know about it. . . .' Her eyes glittered with delight at the tale she told, but Phillip Browne only waved a tired hand at her.

'Stop making things up. You don't know anything. For all you know they're engaged . . . or very much in love . . . or just good friends or even strangers. There doesn't have to be something seamy about everyone you meet, you know.' He often wondered why she thought that way – and the depressing thing was that she was so seldom wrong.

'Phillip, you're an innocent. I'm sure if you check the register of this hotel, they're staying in the same room. They're so far from home, they think they're safe.' And she was right, of course. Audrey was already panicking in her own room, and she rushed downstairs again to hire a second room on a different floor, in Charlie's name. He was laughing half an hour later, when he let himself into the room they shared and looked at her.

'The man at the desk says you're throwing me out.' He was laughing at the explanation they had given him, and he had correctly guessed what Audrey had done in the brief time he had gone across the street to a bar for a drink. 'You've certainly been busy, haven't you?'

She sat on the bed with a look of despair and glanced up at him. 'It's not funny, Charles. They are the last people on earth I would have wanted to meet here.'

'I figured that out eventually, although I'll admit I was slow tonight. I imagine she has a rather loose tongue, dear Mrs Browne, am I correct?'

'Loose and vicious. She'll have it all over San Francisco that I was travelling with you.'

He knit his brows and sat down next to her. 'Do you really want me to move to the other room?' He would have done anything for her. It was hard to remember sometimes that they had other lives to think about, this seemed to be the only reality to them. But he didn't want to do anything that would cause her unhappiness one day, especially if he wouldn't be there to protect her from them. 'I'm really sorry, Aud. I didn't really think we'd run into anyone, certainly no one you knew. . . .'

She smiled at him ruefully. 'The world is very small these days. And to answer your question, no, I don't want you to move into another room. I just want to throw that old bitch off the track so it doesn't hurt my grandfather. But I'm not going to change my life for them, Charles. They don't mean that much to me.'

'They might someday. Once you get home . . .' His voice drifted off. He hated thinking about her having any home, except with him. 'I don't want you to get hurt.'

'I thought of that when all this began, and I cast my lot with yours. If I were really afraid of that, I would still be hiding at home somewhere . . . or I'd be on my way back to the States by now. This is what I want to do' – she sounded proud just to be with him, and she was – 'and you're the man I love, Charles Parker-Scott, and if other people don't like it, that's their problem. As long as we make an effort to see that no one gets hurt' – and the extra room had accomplished that – 'then the rest of what we do is no one's concern but our own.' He smiled down at her and took her in his arms as she spoke the words. He loved that about her. Her courage, her willingness to stick by what she believed. He suspected that she would have tackled anyone in order to stand by what she thought was right, and he loved that about her more than anything. He respected her, as he had respected no one else before.

They went to bed that night and made love passionately for hours, and afterwards Audrey smiled at him and teased, 'I wonder what Mrs Browne would say to that?'

'She'd be desperately jealous, my dear!' They both knew it was true, and Audrey laughed as she thought of it.

'And Mr Browne would harrumph and say . . . "very fine . . . very fine"!'

They fell asleep that night as they always did, safely tucked in each other's arms and, not surprisingly, Audrey dreamed of her grandfather, but by the next morning she had stopped worrying about it. They had done what they could, and if she had to, she would explain it to him when she got home, that Charlie was a friend of James and Vi, that they were 'just friends', that he happened to be in Shanghai at the same time. She was prepared to lie about it, for her grandfather's sake. He didn't need to know that she was deeply in love with the man. It would only have frightened him, fearing that he would lose her again, and Audrey had already long since decided that he would not lose her.

Instead, she turned her attention to the wonders of Shanghai again. It was an incredible place to be, and the people fascinated her as well. There were English and French as well as Chinese, and firms like Jardine, Matheson's and Sassoon's brought in some very proper British types.

'Most of whom don't mix with the Chinese,' Charles explained.

'That seems stupid, doesn't it? I mean after all, as long as they're here.'

He nodded, but things didn't work that way here. 'They're all very colonial in a way. They try to pretend that they're not here. None of them speak Chinese, at least no one I've met, except maybe one man I recall, and everyone considered him a little strange. The Chinese speak English or French to them, and the Westerners expect it that way.'

'It seems rather pompous, doesn't it?' The thought annoyed her, she would have liked nothing better than to learn Chinese. 'What about you, Charles? You speak a few words. Can you understand them here?'

'The accent is different here, but I get along,' he laughed, tossing his trousers on a chair, 'especially when I'm drunk enough,' and with that he crossed the room in two long strides and grabbed her in his arms, 'like now.' He pretended to bite her neck and gabbled at her in Chinese, and they collapsed laughing on the bed. 'All that decadence out there makes me want to attack you all the time, Aud. It's very difficult being here with you.' She laughed and he continued to nuzzle her. They had been so tired during their travels over five thousand miles, and now they were both beginning to revive. She reached out to him hungrily and he held her close, playing his long, graceful fingers on her thighs, until she moaned softly in his arms. She whispered his name as he entered her and their lovemaking went on for hours, until at last they lay spent, and she whispered his name once more as she drifted off to sleep. She couldn't imagine ever loving any man but him. She might as well have married him, because she had given him her heart. Forever and always. It was a love that had crossed two continents, and she would have gone anywhere for him, or to be with him. He sensed that, as he held her close to him, and closed his eyes, listening to the noises of Shanghai.

14

They spent a week in Shanghai, and then moved on to Peking. They left Shanghai by boat, bound for the port of Tsingtao, and they spent a romantic night on the ship, listening to the water lap at the hull, as they made love and then whispered long into the night. Audrey was almost sorry to leave Shanghai, there had been endless sources of wonder there, and Charlie's interviews had gone well there as well. Now, he only had to spend a few days in Peking, and they could begin the long journey back to Istanbul, and then Paris, and London after that, so he could begin his work, and finish the articles by year end, as his contract required. He was getting anxious to get back now, he had a lot of work to do, but as they lay in their bunks on the way to Tsingtao he was not thinking of the articles but only of the woman who inspired him with a passion he had never felt before. He could never get quite enough of her, he loved the way she felt and looked and smelled, he couldn't keep his hands off the silky skin, and deep red hair, couldn't keep his eyes away from hers, his lips from her generous lips . . . every inch of her excited him and he thought he would have done anything for her.

'Will you really come to San Francisco to meet my grandfather?' she whispered to him that night. He had mentioned it earlier and she was already worrying about going back. She couldn't bear the thought of leaving him.

'I'll come if I can . . . when I finish my work. . . .' But he wanted her to stay in London with him. He had decided to go back to London to write his articles and he was hoping to be free after that. He had suggested that she go to London with him more than once, but that was impossible for her.

'You know I can't do that. I have to go back and make sure Grampa is all right. And Annabelle's baby is due in March.' She had to be home for that too. 'Why don't you come to San Francisco to write your articles? Or at least as soon as you're through?' She couldn't imagine that it would take him more than a few weeks, and she didn't see why he couldn't write just anywhere.

'I have a book to do after that, Audrey. I can't just walk off when I feel like it.' The realisation of that depressed him now. He didn't want to do anything that would keep him from her. But he did have his work to think about. He had contracts to fulfil. Somehow they'd work it out. It would make more sense when he got back to London and talked to his publisher, and he would think about it more seriously on the way back, but in the meantime, they still had Peking to share, and their discoveries there took her breath away. It had none of the brassiness and decadence of Shanghai. Peking represented history. The capital of China for eight hundred years – once the home of Kubla Khan – its awesome dimensions alone startled her as they stood in Tienanmen Square, and there were tears in her eyes as she looked at the curving gold roofs of the Forbidden City, which had been the compound of the Emperor's Palace for both the Ming and Ch'ing dynasties for years. She spent hours visiting there and the Temple of Heaven, built entirely of wood without a single nail. It was the building that impressed her most in all of Peking, and it was only five blocks from Tienanmen Square. She walked endlessly, carrying her camera as discreetly as she could, so as not to frighten the children who still thought it a devil box, and took photographs as unobtrusively as possible of everyone and everything in sight. She had been able to replenish her supply of film in Shanghai, and she used most of it in Peking. Particularly once they left the city and drove north, first to the Summer Palace, built by the Dowager Empress just north of the city to avoid the heat of Peking. It was only slightly cooler here, and the thing that fascinated Audrey most was the marble barge that had actually moved across the lake followed by countless other barges with musicians and entertainers playing in the warm night air.

After the Summer Palace, they visited the Ming Tombs, in the Valley of the Ming. The main avenue to the tombs was lined by massive statues of animals, camels kneeling, lions roaring, leopards ready to leap, and twelve human figures, some of them depicting generals of the Ming dynasty. Again, the massive scale of it all, and the incredible beauty and detailing of the work, left Audrey bereft of speech, and more than once there were tears in her eyes, but the sight that impressed her most, that she could barely tear herself from, was the Great Wall. They had gone to Pa-ta-ling, twenty-five miles northwest of Peking, to observe its graceful curves, travelling on as far as the eye could see. The realisation that it had been entirely built by human hands and stretched for more than fifteen hundred miles, separating China from Mongolia, seemed incredible. It had stood for more than two thousand years, and was the width of the four horses ridden by the guards who had patrolled the wall, keeping watch for roving Mongol bands, or the hordes who attempted to breach the wall from time to time. But the sheer grandeur of it, the endless continuity as it seemed to divide the world, was so amazing that she could only look up at Charlie with wonder in her eyes.

'It's incredible, Charles . . . my God, it is surely the most impressive thing ever built by man.' He had always thought so too and standing here with her made it even more special to him now. He had always wanted to share it with someone, and never had before. He had stood here before, five or six other times, always wishing he could share what he felt, the immensity of the hand of history reaching down to him, as it did again now. And she understood that so well, she cared so much, and he knew she felt just as he did, as he took a photograph of her, standing on the Great Wall. And it was only with great reluctance that they left, and at nightfall took the train back to Peking again. It was a short journey back, and she was quiet during the brief trip. It took them a little more than an hour, and she looked up at him as they pulled into the station in Peking.

'I will never forget this day. For the rest of my life, I will remember that wall.' . . . Stretching into forever for hundreds and hundreds of miles. She wanted to thank him for taking her there, but she didn't even know how. He had given her an experience she would never forget for the rest of her life. In fact, the whole time they'd been travelling had been that way, and it made the summer months in the South of France seem so wasted and frivolous. She tried to explain that to him as they lay in their bed that night after a delicious dinner of Peking duck in a restaurant he had heard about but never been to before.

'There's room for both in one's life, Aud. Places like Antibes and places like this. Sometimes I enjoy the balance of both lives.' She wasn't sure she agreed with him. In many ways she preferred this. She was more her father's child than she knew, especially now that she was here, the feelings she was experiencing overwhelmed her that night and she couldn't sleep. She could only think of the Great Wall, and the peaceful pastoral scenes on either side. There had hardly been another human being there, only that remnant of more than two thousand years ago, each stone carefully placed atop the next, wide enough for four horses . . . it seemed to be engraved on her heart, and in her mind. She was awake when he first stirred, and she went back to bed to lie beside him. He was hungry for her, but she seemed distracted after they made love. Her mind was somewhere else. There was something else she wanted to see. She wanted to travel north to see Harbin, it had been another of her life's dreams. She had read a book about it once, and the book had been her father's of course. 'Will we be able to get to Harbin?' she whispered to him in the darkened room. She was remembering her father's albums again and knew for a certainty that he had been there in his youth. He had liked it even better than Shanghai, or so he said, though she wasn't sure why, but she wanted to see it if she could. It was another of her dreams, left to her as a legacy by her father.

'Do you really want to do that, Aud?' Charles did not look enthused. 'We really should start back.' He tried to make it sound as though they had decided that she was returning to London with him, when in fact, for the sake of speedier return, she would have been better off crossing the Pacific by ship and leaving him in Shanghai to travel back to London alone. But she hadn't made up her mind yet. And he wanted to get her to London with him. Going to Harbin could make the difference of her not having time to make the trip back with him. He didn't want any delays and he told her so. 'It isn't sensible.' But she looked heartbroken at what he said.

'How do I know I'll ever get back here again, Charles? Going to Harbin means a lot to me.'

'Why? Just because your father went there. Audrey ... darling, please, be sensible.' But her eyes unexpectedly filled with tears, and he hated disappointing her. He tried to reason with her as best he could. 'It's going to be freezing up there. I was there in November three years ago and it was below freezing. Neither of us is equipped for that.' The excuses sounded lame to her and she didn't want to give in.

'We can buy what we need here. It can't be that cold, for God's sake. Charlie, I just want to see it.' She looked imploringly at him. This was a pilgrimage for her.

'Harbin is seven hundred miles from here. Darling, be sensible.'

But she didn't want to be. 'We've come nearly six thousand miles and at this very moment I am more than eleven thousand miles from home. The way I came, somehow seven hundred miles does not sound like an insuperable distance to me.' She was stubborn when she wanted to be.

'You're being unreasonable, Aud. I thought we'd start back towards Shanghai tomorrow.'

'Charlie, please. ...' Her eyes begged, and he didn't have the heart to say no, but he made her promise that they wouldn't stay in Harbin for more than a day. They would go up, look around, and come straight back, and leave Peking

139

for Shanghai the following morning. She promised to do as he said, and they spent the afternoon buying warm, well-padded clothes. It was more difficult to find clothes here that accommodated Western bodies. In Shanghai they would have had an easier time, but they had to make do. The trousers that Audrey bought were too short, but the fur jacket and warm stockings fit her well, and she was able to buy men's boots that just fit her. Charlie didn't do quite as well, but he insisted he'd be warm enough in the odds and ends they acquired for the brief trip.

And in the morning they took the Japanese-owned Chinese Eastern Railway for the seven hundred-mile journey north across the Manchurian plain. The trip should have taken eighteen hours, but took more than twenty-six, with countless stops and delays, and the Japanese stopping and searching the cars at every station. Their longest stops were at Chin-chou, Shen-yang, Shuang-liao and Fu-yù, but at last just before noon they pulled into the Harbin station. The first thing they saw was a cluster of old Russian women on the platform, with three chubby, rosy-cheeked children in their care, a few dogs sniffing around in the snow, and a bonfire burning nearby where men in Manchurian garb warmed their hands and smoked pipes, sharing the local gossip. There was also a horse-drawn fire engine nearby, the smell of smoke and the frothing at the horses' mouths from their morning's work told them there had been a fire. Charles had also been right, it was freezing here and there was snow on the ground as they left the train and looked around at the long rows of cars and rickshaws. Audrey looked enchanted as they found an ancient car to take them the short distance to the Hotel Moderne, and Charlie looked less than pleased. He would have preferred to have been on his way to Shanghai on the first leg of the journey west, but she had been so stubborn about this that he had decided to indulge her. She had her own mind about some things, and this had proved to be one of them.

As it turned out, the Hotel Moderne was full, since half

of the rooms were being repainted. And they were referred to a small cosy hotel with a bright fire burning in the living room that served as a lobby. There hadn't been any visitors for months, and the old man at the desk was happy to see them. He regaled them with tales of the floods of '32 and gave them one of their two guest rooms, and Audrey rubbed her hands as she looked around and gazed happily at Charlie. 'Isn't it wonderful?' She beamed at him and he laughed. 'It's more like Russia than China.' They had heard a lot of Russian spoken on the way to the hotel, and the town was heavily populated by Russians. It was only two hundred miles from the Russian border.

He looked considerably less delighted than she did. 'I suppose you'll want to go to Moscow next.'

'No, I won't. Now be sensible, Charles. Admit it, wouldn't it have been a shame to miss this?' It looked like a scene on someone's Christmas card, but Charles was not feeling very festive.

He wagged a finger at her as she warmed her hands by the fire. 'We are going back to Peking tomorrow. That's clear, isn't it?'

'Perfectly. And in that case, I want to have a good look around today. Do you have my camera?' He handed it to her, loaded with film, and she picked up her heavy jacket again. It was barely warm enough for the freezing weather.

'Where are we going?' He looked at her with an expression of mock pain. 'I suppose you have the day's torture planned for me.' She always knew exactly what she wanted to do. And the man at the desk had said something about Hu-lan being an interesting place. It was about twenty miles away, but the car that had driven them from the station could be hired for a trip to Hu-lan. She shared the news with Charles and he groaned. 'Can't we stay here? Haven't we come far enough for one day?'

She looked at him in brief annoyance and picked up her jacket and camera. 'You can stay here if you want. I'll be back for dinner.'

'What about lunch?' He looked like a mournful child as he followed her out to the main room, and the wife of the man who had rented them their room immediately began to wave from the kitchen doorway. She had piroshki and hot borscht for them, and after that, Charles was somewhat mollified as they went outside in the freezing air to find the car that had brought them from the station.

Audrey smiled a few moments later as they made their way through the streets of Harbin, glancing at the signs alternately painted in Chinese and in Russian, but in many ways it looked more like a European town than an Oriental one, and here as in Shanghai, one heard an assortment of languages in the streets, French, Russian, less English than in Shanghai, and a Manchurian dialect as well as Cantonese. She was fascinated by the clothes people wore, the fur hats, the odd little coats, and here, as in the rest of China, everybody seemed to be smoking.

The driver they hired showed them the American Bank and drove them towards Hu-lan, but he insisted to Audrey and Charles that the road was blocked before Hu-lan and they would not be able to go all the way. Instead they threaded their way down narrow roads heaped with snow and past picturesque little farms and buildings, as he explained about the soy crop to them. They passed a little stone church half an hour out of Harbin and when Audrey inquired about it, the driver said it was French, and just as he spoke a young girl in a thin silk dress came running into the road, attempting to flag them down. She appeared to be barefoot at first, but as she approached the car, Audrey saw that she was wearing blue cotton slippers and although her feet had not been bound, they were tiny. She was speaking frantically to their driver in a dialect that sounded unfamiliar to Audrey and Charles, and she was waving frantically in the direction of a wooden building.

'What does she want?' Audrey leaned forward, sensing that somehow the child was in danger, and the driver glanced back at her with a shrug.

'She says that bandits killed the two nuns who run the orphanage. They tried to hide in the church and the nuns would not let them.' He spoke in careful English and all the while the young girl continued to wail and wave her arms frantically back towards the church and the adjoining building. 'Someone have to bury them but it too cold now. And someone have to take care of the children.'

'Where are the others?' Audrey spoke quickly as Charles listened to the exchange. 'How many nuns are there?'

The driver spoke to the girl again, speaking up in a loud singsong voice, and she answered him quickly. He turned and translated for Audrey and Charles, who was sorry they had come on this misbegotten leg of the journey.

'She say only the two who are killed. The other two left last month. They go to Shanghai, then to Japan. And next month two more come instead. Now no nuns here at all. Only girl. They all orphans.'

'How many of them are there?'

He asked again, and got the answer with a long sorrowing wail. 'She say twenty-one. Most of them very small. She and her sister are oldest ones there. She is fourteen, her sister eleven. And the nuns dead in the church.' He seemed nonplussed and Audrey looked horrified as she swung open the car door to step outside at almost the same instant Charles grabbed her arm and stopped her.

'Where do you think you're going?'

'What are you going to do? Leave them there alone with two dead nuns? For heaven's sake, Charles, we can at least help them sort things out, while someone calls for some officials.'

'Audrey, this is not San Francisco or New York. This is China, Manchuria in fact. Manchukuo, as the Japanese call it and they are in occupation here. There is a civil war on to boot, there are bandits everywhere, and there are orphans and starving children all over this country. Babies die here every day, and so do nuns. There isn't a damn thing you can do about it.'

She glared furiously at him, wrenched her arm free, and sank into the snow beside the car, looking directly at the shivering girl. 'Do you speak any English?' She enunciated the words carefully and the girl looked at her blankly at first and then began chattering frantically, waving at the church. 'I know. I know what happened.' Christ, how was she going to speak to this girl? And then suddenly she remembered something the driver had said. The nuns had been French. '*Vous parlez français?*' She had studied French in school, and it was rusty but it had got her through the time she spent on the Riviera. The girl answered her immediately in halting French, still waving at the church, as Audrey followed her and spoke slowly, assuring her that she would try to help her, but she was in no way prepared for the sight that met her as they entered the church.

The two nuns lay with their clothes torn off, they had obviously been raped, and after that they had been beheaded. Audrey felt instantly faint as she looked at the pools of blood, and was grateful for the strong arm she felt behind her to support her as she gagged and retched. She turned to see Charlie's pale face and tightened lips, and he growled at her and physically pushed her and the girl back the way they had come, and away from the hideous sight that had met them.

'Get out of here, both of you. I'll get someone to help.' Audrey quickly grabbed the girl's arm and propelled her back outside the church, but now the girl pulled her towards the other building. And Audrey was even less prepared for what she saw here. The moment the door opened, she was instantly surrounded by sweet little Chinese faces, anxiously turned up at her, all of them solemn, and a few of them crying softly. Most of them seemed to be four or five years old, only a few appeared to be around six or seven, and there were at least half a dozen who were barely more than toddlers. Audrey looked at them in amazement, wondering what would happen to them now. The fourteen-year-old and her sister couldn't possibly take care of them all, and now that the nuns were gone, there was no one to help them except a Methodist minister from town who was out in the distant countryside for several weeks. She turned to the girl who had flagged them down on the road, and asked her whom they could call to help, only to be met with enormous frightened eyes and a shake of the head. In halting French once again, she explained that there was no one.

'But there has to be,' she insisted in the voice she had used to run her grandfather's house for almost twenty years. The girl repeated the same answer, explaining that the two new nuns would come the following month. '*Novembre*,' she kept insisting, '*Novembre*.' 'And until then?' The girl turned up empty hands and then turned to look at the children around her, nineteen of them excluding herself and her sister. And then, almost mechanically, Audrey found herself wondering if they had eaten. She wasn't sure when the nuns had been killed, and none of the children were old enough to fend for themselves, except the one who spoke French to her and her sister. And when she inquired, she discovered that none of them had eaten since the day before. Considering that, it was remarkable that none of them were complaining. 'Where is the kitchen?' The girl led the way, and Audrey found a neat, orderly little kitchen with primitive facilities, but a small adequate stove, and a cold room. They had two cows of their own for milk, a goat, and numerous chickens, a huge store of rice, and some dried fruits from the summer before. There was a small supply of meat that had been carefully preserved, and the nuns had done some canning in the fall. In as little time as possible, Audrey made them all eggs, toasted a thin slice of bread for each one, and gave each one a sliver of goat cheese and some dried apricots. It was the richest meal they'd been served in a long, long time, and they looked at her with wide eyes, as she matter-of-factly served them and stood back to observe the scene. She was wearing the apron the nuns had worn, and they stared at her with wide eyes as she prepared the meal, and poured each one a small glass of milk. Only the two older girls held back. They were the ones who had found the two dead nuns, and it was obvious that they were badly shaken. Audrey encouraged them both to eat and at last, reluctantly they took a small plate of eggs and some of the goat cheese, chattering to each other and watching Audrey.

She was cleaning up in the kitchen when Charles came in. He was wearing a grim look and his hands and trousers were bloodstained. 'We wrapped them in some sacks, and put them in a shed out the back. The driver is going to bring some officials out later and they'll take them away. I'll contact the French Consul in Harbin when we go back.' He looked exhausted and upset by the horror of what he had just dealt with, and Audrey quietly handed him a plate with some bread and goat cheese. She was brewing a pot of tea for him as well, but he was sorry she had nothing stronger. He could have used a strong drink at that point, perhaps some brandy.

'They'll have to send someone to take care of the children. There's no one here, Charles. Apparently, there were two other nuns who went to Japan last month, and two others were coming to replace them in November. But now, there won't be anyone here to take care of the children.'

He gestured discreetly to the two older girls. 'They can handle it for a while.'

'Are you kidding? They're fourteen and eleven. They can't take care of nineteen children. They hadn't even eaten since yesterday.'

Charlie looked at her pointedly with sudden fear. 'What exactly are you saying, Audrey?'

She stared right back at him, and there was something hard in her eyes. 'I'm saying that someone has to come here to take care of these children.'

'I got that. That much is clear. And in the meantime?'

'You go into town and talk to the Consul, and tell them to send someone out.' She said it in measured tones and he didn't like the sound of her voice. He had an uneasy feeling that he wasn't going to like what she was going to do. And he was right, he discovered a moment later.

'Where are you going to be while I'm talking to the Consul?'

'Here, with them. We can't just leave them here, Charlie. You just can't do that. Look at them, most of them are two or three years old.'

'Oh for God's sake.' He slammed his plate down and stalked across the room. 'I thought that's what you were saying. Look, dammit. There's a war on here, or damn near anyway. The Japanese are in occupation, the Communists are raising hell. You are an American, and I am a British subject, we have absolutely nothing to do with what goes on here, and if two goddamn French nuns got themselves killed by some bandits it's not our goddamn problem. We should never have come here in the first place. If you had any damn sense we'd be in Shanghai by now, and heading west by tomorrow morning.'

'Well, that isn't what we did, dammit, Charlie, and whether you like it or not, we're in Harbin, and there are twenty-one children here, abandoned orphans without a goddamn living soul to take care of them. And I'm not leaving them until someone else shows up. For God's sake, they'll die here, Charlie. They don't even know how to feed themselves.'

'Who the hell appointed you as their keeper?'

'Who? I don't know. God! What am I going to do, just get back in the car and forget them?'

'Maybe. I told you, there are children starving to death all over China. They're dropping like flies in India, Tibet, Persia . . . what are you going to do, Audrey? Save them all?'

'No.' She spoke to him through clenched teeth. But she had seen enough of those children in the past few weeks and felt desperate each time she did. She was helpless to help them, but this time she was not turning her back. She couldn't. She was staying with these children until someone else arrived. It was a side of her he had never seen, and it was driving him crazy. 'I'm going to stay right here, until someone comes to help, so get your ass back to Harbin and talk to the Consul.'

While he was gone, Audrey put half a dozen of the children down for naps, fed more food to some of the others, straightened up the kitchen again, and watched two of the children milk the cows. Everything seemed to be in good order, and she was pleased to see Charles return at six o'clock, but he didn't look happy as he stepped out of the car, and she wondered what the Consul had told him. She didn't have long to wait to find out. He slammed the door as he walked into the house, and his lips were a long, thin, taut line as he confronted Audrey.

'Well?' He could already tell that she wasn't giving an inch and he wanted to shake her. He had had a hideous afternoon, beginning with the removal of the nuns, and ending with his battle with the Consul.

'He says that he has no control over the Catholic Church, and no responsibility for these nuns. Apparently they've been giving him a hard time for years, and he told them to get out two years ago. He will send someone for their bodies tomorrow or the day after, but he will not take responsibility for the orphans. As far as he's concerned, the orphanage should be "disbanded".'

'Disbanded? What the hell does that mean? Just push them out in the snow to starve?' She had never been so angry at him.

'Maybe. I don't know. Give them to the locals. What are you going to do? Adopt them?'

'Don't be so damn unreasonable for chrissake, Charlie. I can't just walk out on these children.'

'Why the hell not?' He was screaming at her in total frustration. 'You have to dammit, Audrey. You *have* to! We have to go home. I've got my articles to write, you have to get back to the States . . . what are you doing in Harbin with twenty-one orphans?' He sounded so desperate that she smiled at him and for the first time all day she leaned over and kissed him, her anger suddenly vanishing. She was just so worried about the children at the orphanage.

'I love you, Charles Parker-Scott, and I'm sorry I got us into this, but I just can't leave now. We have to get these children settled. We have to. We'll have to ask the people at the hotel if we can find homes for them among the local people.' But if they could have, the nuns would have long ago, and it was obvious that they hadn't. The children stared at them as they argued.

Charles was almost at a loss for words as she stood watching him over their heads. He had never seen her look so independent and stubborn. It was a side of her he had never seen before, and it was beginning to unnerve him. 'Do you propose to spend the night here?' He looked increasingly dismayed. He couldn't imagine how to unravel this tangle they were in, and the afternoon he had spent with the French authorities had been fruitless.

'What do you suggest I do, Charles?'

'I have an idea. Let's find another church and leave them there. There have to be other churches in Harbin.' He was desperate to end their dilemma and get back to Shanghai. More and more he had the feeling that they never should have come, but she looked amenable to his suggestion as the children clamoured around them.

'That's a wonderful idea. You go and I'll wait here. If you can bring someone back with you, then we can leave. Otherwise we can ferry them to the other church in the taxi.' Taxi was a euphemistic word to describe the ancient car that had driven them to the church in the first place. And Charles almost groaned at her suggestion. It was up to him now to find a church where they would be willing to take in twenty-one orphans. It would have been a difficult feat in downtown Philadelphia, and in Harbin it was hopeless. He cursed the day he had ever agreed to come to Harbin, and after a quick cup of green tea, he left to find the driver again and began his search for a church willing to play host to the foundlings.

While he was gone, Audrey changed countless nappies, made them all bowls of rice with some dried meat and broth for their dinner, and attempted to make order in the tidy house that was their home. There was only a slight feeling of chaos since the murder of the nuns the day before, and amazingly the two older girls had taken excellent care of their young charges, except for the absence of meals, which they seemed somehow to have forgotten. The oldest child attempted to explain to her in French all that had happened, how the Communists came down from the hills from time to time and tried to hide in the church, how some of the local Manchurians had tried to take refuge there when the Japanese came two years before, how bandits were everywhere, and killed many people. Ling Hwei, as she was called, explained to Audrey in her halting French, how the Japanese had killed her parents and her three brothers. She and her sister, Shin Yu, were the only members of her family to survive, and the nuns had taken them in, along with the other younger children, some of whom had been orphaned by the cholera epidemic the year before. Periodically, large groups of the children would be moved to the order's mother house in Lyon, or another orphanage they ran in Belgium. They had an orphanage in southern China as well, but Ling Hwei and Shin Yu hadn't wanted to leave Harbin and the nuns had let them stay because they were so helpful.

'Are there other churches where your nuns have friends here in Harbin?' Audrey asked her in French and the girl shook her head, explaining that they were the only nuns in Harbin. Most of the churches in town were Russian Orthodox and run by very old men, Ling Hwei said, and Audrey knew then what she would hear from Charlie when he returned from his mission.

She wasn't far wrong. He came back late that night, and all of the children were in bed, save the two older girls who were whispering quietly in a corner. Charlie looked exhausted, and he met Audrey's eyes with a look of total defeat.

'There's no one, Aud. I went to every church in town. I asked the couple where we're staying. These nuns seem to have led a totally separate life from everyone else, and no one is willing to shoulder their burdens. Food is scarce, people are afraid of the Japanese and the Communists. Everyone wants to mind their own business. No one is willing to come out here to take care of these kids, or take them in, even one by one or in groups. I tried everything, everywhere. The Russian priest told us just to leave them, that they would find their way alone.' He looked miserably at Audrey knowing in advance what she would think of that, and she growled at him in confirmation of his worst fears. He was beginning to wonder if he would ever get her to leave now. 'He said that there are urchins everywhere in China. The strong survive.' Even to Charles, it seemed a desperately cruel thing to say, and they had noticed the misery of the street urchins everywhere, but now Audrey was incensed as she railed at him in the orphanage's simple kitchen.

'What do you suggest? Pushing them out in the snow? Just how well do you think a two-year-old would do as an urchin? Most of these children are barely older than that.' Although they had both seen three- and four-year-olds begging in the streets of Shanghai, Charlie had no more desire to see that happen than she did. He just didn't know how to escape this fate that had befallen them in this far-off place, and he looked sadly at Audrey. He was frozen and exhausted and he hadn't eaten all day.

'I don't know what to say, Aud.' He sank onto a wooden bench and looked at her. Her face softened and she gently took his hand.

'Thank you for trying, Charlie.' It really was an awful dilemma and all of their efforts had come to naught. 'What about taking them to Shanghai with us, and trying to place them there?'

'And what if no one takes them? The streets are teeming with abandoned children. You saw that for yourself. And leaving them there will be no different from leaving them untended here, except that it's not quite as cold. But at least here they have shelter, and enough food for a while, and it's familiar.' Besides, the logistics of travelling almost a thousand miles by train with twenty-one tiny children seemed impossible to him and he wasn't far wrong. 'I don't even know if the authorities here would let us take them. The Japanese are a little touchy about who goes where with whom, at least in groups as large as this one.'

Her eyes suddenly blazed again as she paced the orderly kitchen. 'If they're so touchy, why don't they take care of them.' And then suddenly she remembered Ling Hwei's description of what they had done to her parents, and she realised that it was best if they didn't take the children. They would probably kill them all, as the most expedient way to solve the problem. She sat down on the bench next to Charles with a sigh, with no idea what to do. 'What if we wire the mother house of this order of nuns? Maybe they could send someone to help us.'

'Now there's a thought, if they answer us soon enough. They might have some interim arrangement to suggest. Or someone nearby whom they could send.' His eyes lit up at the thought. 'We'll go to the train station and send a cable in the morning.' Together, they rifled through the desk in the nuns' tiny bedroom, and easily found the address of the mother house in Lyon. It was the Order of Saint Michael, and they had both a phone number and an address. Audrey was even tempted to try to call them. But Charles thought it would be a lot easier to send a wire, rather than struggling with impossible connections where nothing could be heard. Together, in the kitchen, they composed the cable by candlelight that night, and then slept in the two nuns' narrow beds, side by side, shivering in the cold, as Charles prayed for a rapid solution to their problems.

The cable he sent the next day was written in French, laboriously translated by Audrey and Ling Hwei, and although not as elegant as their English version, it explained the essentials to the nuns in France. REGRET TO INFORM YOU

NUNS OF ST MICHAEL AT ORPHANAGE HARBIN CHINA KILLED BY BANDITS IN REGION. TWENTY-ONE ORPHANS REMAINING IN ORPHANAGE IN NEED OF IMMEDIATE ASSISTANCE. PLEASE ADVISE. He had signed it Parker-Scott with no explanation of who he was and only the name of the telegraph office in Harbin. They waited two days for an answer from the nuns in Lyon as Audrey cared for the children and Charlie paced the kitchen. He had already threatened that whether they got an answer or not, he was leaving Harbin with her in one more day, even if he had to drag her to the station.

But the answer finally came – offering no relief at all. He came back to the orphanage to show the cable to Audrey and his face looked grim. He knew what was ahead of him now, and he didn't care what she said. They were leaving.

NOUS REGRETTONS. AUCUNE POSSIBILITÉ DE SECOURS AVANT FIN NOVEMBRE. VOS SOEURS AU JAPON COMBATTENT UNE ÉPIDÉMIE PARMI LEURS CHARGES. L'ORPHELINAT À LINQING FERMÉ DEPUIS SEPTEMBRE. NOUS VOUS ENVERRONS DE L'AIDE FIN NOVEMBRE. QUE DIEU VOUS BÉNISSE. And it was signed. MÈRE ANDRÉ. Charles had almost hit his fist into the wall as he read it. His knowledge of French was such that he was able to understand all that he didn't want to in this case. It said that the nuns in Japan were fighting an epidemic among their charges and the other Chinese orphanage of the Order of Saint Michael had been closed since September. They promised to send help at the end of November, which was still a long time away. They included in the message a blessing for which Charlie did not give one good goddamn. He just wanted to get Audrey the hell out of Harbin within the next day or two, and now he wasn't at all sure how to do it. If he lied to her and told her that help was on the way in a matter of days, then she would insist on staying until they came. And she was too intelligent to be fooled. She would want to see the cable, and when he showed it to her at noon, her eyes were serious as she read it.

'Now what do we do, Charlie?' She looked deeply troubled as her eyes met his. It was a tough one.

He sighed before he answered her, knowing full well that it was going to be a battle. 'I think you're going to have to resign yourself to do something you don't like.'

Her eyes grew hard, but he had already anticipated what she'd say and he was prepared to counter her arguments. 'What does that mean?'

'It means that, like it or not, you've going to have to leave, Audrey. They have shelter. They have enough food to last them for a while, and someone will take pity on them. It's only a matter of a month before the other nuns come.'

'And if they're delayed? If they don't come? If they're killed on the way like the others?'

'That's not likely.'

Her jaw jutted out as she looked at the man she loved. 'Neither is my leaving.'

He sighed again. The last few days had been exhausting and extremely unpleasant for him. 'You have to be reasonable, Aud. We *have* to get back. We can't fool around here forever.'

'We are *not* fooling around. We are taking care of these children.'

'I apologise for the unfortunate choice of words.' A muscle in his neck went taut. 'The fact is we're leaving.'

'*We*'re not. *You* are.'

'The hell I am, Audrey Driscoll.' He stood up to face her and towered over her with a belligerent air. 'You're coming with me.'

'I am *not* leaving these children.'

'The older ones can take care of the others.' He said it in desperation, frightened by what he saw in Audrey's face. There was a stubbornness that genuinely frightened him. He couldn't possibly leave her here in Japanese-occupied Manchuria. Just thinking of what had happened to the two French nuns made him shiver and he reminded her of it now in no uncertain terms.

'I can take care of myself better than that.'

'Really? Since when?'

154

'Since always. I've been taking care of myself since I was eleven, Charlie.'

'Are you crazy? You've been living in a civilised American city, leading a pampered life in the home of your grand-father. What on God's earth makes you think that you're prepared to survive in Manchuria with Communist forces hiding around you, hostile Japanese, bandits everywhere, and people who don't give one good goddamn if you live or die?' He was outraged that she could even think she was equipped to deal with all that. Absolutely nothing in her life had prepared her for this and he knew it, nothing except her own adventurous spirit and her father's damn photo albums. But this was real. Those nuns with their heads cut off in the deserted chapel had been much, much too real, and he wasn't going to let anything like that happen to Audrey. But she was not thinking of herself, only of the chil-dren. She looked at them, and then back at him.

'What makes you think these children are equipped to deal with it if we leave them?' Her eyes filled with tears at the thought. Most of them were so very, very young, and in the past few days she had grown attached to them, two of them were constantly fighting to sit in her lap, and one of them had clung to her in bed all the night before, much to Charlie's dismay, and Ling Hwei and her sister, Shin Yu, were so gentle and trusting. How could she desert them now, and her eyes went back to Charlie now with a look of anguish.

'I know, darling . . . I know . . . it's awful having to leave them. But we have to. The whole country is filled with sorrow and hunger and lost children, but you can't cure it all, and this is no different.'

But it was different. It was different to her. She knew these children now, even if she didn't know their names. And she couldn't have abandoned them any more than she could have abandoned her sister, Annabelle, in Hawaii years before. She had taken her under her wing and had been caring for her for the last fifteen years, with the exception of the past six months. 'I can't leave them, Charlie, I just can't. Even if it means staying here for another month until the nuns come.' His heart sank at her words, and he knew from the look in her eyes that she meant it. And she was no child. She was no eighteen-year-old girl he could push around and tell what to do. She had a mind of her own. It was that which frightened him now. What would he do if she seriously refused to leave China?

'What if they don't come for six months, Aud? That could happen, too. The political situation could get so unpleasant here that they decide to abandon the orphanage altogether, and you could get trapped here for years.' It was a frightening thought even to her, but she was determined not to leave these tiny faces and small clinging hands. She would not leave them to meet their fate here alone.

'I suppose I have to take that risk, don't I?' She spoke with a bravado that masked her own fears, but he watched her in dismay, sensing that something terrible was happening between them.

'Audrey, please. . . .' He took her in his arms and held her and he could feel that she was shaking. He knew she had to be frightened of staying there alone, but he wasn't willing to stay for the next month or two or ten or twelve. He had to get back to London in the next few weeks. He was already nervous about the delay. He had never been in a dilemma as awkward as this one. He couldn't just walk out on her here, that was an awful thing to do, but he couldn't stay indefinitely either. Nor did he want to leave her. He tried to explain it to her as the children clamoured around their legs and she seemed to understand what he was saying. 'I've *got* to go back, Audrey. My work depends on it. And you really have no business staying either. You've told me that all along. What about those responsibilities you talk so much about?'

'Maybe, right now, this is more important.' The way she said it hurt his feelings. Why was she ready to leave him but not these children?

'What about us?' He looked at her sadly. 'Don't you care about that?'

'Of course I do.' She looked hurt by what he had just said. 'You know that I love you,' her voice was husky and she dropped her eyes as she spoke to him, and then she raised them slowly to his again, 'but we have to be honest with each other, too. We would have to leave each other some-time anyway. And if you can't stay here with me, maybe that time is now. All I know is that right now, I can't leave these children, any more than I could have left Annabelle years ago, or you could have left Sean.'

The mention of the little brother he had loved so much was almost a physical blow to him, and she could see him flinch almost as she said it. 'I'm sorry, I didn't mean to hurt you . . . I just . . .' She looked up at him with eyes filled with her own sorrow. 'It doesn't change anything between us. It just means I stay here for a little while before going home.' As much as she hadn't been willing to leave him in Venice or Istanbul, she knew she had to now. She almost felt as though this had been put in her path as a kind of test, just as surviving her parents' death had been . . . and being there for Annabelle . . . and standing by Grandfather. . . .

'What if I marry you now, Audrey?' She looked at him in amazement and he looked ravaged as he said the words.

'Are you serious?' She was stunned.

'If that's what it will take to get you out of here, I am.'

She spoke very quietly, touched, but confused by the offer. 'That's hardly a reason to get married, Charles.'

'It also happens that I love you.'

'So do I. You know that. But after Harbin? Then what? I can't leave my grandfather indefinitely.'

'You don't seem to be having any trouble with it right now.' He looked hurt again and she couldn't remember a worse time in her life than this one.

'This is only for a little while. I'm going home eventually. What about your moving to San Francisco?'

He sighed and looked down at his hands, thinking for

a moment before he raised his eyes to hers again and gave her an honest answer. 'You know I can't do that either. I can't sit in one place with the kind of work I do. I travel all over the world ten months of the year. You would have to come with me. Otherwise, there wouldn't be much point in being married, would there?' But the real point was that they loved each other so deeply. This was the first stumbling block they had encountered, and it seemed insurmountable to both of them.

Her voice shook as she asked him the next question. 'Will you ever forgive me if I stay here?'

'The question is more will I ever forgive myself? I can't leave you here in Manchuria alone, Aud. I just *can't!* He slammed a hand into his fist with a look of anguish. 'Don't you understand that? I love you. I'm not going to desert you here. But I can't stay forever. I have a contract and three deadlines. That's serious business for me.'

'This is serious business for these children, Charlie. It's their lives we're talking about. What if bandits come and kill them?'

'Bandits don't kill orphans.' But they both knew that wasn't always true. Not in China.

'The Japanese might hurt them, too. Anything is possible here. And the reality is that if you can't stay, you may just have to leave me. But Charlie, don't you understand that this is a choice I'm making for myself? I'm a grown woman. I have a right to make my own decisions . . . just as I decided in Venice when I got on the train with you, or in Istanbul, when I decided to come to China. This is my choice, too . . . just like going home to Grandfather eventually. I have to follow my own destiny. . . .' She turned away from him for a moment. 'I only wish . . .' She began to cry at the words. 'I only wish that my destiny were the same as yours. But right now, I don't think it can be.' She turned huge, sorrowful eyes up to his. 'You have to leave me here, Charlie. For the sake of the children.' And then she said something that really shocked him. 'What if one of these children were ours? What if someone could save our child and didn't?' The very thought of sharing a child brought them closer together even as they stood there.

'If we had a child, I would never let you out of my sight again.' He spoke with such intensity that she smiled, and then he suddenly looked worried. 'Is there any chance of that right now?' He had hardly worried about it since Istanbul, but she seemed to have gotten the hang of calculating her dangerous time and she was good about warning him when they shouldn't make love. Neither of them wanted an unplanned child, but suddenly he wondered. The way she had said it brought the possibility to mind, and not for the first time.

'No,' she shook her head, 'I don't think so. But think of it . . . think of these children as though they were ours. Could you ever respect me again if I abandoned them?'

He smiled at how idealistic she was. She didn't understand the Orient at all. And perhaps it was best that she didn't. 'This is China, Audrey. Most of these children have been abandoned, or were sold by their parents for a bag of rice. They would just as soon sell them or let them die as feed them.' The very thought made her ill and she shook her head, as though to deny the truth of what he was saying to her.

'I can't let that happen to them.'

'And I can't stay. Now what do we do?'

'You go home, Charles, back to London, just as we planned before this happened. And I'll stay for a little while, until the nuns come. And then I'll go home via Shanghai and Yokohama. And with luck, by the time I get home, you'll be ready to come to San Francisco for a visit.'

'You make it all sound so simple. What if something happens to you, for God's sake?' He couldn't even bear the thought.

'Nothing will. Leave me in God's hands.' It was the first religious thing she had said to him and he was touched, but the last time he had done that with someone he loved, it had been Sean, and . . .

159

'I'm not sure I'm as trusting as you are.'

'You have to be.' She sounded perfectly calm.

'What about your family? Don't you think you owe it to them to go home now?' He was playing on everything he could, but that didn't work either.

'With any luck, I might still get home by the end of the year. If the nuns turn up in November, I could make it home before Christmas.'

'You're crazy, Audrey.' He had been afraid of that. 'You're being totally unrealistic. This is China, not New York. Nothing happens on schedule. I told you, those nuns could take months to come.'

'I can't help it, Charlie.' Her eyes suddenly filled with tears again, she was tired of reasoning with him. 'I can't do this any other way.' And suddenly as he watched her, she dissolved beneath his eyes and stood crying in his arms as he held her.

'Audrey, please . . . darling . . . I love you . . .' And he did, but he couldn't stay here with her. He had to get back to his own work and responsibilities. This thing had gone too far, and now he just couldn't see it through with her. But he was terrified to leave her alone in Harbin. 'Please, sweetheart, be sensible . . . come home with me. . . .'

'I can't.' Her damp eyes met his and he saw a determination there that stunned him.

'You're serious, aren't you?' His heart sank again. She was. There was no changing her mind. She was staying.

He stayed on for a full week after that, and did everything he could to convince her, but she was entrenched now. She was totally involved in taking care of her young charges, and she had even developed a very competent system. Ling Hwei and Shin Yu were invaluable to her, and she even put Charles to work more than once baby-sitting for half a dozen of the orphans while she milked the cow, or prepared a meal, or went out with the others for some air as they played in the snow in their little fur-lined boots and goatskin caps. The nuns had even knitted them mittens.

Charlie thought as he watched her that he had never seen her as content since he'd met her and he realised now that she was a woman who was used to taking charge, and not in the least afraid of the burden of responsibility. He admired that about her. In fact, he loved everything about her and he dreaded the day he would leave her.

Their last night together was a night neither of them would ever forget. Audrey quietly braced a chair against the door to their room, and they made love until morning in the frigid air of the tiny room, and at last they simply clung to each other and they both cried. He didn't want to leave her and she didn't want to be left, but they were each doing what they had to do. He felt he had to go back to finish his work, and she had to stay here to care for the orphans. It was a decision that hurt them both, and both felt conflicts and regrets but clung steadfastly to their decisions. She was less frightened than sad, and she left Ling Hwei in charge when she took Charles to the station in the morning. She stood beside him, wearing the funny clothes they had bought together in Peking, and he looked at her with tears in his eyes, almost unable to speak as the train chugged slowly into the station. It was heading south to Peking, and then Tsingtao, where he would take the boat back to Shanghai to begin his long journey west. But neither of them were thinking of any of that as they kissed for a last time, and he felt her breath on his face as she spoke his name and smiled through her tears. It seemed incredible that they were finally leaving each other, and she couldn't imagine a moment without him.

'I love you, Charlie. I always will.' She could hardly speak, she was crying so hard. 'I'll see you soon.' But now, even to her, it sounded like an empty promise.

He could feel his heart pound beneath the jacket he wore, and he longed for her again. He couldn't leave her here ... he just couldn't ... a pair of armed Japanese guards patrolled the station and he looked down at Audrey again. 'Will you go with me, Aud? I'll take the next train if

161

you will.' But she only shook her head and closed her eyes with the pain of seeing him go. She wondered suddenly if she would ever see him again. Suddenly she really did feel as though she would never see her own world again, and he felt it too.

'Say hello to Violet and James for me.' But he didn't answer her, the lump in his throat was too large. He only clung to her until the stationmaster shouted out in his sing-song voice and they both knew what it meant. For an instant, they both felt panic sweep over them, and regret, and all the tenderness they had felt for each other for months now. She couldn't bear the thought of seeing him go, but she had to. She knew she couldn't leave those children, and although she hadn't said it to him, she secretly felt that if they had been put in her path, then there was a reason for it. She couldn't imagine what it was now, but she couldn't simply get up and walk away. They were too tiny and helpless, but she was giving up so much just to stay there with them. She was giving up the man she loved, and she felt as though her heart would break as he pulled away from her and hurried towards the train. He had to run up the three steps as the train began to move, and he stood there holding out an arm to her. He would have gladly pulled her up and taken her along, without any of her belongings, but she stood where she was, with tears streaming down her cheeks, waving as he hung out from where he stood, slowly waving an arm, tears pouring down his own cheeks as he left her.

15

The weather in Harbin grew colder day by day, until they couldn't even keep any milk or water anywhere outside. It froze almost instantly and couldn't be used until they thawed it. The children almost never went outside now, and Audrey thought she had never been so cold in her life as November gave way to December, with no sign of the promised nuns. Charlie had been right. This wasn't the orderly life she had been used to in the States. Nothing ever happened on time or when it was supposed to.

The Japanese had come to see them several times to check her passport and question her as to how long she would stay, and she gave them the same explanation each time, 'until the nuns come'. They seemed satisfied and left her alone, although one of them had been inclined to linger and eye Ling Hwei, but his partner had spoken to him harshly in Japanese and they hadn't returned after that. Ling had blushed furiously when Audrey warned her to be careful. She had worn voluminous shapeless clothes since Audrey had arrived but now Audrey suddenly noticed that she had begun to grow round, and in December she confessed, her eyes full of tears, her head bent with shame, begging Audrey not to tell her sister, although it couldn't remain a secret for too much longer. She had 'lain with the Japanese soldier in June', she thought, or perhaps May, which meant that the baby would come in February or March, and Audrey sighed at the thought. She hoped that the nuns would be there by then and she would be long gone. She had already written half a dozen letters to Charles in the two months he'd been gone, and a long-winded saga to her grandfather, begging his forgiveness for staying away so long, and promising never to do it again, but also expressing her gratitude that he had let her come at all. She felt certain that it had satisfied whatever hunger she'd had in her soul. She promised she would never stray far from home again, but even as she wrote it, she thought of Charles and wondered when they would be together again. Surely not as they had been for those months crossing the wilderness of Persia and Tibet and Turkey and China. A time like that would never come again, she was sure, and she was grateful she had had it. In some ways, what she had done was shocking, and had anyone ever known, it would have branded her forever, but no one ever would, hopefully, if the Brownes didn't talk. But she didn't care about them now. All she could think of was Charlie. She didn't regret a moment of what they'd done. She knew he was the only man she'd ever love, and somehow she felt as though they'd wind up together, no matter how insoluble the problem seemed now. But just thinking about Charlie made her heart sing, and just the thought of him made her smile now, in the bleak Manchurian winter. She was still wearing his ring on her finger.

It was a shock when she realised two days before that it was nearly Christmas, and on Christmas Eve she sang carols to the children who sat and stared. Only Ling Hwei and Shin Yu knew 'Silent Night', and most of the songs they knew were French, but the little children were enchanted as the older ones sang, and Audrey tucked them all into bed that night with a motherly kiss and a tender hand. Three of them had had bad coughs for weeks, and with no medicine and so little heat, she worried about them. She took two of them into her bed later that night and they coughed and coughed and coughed, but she wanted to keep them warm with her own body, and in the morning one of them was better. The other had red eyes and a dull look to him, and he didn't answer Ling Hwei when she spoke to him. She was quick to come to Audrey to tell her.

'I think Shih Hwa very bad. We call doctor?'

'Yes . . . yes. . . .' She was always grateful for Ling Hwei's help, the girl was barely more than a child herself, but she seemed to have unlimited love for her sister, and these children, and now for Audrey. She had given Audrey the only treasure she owned, as a Christmas gift, it was a delicately embroidered handkerchief that had been her mother's, and Audrey had been moved to tears as she held it in her hand and hugged Ling Hwei. There were moments when she was glad she had stayed, but there was no turning back now anyway. She had cast her lot with these children, and she would live or die with them, until help came. But she wasn't thinking of herself now, only Shih Hwa who was gasping and grey. He was too feverish to hear when she called his name. She bathed his forehead with towels filled with snow, as she waited for Shin Yu to return with the doctor. She hadn't wanted Ling Hwei to go in case she fell and hurt herself and the baby.

It seemed hours before Shin Yu returned and when she did, it was with an ancient little man in a funny hat with a long beard. He spoke in a dialect Audrey had never even heard, and Shin Yu and Ling Hwei never raised their eyes to look at him. They only nodded when he left, they cried, as Audrey insisted that they tell her what he had said.

'He say Shih Hwa die before tomorrow.' She could see that much herself and she was furious that he was what passed as a 'doctor'. She put on her own jacket and boots and hurried out into the snow a little while later, determined to find the best Russian doctor in town. But when she reached his home, she was told that he was out. It was Christmas they reminded her, and she begged the serving woman to ask the doctor to come to the orphanage when he returned. But he never did. The death of Chinese children caused no one any concern at that time, except their parents, and in this case Ling Hwei, Shin Yu, Audrey, and the children who were old enough to understand. Shih Hwa died in Audrey's arms that night and she cried for him as she would have her own child. Four more died within the next two weeks of what she suspected was croup. It seemed insane that there was nothing she could do. But she couldn't even provide them with adequate steam to loosen the phlegm that was strangling them.

There were only sixteen children there now, including Shin Yu and Ling Hwei, which meant fourteen really, as the two older girls were more helpers than charges. All of them had heavy hearts after the death of the two little boys and three girls, not one of them older than five, and the youngest barely more than a year old. Audrey had sat raging at a heartless God as the baby died in her arms, and it made her think of Ling Hwei's baby now. What would she do with a half-Japanese child, or any child at all for that matter? Children were often sold for as little as a bag of flour. And Ling Hwei herself was barely more than a child, and she hardly looked more than nine or ten. She was delicate and slight, with narrow hips, and tiny graceful hands, and a quick smile now that she was coming to know Audrey better. She loved to play tricks and make jokes, and she always made the others laugh even when they were hungry or sad, and she struggled to learn as much English as she could with Audrey. She was obviously gifted with languages – she had learned French from the nuns, was learning English now, spoke several dialects of her own tongue and, Audrey realised when they were visited again by the Japanese, that she spoke their language, too, though it was embarrassing for her to admit it. It would have been considered traitorous by the others had they known that. But she had learned it from the boy who had fathered her baby. She said that she had met him in the spring, and he had come to the orphanage to visit her often. She had met him at the church, and the sisters had liked him. He brought them chickens, and the goat they still had had been a gift from him. He had been nineteen years old, and she knew that he really loved her. But he had been sent away in July, when she had not known about the baby. Now she had no idea where he was and she hadn't heard from him again, just as Audrey hadn't heard from Charles since he had left in October. It had been several months and she would have thought that she would have had a letter from him by then, although it could have taken that long for a letter to reach her. She had only just then heard from her grandfather at last, who was irate at what she had done, and all but forbid her to come home. He hadn't dared go that far, for fear that she would take him at his word, but she could almost hear his voice tremble in fury as she read the letter, and his hand had shaken as he held his pen. She felt certain that it was rage and not ill health that accounted for the shaky hand she read, and he was so angry that she almost laughed. It was a taste of home just reading the insults and the outrage that she saw there, and she wrote him a long, contrite letter in answer, promising to be home very, very soon, as soon as the nuns arrived, which she felt sure would be at any moment. She had sent another wire to France after Christmas, inquiring as to their progress. As yet, there had been no answer. Undoubtedly they thought she was being impatient, or they had no further word of the two nuns they must have sent some time before. But it was difficult crossing China in winter, as Audrey knew only too well. She had never endured such frigid weather in her entire life as she did in Manchuria that winter. She wouldn't even let Ling Hwei go out now for fear that the intense cold was bad for the baby. It was no secret now, her huge belly told its own tale, and her sister had questioned her with wide eyes. Ling Hwei had told Shin Yu that the baby was a gift from God, just like the little Jesus the nuns talked about, and her sister had been extremely impressed. Afterwards, she asked Audrey if she thought she had done a terrible thing to tell her that and Audrey smiled.

'One day she might not believe that, Ling Hwei, but I suppose for now it will do.' They exchanged a knowing smile, and in an odd way she envied Ling Hwei. She was sorry sometimes that she was not having Charles' baby. Her life was so distant and remote here that the restrictions of the society she lived in no longer seemed to apply and she missed him so terribly now. Night after night, as she lay in the nun's bed, she would think of the nights they had shared, and the days, and the laughter . . . the endless train ride, and the discoveries in Peking, the glorious days on the Orient Express when it all began . . . and their passionate lovemaking in the Pera Palas . . . how far away it all seemed now, and she was desperately lonely without him.

16

The letter that Audrey wrote to Charles on Christmas Eve reached him four weeks later, and he sat reading it late one night in his living room in London. The fire was lit, and he had a glass of brandy in his hand as he read again and again of Shih Hwa's death and Ling Hwei's baby, and then her words. . . . *How I wish that baby were ours, my darling . . . how sorry I am now that we were so careful.* . . . And in an odd way, he knew precisely how she felt. He had reproached himself a million times for everything . . . leaving her in Harbin, not forcing her to come home with him, not marrying her . . . leaving her to the Japanese . . . leaving her . . . leaving her . . . he hadn't had a moment's peace since he had. And finally, in desperation, he had confessed it all to James, who had been deeply shocked by the story.

'You know, it's amazing. . . . Violet was sure it was serious with you two last summer, and I told her she was mad. You know, the girl amazes me sometimes,' he smiled. 'She's almost always right. I wouldn't tell her that though, if I were you . . . it'll make her terribly hard to get along with!' Charles had smiled, wishing he could feel amused by Lady Vi's omniscience.

'I was a damn fool to leave her. It makes me sick thinking of what could happen to her there. I knew it by the time I left Shanghai. I was crazy.'

'You have your own life to lead, Charles.' James was always sympathetic, and particularly now as they sat in a quiet corner of his club sharing a glass of port. 'You can't be expected to spend the next year in Manchuria, tending orphans. Though I must say, I'm surprised at her. I didn't think that was quite her thing either. If you told me she had stayed on to take photographs, I could believe that quite easily, but not this. . . .' He smiled gently at his old friend. 'She's a good soul to take those children on, isn't she?'

'She's a damn fool,' Charles had said darkly. And Violet had returned the compliment to him when her husband told her the story.

'He did *what?*' She had shrieked the words as James looked at her in amazement. 'He *left* her there? In occupied Manchuria? Is he *crazy?*'

'Darling, she's a grown woman after all. She has a right to make decisions for herself, and she made that one.'

'Then why did he leave her? He took her there to begin with, he could have damn well stayed with her till she came home.'

'Apparently, going to Harbin was her idea, and she absolutely refused to leave the children.'

'I should hope so.' Vi understood perfectly and thought her a saint for staying.

'He couldn't very well violate his contract, and abandon all his responsibilities.' He would have excused Charles of anything, far more than Charles was willing to excuse himself. Charlie completely agreed with Lady Vi, and thought himself the worst bastard on earth for leaving Audrey in China. Not a day went by that he didn't reproach himself for leaving. But there was no reproach in her letters to him. Particularly the one she had written to him at Christmas. It was tender and gentle and loving, and it was obvious that she was anxious for the nuns to come. She had already been there for over two months, and she was worried about getting home now.

Charles answered her as often as he could, but there seemed to be so little to say to her. For a writer, he found himself bereft of words, whenever he sat facing a sheet of paper with her name scrawled across the top, *My darling Audrey* . . . And then silence. What could he say to her? How desperately sorry he was? What a huge success his latest book was becoming? That he had been invited to India in the spring and Egypt in the fall? . . . that Lady Vi and James wanted him back the following summer? It all seemed so stupid and inconsequential, and he missed her so desperately. He felt as though someone had torn a limb from his body the day he left her. And he kept remembering again and again what she said before he left . . . 'what if those children were ours' . . . and then what she said about Ling Hwei's baby, that she wished it were she having his child. And the agony was that he wished the same thing now. He knew there was no point in asking her to marry him again, or to join him in India, or Egypt. She couldn't go. She had to go home to the family whom he felt took such terrible advantage of her. He had secretly come to hate Annabelle for demanding so much of her, for expecting Audrey to rear her children, tend to her house, do everything for her. When would Audrey get a chance for her own life? And when would he see her again? It was that which tormented him most, and which led him to the cognac bottle every night before he went to bed. He couldn't bear the emptiness of his bed, as he remembered their nights in Venice and Nanking, and Shanghai . . . and the endless hours on those tiny trains . . . he did nothing except work and think of her. He hardly went out any more at all, and Lady Vi finally stopped berating him for leaving Audrey in Harbin because she could see he was suffering enough without her assistance. He had lost weight, and he had a bleak look about the eyes which worried James.

Lady Vi finally wrote to Audrey herself, and Audrey was thrilled to get the letter, relieved to have her friend in her confidence about her love for Charles, and she wrote to Lady Vi whenever she had a free moment and had already written to Charles, which wasn't often. Or not often enough. And Vi would call Charles whenever she got a letter from Audrey.

'What did she say?' By mid-February, he sounded grim when Violet called him.

'The nuns hadn't arrived yet when she wrote. Of course they could have arrived by now. I certainly hope so. Poor girl. She is really quite the bravest soul I know.' And Violet said as much when she gave a dinner party and invited Charles, and his illustrious publisher, Henry Beardsley as well. She had met him before and rather liked him. He was a powerful, blustery man with a brilliant mind and a somewhat common manner. But he made excellent dinner conversation and James thought it was fun to mix in some 'fresh blood' with their aristocratic friends. And this time Beardsley had surprised them by asking if he could bring his daughter, Charlotte. She was an attractive girl in her late twenties, extremely well groomed, and dressed in the latest fashion, although not beautiful in the classic sense. But she was attractive and very bright. She had gone to college in America, Vassar, and had a Master's in American literature, which made her useful to her father in his business. He was obviously very proud of her, and Vi was surprised to learn that she still lived at home with him. She was twenty-nine years old, she admitted candidly, and her father was widowed.

'Actually, I would have preferred law school.' She smiled across the table at Charles, in answer to Vi's question about Vassar. American colleges had always fascinated her. 'But my father objected. He said he didn't need another solicitor in the house, but one day he would need a managing director.' Father and daughter exchanged a knowing smile. It was no secret in publishing circles that he was grooming her for the role, and Charles had met her before. But most of his dealings were with her father, and he had never been as impressed by Charlotte as he was that night. She was extremely bright, and very pleasant, and it was obvious to Violet that she was extremely interested in Charlie.

'Oh for heaven's sake, Vi . . .' James gave her a disparaging look as they got undressed later that night. 'You're always imagining romance in the air.'

'And am I right? Besides, I didn't call it romance this time, did I?'

'What's that supposed to mean?' He looked at her with interest. He enjoyed her company more than anyone else he knew. Aside from being husband and wife, they had been best friends for years now.

'To tell you the truth, darling, I'm not sure. If you want to know what I really think, I think she's as cold as ice and she likes who Charlie is. She's twenty-nine years old, she's smart as hell, has plenty of money, and she needs a suitable husband. Charles would be perfect for her.'

'Good God, you certainly don't waste time. I hope she's not as analytical as you are.'

'Don't be too sure.' She gave him a Mata Hari look and he laughed as she swept off to the bathroom in a cloud of French perfume and pink satin peignoir.

But two weeks later, he wondered if Violet weren't more perceptive than he gave her credit for when he ran into Charles having lunch with Charlotte Beardsley.

'Very nice to see you again, Miss Beardsley. . . . Charles, old boy, behaving yourself?' They chatted for a few minutes and he moved across the room to the group he was meeting for lunch, but he noticed that Charlie looked relaxed and seemed to be having a good time, and when he questioned him about it the next day, Charlie attributed it all to business.

'She's a good-looking girl.' James was fishing and Charlie laughed as they stretched their legs out in front of the fire at their club.

'Don't be silly, and you can tell Lady Vi to call off the hounds as well. Charlotte wants to start handling my contracts for her father. She says he's getting tired, and my work is rather clean-cut and direct. I don't see any harm in handling it with her, and she gets on well with my agent, cousins or something of the sort.' Charlie didn't seem to suspect any ulterior motive, and James insisted to Lady Vi that this time she was wrong. But Violet refused to believe it.

'Don't be silly, Vi. And I can tell you, all he thinks about these days is Audrey. Any news from her today?' It was March by then, and they were all beginning to wonder if she would ever be able to leave Harbin.

And so was she. She had been asking herself just that for weeks, as the freezing weather held and Ling Hwei came closer and closer to having the baby.

17

It was mid-March and Audrey was lying in bed in Harbin, thinking of Charlie and the nights they had shared, when she heard a thump and a soft crash in the kitchen beneath her room. She sat up in bed and listened, her mind instantly alert, fearing that the Communists had come to hide there, or worse yet, bandits, as they once had in the church, when they killed the nuns. Her entire body stiffened, and her hand closed around a gun Ling Hwei had given her several months before. She wasn't sure where she had got it but she didn't question her about it. She was just very grateful to have it.

She heard another muffled bump, and then a sound as though someone were dragging something very heavy across the floor beneath her. There was no question now. There was someone in the house with them, and as she tiptoed out of her room in one of the nuns' heavy wool nightgowns she had appropriated months before, she saw Ling Hwei tiptoe out of the room she shared with half a dozen of the younger children. Her body was distorted by her baby now and, with a stern look, Audrey waved her back to her room in silence. She didn't want her getting hurt, and the memory of the beheaded nuns came rushing back to her now, as she wondered who was downstairs. There had been no major Communist skirmishes in the area since she'd been there, but the Japanese had been tightening their rein for a while. All she knew was that there was an intruder in the house, and she tiptoed down the stairs with her pistol loaded and cocked, ready to shoot whomever she met, her whole body tense, her eyes darting into the darkened room beneath them as she came down the stairs. Her heart was pounding so loudly in her ears that she wondered if she would hear the intruder in time to defend herself, but suddenly she could hear heavy breathing as she saw his shape outlined by the window. With her finger on the trigger she hesitated for only an instant. She realised suddenly that there could be no hesitation, she would have to kill him, but his voice called out to her sharply in the dark. He knew she had seen him, and what startled her was that he had spoken to her in French, assuming that she was one of the nuns.

A growling breathless voice had said to her, as though in pain, '*Je ne vous ferai pas mal.*' I won't hurt you. He had an odd accent she hadn't heard before, but he had spoken clearly. But there was no way to know if he had come in peace or if he was lying to her.

'*Qui êtes-vous?*' she whispered into the darkness as her heart pounded like jungle drums. She had asked him who he was and she had no idea what he would answer.

'*Le Général* Chang.' He spoke up in a clear voice this time, but she did not lower the pistol that she was still keeping trained on him.

'*Que faites-vous ici?*' She asked him what he was doing there and waited for his answer.

'*Je suis blessé.*' There was a long silence then, after he told her he was wounded, and coming down the last few steps she grabbed a candle and lit it awkwardly with one hand, still watching his form, as she kept the pistol pointed at him.

She warned him not to move and held the candle high, and all she could see was a stocky man of medium height in what looked like Mongolian costume. There were pools of melting snow around where he stood, and suddenly in the guttering light she could see a huge bloodstained gash on his shoulder. It was wrapped in bloody rags, and he was holding it awkwardly as he looked at her. There was a large pistol shoved into his belt, and a large sword hung at his side, a long strap of bullets over one shoulder, but he held none of his weapons out in defence against her. He only watched her with cautious eyes and asked her if she was one of the nuns of Saint Michael. She wasn't sure whether or not to pretend she was, and then she decided to be truthful. She shook her head, still staring at him in terror, and upstairs she could hear Ling Hwei moving around now. She was terrified that he might see her and hurt her, but he didn't seem ready to hurt anyone. He looked as frightened as Audrey felt as she held the pistol and the candle.

'May I stay here until tonight?' he asked her in French, and she had the odd feeling that he had been there before. And his next words confirmed that suspicion. 'I can hide in the meat cellar, as before.' He looked pleadingly at her and she could see loops of gold embroidery on his fur cap. His jacket was more ornate than most she had seen as well, although with the blood stains he looked somewhat dishevelled. She remembered his words again now, and thought to question him before she agreed to let him stay. She could not let him put the children in danger.

'You are a general you said?'

'I am general of my province, and loyal to the Nationalist Army.' He was one of Chiang Kai-shek's followers then, and had obviously been fighting the Communists somewhere. She wondered what province he meant, but he explained as she watched him. 'I am from Baruun Urta, across the Kyhingan Mountains. We came to meet with some of General Chiang Kai-shek's men, but we met with Japanese troops. I have three men waiting for me in the church. If you will not let me stay, they will help me. Do not fear.' He was oddly polite, and his French was far more fluent than hers, which seemed odd for a Mongolian general. 'The sisters have let me stay here before. I have been twice when we came this way, but I do not wish to endanger you or the children. If you wish me to go, I shall.' He attempted to stand erect, but she saw him wince and he seemed to stumble from the pain in his shoulder.

'Did anyone see you come here?' She was trying to decide what to do, as Shin Yu came down the stairs and stood just behind her. She was startled to realise that it wasn't Ling Hwei, and Shin Yu attempted to say something to her, but Audrey waved her upstairs as she attempted to concentrate on what the Mongolian general was saying.

'I do not believe we were observed, mademoiselle.' He looked weak, and she could see that the shoulder was bleeding profusely. 'We will not trouble you. We need only a place to rest until nightfall. We are travelling on foot, and we must return to our people.' Whatever their mission had been, it was accomplished. But she was afraid to let them stay. What if it brought them reprisal from the Japanese? So far no one had bothered them and she was anxious to keep it that way for the sake of the children, but the man was obviously wounded and wouldn't make it very far without shelter and respite.

'Put down your arms.'

'Pardon?' He sounded startled and acted as though he didn't understand, as Shin Yu came down the stairs again and Audrey waved her back upstairs.

'I said put down your arms, your pistol and your bullets and your sword. I will not let you stay otherwise.' He thought about it for a moment looking long and hard at her with an unreadable face.

'And do you propose to defend me?'

'I do not know who you are. I cannot let you hurt these children.'

'We will bring them no harm. My men will hide in the shed outside, and I will stay here in the meat cellar if you let me. I am the general of my province, mademoiselle. I am a man of honour.' He spoke with such civility that the incongruousness of the situation struck her with full force, but she could not relax her guard. She had only his word as to who he was. For all she knew he could have been a bandit, and perhaps they would have had no qualms about attacking her and the children. 'You have my word. You and the children are safe. I need only a few hours to recover my strength.' And then looking at her, he knew that he would not win the battle. He removed the pistol from his belt, the sword from its scabbard, and with more difficulty slipped the strap of bullets off his shoulder. What she did not know was that he had another pistol concealed beneath his jacket and a razor-sharp knife hidden in his sleeve, but he had no intention of using them on her. Nor would he have been foolish enough to leave himself unarmed. He knew better than that, and had she thought about it for any length of time, she would have suspected that he had other weapons.

'How do I know you will not hurt the children?'

'You have my word, mademoiselle. We will not harm you.'

'What about your men?' She was remembering the beheaded nuns in the church when she and Charles had first come here.

'I will speak to my men, and they will conceal themselves quickly. No one will see them, I promise you.' And then he smiled at her. He had an odd, interesting face, with narrow eyes and high cheekbones, he looked entirely different from the Chinese around Harbin, or the others she had seen in Nanking or Peking or Shanghai. 'We are adept at this.' Not too adept, though, she thought, or he wouldn't have been wounded.

'Do you need clean dressings for your wound?' She still stood cautiously by the stairs, and had told him to back away from his weapons. He sidled along the wall to the other side of the kitchen, and keeping her pistol pointed at him, she collected his gun and his sword, and then retreated back to the foot of the stairs as she heard Shin Yu call her again. The child was obviously frightened by the commotion. She called to her that she would be right there and turned her attention to the Mongol general again.

'If you have some clean rags . . .' he began hesitantly, 'but I think this will do. . . .' He motioned to the blood-soaked strips of blanket covering the wound then, and Audrey turned her gaze to it as she held the candle high. She saw then that he was not an unattractive man, but she wasn't sure she could trust him. Yet there was something honest and straightforward about his gaze. 'I have children of my own, and I told you, mademoiselle. I have been here before. The sisters knew me well. I was educated in Grenoble as a young man.' It seemed remarkable that he had, and had yet returned to this primitive and uncomfortable part of the world, but something told her that he was telling her the truth.

'I will give you some clean rags for your wound, and some food. But you must leave tonight.' She looked at him firmly, and spoke to him as she would have to one of the children. 'You have my word. I shall speak to my men now.' Before she could say another word, he disappeared, and she could see only a shadow darting to a shed standing between the orphanage and the chapel. She took the opportunity to cut two towels into strips, pour out a bowl of water, and slice some cheese and bread and dried meat, and when he returned she pointed to all of it standing on the kitchen table. She was boiling some water for green tea, and he seemed weak as he sat down on the kitchen bench, and looked gratefully up at her. 'Thank you.' He hastily ate the meat and cheese, and looked too tired to change the dressings, but Audrey was too frightened to do it for him until she saw him untie the strips of blanket and reveal the ugly wound. He had obviously been struck by a sword, and the gash it had left was red and raw and angry. He had some powder in a small tin in his pocket which he shook into it after she handed him some of the strips of towel soaked in water, and together they cleaned it, and she quietly bound the wound up again as he watched her. 'You are a brave woman to trust me. How did you come here if you are not a nun?'

She explained to him about the nuns who had been killed, and told him that she had been visiting Harbin. She did not tell him about Charles having come here with her. And she kept her eyes on the bandages as she worked. She was aware of a certain rugged beauty about the man, and a virility that she had never felt before from anyone. It was almost as though he exuded manly powers, and she was torn between fear and admiration of him. In some ways, he was a frightening man, one sensed that he would have leapt like a tiger and killed with one swift move, and yet, as he talked to her, he seemed very gentle. He had powerful hands and an interesting face, and she watched him as he made his way quickly to the meat cellar. He had told her the truth. He knew exactly where it was and how to get into it. He looked at her for one last time, and then closed the door quietly behind him, descending into the darkness as she stood alone in the kitchen with the bowl of blood-soaked water and rags the only reminder that he had been there. She swiftly poured the water into the snow outside the kitchen, and covered the red stain with more snow, burying the rags along with it. It would be spring before anyone discovered the bandages he had used, and he would be long, long gone by then. She went back into the house, and Shin Yu was waiting for her, frantic now, with huge eyes filled with fear.

'It is Ling Hwei,' she explained, 'it is the time. Her baby from God is coming now ... she is very sick ... oh, very, very sick, Miss Audrey. ...' Audrey ran up the stairs in her nightgown, still carrying her weapon and the general's, she dumped them all under her bed, and covered them with a spare blanket, and ran to the room where Ling Hwei slept, only to find the other children still asleep, and the young girl, clinging to her thin blanket in pain, her teeth clenched and her eyes wide with agony and terror. Audrey ran a gentle hand across her forehead, and the girl made no sound, but she writhed as though in terrible pain, her hands suddenly grabbing Audrey's.

'It's all right ... it's all right ... I'm going to take you to my room.' She swept the girl into her arms, and went quickly to her own room, asking Shin Yu to stay with the other children. She was afraid for her sister and she wanted to go along, but Audrey knew that it was best if she did not observe what Ling Hwei would go through. For months she had stared at those narrow hips and feared that the birth would not be easy for her. She had wanted to call one of the Russian doctors to the girl when the time came, but she knew from her earlier experience that they wouldn't care about this Chinese girl. She was no more special than anyone else, and babies were born at home with the help of mothers and sisters and cousins. But this girl had only Audrey to help her, with no experience at all. She had never even seen a baby born, and she sat holding her hand as she wrestled with the contractions in silence. Never did she make any sound, and Audrey wished that she would have. When the other children began waking up, Audrey asked Shin Yu to watch them and prepare their breakfast. She prayed that the general would not emerge from his hiding place, and she had no reason to think that he would, except that she was nervous about it all morning. But she could not leave Ling Hwei, the girl was obviously in terrible pain, and now in spite of herself she was moaning hoarsely and she seemed to be delirious, and she rolled and shrieked, grabbing at Audrey's arms and begging her to help her.

At last in the late afternoon, thinking that it was taking an unusually long time, she forced Ling Hwei to let her look to see if the baby was coming. The girl cried pathetically like a little child, and Audrey was suddenly reminded of the sobs of Shih Hwa before he died, but Ling Hwei wasn't dying, she was giving birth to the baby she had conceived with the young Japanese soldier the year before, and Audrey was sure that as she lay in agony she bitterly regretted what she had done, but it was too late now and there was no sign at all of the baby's head when she looked, even though Ling Hwei had been in labour for more than twelve hours.

Shin Yu put the children to bed for Audrey that night, after caring for them all day. She would come and check with Audrey from time to time, and get instructions and check on her sister, but Audrey would not let her see her. She had eaten nothing herself all day long, and Ling Hwei had refused even tea. All she would accept once in a while were tiny sips of water, but now she was crying pathetically most of the time, and Audrey was so distraught that she did not even hear the footsteps behind her in the room, as the general entered it on silent feet at midnight. She jumped with a stifled scream as she saw his shadow on the wall, and it was too late to reach for the pistol she had concealed beneath the bed. She leapt to her feet and wheeled to face him, but his face was peaceful when she did.

'Don't be afraid.' His eyes went swiftly to the struggling girl and then back to Audrey. 'One of the children?'

Audrey nodded, as the girl cried. It had gone on for nineteen hours now, and there was still no progress. 'She was raped by the Japanese.' She didn't want to tell him the truth, that she had willingly slept with one of them, for fear that he would hurt her.

'Animals.' He spoke softly in the stuffy room. The room was pungent with Ling Hwei's sweat and hard work through the long day and night, and she looked at him now with unseeing eyes. The pains never seemed to relent any more and for the last hour, Audrey had been crying with her. She had never felt so helpless in her entire life, and she glanced at the general now as he watched Ling Hwei for a moment. 'She works hard.' He looked as though he knew what it was about, and Audrey turned to him hesitantly. She still wasn't sure if she could trust him, although he had kept his word through the day, keeping to his hiding place in the cellar. She wondered if he was perhaps as honest as he seemed and if he could help the girl struggling with her baby.

'She's been in labour since last night, when you arrived. Almost twenty-four hours now.' Audrey felt despair creep into her voice. She was frightened for Ling Hwei, and she herself knew nothing of what to do for her, other than to hold her hand and wait for the baby to be born. But she had no idea how to relieve the agony that the girl was in, or even if one could have.

'Can you see the child's head?' Audrey shook her head, and he nodded. 'She will die then.' He spoke gently, but without surprise. In his forty years he had seen a great deal of life, birth and death, and war and despair and starvation. His shoulder no longer hurt quite so much, and he looked more rested than he had the night before, but Audrey looked anguished by what he had just said to her.

'How do you know?' she whispered.

'It is written on her face. My firstborn took three days to come. A son.' His eyes and mouth remained serious. 'But she grows weak, and she is young. I can see it.' His eyes narrowed as he watched, and then glanced at the American woman.

'We should have a doctor.'

He shook his head. 'They will not come. And they cannot help her. They can save the child, but no one will want a Japanese bastard.'

'What do you mean?' She wondered if he would have let her die as she looked from General Chang to Ling Hwei. 'Can something be done?' Audrey knew nothing of the procedures of delivering a baby and was sorry she hadn't listened at greater length to her sister's tales. But Annabelle had had an easy time, it seemed, and they had given her chloroform during the delivery. There was nothing like that here, and she turned to the Mongolian general now, thinking that he was precisely what her image would have been of a warlord. He seemed to be considering the situation, weighing matters that Audrey could not know, and then his eyes met hers. 'You can cut her.' It sounded horrible to Audrey and she wasn't sure what he meant as he went on. 'With a clean sword. It should be done by a woman, or a holy man, but you do not know how, I can see that.'

'Do you?'

'I have seen it done. They cut my wife once. With my second son.'

'And she survived?' That was all Audrey wanted, to save this girl, and to relieve her of the child who was causing her so much pain. Shin Yu knocked softly on the door and Audrey sent her away with muffled words. She didn't want her to see the general there, or for her to see her anguished sister.

'Yes.' He nodded in answer to her question. 'She survived. As did the child. Perhaps this girl will, too, if we do it quickly. First, you must press the child down.' Without ceremony, but with gentle hands, he went to Ling Hwei, said only a few words to her, and then looked down at the small mountain of her belly. He felt where it began, and then suddenly, without warning, as she began the next pain, he crushed his full weight down on her as she screamed, pushing the child down so that it would come out. She objected violently, but he did it two more times, as she fought him, and Audrey feared that he would kill her with the pressure of his powerful body, but this time when he bid Audrey to look, she could see a small spot of the baby's head, there was a tiny bit of black hair and she grinned up at General Chang with relief. 'I can see the baby.' He said nothing, but applied pressure two more times, and the circle of the child's head grew, and then he stepped back and looked at Audrey.

'You will need clean towels, sheets, rags.' She took that to mean that the baby was coming, and when she returned with her arms full, she jumped as she saw him make a single gesture and flick a long-bladed knife out of his sleeve and pass it through the candle's flame again and again until she could only imagine how hot it was, but this would make it clean, when he made the incision. She realised then that the weapons he had given her had not been all he carried, but she said nothing now. He had been true to his word so far and if he helped her with Ling Hwei she would owe him a debt forever. He held the blade aloft now, and Audrey was not entirely sure where he would apply it. 'See if you can see more of the baby's head now,' he instructed her, but the spot had not grown since he had stopped pressing on Ling Hwei's belly, and the poor girl was crying hideously in ever greater pain as the baby fought to come out and got nowhere. 'Hold her legs.' He spoke in a firm, hard voice, and for a moment, Audrey was frightened. She was trusting this man, and she had no reason to other than the fact that she seemed to have no choice. There was no one else to help her.

'What will you do to her?' Audrey was afraid but something in his eyes reassured her.

'I will try to make an opening large enough for the baby's head to pass through. Hurry, we can't let the blade get cold.' Audrey hesitated for only an instant, and then with soothing words, she sat down next to Ling Hwei, with her back to the girl's head, and held her legs back as hard as she could. But Ling Hwei presented little resistance. She had no strength left with which to fight them, and as Audrey watched him work, his hand moved deftly with the blade. There was no blood at first, and then suddenly a great gush of it rushed into the towels he had told her to place there. And now, in a strained voice he told Audrey to press on her stomach as he had, and when she was too gentle he shouted at her, caught up in the urgency of it now, too. God only knew how many people this man had killed, and yet he was fighting for one life now, with Audrey. Audrey held her breath and pressed as hard as she could, and he heated the blade again and cut even further, and then with horrible moans coming from Ling Hwei, the top of the baby's head appeared, and then slowly its forehead, two tiny little ears, a nose and mouth, and the entire head was free as Audrey watched in amazement and he ordered her to continue pushing. There was silence from Ling Hwei now, she had lost quantities of blood and the pain had finally become too great. She was unconscious as her little girl came into the world, and the general held her victoriously aloft, as though he had conceived her himself, smiling broadly at Audrey. They wrapped her swiftly in a blanket and cleaned her off with one of the clean towels as she whimpered and then cried and Audrey felt the tears course down her cheeks. She was amazed to see fingers of light streaking in through the window. They had been working together since midnight, and General Chang had saved Ling Hwei and her baby. But his eyes were serious now as he observed the girl, and then examined the wound he had made with his knife. He looked at Audrey and did not tell her what he feared. But she had bled terribly and he doubted that she would live now. Only the baby would survive, unless the young girl was very, very lucky.

'You must sew her,' he told her quietly. Audrey swiftly fetched the only needle she had and strong white thread, and passed the tip of the needle into the fire as he had done with his knife, before sewing up the incision. It was the most difficult thing she had ever done, and with every stitch her hand shook and she prayed for the girl. It would be so unfair if she died. It couldn't be. The tears burned Audrey's eyes and it seemed to take a long time to make the necessary repairs, and then gently she cleaned her with cool water and a clean rag. She cleaned her whole body, and then wrapped her in blankets as the general held the sleeping child as though she were his own. Neither of them seemed to remember that she was half Japanese, and neither of them cared. She was a new life, their child, the life they had saved in a night of hard work together. 'You did very well.' His voice was gentle as he watched Audrey with the unconscious girl. Ling Hwei was very pale. Audrey turned her eyes to his, with frightened questions.

'She looks so pale.'

'She has lost a great deal of blood.' So had he with his shoulder, but he was a man, and he had lost blood before. Women in childbed were a different matter. His brother had lost two wives that way, but he had two sons. He looked down at the baby then, remembering his own when they were born, and the first time he had held them. It seemed so long ago now, his youngest was eighteen and was in the mountains with Chiang Kai-shek's army, but the feeling was still the same, the feeling of awe that such a thing could occur at all, a new life erupting out of an old one.

'Will she be all right?' Audrey's voice was soft as the candle sputtered and she let it go out. The light of the dawn was enough for them to watch her.

'I don't know.' And then he looked down at the baby. 'She must have milk if she cannot have her mother.' And when Shin Yu came to the door a little later, she asked her to have one of the children milk their cows, but General Chang thought that the goat's milk would be easier for her to take, so Audrey had them bring both and then she looked at him in dismay. They had no bottle with which to feed her. By a miracle they found a leather glove that one of the nuns had worn, and after Audrey made them boil it on the kitchen stove, they were able to pour the goat's milk into it and the baby suckled it happily and then went back to sleep. Ling Hwei had not woken up yet, and as Audrey watched her she knew that she would not survive the ordeal she had suffered with the birth of the baby. The general returned to the meat cellar for the day. It was too late for him to leave now, and only Shin Yu knew that he was there. When he came back after nightfall, Audrey was still at her post, feeding the baby every few hours and nursing Ling Hwei, who barely seemed to be breathing and hadn't regained consciousness since the birth of the baby. Chang held the infant that night, and nursed her with the glove as Audrey silently held Ling Hwei in her arms, and watched her until she uttered a soft sigh and died. Audrey held her there for long after that, thinking of what a sweet child she had been, and of the pain of the child who now had no mother. The thought of it hurt her to the core, as she thought of her own mother and the lonely existence for Ling Hwei's baby, growing up in the world with no one to love her, condemned by Japanese and Chinese alike, in a society where girls were sold for rice or beans or flour. The tears ran down Audrey's face, as she covered Ling Hwei, and clung to her tiny baby. Chang went downstairs and made tea for them and when the dawn came, she woke Shin Yu and told her. The girl cried, hid her eyes and clung to Audrey. Audrey felt her pain, remembering how Annabelle had been when their parents died. And General Chang watched them. He had been there for two nights now, and each time he planned to go, something had happened to detain him. He spoke to Audrey briefly before disappearing again for the day, and looked at her urgently this time.

'I must go at nightfall. My men will be impatient.' She had been leaving food for them in the shed near the church, but she had never seen them. He had been true to his word so far, and she no longer feared him. Not after what they had done together. There was a bond between them now, which neither would ever forget. And it created something special between them.

'Thank you for your help.' Her eyes looked deep into his, and expressed her gratitude and something more.

'What will you do with the child?' He looked at her strangely, curious about her now. She was an unusual woman in many ways, and he still did not understand how she had come there. She had come from so far away, and she was so serious about her responsibility to her charges. 'Will you keep her?'

It seemed a strange question and Audrey searched his eyes. 'I suppose she'll be one of the children here, in the orphanage. She's no different than they are.'

'And you? Are you not different now? Is she not a little bit yours after you saw her born?' He searched her eyes and slowly Audrey nodded. He was right. She had felt differently since the baby had been born, as though a part of her had been fulfilled. But she had been so upset about Ling Hwei that she hadn't rejoiced in the baby as she otherwise might have.

'Perhaps you will take her with you one day, and give her a better life.' He said it as though he hoped she would, as though the baby was something they had shared and he didn't want Audrey to leave her behind when she left China.

She sighed, knowing the impossibility of that. 'I would like to take them all home with me when I go. But I can't. When the nuns come, I must go.' Her eyes begged him to understand, yet she felt as though she were letting him and the children down.

'You will condemn her to a life of starvation and ignorance here, mademoiselle? She will be fortunate if you take her with you.' His eyes were so intense and she felt strangely drawn to him, as though he were someone she had known for a long, long time, as though he were part of a familiar world. Not a Mongol warlord. Or was this the only world familiar to her now, she wondered, as he looked at her with wise eyes. 'I was fortunate to have been sent to Grenoble.' He smiled sadly at her. 'I would like to see something like that happen to this baby.' He knew too well the life she would lead if Audrey didn't save her.

'And yet you came back?'

'It was my obligation. But this baby has no one here, and no one will want her if she is half Japanese.' He could see the difference in her even at birth. She did not look pure Chinese, as of course she wasn't. 'Perhaps one day they will kill her for that. Save her, mademoiselle. When you go, take her with you.' It irked her that he should press her. She didn't even want to think of that now. Ling Hwei had just died and she had all the others to think of, too, not just the baby.

'And the others?'

'You will leave them as you found them, but she was not here when you came. Perhaps she is yours now.' It was as though he were fighting for this small life, the life he hadn't even wanted to save at first, but now she was theirs. And as Audrey held her to her breast all that day, she kept remembering his words, and she found herself clinging to the tiny baby. They had to report Ling Hwei's death to the local officials, but she was afraid to with Chang and his men there. Instead she wrapped her in blankets, and put her in one of the sheds outside. She would report it the next day when they were gone. In the meantime, she had her hands full with Shin Yu's grief, and the other children to care for, and now the baby. It even distracted her from thoughts of General Chang all that day, which was just as well, because all her thoughts of him seemed to confuse her. That night, when the children were in bed, Chang came to her door and knocked softly. He reclaimed his pistol and his sword and looked at her for a long time. He had respect for this woman and wondered if they would meet again. She was more beautiful than the women he had met in Grenoble, and in those days, in his youth, he had pined for his own kind. But now she reminded him of a time long gone, and he reached out and touched her cheek with his hand, and she had never felt a more gentle touch or seen kinder eyes. She realised now at last that she had nothing to fear from him all along. She realised also how attracted to him she was, but they both knew that nothing would come of it.

'*Au revoir*, mademoiselle. Perhaps we shall meet again one day.' He would have liked nothing better, but he had another life to return to, a life where there was no place at all for her, and never would be.

'Where will you go now?' There was worry in her eyes, and concern, and admiration and affection.

'Back across the mountains to Baruun Urta. We will come back this way again sometime, but you will be gone by then, back to your country.' Their eyes met and held for a long time, and she had a longing for him that almost frightened her it was so strong, but she had never known anyone quite like him. Even the memory of Charles seemed dim at that very moment.

'Take care of your shoulder, General.' He smiled at her, and looked down at the baby in her arms. The little girl slept there, content and warm, like a little angel.

'Take care of our baby,' he whispered to her, and touched her face gently with his hand, caressing her with his eyes, and a moment later he was gone, and she heard only a faint crunching in the snow, and then nothing, as she lay in her bed, with the baby held to her bosom, keeping her warm in the freezing air, and remembering all that he had said to her . . . take care of our baby . . . our baby . . . and as she thought of it, she felt a love in her surge up inside as it never had before, a love for the sleeping child in her arms, and the memory of the Mongol general who had saved her. Audrey lay back against her pillows and slept . . . dreaming confused dreams of her grandfather, and the baby, and Charles . . . and the general.

18

Mai Li was two months old when the car that had once driven Audrey and Charles from the station drove up in front of the orphanage and two nuns stepped out, in heavy navy blue habits with warm black cloaks and starched white coifs. They had come not from France or Japan, or the other house in China, but from Belgium, and they had taken a long, long time coming. A cable had warned Audrey the month before that they were on their way, but God only knew when they would arrive, and they were amazed to find Audrey there and not their sisters as they got settled. It was odd explaining everything to them, and showing them around, and Audrey found that she felt possessive about each of the remaining sixteen children. They were 'her' children now, especially the younger ones who had come to depend on her so totally, and Shin Yu who looked up to her as she had Ling Hwei, and Mai Li who smiled now every time Audrey or someone spoke her name. She was a happy, gregarious little baby, and she was well fed and well loved by all of the others.

Audrey explained to the nuns how she had come to be there, and they were stunned by the decency that had led her to stay with the children. She explained only that she had been travelling with 'friends', and the friends had returned to England seven months before, while she had stayed. She was free to go now, but she found that it was too painful to tear herself away. She couldn't bear the thought of leaving them now, and Shin Yu had begun teaching her Chinese. Haltingly, she told her how sorry she was to be leaving, and the pretty young girl looked at her sadly. She had lost everyone she loved now, her parents, her brothers, her sister, and now Audrey, who had become something of a guardian angel.

'You will have Mai Li here with you, Shin Yu,' but Shin Yu quickly shook her head and there was an ugly look on her face. She was twelve years old now, and she had grown up a great deal in the months that Audrey had been there.

'Mai Li bad baby . . . *bad baby!*'

'How can you say that?' Audrey reverted to French, shocked at Shin Yu's reaction.

'She is not Chinese, and she is not God's baby. She is Japanese. That why Ling Hwei die, to punish her for Japanese baby.'

'Who told you that?' Audrey looked shocked at the interpretation, and there had been no one on hand to gossip with her. But Shin Yu pointed to her eyes now.

'I see. Mai Li not look Chinese. She Japanese. And I remember boy Ling Hwei like. . . .' She looked sorrowful as though she herself had been disgraced. 'Ling Hwei lie to me. That not God's baby.'

'All babies are God's babies. And your sister loved you very much, Shin Yu.' Shin Yu did not answer, and Audrey found herself thinking of what General Chang had said, that the child would be spurned because she was neither Japanese nor Chinese. It broke her heart to think of it now, that the baby she had come to love so much would never be accepted by her own people. It made Audrey more and more pensive as she packed her things and got ready to go.

And that afternoon, she went to the telegraph office to send two cables. The first was to Charles, because she wanted to tell him that she was free now, and would be returning to San Francisco shortly. She knew he would be relieved to hear it, and she didn't want him to have the agony of waiting for a letter, which could take weeks to reach him.

The message she sent him was simple and direct. NUNS FINALLY HERE. LEAVING HARBIN SHORTLY, RETURNING TO SAN FRANCISCO VIA YOKOHAMA. ALL WELL. I LOVE YOU ALWAYS. AUDREY. And to her grandfather much the same, assuring him that she would give him the exact date of her arrival when she knew it.

She was startled when, two days later, a boy arrived, running from the telegraph office with a cable for her clutched in his hand. She gave him a coin for bringing it to her, and he left with a delighted grin as, with trembling hands, she opened the fragile slip of paper they had sent her. She was terrified the news would be about her grandfather, and the possibility of having stayed too long in Harbin terrified her as she read the words. And then suddenly, her eyes filled with tears and she turned away as the nuns watched her, and then discreetly shooed the children away, and one of the sisters returned to speak to her gently.

'Is it very bad news, mademoiselle?'

Audrey shook her head and smiled through her tears. 'No . . . no . . . it is not that . . . I was afraid at first that it might be my grandfather, but it is not. It is something else entirely. I was just surprised,' she fought back fresh tears, 'and very touched.' The cable had been from Charles and she went to her room to read it alone again, and then she went for a long, long walk. She knew she would have to answer him soon, and a letter would not reach him quickly enough. He deserved an answer sooner than a letter would reach him. She had been completely taken aback by the message in his cable.

THANK GOD. WILL YOU COME HOME VIA LONDON? HAVE SERIOUS PROPOSAL TO DISCUSS WITH YOU. WILL YOU MARRY ME? I LOVE YOU. CHARLES. It said everything she wanted to hear, and yet she knew she couldn't do it. At least not yet. She had been reading between the lines in the letters her grandfather sent. His hand seemed to shake more each day, and he suddenly sounded very frail. He was clearly depressed and no longer believed she was coming home. She absolutely could not go home through London. But to say so in a telegram would be so blunt and unkind and so difficult to explain. If only he would let her go home as quickly as she could and then evaluate the situation there. She already knew that Annabelle was furious with her for not coming home before the birth of their little girl, named

Hannah, after their mother. But she had a husband and servants and even a mother-in-law to help her if need be, although Harcourt's mother really wasn't very helpful, and the children Audrey had stayed with had had no one at all. But Annabelle wasn't likely to understand that.

It wasn't Annabelle who concerned her anyway. It was her grandfather, and she tried to convey that to Charles in the agonising telegram she sent him the next morning.

DARLING, I WOULD LOVE TO COME HOME THROUGH LONDON, BUT I CANNOT, GRANDFATHER NEEDS ME AT ONCE. I MUST RETURN QUICKLY TO SAN FRANCISCO. CAN YOU FORGIVE ME? I WILL CALL YOU IMMEDIATELY FROM HOME TO DISCUSS YOUR PROPOSAL. IT SOUNDS WONDERFUL. CAN YOU COME TO SAN FRANCISCO TO SEE ME? WITH ALL MY HEART. AUDREY.

It seemed an inadequate answer and she feared that he would be hurt by her not coming home through London, but there was just no other way ... nor could she see an easy way to desert her grandfather in the near future to get married. Realistically, he would expect her to stay home, at least for a little while. And although she wanted nothing more than to be married to Charles, it was painful to have to make such agonising choices. And there were others which were almost as painful, or perhaps even more so.

General Chang's words kept echoing in her ears when they had spoken of the baby they had delivered together. ... 'Take her with you, mademoiselle.' But she didn't see how she could now. She had also thought of taking Shin Yu home with her, but when she had even mentioned it, Shin Yu had looked frightened. She didn't want to leave China. All she knew was Harbin and its surroundings. She wanted to be here with her own kind. She was even used to the orphanage now, as many of the children were. They didn't have a bad life there. All they did not have was a mother and a father. And Audrey had been wonderful to them in the long months she was there. The nuns assured her that her place in heaven was secure after what she had done for the children.

Audrey cabled to Shanghai for reservations at the Hotel Shanghai, and a cabin on the *President Coolidge* bound for Yokohama. There was no time to waste now, and two weeks after the Belgian nuns arrived, she had packed all her things, and had only one night left to spend with the children.

'We will pray for you, Mademoiselle Driscoll.' They had a festive dinner for her that night, and all the children sang songs. They were very fond of the younger of the two nuns, and not quite as sure of the other, who was inclined to be a bit more strict with them, and they adored Audrey whom they were all used to by now. It was going to be a tearful farewell at the station the next day, but they had all promised to come with her to see her off.

Before bed that night, Audrey warned the two nuns about General Chang, lest he return, that they need not fear him. And for the first time, she put little Mai Li's basket in a room with some of the other children. If she woke in the night, one of the two nuns would hear her and could feed her the goat's milk she so enjoyed. But it was time for Audrey to wean herself from her. She had to fight herself all night not to answer the anguished cries she heard, and she knew that the baby was crying for her. For two months she had held the child in her arms almost night and day, and Audrey was the only mother she knew, and now she was going to lose her. It tore at Audrey's heart as she lay awake all night, longing for the child with the silky black hair and huge black eyes in the delicate face that broke into huge toothless smiles each time she saw Audrey. It took every ounce of courage she had to tiptoe into the room the next day and look into her basket. And when she did, the baby was looking up at her, with wide questioning eyes, and Audrey could bear it no more. She took the baby out of the basket and held her tightly in her arms, crooning softly to her as tears poured down her cheeks. All she could think of was the sweet child who had given her life to give birth to this baby, and Audrey had never loved another human being as she loved this one. She was so distraught as she held the infant that she did not hear the sister sweep quietly into the room behind her. She watched Audrey cry for a little while and then came to put an arm around her.

'Take her with you, mademoiselle . . . take her . . . you cannot leave her.'

'I know.' They were anguished words as Audrey turned to face the older of the two nuns. Her eyes were damp as well and she looked gently at Audrey.

'You must not leave someone you love so much. And she will have no life here. She will be shunned by all in time. She is neither Japanese nor Chinese. But she is yours, she is yours in your heart and that is the only thing that matters.'

'And in San Francisco?' She asked herself more than the nun, but all she could hear now were the general's words, 'Take her when you go . . . take her when you go. . . .' 'What will they do to her there?'

'You will be there to protect her.'

And Grandfather? And Annabelle? . . . And Harcourt? . . . And Charles? Would he understand it? But all she could think of was this tiny baby she loved so much. They were right. She couldn't leave her. She couldn't. She looked at the nun as tears poured down her face now, clinging tightly to Mai Li. 'What will I do? How do I take her with me?'

The nun smiled through her own tears. She thought Audrey the most amazing woman she had ever met, and she was. 'We pack her clothes and her basket and you take her, with a supply of goat's milk and your love.'

'Don't I need papers for her? A passport?' She was leaving in two hours, and she had thought of none of this, and suddenly she wanted to take Shin Yu, too, and all of them, but she knew she couldn't. But Mai Li was different, Mai Li had been hers from the beginning, and if she left her here, no one would ever love her. The very thought tore at Audrey's heart as the nun watched her.

'We will give you a paper, certifying that she is an orphan, from this orphanage, and you present it to the officials in Shanghai when you leave. They will not stop you. They do not want her. And in your country, if she is in your protection, and you promise to adopt her, you can get her in. It will be easier going home as you are, rather than crossing so many borders going back the way you came.' It all seemed so simple, and suddenly Audrey's hands flew as she packed for the baby as well as herself.

In less than an hour they were all at the station, and there were no dry eyes. She had given the nuns an enormous draft on the American Bank in Harbin. She wanted the money used for the children, and she explained to Shin Yu that if she changed her mind and wanted to go with her, she would take her, too, or send for her anytime she wanted. But Shin Yu shook her head as she cried, and clung to the young nun's hand. She wanted to stay here and she refused to kiss Mai Li. All the other children kissed Audrey goodbye as she cried, and at last Shin Yu did too, and Audrey was still sobbing as the train pulled away and she clung to Mai Li in her arms.

She knew she would never return here again, or she was not likely to, and she was leaving them all behind . . . all the children she had loved and cared for, for eight months, the memory of Ling Hwei . . . and General Chang . . . she looked down at the sleeping babe as she thought of them all, and closed her eyes as she began her journey home at long last, with Mai Li secure in her arms as she thought of those she was leaving and those to whom she was returning, wondering how she would bridge the two worlds in one lifetime.

19

Audrey spent one night in Shanghai at the Hotel Shanghai before boarding the *President Coolidge* the next day. She had travelled from Harbin to Peking and from there she had taken one of the new sleeping cars direct to Shanghai. She did not want to waste time now. And once in Shanghai, all she could think of was Charles. She remembered the time they had spent there, and she kept thinking that she had had no answer to her cable telling him that she could not come through London. But she had other things to think of now. The nuns had been true to their word, and the paper they had given her in Harbin satisfied the local officials as to Mai Li's origins. They gave Audrey no problems at all about taking her out, nor did the Japanese. She was amazed at how easy it was, and she heaved a sigh of relief when she boarded the *President Coolidge*. It was almost June, and she had been gone almost exactly a year. She had cabled ahead what ship she would be arriving on, and she was going to try to call them from Honolulu when the ship docked there.

They docked at Kobe first, two days after leaving Shanghai, and from there they went on to Yokohama, and from there they sailed straight for Honolulu, and as Audrey settled down in her cabin with Mai Li, she felt as though she were almost home. She met very few people on the trip, and she kept to her cabin with the baby most of the time. She walked the decks to get some air, and chatted with a few people along the way, but she took her meals in her cabin so as not to leave Mai Li alone, and she didn't want any strangers babysitting for her. So it was a quiet trip for her, and she was lost in her own thoughts most of the time. She rejoiced in the ship's well-stocked library, and caught up on many of the books she'd missed in the last year, like *God's Little Acre* by Erskine Caldwell, *Lost Horizon* by James

Hilton, and *Tender Is the Night* by F. Scott Fitzgerald, and they arrived in Hawaii in just under twelve days. They stayed on board for the night there, and set sail again the next day, and it seemed like a mirage to her when the ship slipped into the San Francisco Bay six days later and moored at the Embarcadero. Her heart was pounding as she looked at the dock, wondering if anyone would be there. She had tried to call her grandfather from Honolulu but hadn't been able to get through so she sent a cable instead. And then suddenly tears leapt to her eyes as she saw him. The familiar figure with the silver-headed cane stood on the quay as they docked, alone, staring at the ship, and had she been closer she would have seen the tears rolling unchecked down his cheeks. But his eyes were dry when she met him.

She came slowly down the gangplank with trembling knees, clutching Mai Li close to her, as she always did, and the child looked like a tiny round bundle. One couldn't even see what she was, and Audrey stopped and looked at him, as the tears poured down her face. He looked frailer than he had a year before, but he was still distinguished and erect and the grandfather she had loved so dearly for a lifetime. She wanted to hurl herself around his neck, but she was afraid as she approached him. She knew how great his pain must have been to have her gone for so long, and she wondered if he would ever forgive her. And yet he had come to meet her, and he was standing there, which surely had to mean that he forgave her. She had come back to him after all, unlike her father. She had been acutely aware of that, and it was precisely because her father had not that she had. She felt she owed him that, and she wanted to make up to him for what he had lost, although it cost her something so dear to come home to him as she had. She could only begin to imagine what Charles had thought when he got her cable refusing to come to London. First, she had insisted on staying in Harbin, and then she had insisted on coming home to her grandfather without going through London. But as she stood looking at her grandfather from the bottom of the gangplank she knew she had done the right thing, and she walked slowly towards him, holding Mai Li gently against her chest, with her eyes locked in his as he scowled fiercely at her. He said not a word to her as she approached him, and they stood looking at each other for what seemed like a very long time, as her lip trembled and she put her arms around his neck, and then suddenly the floodgates opened wide, and she couldn't stop crying as he slowly put his arms around her, and his eyes were undeniably damp when she pulled away again.

He could barely speak as he looked down at her with the dignity she had remembered so well, as she thought of him on lonely nights in Harbin. 'I never thought I would see you again, Audrey.'

'I'm sorry it took so long, Grandfather.'

He nodded, pulling himself up to regain control, but she saw that he leaned heavily on his cane, and she watched his eyes travel to the bundle in her arms. It was Mai Li, still sound asleep as Audrey held her. 'What is *that*?' He frowned, and waved his cane in her direction.

Audrey smiled hesitantly at him and felt her heart pound as she turned so he could see the delicate little face leaning against her bosom, all but concealed by the silk bindings that held her strapped to Audrey. 'This is Mai Li, Grampa.' He almost reeled backwards at the words, and looked at Audrey in horror.

'You were right not to have come home.' He barely spoke above a whisper, and for an instant Audrey feared he would have a stroke right there at Embarcadero. 'You're a disgrace to your family! Muriel Browne was right . . . I didn't believe her when she told me . . . all that rubbish about murdered nuns and abandoned orphans!' She had never seen such fury as what she saw in his eyes and she was shaking her head, astonished at what she was hearing. It had never dawned on her that he might think Mai Li was hers. But she had caught the words *Muriel Browne*, and she wasn't pleased at that either.

'Just what exactly did Mrs Browne tell you?' There was fire kindling in her eyes now too.

'That you were travelling with a man.' He looked down at Audrey with open rage. 'I told her she was mistaken. You have no decency and no shame, Audrey, and to come with *that* . . . with that bastard . . .' He spluttered, unable to say the rest of the words, but she had never seen him taller. 'How dare you!'

'How dare I what? Love this child, Grampa? Is that a sin? No, she isn't mine. She is one of the orphans, and if I had left her in China, someone would probably have killed her, or let her die of disease or starve, or perhaps they'd have sold her as a concubine, if she lived that long. She's half Japanese and half Chinese, and I brought her home with me because I love her.' She was crying again, and she backed away from him in shock at what he had said to her.

'I didn't know . . . I thought . . .' Tears slowly welled up in his eyes too as he saw something in her face he had never seen there before, a blind love, a raging passion, a love for the child that reminded him of what he had felt for her when she had come from Hawaii to live with him. 'I . . .' He turned away from her slowly, feeling grief and relief well up in his soul. It was so good to see her again. He had thought she was lost to him forever, and now she had come home to him with this child, and he had thought . . . He turned to look at her again, and she stood so young and proud, holding the baby in her arms, and his heart went out to her as it always had. And he looked deep into her eyes. 'I'm glad you came home, Audrey.'

She smiled through her tears, and walked slowly towards him. 'So am I, Grampa . . . so am I. . . .' He put an arm around her shoulders and led her to his car. She got in first, holding Mai Li close to her and he got in behind her. He had brought the Rolls to the pier, and they let the chauffeur look for her bags. She had gone through Customs on the ship, and now it was up to him to get her things. There had been no problem with Immigration clearing Mai Li, and

Audrey sighed as she sat back against the luxurious leather seats and looked at her grandfather. It seemed a lifetime since the last time she had been here and saw him watching her now, almost as though he were afraid to believe she were sitting beside him.

'Is she all right?' He stared at the sleeping child, trying to get a glimpse of its face. And Audrey was touched by his concern.

'She's fine.' She smiled up at him and then leaned over to kiss his cheek, smelling the aftershave that always reminded her of him, as he felt the delicate silk of her skin next to his and almost closed his eyes with relief.

'What ever possessed you to bring home a baby?'

'Just what I said to you, Grampa. I couldn't leave her. They would have killed her in China.' The words shocked him into silence as the baby stirred and let out a little muffled sound, and Audrey turned her gently so he could see her. She had beautiful, delicate little features and he stared down at her in fascination, and then at his granddaughter.

'You're sure she's not yours, Audrey?' She had been gone long enough to have her, and Muriel Browne had said . . .

Audrey smiled. 'Positive. I wish she were.' He looked shocked and she laughed. 'Just to give Mrs Browne something to talk about.'

He didn't answer her at first, and then he sighed, glancing out the car window at the ship that had brought her home, and then back at her. 'For a time, I thought she was right. She said he was a well-known writer.' His eyes searched hers and something he saw there made him wonder.

'She was referring to a friend of my English friends, Charles Parker-Scott.' Her heart turned over as she said his name, and her grandfather watched her eyes, but she gave nothing away. Not yet anyway, and then she sighed and leaned back against the seat again as her grandfather glanced back at the baby.

'What did you say her name was?' He was fascinated by her, far more so than he was by Annabelle's baby, who was almost exactly the same age. But she looked just like Harcourt, and she was always crying.

Audrey smiled at him. 'Her name is Mai Li, Grampa.' It seemed so amazing to be sitting beside him again, and even more so, holding Ling Hwei's baby.

'Molly?' He scowled, looking at Audrey. 'Molly?'

'That'll do.' They exchanged a long look, and suddenly he reached out a hand and took Audrey's strong young hand in his own frail one. He was eighty-two years old now.

'Don't ever leave me again, Audrey.' He had wanted to say it with force, even with anger, but the words came out like a plea from the heart, as Audrey's eyes filled with tears and she kissed his cheek.

'I promise, Grampa . . . I promise. . . .' She had to force herself not to think of Charles as she said it.

20

'She did what?' In London, Lady Vi looked at James in shock. He had just told her something he knew he shouldn't, but he felt so badly for Charles that he had to share it with Violet.

'She turned him down. He sent her a cable asking her to marry him, and come home via London, and she wired back saying she couldn't.'

'Couldn't come back through London, or couldn't marry him?'

'Both I suppose. I didn't ask him that precisely. Besides, he was quite drunk when he told me, poor chap. He's in terrible shape. I think he was holding out the hope to himself that when the nuns came, she'd come back to him here. And that takes care of that, I'm afraid.'

'But she has that grandfather of hers, you know. Perhaps she had to go home and see him first. That could be.' Lady Vi had very sensibly hit the nail on the head, but James shook his head, having heard Charles's highly inebriated interpretation the night before. He had apparently been drunk for several weeks, according to mutual friends, and James had gone to his flat to see him, while Lady Vi dined alone with her mother.

'I don't think Charlie sees it that way. He sees it as a rebuff. In fact, I think he sees it as rather more than that. According to him, the romance is over.'

'Oh, my God.' Violet could easily imagine what that would do to Audrey. 'Is he going to America to see her?'

'I don't think so. In fact, I doubt it. He has that contract for the Indian book, and he ought to be leaving soon on that.'

'And I can just imagine who's going to be following him everywhere. . . .' She looked disapprovingly at James, and he shook a finger at her.

'Now, Vi, Charlotte may not be your sort, but she's a bright, interesting woman, and she may do Charles some good right now.' It was what Charlotte herself hoped, although Violet did not share that opinion.

Charlotte had finally taken the bull by the horns herself and gone around to Charlie's flat with boxes of breakfast pastry, a huge basket of fruit, and she had made him fresh orange juice and fried eggs and crumpets, with mugs of steaming black coffee, and she had let him pour his heart out to her. They were becoming friends over his books, and he thought of her almost as a man. She was intelligent, level-headed, an extraordinary businesswoman, and a very sensible person to talk to. And she was absolutely nothing like Audrey.

'Everything else comes first with her . . . came first. . . .' For the first time, he forced himself to speak of her in the past tense. He hadn't seen her in nine months and it was time to stop kidding himself that he would see her again. He wouldn't, unless he went to San Francisco, and he refused to do that. Besides, he didn't have time now, Charlotte and her father felt he should be out in India when he finalised the research for the book, in order to get the mood of the book right, and she thought he should leave at once. Besides, he had to get it finished before he went to Egypt in the autumn. Charlotte had a great many plans for him, and none of them included a trip to see Audrey.

'You'll feel better when you get away,' Charlotte said matter-of-factly as she poured him another mug of the steaming brew, and he looked at her gratefully. She was just what he needed just then, tender, loving care and a sharp mind. She was ready to organise everything for him, and she seemed to understand perfectly what a writer's needs were. She didn't expect him to do anything except write, and she was prepared to help him get the peace and quiet he needed to do it. She had even offered him her country house, if he needed some quiet time by himself, and she reminded him of it again now. 'You know, it might do you good, Charles. A change of scene, a breath of air . . .' She smiled at him, and he sighed and sat back in his chair.

'What did I ever do to deserve all this?' It was in such sharp contrast to what he viewed as Audrey's desertion.

'You're one of the most important writers we have, and it behoves us to take good care of you, doesn't it?' She even sent the Beardsley car around for him, to drive him down to the hunting box she had lent him. He had insisted that he could drive himself, but she thought he shouldn't worry about anything at all, and as he sat in the backseat of the Rolls pouring himself a drink, he had to admit that he enjoyed it. But as soon as he arrived, the memories of Audrey flooded his mind again, and he went for a long, lonely walk at sunset, wishing he hadn't come. All he could think of now were those last days in Harbin, wishing he had stayed, wishing that she was still with him.

He walked slowly back to the house after dark, sorry he hadn't driven himself down. Suddenly all he wanted to do was go home. He appreciated what Charlotte had done, but he didn't belong here. He wanted to go home to his own flat. It seemed stupid to sit there all alone for two days, supposedly relaxing. He thought about calling James and Vi and inviting them down to spend the day with him the following day, but as he opened the door, he saw a roaring fire in the fireplace that hadn't been there before, and he suddenly wondered who had built it. He strolled into the living room with a puzzled air, and jumped when he heard a voice directly behind him.

'Hello, Charles.' He turned to see Charlotte standing behind him in a slinky grey silk dress, holding out a glass of champagne to him. It was very much like something he had seen recently in a film, and he smiled as he walked towards her. She was a very attractive woman, and he suddenly saw her in a different light as she spoke to him in her husky voice.

'I didn't realise this was part of the arrangement, Charlotte.' He took the glass from her and stood very close to her, looking into her eyes. She was a blonde with big dark brown eyes. But they were the eyes of a very wily woman.

'Actually, it wasn't.' Her voice was silky, and he noticed that she had put a record on while he was out walking. 'I just thought I'd come down to see how you were doing.' They both knew that there was more to it than that, but suddenly he didn't mind. He had been so lonely for so long, and he was tired of aching over Audrey.

He sat down beside her on the couch, and halfway through the bottle of champagne, they moved into the large, comfortable bedroom. It was Charlotte who peeled away his clothes, who slid her hands expertly over his body, who used her lips in ways that drove him mad, and left little bites on the insides of his thighs, and when he plunged into her, it was Charlotte who screamed with delight, and then brought him towards her again, and again and again as the night wore on. She was relentless as she devoured his flesh, but in many ways, she was exactly what he needed. She wanted only one thing, and that was to please him, in every way she knew how. And she did. His body had never felt quite the same thrills, except . . . but he didn't allow himself to think of that any more. For him, it was over.

21

Audrey's reunion with Annabelle was not quite what she had expected. She knew that her sister was angry at her for not coming home, but she had not realised the extent of her fury. Things had changed in the past year. Much more than Audrey had expected. Harcourt's little affair in Palo Alto had been found out, as had his next two affairs with Annabelle's closest friends. And the warfare between them was open now. She had had an affair herself, she told Audrey casually as she sipped a drink in her grandfather's living room. Prohibition was over, and everyone was drinking much more openly now. Annabelle liked going to restaurants with her friends and ordering drinks and lunch, sometimes as many as four, and Audrey was shocked as she watched her. She wandered around like a nervous cat, holding her glass, and talking about the man she had slept with.

'What's happened to you, Annie? I haven't been gone that long. Are you that unhappy with Harcourt?' It was heartbreaking. Audrey had never cared for him herself, but he had been Annabelle's choice and they had two children after all. 'Do you think things will straighten out?'

Her younger sister shrugged a disinterested shoulder. 'Maybe.' She was wearing a fashionable suit, and Audrey noticed that her clothes were very expensive. One of her revenges against Harcourt was to spend as much of his money as she could, and she was doing a good job of it, from what Audrey could see at that moment.

'How's the baby?'

'She cries all the time.' Annabelle's eyes met Audrey's and there was something there that Audrey didn't like, but she couldn't put her finger on it yet. It was as though Annabelle had changed radically in the last year into a spoiled, nasty girl. All the sweetness of her youth seemed to have disappeared and Audrey was heartbroken to see it.

'I'm sorry I didn't come home in time to help you, Annie.' Her voice was gentle and she was sincere, but Annabelle didn't believe it.

'I'll bet you are.' She smiled nastily at her older sister. 'I hear you had a few good times yourself while you were over there.'

'What's that supposed to mean?' Audrey was still shocked at the hostility in her voice.

'Muriel Browne says you were shacking up with some guy in Shanghai.'

'How nice of her to say that.' Audrey began to look angry.

'Is it true?' Annabelle's eyes glittered meanly as she asked and Audrey shook her head. Not the way they described it anyway. She wasn't 'shacked up with some guy', she was with the man she loved.

'No, it's not.'

'You must have been doing something over there, and I don't buy that crap about the orphans.'

'Too bad, Annabelle, because that's just exactly what I was doing.'

'Is it?' Her eyes narrowed as she looked at her sister. 'I think maybe you didn't want to be bothered with your responsibilities here, so you dumped all of us. You probably hoped Grampa would drop dead and you could cash in when you came back. Rotten luck, he's still around, and so am I. And if you think I'm going to take care of him for you, you're crazy.' Audrey got to her feet, horrified at what she was hearing.

'What's wrong with you? What's happened in the last year? What happened to the Annabelle I knew?' She walked over to her and had to remind herself not to stare at her.

'I grew up.' Annabelle looked indifferently at the sister whom she felt had abandoned her. After giving her fourteen years of her life, Annie wanted more, and Audrey didn't have it to give her. It was time she stood on her own two feet, but Audrey was appalled at how she was doing it. She was turning into an expensive whore, a bad wife, a rotten mother, and an ingrate.

'I don't call that growing up. I call it disgusting. You'd better think twice about where you're going, Annabelle. You're about to destroy your marriage, and probably your children's lives at the same time.'

'What the hell do you know about that, Miss Eternal Virgin.' Audrey wanted to put her hands around her neck and throttle her, but Annabelle was saved by the fact that their grandfather walked in, and Audrey restrained herself. He sensed that there was something heavy in the air, and in order to lighten it, he asked Annabelle if she had seen Molly. 'Who's that?' She looked at Audrey in confusion, and Audrey looked at her with fury barely concealed in her eyes as she stood up.

'My daughter.'

'What?' It was a shriek you could have heard through the whole house and their grandfather barely concealed a smile.

'I wouldn't exactly say that, Audrey.'

'She is indeed.' There was something intransigent in her voice and face as she looked at him and then her sister.

'Where is she?' Annabelle couldn't believe her ears, and she flew upstairs to Audrey's room to find the tiny almond-eyed bundle asleep in the basket Audrey had set up beside her bed. Annabelle was back downstairs again in a moment. 'Well, I'll be damned. Muriel Browne was right, then ... and what's more he was a Chink!' Annabelle seemed to gloat over her sister, as Audrey looked at her with empty eyes.

'Muriel Browne was not right, Annabelle. Mai Li was one of the orphans I took care of.'

'I'll bet.' She laughed meanly at what she thought was her sister's disgrace, and Audrey watched her as she straightened her hat in the mirror.

'Why do you suddenly hate me so much, Annabelle?

What have I done to you?' There was pain in her voice as she asked her, and her younger sister pivoted slowly on one heel as she turned to look at Audrey.

'You deserted me, that's what you did. You dumped everything on me, the house, the kids, the servants, you ruined our holiday, my life . . . hell, you even ruined my marriage. . . .' And it was obvious that Annabelle believed that.

'And how did I do that?'

'You dumped everything on me, and then you left, bang, for a whole year. You didn't give a damn that I was pregnant, that I needed you, that. . . .' She shrugged. 'What difference does it make?'

'It makes a big difference to me, Annie.' Audrey spoke sadly as their grandfather watched them. 'When I left here, I had a sister. Now I don't, from what I can see. I thought we were friends, enough so that you would understand that I needed to get away. Those aren't my responsibilities you're talking about. They're yours.' But she didn't see it that way.

'They didn't used to be.'

'That's the whole point. It was time you learned to take care of your own life . . . Harcourt wants you to. . . .'

'To hell with Harcourt.' She tossed off her drink and walked to the door, with a glance over her shoulder at Audrey. 'Come to think of it, to hell with you, too. You didn't give a damn about me while you stayed away, and now I don't give a damn about you.' And as the door slammed behind her, Audrey wondered if she ever had. She walked slowly back upstairs, as her grandfather watched her.

22

In the first days back, there were moments when Audrey felt like a total stranger. Two of the maids she had hired for her grandfather before she had left had quit while she was gone, and his ancient butler had finally retired. But it was not so much the changes in the household that shocked her, but the changes in the world. She felt as though she had been on another planet for the past year, and now everything was moving much too quickly. Nothing but the sketchiest reports of world events had reached her in Harbin, and none of it told her anything of what was happening in America.

The economy had finally improved, and San Francisco appeared to be in grand spirits when she returned. Her grandfather still complained about Roosevelt, of course, and he thought his 'fireside chats' absurd, but when she insisted that the country was healthier, he only growled and told her to 'wait!' It was obvious to him that FDR was going to cause trouble, albeit of an unspecified nature.

Only days after her return, there were reports of a Nazi Blood Purge in Germany, which exterminated all of those allegedly guilty of plotting against Hitler. There were nearly a hundred of them, and the world was shocked at their summary disposal. On July sixteenth a general strike was called in the States, which began in sympathy with the international longshoremen. Nine days later Austrian Chancellor Dollfuss was killed, and Berlin denied any involvement. On August second, Germany's President Hindenburg died, and in a little over two weeks Adolf Hitler was voted into the presidency, although he retained his previous title as *Der Führer*. Air France had been formed, and in the States, both American and Continental had appeared. Several new trains had sprung into being, though none of them as elegant as the Orient Express. And all in all, Audrey's head swam just trying to keep up with it all, and catch up on what she had missed during her lengthy absence.

But more than anything, she herself seemed to have changed. She felt less involved in life here, and San Francisco suddenly seemed terribly insular and provincial. People gossiped all the time about each other's wardrobes and husbands and dinner parties, and somehow Audrey couldn't seem to get involved in it any more. She couldn't even make the pretence. All she could think about was Charles, but he had steadfastly not answered her last two letters.

And whereas before she had gone through the motions and made the social rounds from time to time, now all she wanted to do was keep to herself and stay home with her grandfather and the baby. He noticed it too. At first he just thought she was tired from the trip, but he began to watch her more closely as July drew to a close. She'd been home for more than a month by then, and had looked up none of her old friends. He wondered if she had fallen in love with someone during her trip, and he prayed that it was not some Oriental. He still worried at times about the baby, but she did not appear to be Eurasian, she had marked Oriental features, and he had to admit that she was awfully appealing. She was a happy, smiling, little thing and Audrey never let her out of her sight, and he persisted in calling her Molly.

It amazed her to realise how many people suspected the child was hers – not that she cared. The people with small minds thought she had stayed away to give birth to an illegitimate Chinese child. It amazed her to think they would even think of that. She hadn't even considered it before she came home with her.

Annabelle did not come to the house again while Audrey was there, although she read in the papers that she had gone to Carmel with friends. And their grandfather didn't question either of them, although he knew of the rift that had come between them. Audrey never complained, and she was too busy moving everyone to the lake for him. He only wanted to spend a few weeks there this year. He was more easily tired now, and he was afraid that he wouldn't feel as well in the altitude. He was eighty-two years old now, and he had slowed down a great deal in the past year, although his opinions were just as strong. And when they got in their first violent argument over Earl Grey tea one morning at the breakfast table, Audrey sat back in her chair and laughed, and she looked happier than she had in weeks.

'It's just like old times, isn't it, Grampa?' She remembered their battles about Roosevelt just before she left and she looked benevolently at him as he concealed a smile from her.

'You're no smarter than you were a year ago. But then, running around the world like a fool never did anything for Roland either. At least he was smart enough not to come home with any foreign brats.' But there was no meanness as he spoke, and Audrey didn't bridle as she might have a few weeks before. She had watched him play with the baby when he thought no one was around, and he delighted in her little cooing sounds, and insisted that she had already said his name. 'She said, Gramp, Audrey! I know she did . . . bright little thing . . .' He thought Audrey had taken on a tremendous burden in bringing her home though, and when she tried to describe the fate she would have had to leave her to, he felt sorry for them both. Audrey for what she had taken on, and the child who would never be accepted in the States, or so he thought.

'She'll grow up as my own, Grampa.' But that was just what he feared.

He shook his head slowly, as they talked about it one night, up at the lake. 'It doesn't work like that. And even if it does, no man will marry you now. They'll all suspect she's yours.'

'Would that make me so terrible if she were?' She sounded tired now. One had to fight so many things here, prejudice and selfishness, and what everyone said all over town. In China it was so much simpler worrying about bandits and floods and running out of food or clean water. Life seemed so much more complicated here. But she had already begun to forget the difficulties of her life in Harbin, the terrors, and the agony of helplessness and loss when Shih Hwa and the others died . . . her sorrow over Ling Hwei . . . all she remembered now were the little faces she had loved so much . . . the little ones . . . and Shin Yu. She wondered so often how they were. She had sent another draft to the American Bank in Harbin as soon as she arrived, to provide for anything they might need, but it seemed so little to do for them. 'How can people begrudge Mai Li a decent life here, Grampa?'

'Because she's different from them, Audrey.' He spoke quietly now. 'That frightens some people a great deal. Not everyone has the open mind you do.'

'I'll be there to protect her, Grampa.' Just as she had been there for Annabelle, for as long as she could. And he patted her hand.

'I know you will, child. Just as you are for me, and Annie, and everyone. You're too good to all of us.' It was the first time he had ever said that to her and she was touched by it. 'Your heart is too big. You ought to start thinking of yourself now, Audrey.'

She laughed softly in the clear mountain air, as they sat on the porch in rocking chairs looking up at the stars. 'Don't tell me you're worrying about my being an old maid too.'

He smiled. It wouldn't do any good if he were. He knew her too well, and she would do exactly what she wanted with her life, particularly once he was gone. And there weren't many men who would have been big enough for her, big enough in mind and in heart and in spirit. He glanced over at her as they sat and rocked, and he saw the beauty that had sharpened in the last year. She was more than just beautiful now, there was something about her that glowed from within. She was striking and suddenly very, very lovely.

'You're a handsome girl, Audrey. You should find the right man one day.'

She almost told him then about Charles, but she didn't want to worry him. He was getting so old and frail after all. She didn't want him to think he prevented her from marrying. She owed him that much.

'Shall we go in, Grampa?'

'I suppose so, my dear.' He looked at her tenderly, knowing full well how good she was to him.

Tahoe was the same as it had been every year she'd gone there with him. The Dollars entertained as they always did. The Drums were there, and the Allens. But Audrey seldom went out, and she never saw them. She stayed home with her grandfather, and Mai Li, who was becoming 'Molly' to everyone now, even to her. The baby was six months old and laughing and smiling most of the time. And she began crawling the day they went home. It was the same day the *SS Morro Castle* caught fire off New Jersey and went aground. It was a terrible tragedy and hundreds of lives were lost. Audrey listened to reports of it on the radio, and the newspaper photographs of the disaster were grim. But the nation was even more upset less than two weeks later when Bruno Richard Hauptmann was caught, for possession of the ransom money paid in the Lindbergh kidnapping two years before. The Lindbergh child had been killed, of course, and the drama had caused untold grief, and there was no way of knowing whether Hauptmann was truly guilty or not, but the authorities seemed to think he was. Audrey and her grandfather discussed it at great length, and she was playing with Mai Li, and thinking about it later in the afternoon when the butler came to tell her that there was a telephone call for her. He did not know who the gentleman was, he informed her with a disapproving air, and she followed him to the phone after entrusting Mai Li to one of the maids.

'Hello?' She was still thinking of the Lindbergh affair when she answered the phone with a puzzled frown. 'Who is this?'

There was a brief pause. And then her heart stopped when he spoke. It was Charlie.

23

'Audrey?' Her heart pounded in her ears at the sound of his voice, and her mouth was so dry she could barely speak.

'Yes.' He sounded so close. 'Where are you?' There was no need to ask who it was. She would have known his voice anywhere. She heard it every night in her dreams, and she heard it now, barely louder than her thumping heart as she listened.

'I'm in California. Los Angeles actually.' He sounded more British than he had before, and the memories of him washed over her in waves. 'How long have you been back?' He hadn't corresponded with her since receiving her second cable from Harbin. There had been nothing left to say, as far as he was concerned, after she refused his proposal of marriage. And he had debated lengthily about calling her now. It had taken him two days to make the decision. Two agonising days, trying to force himself not to call her. But eventually he couldn't stand it. He had rushed back to his room, picked up the phone and asked the operator for her number as he held the phone with trembling hands, and now there she was, her voice just as he remembered.

'I came back in June.'

'Your grandfather's well?'

'More or less. He's got very frail in the past year.' She sighed and then added, 'He was happy to have me back.' For a moment, Charlie only nodded . . . he was thinking of all the conversations they had had about her grandfather and her sister and her duties in San Francisco.

'And your sister?'

Audrey sighed again. 'She hasn't got any easier. Actually . . .' She tried to find the right words, 'she's changed . . . I don't think her life is going very well.' It didn't surprise him. She had always sounded like a spoiled brat, and maybe now, with a little distance, Audrey saw it more clearly. 'What about you? How long are you here for?'

'Just a few days. I flew to New York, and then out here. They're talking about doing a film of one of my books. It's very flattering actually.'

She smiled, her eyes closed, imagining the handsome well-chiselled face before her. 'Are you in it, Charlie?'

He laughed at the thought. 'God, no. What a thought.'

'You'd be wonderful.' Her voice was so gentle and so silky that it made his heart ache. He wanted desperately to see her.

'And you? What are you doing with your life now?' It seemed strange to be catching up like this. Once upon a time, not so long ago, they had been closer to each other than to any other human beings on earth. But now, it had been eleven months since he'd seen her.

'I'm doing what I've always done. Taking care of Grandfather and . . .' She had been about to say Mai Li, and then realised that he didn't know about her, and it seemed difficult to explain over the phone. Something stopped her from telling him.

'And your sister?'

'More or less.' It was just too difficult to explain and there was a sudden silence as he debated whether or not to ask her then decided to throw caution to the winds. He had come this far, he might as well. . . .

'Audrey? . . .'

'Yes?' She waited.

'Do you want me to come up?'

She felt as though someone were squeezing her heart as she nodded. She didn't have the strength to say no. She wanted to see him, even if it was only for a moment, no matter how hopeless it was, or how bogged down she was in San Francisco. 'Yes . . . I do . . . more than anything.' She wasn't afraid to let him see how much she still loved him. 'Can you do that?'

'I think so. I finish my business here tomorrow. I could fly up tomorrow night. Are you free then?'

She laughed at the question. She was free for the rest of her life, especially for Charlie.

'I think I can arrange it.' She sounded as she always had, the little edge of humour blended with the sexiness of her voice. She didn't have the raw sensuality of someone like Charlotte, but they were two very different women. Charlotte was someone to play with, to talk to, to work with . . . but Audrey . . . Audrey was a piece of his soul, a part of his flesh, the most important part of his being. 'Can I pick you up at the airport?'

'Do you want to?'

'I'd love it.'

'I'll let you know what time I'm arriving.'

'I'll be there . . . and Charlie?'

'Yes?'

'Thank you.'

His heart went out to her, and he hung up feeling like a schoolboy again, desperately glad that he had called her. The next day dragged by interminably for both of them. She went downtown with her grandfather and took Mai Li to the doctor for a vaccination. She thought about going to the hairdresser before picking him up, but that seemed too much like something her sister would have done, and she would have met him feeling like a stranger. Instead, she wore a new grey wool dress, her pearls, and wore her copper hair waving to her shoulders as he liked it best. She carried a fox jacket over her arm as she parked her car and walked into the airport. Unconsciously she felt his gold signet ring, still on her finger. Even her grandfather had noticed it, but he had never asked her where it came from. She had ten minutes before his flight arrived, and all she could do was pace up and down, thinking of the last time she had seen him. She remembered his face as the train pulled away in Harbin, the tears on his cheeks, the look in his eyes . . . and then suddenly they announced his flight, and Audrey felt an electric current shoot through her.

She stood, watching people emerge, having walked from

the plane to the gate, and she almost held her breath as a handful of men brushed past her . . . and then suddenly there he was, the jet-black hair and deep-set eyes . . . the mouth that had kissed her so often and in such tender places. She stood breathlessly watching him, and then before she knew what he had done, he had taken her in his arms and kissed her. He held her as tightly as he had a year before, and they stood for a long, long time, unable to speak, and remembering what they had shared in another lifetime.

'Hello.' He looked down at her finally with a small boyish grin as people eddied around them, and she laughed at the look in his eyes.

'Hello, Charlie. Welcome back. . . .' But to what? To her life? And how long would he stay? A day? Two? Three? She knew almost as soon as they met that in a moment they would be parting again and it made everything bittersweet as he watched her and followed her to her car parked outside. He was carrying only a raincoat, a small overnight bag, and his briefcase. 'How's the film?'

'I'm not sure. We signed a contract, but those people are so crazy, I have trouble believing they mean business.' She smiled at the thought. It was nice to know that he was so successful. It was a side of him that she admired, although there were other things about him she loved even more. 'Are you excited?' She unlocked her car, and slid behind the wheel, unlocking his door for him, as he piled his things in the back seat and climbed in beside her.

'Yes, I am.' But he was far more excited to see her. He had even privately accused himself of agreeing to the film deal just so he could come to California, not that he would ever have admitted that to Charlotte. She seemed able to tolerate any of his foibles, except hearing him talk about Audrey. She never failed to remind him that Audrey hadn't come to him when he asked her. In her eyes, it was an unpardonable sin. He found himself thinking again now how different they were as Audrey backed the car out of its parking space and drove towards the city. She saw him watching her when she glanced at him and they fell silent as she drove.

'I'm not sure what to say, Charlie.'

'About what?' But he knew. She had always been very direct with him and he sensed that she was going to be again now.

'About what happened . . . the telegrams. . . .'

'What is there to say? Your answer was pretty clear.'

'But were my reasons?' She had always felt that he didn't understand, and in some ways he didn't. 'Do you know that I would have given my right arm and my heart to drop everything and marry you last year? But I couldn't just run off to London and leave Grandfather again. I'd been gone for a year . . . and he's so old, Charlie, and so frail. . . .'

'I don't understand the sacrifices you make.' He glanced out the window, remembering again the pain of her refusal. 'That was the second time you'd turned me down.'

But she disagreed. 'The first time was never a serious proposal. You were just desperate to get me out of Harbin, and you'd even have married me to accomplish that.' She smiled at him and he didn't deny it. She knew him very well. Better even than Charlotte. She knew a different side of him than Charlotte did, a gentler side than Charlotte knew in him. He liked the way Audrey made him feel, the gentleness in her soul, the integrity, the goodness. And suddenly he turned to her with a smile.

'You know you are the most stubborn woman I have ever met, Audrey Driscoll.'

She grinned broadly and glanced at him before turning her eyes back to the road. 'Is that a compliment or a statement?' He laughed and shook his head.

'Neither. It's an accusation.' And then suddenly he laughed again. 'You're a bitch, damn you . . . a bitch!' He grabbed a handful of her hair and pulled her head backward just enough to catch her attention as he kissed her on the neck. 'Do you know I was drunk for a month after that damn telegram of yours. A month!' And he did not tell her that Charlotte had come to his rescue, or in what way. She had nothing to do with what he felt for Audrey.

Her face grew serious as he let her mane go, and they approached the city. 'It wasn't easy for me, Charlie. It was the hardest thing I ever did . . . that and staying behind in Harbin.'

'That wasn't so hard. You were so vehement about what you believed you had to do, I didn't think you ever had any regrets.'

'Are you serious? After eight months there, you don't think I had regrets? You're crazy. But I thought I did the right thing. I paid a hell of a price though, didn't I?' She looked directly into his eyes as they stopped at a red light. And she had got an enormous reward too . . . Mai Li . . . she looked at Charlie pensively. 'Where are you staying, by the way?'

'The studio made a reservation for me at the Saint Francis. Is it all right?'

'Excellent.' And immediately, in unison, they both thought of the Gritti and the Pera Palas, but neither of them said a word. Instead, he looked at her thoughtfully.

'Will you have dinner with me tonight, Aud?'

She nodded. It was odd making dates with him, after all those months of travelling together. It had been so much like being married, and now they had made a step back to the days at Antibes when they first met and neither of them quite knew what the other was thinking. Although he had noticed his ring still on her finger.

'Will you come and meet my grandfather first?'

'I'd like that.' He said it slowly. He wanted to meet the man to whom he had lost her. And when she left him at his hotel, he kissed her gently on the lips and her heart soared in spite of all the sensible things she said to herself on the way home. She didn't want to let herself fall in love with him all over again . . . he was only there for a few days . . . there was no point . . . but there was no stemming the tides of what she felt, and had felt since the first day she'd met him.

Her grandfather saw her coming in, and looked up from the evening newspaper he was reading with a frown. 'Where were you, Audrey?'

For a moment, she didn't know what to say, and then decided to tell him the truth, or some of it at least. 'I went to pick up a friend at the airport.'

'Oh?' The scowl deepened.

'Someone I met in Europe. He's just here for a day or two.'

'He? . . . do I know him?'

'No,' she smiled. 'But you will shortly. He'll be here in an hour for a drink. He said he'd like to meet you.'

'Obviously a young fool.' He pretended to be annoyed and she refused to be fooled. She knew he liked meeting her friends from time to time, and he often chided her for not going out more, but there was no one she was interested in. No one even began to compare to Charles. The men she knew paled in comparison. And now he was here . . . she glanced at her watch, and decided to run upstairs and see Mai Li before changing for dinner.

As though he read her thoughts, her grandfather spoke to her through his newspaper. 'She got a new tooth today.'

'The baby?'

'No, the upstairs maid.'

Audrey laughed. 'For six months, she really has quite a few.'

'She's very advanced. Mrs Williams,' (their housekeeper) 'told me so. She says her grandson has no teeth or hair, and he's almost a year old. You watch her, she'll walk before her first birthday.' It touched her to see how proud he was of the baby she had adopted. He was much more interested in her than in Annabelle's brood, and he didn't even seem to mind the fact that she was Chinese any more. He went for strolls with Audrey from time to time, and helped her push the pram.

'I'll be down in a little while, Grampa.'

And when she came down again, she was wearing a

cocktail dress she had bought at Ransohoff's and never worn. It was a slinky black silk with broad shoulders and a diamond-shaped cutout in the back. It was beautifully cut and it suited her to perfection. Her grandfather noticed how well the dress looked and how carefully her hair was done and he correctly surmised that their guest was someone important . . . to Audrey.

'Who did you say he was?' he asked her just before the bell rang.

'Charles Parker-Scott. He's a writer.'

'Haven't I heard that name before?' He scowled pensively just as the doorbell rang and Audrey walked into the hall just as the butler opened the door, and Charles stepped in. Their eyes met at once and it was obvious that he was struck by how lovely she looked. It reminded him of a thousand other moments they had shared, but he wasn't quite sure she had ever looked quite as beautiful as she did that evening.

'Hello, Audrey.' He felt like a very young boy as she smiled, kissed him on the cheek, and ushered him into the living room to meet her grandfather.

'Charles Parker-Scott, my grandfather, Edward Driscoll.' The two men shook hands and sized each other up. Both were favourably impressed, although each had hoped not to be. Especially Charles, who had wanted to form an instant dislike for the man who had kept her from running off to London.

'Good evening, sir. How do you do?'

'Very well. Why do I know your name?' He wondered if Audrey had mentioned him before or the man was well known. He couldn't remember. And actually it was a case of both, but Charles was far too modest to say so.

'Charles is an author, Grampa. He writes wonderful travel books.'

The old man frowned and then nodded slowly. It rang another bell too, but he couldn't remember what, and Audrey was relieved that he couldn't. She was sure that

Muriel Browne had mentioned his name after they had met in Shanghai, and she didn't want to remind her grandfather of that now, or he might well figure out just how important Charles was. Her grandfather was no fool, and she knew he suspected that she had been involved with a man during her time abroad, although he no longer asked her.

'In fact, he just sold one of them as a film and that's why he's in California.' The butler brought them all drinks and Charles chatted easily with the elderly gentleman, watching the sharp eyes and elegant hands that fluttered a little as he held his drink, but as he stood up to show Charles his library, he didn't look nearly as frail as Audrey claimed, and he wondered suddenly if she used him as an excuse. Perhaps she simply didn't want to get married. But he knew her better than that. And he followed Mr Driscoll to the shelves of his old books and first editions and beautiful leatherbound volumes that he had collected over a lifetime. He was enormously impressed with the quality of the collection. The whole house was lovely, in fact, and filled with beautiful antiques and treasures, many of them collected by Audrey's father on his travels, and others gathered here and there by her grandfather and his wife, or their parents before them. He had actually never suspected that she came from a home quite as fine as this, she was so quiet and well-bred and unassuming.

'You have a beautiful collection, sir.' They sat down again and Charles smiled. He liked the old man, in spite of himself, and Mr Driscoll smiled. He was sorry Audrey didn't have more men come to visit. It was nice seeing a young man from time to time, it reminded him of Roland in his youth . . . so long ago . . . in fact, he decided, as he looked at Charles, this young man was astonishingly like him, and he said so.

'You know, you're very like my son. Has Audrey told you that?'

'Not really . . . except that we both love to travel.'

'Damn fool . . .' Edward Driscoll's brow clouded and

Charles feared that he had said something too painful, and then the old man looked up and glanced at Audrey with relief. 'At least she came to her senses. Did you know she actually went to China?' Charles repressed a smile and nodded solemnly at the tale. 'Spent close to a year in Manchuria in a place called Harbin . . . and even came back with a baby.' And with that, Audrey thought Charles was going to fall out of his chair. He grew so pale that Audrey wanted desperately to explain, but her grandfather didn't let her. 'Cute little thing. We call her Molly.'

'I see.' Even Charles's lips had gone white, and Audrey wanted to reach out a hand and touch him, but all she could do was attempt to explain, as though very little hinged upon her explanation.

'She was one of the orphans where I was . . . or actually one of the children . . . an older one . . . gave birth to her . . . but she died in childbirth. . . .'

'Audrey!' Her grandfather was shocked. 'You needn't bore your guest with the details.'

And then, for lack of something better to say, she glanced at Charlie desperately. 'Would you like to see her?' She could see that he was about to decline, but her eyes begged him not to and he stood up awkwardly.

'All right.' He followed her silently to the staircase, and walked upstairs, and it was only after reaching the second floor that he spoke in a whisper to Audrey. 'So that was it . . . why the hell didn't you tell me instead of letting me make a fool of myself. What is she? Half Chinese?'

'Yes.'

'He's right,' he spoke to her through clenched teeth and grabbed her arm as they reached her bedroom door, 'you are a damn fool. How could you do a thing like that? Why didn't you get rid of her before you came home?'

Her eyes filled with tears. She knew what he thought, and she didn't want to have to defend herself to him. 'What would you suggest? That I kill her? I brought her home because I love her, and I'm not the damn fool . . . you are.'

She strode across the room, and picked the baby up, as the young maid who helped her with Mai Li discreetly left the room. Audrey held the baby in her arms, and was instantly met with a broad smile and a gurgle. She had a beautiful little Oriental face, and it was difficult to say if she was Chinese or Japanese, or simply very, very pretty. But Charles looked puzzled as he looked at Audrey's face and then the baby's.

'She's not ...' He felt suddenly very foolish, and very ashamed of the assumption he had made ... but it would have made it easier to swallow her refusal to come to London. He wanted to believe anything, except that she had given him up for duty. 'Audrey ... I'm sorry ... she isn't your baby, is she? I mean, not the way I thought. ...'

Audrey sadly shook her head, still wishing, as she often did, that she was. 'She was Ling Hwei's, and she died giving birth to her before I left. The father was Japanese ... a soldier ... and I just couldn't leave her there. You know what would have happened.'

He nodded. Only too well. 'I understand now. Why didn't you tell me?'

'I would have, but after the telegram, you never answered my letter, and I didn't know how you'd take it.'

He smiled at the obviously happy child, nestled in Audrey's arms.

'She's so sweet. How old is she?'

'Six months. Grampa calls her Molly.' They both smiled. This was like a gift to remind them of the time they had shared in China. He was gently rubbing her fat little cheek with his finger and she was trying to work it into her mouth to rub it on her new teeth as he laughed and tickled her and she giggled. 'Would you like to hold her?' He looked hesitant at first, but she handed the baby to him, and Molly squealed with delight, and then cooed as he held her silky little cheek close to his own, and then gently kissed her. She smelled of soap and baby powder and everything about her looked clean and pretty and loved, and he now understood what Audrey had been doing since her return. As he looked around the nursery, he saw dozens of photographs she had obviously taken of her with the Leica. 'Isn't she wonderful, Charlie?' They were suddenly friends again, as he laid the baby down on the bed, and they sat there together, watching the baby rolling around, and grabbing her toes with happy gurgling. They both laughed and looked at each other with the same tenderness they had once shared, and Audrey dared to tell him what she still felt, now more than ever. 'I still wish she were yours, Charlie.'

'So do I.' His eyes met hers, and he loved her just as much as he had before, perhaps more, and seeing her with the baby did something to him. He ached for her even more, and they had to tear themselves away to join her grandfather again. They gave him a full report on Molly's antics and everything she'd been doing, and he grinned delightedly and bragged of her accomplishments to Charlie. One would have suspected that he had been shocked when she first arrived. To listen to him, one would have thought that the baby was the prize of his own bloodline.

'She's the best little girl in the world.' And then he smiled at Audrey. 'This one wasn't bad either, but it's been a while. . . .' He gazed fondly at her, and eventually they stood up, and Charles told him how happy he had been to meet him. They had dinner reservations at the Blue Fox, but neither of them seemed interested in where they ate. Suddenly, she was filling him in on everything, all her last moments in Harbin, Molly's birth, even the appearance of the Mongolian general.

'Good God, you could have been raped.' Or murdered. But he didn't say it.

'Looking back at those eight months, I suppose I could have been a lot of things . . . but I don't know, Charlie . . . it seemed the right thing to do at the time. And I got Molly out of it.' He smiled. It had touched him to see her with a child, and it made him hungry for all he had once dreamed of with her.

'And now, Aud? What are you going to do with the rest of your life?'

'I don't know. Stay here. As long as Grampa is alive anyway.'

'He's a wonderful man.' He said it almost sorrowfully and she smiled.

'I know . . . that's why I came home to him. I owe him everything.'

'Even your future, Audrey? Somehow that doesn't seem right.'

'My present in any case.'

'And Annabelle? What does she feel she owes him?'

'She doesn't think that way, I'm afraid.'

Charlie smiled ruefully at her. 'My luck I'd fall in love with the dutiful one.' And then, over dessert, he took his courage in both hands. 'Can I tear you away for a while, Aud?'

'Like how long? A weekend in Carmel, or a year in the Far East?' They both smiled. It was quite a contrast between the two. She would have preferred to go to the ends of the earth with him, but it was impossible. She couldn't leave for more than a few days.

'I've just come back from India, doing research for the next book.'

'It sounds interesting.' But she knew there was more to it than that.

'. . . and I'm going to Egypt next.' He paused, and reached for her hand. 'Will you come with me?' Her heart stopped just listening to him. She wanted to do that more than anything. She would have gone anywhere with him. But Egypt would have been fabulous.

'When do you go?'

'By the end of the year, or perhaps in the spring. Does it make any difference when I go?'

She sighed. 'Probably not. I can't imagine Grandfather sitting still for another trip, especially after what happened last time, with my extending it by eight months in Harbin.'

He was suddenly annoyed at her again for doing that, if it meant she couldn't go away with him. 'I don't know, Charles . . . I just don't see how I can . . . and I have Molly to think of now.'

'Bring her along.' He sounded as though he meant it, and Audrey smiled and kissed his cheek.

'I will always love you, Charles. Do you know that?'

'It's difficult to believe sometimes.' He sat back in his chair and looked at her. 'And I don't want you to give me an answer tonight. Just think about it . . . think about Egypt in the spring. Can you think of anything more romantic than that?' She shook her head and smiled.

'You don't have to sell it to me, Charles. That has nothing to do with it. I would be happy in a cow pasture in Oklahoma with you.'

'Now there's a thought.' He laughed, and their mood lightened suddenly, and he suggested that they go dancing in his hotel. The moment their bodies met, she felt all the same magic happening again. Their lips met, and their bodies touched, and she wanted him just as she had for the past year. It was more than she could bear just being this close to him again, and when he looked down at her she smiled up at him.

'I don't think I'm ever going to be able to resist you, Charles. It's going to be very awkward if you marry someone else one day.'

'There are ways of preventing that,' he said seriously in her ear, and then led her quietly from the room. They spoke for a moment in a corridor. He didn't want to do anything foolish with her, and yet their hearts always seemed to be on the line. But as she nodded, he quietly slipped his room key into her hand, and then walked to the desk and asked for another one as she took the elevator upstairs, looking terribly sedate and very beautiful and the elevator operator admired her. It would never have occurred to him that she wasn't someone's wife, and she thanked him as she got out, her heart pounding again, and let herself in Charles's room just as he arrived on the floor and followed her to the room. He opened the door and found her standing there in her elegant black dress and a sheepish smile.

'Imagine if someone saw me doing this! I'd be tarred and feathered and thrown out of town!'

'I suspect you're not the first, you know. But as I said before, there are ways of preventing this. . . .' And there was specifically one he had in mind, but they both forgot everything as he took her in his arms, and a moment later, their clothes lay in a heap on the floor and she was clinging to him. It had been a lifetime and a year and several oceans and continents since they'd met, and suddenly she couldn't remember how she had managed to live without him for all this time. And he knew all too well how empty his life had been without her. It was four o'clock before she was able to pull away from him again, and glancing at his watch on the bedtable, she murmured unhappily.

'Dammit . . . I have to go home. . . .' It wasn't like their life in China, where they had existed as man and wife for months. This was pretence and appearances and propriety, and it seemed very strange to them. But he watched her get dressed as he smoked a cigarette and then hastily put on his own clothes to take her home in a taxi, and once there, he kissed her in the cab, and then watched her slip into the house with her key. He watched the light go on in her room upstairs and she pulled back the lace curtain to wave to him, and as he rode back to his hotel he felt desperately lonely, not having her beside him.

The bed still smelled of her perfume and their flesh, and he found a strand of long red hair cast over his pillow, like a gift she had left him. He wanted to call her, to bring her back, to lie next to her again, but that didn't happen until the following afternoon when he met her again and they went back to his hotel room as discreetly as they could. They lay there until ten o'clock that night, and then ordered room service as she sat wearing his robe and sharing a cigarette with him. It felt good just being there with him, but there was something very serious in his eyes tonight, and as he turned to her when the waiter left, she knew something was wrong. She knew him too well for him to fool her for very long.

'What's the matter, Charles?' Her voice was as gentle as it had always been.

'There's something I have to say to you.'

'It can't be as bad as all that.' She reached out a hand for his, but he was too nervous to leave his hand in hers, and he suddenly stood up and began walking around the room, looking at her and then finally he sat down and looked into the blue eyes that had haunted him for so long.

'I have to go to New York tomorrow afternoon.' The words sliced through her like a knife.

'I see.'

'I have meetings to attend with an American publisher, and they moved them up by a week.' She wondered if he was going to ask her to go with him, but it was much worse than that. 'And I think we should both know where we stand when I go. We can't go on like this, Aud. . . . The last year, without you, was the most difficult year of my life, except the year after Sean died.' He was being honest with her. 'And it won't be easy now, leaving you again. We can't keep doing this.' She wanted to ask him why not, why they couldn't just let it go on this way for a while, until she felt she could leave her grandfather . . . until . . . until what, she asked herself. There was no easy answer to the problem. 'I want to marry you. I want you to come to England with me. I understand that it could take a while . . . a month, maybe even two. I could live with that. But I want to marry you, Aud. I love you with everything I have to give.' It was everything she had always dreamed and she knew he was the only man she would ever love. But she couldn't do what he asked . . . couldn't . . . why couldn't he understand that, and let it go for a while?

Her eyes rapidly filled with tears as she shook the copper mane, and gently touched his cheek with her fingertips. 'Don't you know how much I love you, Charles? . . . how badly I want exactly the same things you do? . . . but I can't . . . I *can't*!' She stood up and walked across the room, staring blindly out the window at Union Square far below. 'I can't leave Grandfather, you don't understand that?'

'Do you really think he expects that of you? He's not that unreasonable, Aud. You can't give up your life for him.'

'It would break his heart.'

'And mine?' Charles's voice was soft, his eyes bright with unshed tears. She couldn't answer him.

'I love you.' Her eyes begged him to understand as her lips said the words, but he only shook his head.

'That's not enough. It'll kill us both. Will you marry me?' There was no dodging him, and she couldn't give him the answer he wanted. It was a sacrifice she had to make . . . just like staying in Harbin for eight months, only much, much worse. . . . 'Audrey, answer me.' He stood staring at her with a terrifying look on his face. It was a look that said he meant what he was asking her, that there wouldn't be another chance . . . that this was the last time. . . . 'Audrey?' They stood there across the room from each other now, with a universe separating them, or it might as well have been.

'Charlie, I can't . . . not right now. . . .'

'Then when? Next month? Next year? I've never wanted to marry anyone . . . until you . . . and now I will offer you everything I have to give . . . my life . . . my home . . . my heart . . . whatever fortune I have . . . my royalties . . . everything I have to give is yours . . . but I won't wait another ten years . . . I won't waste my life and yours, waiting for that man to die. Somehow I have to believe that he would want better than that for you. Do you want me to ask him myself? I'd be happy to do that too.' But she shook her head.

'I can't do that to him, Charles. He would tell me to go. And then he would die. I'm all he has.'

'You're all I have.'

'And you are the only man I'll ever love.'

'Then marry me.'

She stood there watching him interminably, but she shook her head and then quietly sat down and began to cry. 'Charlie, I can't.' He turned away from her, and stood looking out the window at Union Square.

'Then it's over for us, when I leave. I don't ever want to see you again. I won't play this game with you.'

'It's not a game, Charlie. It's my life . . . and yours . . . think of that before you shut me out like that.' She was talking to his back, and he only shook his head, and then finally, he turned to look at her again and there was grief in his eyes.

'To leave you in my life, on the edge, taunting me, will torture us both, and what will we have? Emptiness . . . promises . . . lies . . . you said you wished Molly were mine, well so do I . . . and one day I want children of my own and so do you . . . we won't have them like this, or we shouldn't anyway. I want a real life, with a real wife, and children when that seems right . . . just like James and Vi.' It all made perfect sense to her.

'Then come to live in San Francisco with me.'

'And do what? Work on the local newspaper? Sell shoes? I'm a travel writer, Audrey. You know what my life is like. I can't do what I do, just living here. One of us is going to have to make a sacrifice, and this time it has to be you. You have to come with me.'

'Charlie, I can't.' Audrey could barely speak she was crying so hard.

'Think about it. I'll be here until four o'clock. My plane leaves at six.' It was less than twenty-four hours and nothing drastic was going to change in twenty-four hours.

'That's not going to change anything. You're being unreasonable.'

'I'm doing the best thing for both of us. You have to make up your mind.'

'You act as though it's a choice I have, when I don't . . . as though I were being capricious or whimsical . . . when all I'm doing is facing my responsibilities here.'

233

'What about your responsibilities to me? . . . to yourself . . . even to that child? Don't you owe each of us something more, the guts to go after what you want . . . if it really is what you want.'

'You know it is.'

'Then come with me. Or at least promise you'll come soon.'

'I can't promise that.' She covered her face with her hands, thinking of the dilemma she was in. 'I can't promise you anything.'

He nodded. He had understood the risk when he'd come. But at least it would be over now. She would either agree to marry him, or he would close the door on everything he felt for her. He wasn't going to play games with her any more, or with himself. He owed himself that much.

There was silence in the cab when he took her home, and he touched her face very gently before he kissed her goodnight. 'I'm not doing it to be cruel . . . but we have to make a clean break, if that's what it's going to be . . . for both our sakes.'

'Why?' She didn't understand. 'Why now? Is there someone else?' That possibility hadn't even occurred to her until that point, but he shook his head.

'I'm doing it because I can't live without you, and if I have to, then I'd better get used to it. Starting now.'

'You're being unfair.' But she had thought that when he refused to write to her when she had turned down the proposal he had cabled to Harbin. 'Look at the responsibilities I have.'

'There will always be something, Aud. You have to make a choice now.'

She shook her head, looking griefstricken and he followed her out of the cab and kissed her on the front steps. 'I love you.'

'I love you too.' But there was nothing she could do. And when she went to her room, she took the sleeping baby in her arms, feeling her warmth next to her, and listened to the little purring sounds of her breath. She was thinking of everything he had said, about wanting to marry her . . . about the children he wanted to have . . . it was just rotten luck that he wanted everything now, and she sat at the breakfast table the next morning, staring woodenly at her plate, having slept barely at all, and her grandfather stared at her with a fierce frown to mask his own worry. He sensed that she was very unhappy.

'Did you drink too much last night?' She shook her head and attempted to smile at him. 'You look terrible. Are you sick?'

'Just tired.'

And then suddenly, there was an odd tone in his voice, as though he were suddenly afraid, and she felt sorry for him. 'Are you very fond of him?'

'We're good friends.'

'And what does that mean?'

'Actually,' she smiled halfheartedly, trying to get him off the track, 'I'd rather not talk about it.'

'Why not?' Because it hurts too much. But she didn't say the words to him.

'We're just friends, Grampa.'

'I think there's more to it than that, from his side anyway. Damn good thing if not from yours.'

'What makes you say that?'

'That's no life for a decent girl, running all over the world with a man like that, chasing camels and elephants . . . think of the stench!' He looked horrified and she laughed at the thought.

'I'd never thought of it quite that way before.'

'Besides, it wouldn't be good for the child.' . . . Or for him. She knew he was thinking of that too. And he had a right to, after all. He was almost eighty-three years old now and he needed her. She knew that only too well.

'It's not serious, Grandfather. Don't worry about it.' But he did anyway. She could see it in his eyes. And she felt a lead weight in her heart, when she called Charlie at noon.

She had promised to meet him for lunch downtown, and when she did, they found they both looked grim. They both had a lot on their minds. They made small talk for a very short time and then he looked at her. They hadn't even ordered their lunches yet.

'Well?'

She looked at him, wanting to put it off, but there was no escaping it. 'You know the answer, Charles. I love you. But I can't marry you. Not now.' He nodded, bereft of speech, and his eyes were dry as he looked at her.

'I had a feeling you would decide that way. Because of your grandfather?' She nodded silently. 'I'm sorry, Aud.' He reached out a hand to touch hers and then he stood up. 'I don't think we should have lunch. Do you? There's an earlier flight I can catch if I hurry.' It was all moving too quickly for her now, and she could see unspoken anger in his eyes, and fury and hurt and revenge, and she felt as though she were ricocheting off the walls as she followed him out. Suddenly she was in a cab, and everything was moving too fast. She was standing in front of the house, with Charles standing outside the cab. He was looking down at her with raging hurt in his eyes and she moved to kiss him goodbye. But he took a step back from her and put up his hand as though to ward her off, shook his head, and then disappeared into the taxi again with only a murmured goodbye. As she stood watching him, the cab shifted into gear, and suddenly after all that time, all those moments, all those miles, and so much love . . . he was gone. Forever.

24

As Audrey walked into the front hall of her grandfather's house and the butler quietly closed the door, she was aware of a ruckus in the upstairs hall, and she noticed a stack of boxes and trunks waiting at the foot of the stairs. Suddenly, she realised that her sister was standing watching her from the library doorway. It was the first time they had seen each other since their unpleasant encounter right after Audrey got home, and Audrey looked at her cautiously now, wondering what she was doing there, and if she were leaving on a trip with that huge stack of bags, and then suddenly, with a sinking heart, she knew what had happened.

'Is something wrong?'

'Harcourt left me.'

Audrey nodded, not surprised anymore by anything, but only puzzled by what Annabelle was doing there. She was still deeply disappointed in her sister. 'Then why are you here?' Her tone told a tale of sorrow that Annabelle did not understand, and wouldn't have cared about anyway. Besides, she was too wrapped up in her own problems.

'I didn't want to stay in Burlingame. I hate that place.'

'Did you try the hotels?' Audrey sounded bitter as she spoke, and Annabelle looked startled.

'This is my home too, as much as yours.'

'Did you ask Grandfather if you can stay here?'

'No.' His voice reached them. Neither of them had realised that he was at home. 'She did not. Would you care to explain that to me, Annabelle?' They both suddenly felt as they had as children, when he caught them doing something they shouldn't. Audrey wondered if she had been unduly harsh, and Annabelle knew she should have called before simply arriving.

'I . . . I tried to reach you this morning, Grampa, but . . .'

'That's a lie.' He looked at her with severe annoyance. 'At least have the good manners to tell the truth. Where is your husband?'

'I don't know. I think he went up to the lake with friends.'

'And you've chosen to desert him?'

'I . . .' It was awkward explaining it all to him in the hall, but he showed no inclination to ask her to sit down. 'He said that he wanted a divorce.'

'How amenable of you to grant it to him. Do you realise that you are under no such obligation?' She nodded.

'But I. . . .'

'You want out?' He put the appropriate words in her mouth and she nodded. 'I see. How convenient. And now you come home to me, and your sister, is that it, Annabelle?' She blushed faintly and nodded again. 'For any particular reason? The address perhaps? . . . the excellence of my staff? . . . the advantages of a house in town . . . or perhaps because your sister oversees your children so well?' He knew her well and Audrey almost laughed at Annie's obvious discomfort.

'I . . . I just thought . . . maybe for a little while. . . .'

'How little, Annabelle? A week? Two? Less perhaps?' He was enjoying his effect and Audrey almost felt sorry for her sister. Almost. But not quite. She no longer merited a great deal of pity. She was too unkind and too spoiled, she drank too much, and she was too often vicious. 'How long do you intend to stay here?'

'Until I find a house?'

'Don't ask me, tell me . . . very well then. Until you find a house. I agree to let you stay here, but see to it that you find one.' He glanced at Audrey as soon as he said the words and saw the triumphant look on Annabelle's face. 'And see to it that you don't impose unduly on your sister.' They were wise words, the only problem was that Audrey and Annabelle did not share the same interpretation of 'unduly'.

Within the next two hours, she had managed to park both of her children in Audrey's room. Little Winston was attempting to destroy all of her books, and Hannah had been dumped in Molly's crib, and the hostess had just bitten the guest in the toe and drawn blood, much to Annabelle's horror.

'Chinese gutter brat!' she screamed, and without further ado, Audrey slapped her. One good, hard crack across the face, which was exactly what was needed. She was slightly more subdued after that, but it was five o'clock before Audrey could close her bedroom door and get some rest, and think about what had happened with Charlie. It was difficult to believe she had seen him only a few hours before, and as tears fell on her pillow, she wondered if she would ever see him again. It seemed very unlikely. And suddenly realising what it meant, and that she was trapped now in her life with her grandfather and Annabelle, she began to sob, thinking of the man she had lost and knowing that he was gone forever. Her eyes were still red when she went down to dinner that night, but no one noticed. Her grandfather was lost in his own thoughts, and Annabelle regaled them all with ugly tales of Harcourt's infidelities, and by the time dessert was served, Audrey actually felt ill. The next few months were a nightmare. None of the nurses Annabelle hired ever stayed. They detested Annabelle, and her children were hardly more endearing. The other servants resented the new arrivals and the extra work they made, and Annabelle was constantly out, and always leaving Audrey saddled with her children.

Even her grandfather seemed to find it all wearing, and he took less and less interest in little Molly, who had given him so much joy only months before. But now almost nothing seemed to bring him joy. Audrey felt unable to cheer him. Her own heart seemed to drag daily, and only Molly brought her any comfort. All she could think of was Charles. She had attempted half a dozen letters to him but threw them all away. What could she say to him? Nothing had changed. Nothing was ever going to be different. And now, to add to her miseries, Audrey was afraid that her grandfather was failing. He paid no attention to politics any more, seldom read the paper, and never went to his club for lunch. Audrey mentioned it to Annabelle several times, but she didn't seem to notice. She was far too busy going out with her own friends and every single man in town. She had gone to the opera house several times, all the chic restaurants, several dances, and she didn't want to hear about her grandfather, or her sister, or her children.

'Look dammit.' Audrey was losing patience with her by Christmas Eve, when she announced that she was going out with friends, and didn't have time to dine with her grandfather and Audrey. 'You could at least spend an hour with him, Annie. Don't forget,' there was ice in her voice that had never been there before, 'he supports you.'

'So what? He doesn't have anyone else to support, does he? And he supports you too. You spend time with him. You have nothing else to do.' She had nothing but contempt for her older sister. She had been there taking care of her all her life, and she didn't see why things should be any different now. She was an old maid anyway, wasn't she? And no man would want her now, now that she had saddled herself with that stupid Chink baby. She didn't make any bones about it to her friends, she had even insinuated more than once that the baby might be Audrey's. But Audrey didn't care. She loved Mai Li as though she were her own baby, and she didn't give a damn about local gossip. She was only sorry to see Annabelle ruin her life, whoring around, but no amount of lecturing or entreating seemed to reach her. She was determined to waste her life on weak men and strong drink, and Audrey had given up trying to change her. She was a spoiled, unpleasant girl, and Audrey had Mai Li to cling to now. It hurt her to see the way Annabelle lived, but she realised that there was nothing she could do about it, and she admitted to herself now that Annabelle had always been spoiled. Only the drinking and her recent excesses had made her worse. But it saddened her to see it. The divorce was a bitter one, and Harcourt had appeared at the house more than once, raging against Annabelle and her lawyers. Her grandfather instructed the butler not to let him in any more. He was usually drunk when he showed up anyway, and he instigated ugly scenes between himself and Annabelle, neither of them making much sense, but throwing lamps and pieces of jade was something her grandfather would no longer tolerate, he told Audrey.

'I'm sorry you have to put up with it at all, Grampa.'

'I suppose I should buy her a house somewhere,' he sighed, 'but I'm too old to worry about it now. And I'll be gone soon anyway. You and she will both own this house when I'm gone, and it's certainly big enough for both of you, and your motley crew of children,' he smiled. He was leaving them joint ownership of the Tahoe house too, though Audrey wasn't very sure of the wisdom of that. She would have much preferred to live elsewhere alone, and not share anything with Annabelle, who was certainly no pleasure to live with. But she didn't say anything to her grandfather about that, except to chide him for saying that he would be gone soon, but she was afraid he might be right. He had lost considerable weight in the past few months, and he was beginning to sleep all the time. She had to rouse him now to take his daily walk, and most of the time when she and Mai Li came in to see him before dinner, or in the early afternoon, he was sleeping. Mai Li was walking now, and teetering on tiptoe as she careened across the room, her hair still standing straight up, and her eyes wide with delight. On Christmas Eve, Audrey had dressed her in red velvet, with a tiny red satin bow in her silky black hair, white stockings and tiny black patent leather shoes. It was a long, long way from Harbin, where she had been born. Audrey looked at her with pride and handed her to her grandfather. Little Hannah was already asleep in her bed, and Winston had been taken back upstairs by the maid in disgrace, after breaking a crystal decanter and his great-grandfather's composure. The other two children still had no nurse, and Audrey took care of them most of the time, since Annabelle was never there. He looked at Audrey now, with Molly, as everyone now called her, on his knee.

'Where's your sister tonight, Audrey?'

'I believe she went to a dinner at the Stantons'.'

'How unusual for her to be out,' he said sarcastically and knit his brows as he looked at Audrey. 'You ought to do something more with your life than baby-sitting for her brats all the time, Audrey.'

'She'll get things sorted out eventually, Grampa.' But she no longer believed it herself. She was going to have to put her foot down, but she hadn't wanted to cause any problems in the house. It made him nervous whenever that happened. Most things made him nervous these days, the doorbell, the phone, the sound of cars outside. He complained about everything moving too quickly, and everything being too loud, in spite of the fact that he was slowly losing his hearing. But he remembered a far gentler world, and suddenly all of the changes around upset him. Audrey reassured him as much as she could, and she had her hands full keeping him happy and well cared for. It was more difficult now to find people to work in the house, people weren't as desperate as they had been a few years before, and they preferred to work in factories or stores. They didn't want the restrictions of working as domestics. And more than once now, Audrey found herself scrubbing a wall, or beating a carpet, or using the Hoover in the rooms that she lived in. But there was no sign of that now as she sat in a dark blue silk evening gown beside the fire on Christmas Eve, as Edward Driscoll was dozing. She sent the baby upstairs to bed, and they sat that way for a long time, as she sipped a glass of sherry, and thought back to the previous year when she had been in China singing Christmas carols with the children in the orphanage. Thinking of them brought Charlie to mind again, and she wondered if he was already in Egypt. Her heart was heavy just thinking about him, but she knew now, that it was over. She had taken off his ring months before and put it carefully in her jewel box. She had had a Christmas card from James and Vi, and they didn't mention him at all. They only said that they hoped to see Audrey again in 1935, and urged her to come and visit them in Antibes the following summer. She would have liked nothing better, but with her grandfather slowing down she couldn't imagine leaving him for the summer.

On the Ides of March, Mai Li became one year old, and two days later, Edward Driscoll had a stroke that left him without speech and paralysed on his left side. His eyes looked at Audrey in anguish as she moved quietly about his room giving instructions to the nurses and waiting for the morning and evening visits from the doctor.

It had taken her two days to find Annabelle to give her the news. She had been in Los Angeles for a week, going to the races with friends and she hadn't been sleeping in her hotel room at night, or even bothering to answer the messages Audrey left her. Audrey was livid when she finally found her.

'What if something happened to one of your children?'

'You're there, aren't you?' Faithful Audrey who never went anywhere and could always be counted on. She suddenly felt a boiling rage spill over in her, and had Annabelle been there, she might have slapped her. She was making a spectacle of herself all over the state, with both single and married men, and she seemed to be just as outrageous as Harcourt, who was having a flagrant affair with the wife of one of his best friends, and seemed to be in the gossip columns almost daily. It was too bad they hadn't stayed married, Grandfather had commented once, they deserved each other. But now, it wasn't Harcourt Audrey was thinking of when Annabelle finally returned her call with an air of boredom.

'Grandfather had a stroke two days ago, Annie. You'd better come home now.'

'Why?' Audrey could feel her whole body go rigid as she listened to her sister's voice.

'*Why?* Because he's a very sick old man and he might die,

243

that's why. And because he's taken care of you all your life, and you owe him something for that, or hadn't you thought of that before?' Annabelle was the most selfish human being she'd ever known, and she was slowly beginning to hate her.

'There's nothing I can do for him, Aud. And I'm rotten around a sick room.' Audrey had discovered that when little Winston had got chicken pox and then passed them on to both Hannah and Molly. Annabelle had gone to Santa Barbara for a three-week holiday, leaving all three in Audrey's care. She had not even called once to see how they were doing.

'You belong back here.' Audrey's voice was like ice now. 'Not whoring around LA. Now get your ass back here tonight. Is that clear?'

'Don't talk to me like that, you jealous bitch!' Audrey was shocked at the venom in her sister's voice. There was no longer a vestige of kindness between them. 'I'll come back whenever I damn well want to.' For what? Her inheritance? But as Audrey thought the words, she realised something she had known before. She could never have lived in that house alone with her sister. Once her grandfather was gone, she was going too. There was nothing to hold her there, or even in San Francisco. She owed Annabelle nothing. She had given her half her life and there was nothing left to give her. It was time Annabelle took care of her own responsibilities, and her own children.

Audrey sat thinking for only a moment and then nodded. Something had ended for her just then. It was the end of an era. 'Fine, Annabelle, come home whenever you like.' And as she hung up, she felt as though she had been talking to a stranger.

25

Her grandfather lingered until early June, and then finally breathed his last, as Audrey held his hand and gently kissed his fingers. Even as she closed his eyes, and felt the tears roll down her cheeks, she knew it was a mercy. He had been such a powerful man once, so strong and proud, that to live trapped in a useless body with a failing mind and with a mouth that could no longer speak was the worst kind of prison she could think of. And it was time for him to be free. He was eighty-three years old, and very, very tired of living.

Audrey saw to all the arrangements with a heavy heart. She had never realised how many terrible details there were, everything from selecting the casket, to the music for his funeral service. There was a minister they had all known who read the eulogy at the funeral service, and Audrey sat in the front row in a black hat with a black veil, wearing a severe black suit and black stockings and shoes. Even Annabelle looked serious on that day, although she looked far less so at the reading of the will, and she smiled cheerfully at Audrey as she crossed her legs and lit a cigarette. He had left a far greater fortune than either of them had hoped for. There were the houses in San Francisco and Meeks Bay, at Lake Tahoe, as well as quite a lot of very solid stock that the girls could live on for the rest of their lives, if they were careful. Audrey was particularly touched that he had left a small, specific bequest to Mai Li, and had referred to her as 'my great-granddaughter Molly Driscoll'. Tears filled Audrey's eyes as she listened, but Annabelle didn't appear nearly so touched. There was a clause that said that either of the girls could buy out the other's share of the houses, but otherwise they could live there together. And Audrey knew for certain that she would not do that.

Quietly, over the next few weeks, she packed up her

things, and put them in boxes in the basement. There were packing boxes and steamer trunks, and a box of the clothes Mai Li had outgrown. There were even her father's albums, carefully wrapped in tissue paper and then linen, and stored away. She would only take a few trunks with her, and her plan was to go to Europe for a few months, and then she would decide what to do from there. She wanted to see Violet and James, and more importantly, she wanted to see Charlie. She wanted to see him more than anything. She was free now, and she had none of the encumbrances she had had before, except Mai Li. She had heard nothing from him since he'd left San Francisco in September. Her heart still ached when she thought of the proposal she had felt obliged to turn down, and she wondered if he would even be wiling to see her. She hoped so. He was the main reason for her going to Europe.

It was late July by the time she finished all the odds and ends that she had to attend to. Everything was packed and put away. Her affairs were in order, and she had done whatever she had to do for her grandfather's estate, and then finally she sat down with Annabelle one day. Annabelle was dressing to go out and Audrey thought she was wearing too much rouge. There was a trouser suit spread out on the bed, and a creamy silk shirt, and she was doing her hair in an upsweep. She had been copying the style of Marlene Dietrich a lot these days, and she was creating almost as much sensation in San Francisco as Dietrich was in Europe.

'You're too pretty to wear trousers.' She smiled at her younger sister and sat down, and Annabelle eyed her suspiciously. They had spoken little since their grandfather died, and there had been an item in the paper about her the day before, something about her flirting with somebody's husband, and she wondered if Audrey was going to give her a lecture.

'I'm in a hurry to go out, Aud.' She spoke nervously and avoided Audrey's eyes. A cigarette burned in a pink ashtray on her mirrored dressing table and in the next room they could hear Winston and Hannah and Molly playing and fighting over their toys. They were a rough little crew, but they had been good company for Molly and Audrey knew she was going to miss them.

'I won't take much of your time, Annie.' She was wearing a plain black silk dress and she looked older than her years as she looked at her younger sister. She was wearing black to mourn the grandfather they had just lost, but Annabelle seemed not to remember. 'I'm leaving for Europe in a few days. I thought I'd let you know.'

'You're *what*?' She looked horrified, which seemed amazing to Audrey. They hardly saw each other any more, and when they did it wasn't pleasant. 'When did you decide that?' She swivelled on the seat to her dressing table and stared at her sister, with one eyebrow painted on and the other one missing. Audrey smiled at her.

'I decided a few weeks ago. There isn't enough room in this house for both of us, Annie. And there's no reason for me to be here any more. I stayed for Grandfather's sake, but he's gone now.'

'What about me?' Audrey stared at her in dismay, surely she couldn't still expect Audrey to stay and take care of her. 'What about my children? Who'll run this house?' So that was it. Audrey almost laughed at the horror on her face.

'I guess that's all up to you now, Annie. It's your turn. I've done it for eighteen years.' She was twenty-nine now, and she had been running her grandfather's house since she was eleven. More than that, she had been taking care of Annabelle's children for her since she had moved in ten months before, and it was high time Annabelle took care of them herself. 'It's all yours now.' She stood up with a small, wintry smile. She still felt the emptiness of their loss and each time she walked down the hall, she missed him. She couldn't even go down to breakfast any more. She choked looking at his empty place and waiting for him to arrive, to argue with her over what he read in the paper.

'Where are you going to go?' Annabelle looked frankly panicked.

'England. The South of France after that, and then I'll see.'

'When are you coming home?'

'I haven't made up my mind yet. Probably not for a few months. I have no reason to rush back now.'

'The hell you don't.' She slammed her hairbrush down on the table and stood up. 'You can't just walk out on me like that.'

Audrey stood up and looked down on her much smaller sister. She was smaller in stature as well as spirit. 'I didn't really think you'd notice.'

'What's that supposed to mean?'

'We're not exactly close any more, Annie, are we?' Her voice was gentle and her eyes were sad. It wasn't supposed to have ended up that way, but it had. There was nothing between them any more, nothing except unpleasantness and hard feelings and mutual disapproval.

'Why are you doing this to me?' Annabelle started to cry and her mascara started to run in black rivers down her cheeks. She looked awful as she sat down again and stared up at Audrey. 'You hate me, don't you?'

'No, I don't.'

'You're jealous of me because you never had a husband.'

Audrey suddenly laughed in the dressing room that reeked of perfume and cigarette smoke. She had never wanted a husband like Harcourt, and the only man she'd ever loved had been Charlie. 'I hope you don't believe that, Annie. I don't begrudge you what you've had, and I hope you marry again one day, a little more wisely this time perhaps,' although that seemed unlikely given her taste and wild behaviour. 'It's just time for me to go. I guess I'm like Father. I need to move around.' She didn't tell her about Charlie.

'What'll I do with the children?' she wailed.

'Get a nurse for them.'

'No one ever stays.' Audrey was sorry for her, but she wasn't willing to stay either, and it might be good for

Annabelle to have to take care of her children herself for a change. Audrey was rejoicing at the prospect of being alone with Molly. She was beginning to talk now and each moment she spent with her was a pleasure.

Audrey stood for a long moment, looking down at her sister. 'I'm sorry, Annie.'

'Get out of my room!' Annabelle shouted at her, hurling her hairbrush at the door. 'Get out of my house!' Audrey closed the door softly behind her and she heard the sound of breaking glass shortly after.

Four days later, she closed the last of her bags, and looked around her room. She had no regrets. She could hardly wait to leave, even though Annabelle had come sobbing to her the night before, begging her not to go. Two of the maids had quit once they knew Audrey was leaving, and both the cook and the butler had retired the month before, shortly after her grandfather's death. It was time for all of them to start afresh, Annabelle as well as Audrey, and for the first time in her life she was being forced to stand on her own two feet. As she put her bag in the hall with a sigh, Audrey wondered how she would manage. And as she looked down the hall, she wondered when she would see this house again, if ever. And it would surely no longer be the same. Once Annabelle got used to being on her own, she would probably go wild and sell everything in it, or throw everything out and redecorate, and it was unlikely that she would be decent enough to ask Audrey's permission.

Annabelle did not get up to say goodbye to her before she left, and the children were still sleeping. Audrey quietly dressed Mai Li, and they had breakfast in the kitchen, and the chauffeur drove them to the airport with all their things. She had decided to fly to New York to save time, rather than take the train, and then they would board the *Normandie*, the French line's newest and most wonderful ship, and she planned to get off in Southampton. She was hoping to see Charlie as well, and she was planning to call him as soon as she got to London. Perhaps he was too angry with her and the damage could not be repaired. But she had to try. She owed herself that much. He was the only man she had ever loved, and it was worth one more try to see him.

She shook hands with all of the servants before she left, scooped Molly up in her arms, and walked down the front steps with the child in one arm, and her vanity case in the other. It was the same vanity case she had taken with her to China and she smiled to herself now as she remembered the endless trip on the trains, clutching the useless object on her lap as Charles threatened to toss it out or trade it for a couple of fat chickens. She could hardly wait to see him now. And the long flight to New York seemed to pass in minutes as she thought again and again of her final destination. She had no regrets about leaving San Francisco, and she could feel her heart thump as the plane got under way. There was something so exhilarating about going away . . . travelling anywhere . . . she had the same feeling when they boarded the ship in New York, and she remembered meeting Violet and James only two years before on the *Mauretania*. But this time there was no one who particularly interested her on the crossing and although the *Normandie* was extraordinary in every way, she spent most of her time with Mai Li, or reading in a deckchair while Mai Li played nearby, and she ate most of her meals in their cabin. She didn't want to leave the child with an unfamiliar maid while she went to dine, and she was perfectly content to lead a solitary life. Most of the time she still wore black, and she was lost in her own thoughts, and anxious to see Charlie. She hadn't seen him since he left her on the pavement and drove away, after she turned down his proposal. The very thought touched her heart again, and she felt the same dull ache she always felt when she thought of him. But it was exhilarating docking in Southampton. She was only hours away from him now, and the trip to London sped by. It was only a little while later that she checked into Claridge's again, as she had before, and asked the operator to connect her with his number. He was out when she called, but it was still only midafternoon.

He was probably out for the afternoon or perhaps even away for a few days. If she didn't reach him by the following day, she could send a note to his flat, or ask Violet and James if they knew where he was when she called them in Antibes, which she finally did late the next day. Lady Vi came on the line, and it was a terrible connection.

'Violet? . . . Can you hear me? . . . It's Audrey . . . Audrey Driscoll . . . What? . . . What did you say? . . .'

'I said . . . where . . . are . . . you?' The line kept fading in and out, and Audrey could barely hear her.

'I'm in London.'

'Where are you staying?'

'At Claridge's.'

'Where? . . . never . . . mind . . . When are you . . . coming . . . down?' They had been in Antibes since June, and Audrey imagined that it was as festive as ever.

'Maybe at the end of this week.'

'What?'

'This weekend.'

'Jolly good. How are you?'

'Fine.' She had wanted to tell her about Molly, still hadn't, and now it would have to wait. It was an impossible subject to tackle with a bad phone connection to the South of France. 'How are you and James, and the children?'

'We're fine . . .' The line faded out completely then, and all Audrey could hear was something that sounded like 'edding.'

'What did you say? . . . this is an awful . . . connection. . . .'

'Yes . . . it is . . . I said . . . we just came back . . . from . . . edding.' The line did it again, and Audrey almost groaned in exasperation.

'From *where?*'

Suddenly like clouds parting to reveal the sun, the connection improved and Audrey almost fainted as she finally heard the words clearly. 'Charlie's wedding.'

'What?' She sat rigid on the bed, as though someone had slapped her.

'I said . . . we just got back from Charlie's . . . wedding . . . it was lovely. . . .' Oh, God . . . oh, no . . . no . . . please God . . . not Charlie. . . .

'I . . . oh . . .' It was almost like a physical blow and for a moment words failed her.

'Are you there? . . . Audrey, can you hear me? . . .'

'Yes, barely . . . Who did he marry? . . .' Not that it really mattered.

'Charlotte Beardsley . . . his publisher's daughter . . .' There was no point attempting to explain that the girl had been chasing him for two years and had followed him to Egypt and literally camped at his feet. James said that it would never last, that it was an obsession she'd soon tire of when she knew him better, and he couldn't imagine why Charles had given in to her, except that somehow Vi suspected there was a reason. 'They got married in Hampshire. . . . We just got back.'

Audrey was still painfully quiet at her end, and fighting to hold back the tears that choked her. 'That's nice. . . .' Her voice was too faint for Violet to hear her and this time it had nothing to do with the connection.

'When are you coming down?'

'I don't know . . . I . . .' She suddenly remembered why she had come to London, and there was no point staying there now. That was why his phone hadn't answered. She shuddered at what it would have been like to have been answered by Charlotte, now Charlotte Parker-Scott. And suddenly all Audrey wanted was to get out of London. 'What about tomorrow? Is that too soon?' She glanced at Mai Li playing in the room beyond, and decided that she'd better say something.

'That's lovely, Audrey! Will you fly?'

She was in no hurry now. 'I'll take the train. And Violet . . . I'm bringing my daughter.'

'Your what?' The line had begun crackling again.

'My daughter!' Audrey shouted.

'Tell me when you arrive. Anything you bring is fine. We have lots of room for you.'

'Thank you . . .' Her lip trembled as she said goodbye. 'I'll see you tomorrow.'

'*Au revoir*. We shall meet you at the train.'

'Fine.' They both rang off, and Audrey sat staring into space for a long, long time, thinking of what she had heard from her old friend. It seemed unbelievable somehow. Charlie, whom she had loved so much, whom she had come to see, was now married to a woman named Charlotte.

26

The train arrived at the station in Antibes at exactly eight forty-three the next morning. Audrey was sitting by the window in a light blue linen dress and espadrilles she had bought when she was in Antibes two years before, and Mai Li was wearing a pink cotton dress with a white pinafore and a pink bow in her hair, and she looked like a little Chinese angel. She sat on Audrey's lap as the train pulled in, and she looked fascinated by the activity beyond. Audrey glanced out, hoping to see Violet and James, but she couldn't see them at first, and went about the business of finding a porter to unload her bags. She and Molly were already on the platform when she saw them. They hadn't changed a bit. And Violet looked exquisite in a diaphanous white dress with a huge white hat, and a pink scarf around her neck, barely concealing a rope of pearls the size of moth-balls. James was wearing a navy and white shirt, loose white trousers, and navy espadrilles, and he looked much more French than English. It was Violet who ran to Audrey first, and she stopped suddenly as she reached her and saw Molly in her arms, her eyes wide with fascination as she stared at the beautiful lady.

'Hat!' she said as she pointed and they both laughed as Violet turned questioning eyes to Audrey.

'And who is this?' She didn't look accusing, only curious, as James told the porter where to take the bags.

Audrey laughed. 'I tried to tell you on the phone yesterday, but the connection was so awful. This is my daughter, Molly.'

'My, my . . .' Violet looked naughtily at Audrey and waggled a finger. 'So that's what you were doing over there. I must say . . . she's very pretty . . .' Violet leaned forward as she stroked the silky black hair. 'Darling, who was her father?'

'Actually, I'm not sure.' Violet's eyes widened further in surprise at Audrey's answer. 'I think a Japanese soldier.'

Violet pursed her lips at that. 'You mustn't tell anyone that. Pretend it was a well-known philosopher. Or someone in government, someone terribly important.'

'I say, who's this?' James had come upon them and gave Audrey a warm hug and a kiss on the cheek as he glanced at the baby.

Violet answered for her. 'Look, darling, Audrey's had a little Chinese baby.' Audrey laughed at the description, and decided to save her reputation before the game went too far, although neither Violet nor James seemed upset to think that she'd had an illegitimate Chinese baby. It was amazing how open-minded they were, and Audrey found herself wondering if anything would shock them.

'Actually, her mother died at the orphanage while I was there, and I brought Mai Li home with me and adopted her.'

James smiled at their old friend as he led her to the car, and Violet played with Molly, tickling her as she giggled. 'Your grandfather must have been pleased.' Audrey laughed at the memory of his initial reaction, but he had been good to Molly after that . . . even remembering her in his will, as 'my great-grandchild Molly Driscoll' . . . Audrey had been so touched.

'He got used to her eventually. He loved her very much.'

Violet frowned at her then, as they settled into the enormous Mercedes. 'Charles didn't say anything about her to us, after he was out to see you last September. How like him.' She looked at James and they laughed as Audrey fought not to let the pain she felt show on her face. She felt rooted to the spot just hearing his name, and hoped they wouldn't tell her about the wedding. Yet eventually, she'd have to know, she'd want to know, at least who he had married and why. There had to be some deeper explanation. It didn't seem possible that he had just fallen in love in the past year, and run off to get married. He wasn't that sort of person, at least . . . she fought heroically to push him from her mind and turn her thoughts back to James and Violet. They drove to the villa and the three of them chatted. Audrey was enchanted to find that very little had changed there. The room they gave her was the same one she'd had before, with a peaceful view over the Mediterranean, and they opened a door between it and the adjoining guest room, giving her a room for Mai Li as well, although they hadn't been expecting her. But they were enjoying a lull between houseguests, having just come back from Charlie's wedding. Finally, as they watched the sunset on the terrace, she asked Violet about the girl he had married. She had to know something about her . . . had to . . . and James was inside opening wines for their dinner so that they could 'breathe' before he served them. He was especially fond of Haut-Brion, which they had laughingly called O'Brien the summer she was first there, and Mouton Rothschild, which he liked even better. They ate and drank extremely well in the South of France, but Audrey wasn't thinking of any of that now.

'Charles never mentioned a woman to me when I saw him in San Francisco.' She said it hesitantly, embarrassed to admit how much it mattered to her, even to Lady Violet.

'Charlotte's been chasing him for a couple of years now.' She was cautious at first, watching Audrey's eyes, but they seemed to be veiled, and she looked away, out over the water. Violet gently laid a hand on hers. 'You aren't still in love with him, Audrey, are you?' There was no point pretending, Violet would have suspected anyway, and she turned her gaze back to her friend with eyes full of pain, and tears brimming on her lashes. 'Oh my dear . . . oh Audrey, I'm so sorry . . . and I told you so bluntly on the phone. Somehow I assumed it was all over for both of you. He was so definite about it when he came back from San Francisco.'

Audrey looked deeply troubled as she looked at her friend. 'What did he say?'

'Not much in fact, except that it was over. You were settled there, and he had his own life to lead. And I must say, he went about it with a vengeance.' Audrey nodded, understanding only too well why.

'He asked me to marry him again. . . .' She turned anguished eyes to Lady Vi. 'But Violet . . . I couldn't. How could I leave my grandfather then? It wouldn't have been right . . . I just couldn't. I suggested he live in San Francisco for a while. But of course he couldn't do that either . . . we were both trapped by our obligations.'

'And he left in a huff, I suppose.' Violet knew him well and Audrey nodded.

'He was furious. Of course he was hurt as much as angry, but he refused to understand what held me there.'

'You have to realise, Audrey, the man has no responsibilities of his own . . . never has had . . . except of course his brother. But he was practically a child then himself, and he didn't yet have the taste for travel. Once you get that, you never settle down. I'm not sure he ever will actually. At least not in a conventional sense. The amazing thing about you is that you like all that mad jauntering about as much as he does.' Audrey smiled and wiped her eyes with the handkerchief she had in her pocket. James watched them from the dining room, thinking what a lovely portrait they both made. He stood drinking a *kir*, sensing that confidences were being exchanged and not wanting to interrupt them.

'The damn stupid thing,' Lady Vi went on, she was not going to hide her feeling from Audrey. She had made no secret of how she felt almost from the beginning. She had even been frank with Charles, once, but he had refused to believe her. 'The stupid thing is that I don't think that woman loves him. She wanted him . . . oh God, yes . . . she wanted him desperately, like an object one must have, or a fabulously dear piece of land . . . a castle perhaps . . . or a mountaintop one must climb. I think she sees marrying Charles as an achievement.' Audrey was intrigued as she listened to her friend.

'But apparently he must love her.' She blew her nose again and dabbed at the eyes that refused to stop crying. But it felt good to be candid with her friend. She had to talk to somebody about him.

'You know,' Lady Vi squinted at the sun as she sank back in her chair with a pensive look. 'I've never been quite certain he does. I think he's convinced himself. And she certainly makes life easy for him. Good Lord, she does everything for the man except put his shoes on for him. It's really quite disgusting.'

'And in contrast there I was refusing to give an inch, standing by my grandfather till the end.'

'It's hardly something one would condemn you for.' Lady Vi was stilly angry that Charlie had married Charlotte Beardsley. She had cried copiously at their wedding, but not because she thought the ceremony touching. James had warned her about being too outspoken about it, or they would lose Charlie's friendship. He seemed determined to defend the girl no matter what. Perhaps because he knew no one else would.

'Is she very beautiful?' Audrey looked like a heartbroken child as she asked and Lady Vi shook her head.

'No, she's not . . . handsome perhaps . . . or maybe attractive is the better word. And she's very expensively put together. All the latest styles, and everything terribly costly. I think her father has spoiled her rotten. And of course they have a great deal of money.' Lady Vi said it as the supreme condemnation, but what she was saying of course was that they had money and no class, although she would never have put it as bluntly to Audrey. 'And Charles says she has an excellent head for business. She has taken over handling his books, and she's done extremely well for him. She's even sold the film rights for two of his novels, which is something Charles would never have thought of on his own.'

'It sounds as though she's good for him.' And then she asked what she really wanted to know. 'Is he happy?'

Lady Violet thought about it for a long time and then

looked her friend in the eye. 'No, he's not. He says he is, but to be honest with you, I don't believe him. James would kill me for telling you that, but it's what I think. I think he's fooling himself about what he feels for her. I think he made up his mind to get married, and she was there, dancing through hoops for him, so he told himself it was right. But there's no joy there, no spark, no excitement . . . it's not what you shared, from everything I understand. When he talked about you, he either looked as though he were in heaven or in hell, and most of the time, he was,' they both remembered when she had refused to leave Harbin, 'but there's none of that now. He only looks half alive. Numb actually. Although he claims to be having a wonderful time. But even if he is, he won't be for long. I think that behind the mask Charlotte Beardsley is a very difficult woman. I think there are reasons why she hasn't been married until now. I think she went after what she wanted in life. She wanted a career, and she has one, a big one, and then she decided she wanted a husband and she got that. But what she'll do with him now is beyond me. She'll have him like a puppet on a string eventually, and Charlie will hate every minute of it. She's going to turn him into a factory for books and films, and making pots of money. It's the only thing she understands really . . . she doesn't understand what makes people like you and Charles tick, that marvellous wander-lust that takes you all over the world, just sniffing out funny smells and taking photographs of unusual people.'

'Taking photographs of what?' James had finally joined them after all, and he looked suspiciously at his wife. He had made a great point of telling her not to discuss Charles with Audrey. There was no point digging into old wounds. He knew Charlie was still sensitive on the subject, and Audrey might well be too. It was obviously an affair that had meant a great deal to both of them. And the only thing he regretted on their behalf was that they hadn't worked it out. They were both so very much alike, and Charlotte was so very different.

The two women didn't speak of it again, but everything Vi had said stuck in Audrey's mind, as she tried to tell herself again and again that it was over, that she couldn't love him any more . . . he was married.

But it still seemed impossible to believe. All she could remember were the endless hours of making love on the Orient Express, or the wonders of watching the sun come up as they hovered on a mountaintop in Tibet, sitting in a tiny uncomfortable little train. She was so grateful to have done it all now. Without that, she would have no memories to draw on. Again and again she thought of what Vi had said, about Charlotte making life so easy for him . . . 'she was dancing through hoops for him' . . . and yet that still didn't seem like an adequate reason to get married. He was different from that, she knew, and it wouldn't have been reason enough, unless she had driven him to it by refusing him again, and he had done it out of anger. But he was more sensible than that as well, and she lay in her bed at night thinking about him, and telling herself that it didn't matter why he had married Charlotte. He had. And now Audrey had to forget him.

She tried unsuccessfully to put him out of her mind during the pleasant weeks at Antibes, and she was greatly intrigued when they caught a glimpse of Wally Simpson, and Edward, Prince of Wales. He said a few words to James when they met, and Audrey was introduced to both of them. James seemed to think she'd have something in common with Mrs Simpson because they were both American, although Mrs Simpson did nothing more than shake her hand, Audrey was stunned by how elegantly dressed she was, even in Antibes. She looked as though she had just stepped off the cover of *Vogue*, in a linen dress and perfectly groomed hair, a small elegant straw hat, and shoes that were obviously custom made, and she was struck by her beautiful pearls, and by how adoringly the Prince looked at her as they walked away. He was an extremely handsome man, and Audrey was excited to have met them. She chatted with Vi about them at length, and they discussed the extent of the scandal. Mrs Simpson was of course divorced, and everyone was shocked at the Prince's involvement with her. She had hoped to catch a glimpse of the Murphys again too, but tragedy had hit them hard that year, and she never saw them. They had lost their son, Baoth, to spinal meningitis in March that year, and their older little boy, Patrick, had had a relapse of tuberculosis. The gilded life had grown suddenly tarnished.

But another couple arrived at the villa to distract them. They were good friends of Violet and James, or at least she was. She had been the Baroness Ursula von Mann and she and Vi had gone to boarding school together as young girls. She had only recently married an economist named Karl Rosen. She was now 'merely' Ursula Rosen, or Ushi as she was called. She had blonde curls, big green eyes, freckles, dimples and a wonderful laugh and she told shocking stories about her friends and family in Munich. They had a large schloss, and she came to the South of France every year, she explained in her German accent, and now they were on their honeymoon. They had been to Vienna and Paris, and now they were here, and in September they were going to Venice and Rome and then back to Berlin where Karl lived. Her father had insisted on buying them an enormous house, and apparently he was concerned but not overly upset that Karl was Jewish. There were admittedly some ripples in Germany just then about Jews, she explained, and her father had warned her not to irritate any of the important Nazis when they met. She had strong anti-Nazi opinions which she could only voice here, in the South of France, but none of them felt that Hitler was going to bother Jews of any stature. Karl had a doctorate after all, he had written several books, he taught at the University of Berlin, and he was an important man in Germany. He was also very funny when he drank a lot of champagne, and the five of them had a wonderful time in the villa. Audrey was relaxed and happy and suntanned during the last week of August, as she tried to decide what to do next. She had left herself open to spend several months in London with Charles, and now that wasn't going to happen.

'Come to Venice with us,' Ushi suggested as they lay on the terrace soaking up the sun. She was wearing Karl's straw hat over her golden curls and she looked extremely pretty.

But Audrey laughed at the suggestion. 'On your honeymoon? Now there's a thought. I'm sure Karl would be thrilled.'

'*Ja*, I'm sure he would be.' His voice boomed from the doorway and he came to perch on Ushi's chair. 'Why don't you come with us, Audrey?'

'I can't do that, Karl.'

'Why not?'

'You two should be alone. It's your honeymoon, for heaven's sake.' He leaned over and whispered for all to hear. 'We could make a *ménage à trois, ja?*'

'*Nein.*' She laughed, and turned to see a car pull up, and two people alight. The man had his back turned, and the woman was tall and thin, with a large picture hat, and a very tailored white dress with broad shoulders. She heard the sound of English voices as Vi greeted them in the garden and they went into the house as one of the servants carried their luggage. Vi hadn't told them there would be more guests and she wondered if she should offer them Molly's room. Vi was such a good sport about unexpected houseguests that Audrey wondered if these newcomers had actually been expected.

'Do you know who they are?' Ushi asked Audrey lazily and she shook her head. 'Neither do I.' And then she smiled at her new friend. 'I'm so glad we met you, Audrey . . . and little Molly.' Ushi hoped to have a baby soon and they were already trying to get her pregnant. They wanted six children, they had already agreed, and they wanted to get started as soon as possible. Ushi was thirty-one, after all, and Karl was thirty-five. They were both exactly the same age as James and Vi. Audrey was the baby of the group at twenty-nine, and they teased her from time to time about it. But as they chatted now, Violet suddenly came out to where they sat, with a large pitcher of lemonade and a nervous glance in the direction of Audrey. Ushi saw it first, but Audrey didn't seem to notice as she poured the fruit juice into glasses for them all, and chatted amiably with Karl. The newcomers stepped out onto the veranda, and the man who walked out behind the well-dressed Englishwoman looked visibly shocked as he saw Audrey. The others were aware of it before she turned around, and when she did, she stood rooted to the spot, and dropped her glass which shattered on the terrace and cut her foot badly. Everyone rushed forward to help her to her seat, and Karl proffered a white damask napkin to stanch the blood, but she insisted that someone get a towel, she didn't want to ruin Violet's napkins.

'Oh for heaven's sake, Audrey, don't be a fool.' She applied the napkin to the gash herself, and there was suddenly confusion and fuss everywhere, as their eyes finally met. There was no avoiding it forever anyway, and Violet felt Audrey's pain as she proffered a hand to Charlie.

'Hello, Charles. Sorry for the drama as you entered. I'm not always that clumsy.' She smiled and felt her whole body shake as she looked at him and then his wife, and no one made any move to introduce them. There was an electricity in the air that was almost painful. 'How do you do, I'm Audrey Driscoll.' She held out her hand and the tall, attractive young woman looked her over and then shook her hand. There was nothing warm in her eyes as she looked at Audrey.

'I'm Charlotte Parker-Scott. How do you do?'

'Well, everybody, shall we move inside while they clean things up?' There was glass all over the terrace, and Violet was a nervous wreck. 'Everyone wear shoes, please.' She was shooing them all inside and Audrey apologised profusely for the chaos she had created. They both knew why, and Ushi also sensed that this man's arrival had caused Audrey great pain, but one could read nothing on her face as she hobbled inside with Karl's assistance. He offered to carry her but she declined, taking refuge in her room to clean up, and put on a bandage. Vi joined her there moments later, with a look of anguish on her face as she wrung her hands. 'Audrey, I had no idea . . . you must believe me . . . so like Charlie to show up like that . . . they weren't expected. . . .'

'It doesn't matter. It would have happened sooner or later.'

'But not here. For heaven's sake, you came here to forget him, or at least I assume so.'

'Maybe this is the best cure. A vaccination of Charles Parker-Scott.' And then, as she held a damp cloth to her cut foot she looked unhappily up at her friend. 'She's a very pretty woman, Vi. I suppose that explains it.'

Violet waved a frantic hand. 'Don't be ridiculous. She isn't one tenth as pretty as you are. And she's as cold as an iceberg.' Even in the few moments she had seen her, Audrey had sensed that about her. She was businesslike and cool, and very much in control. 'They're only staying the night. I told Charles they can't stay. I can't have you made uncomfortable like that.'

'Don't be ridiculous, Vi. Besides, I want to travel a little bit anyway. And Ushi and Karl suggested that I go to Italy with them.' She didn't want to go with them, she didn't think it was fair to them, but it was better than staying here now, and she could use them as an excuse to leave, and then part company with them after a day or two. But she didn't want to stay here with Charlie and his new wife, that much was certain.

'Please, Audrey, please . . . they'll leave tomorrow, I swear. . . .' She felt terrible about the pain that had been caused her friend, enough for her to drop her glass and cut her foot. But worst of all had been the look on her face when she first saw Charlie. It was a look of such anguish and despair that it took one's breath away. The magnitude of her loss was written all over her face, and Charlie couldn't possibly not have seen it. Unfortunately, Charlotte had seen it too, and she was discussing it with Charlie in an undertone on the terrace at that moment.

'You didn't tell me she'd be here.' She knew precisely who she was, and she suspected just how much she had once meant to Charlie. She had recognised all the signs when he'd returned from San Francisco the year before, and she had taken full advantage of his determination to put her behind him. She didn't want the memories revived now. She had won him, and she was going to keep him.

'I had no idea.' He was painfully quiet and their eyes met. 'It never occurred to me that she would be.' He had been wondering about it himself, how she had managed to leave her grandfather in San Francisco.

'I think we should go to a hotel.'

But his face set in a way Charlotte didn't like. 'I'm not going to run away from her, Charlotte.'

'And I'm not going to live under the same roof with her.' Charlotte's eyes were like black rocks and her jaw was tense as she spoke through clenched teeth. 'Besides, it's not good for me to get nervous.' He looked at her and sighed. It was going to be a long six and a half months. Whenever she reminded him of her condition she was able to get her way, and Charlie wasn't going to risk upsetting her now.

'Let's just try it for tonight. If it's too difficult, we'll go to a hotel tomorrow. I promise. But if we leave now it will be obvious to everyone, and it will upset Vi and James.'

Charlotte was smart enough not to push him, and she stood watching Charles with piercing eyes, particularly when Audrey emerged from her room a few minutes later in a white linen trouser suit *à la* Dietrich. The snowy white set off her deep tan and her copper hair, and Charlie thought he had never seen her look more lovely. He turned away and went inside to help himself to another drink. Charlotte was right. This wasn't going to be easy.

Audrey spent the rest of the afternoon out shopping with Ushi and Karl, and when she came back, she took Molly to the kitchen to feed her. All of Vi's maids were in love with the little girl so there was a constant array of adoring baby-sitters, but Audrey didn't like to leave her very often. It was comforting to fall back into her routine now, cutting up little bits of cooked chicken for her, and smiling when she laughed and played peekaboo with her napkin. Molly was the only sunshine in Audrey's life, and she realised now that she always would be. It was excruciating to be here with Charles, and it took every ounce of courage she had to go down to dinner that night. She took special care to look her best. Despite what Vi said, she found Charlotte formidable competition. She wore exquisite clothes, and had impeccable taste, and Audrey felt dowdy beside her. She was one of those women who just reeked of money and power, and if it weren't for her brilliant mind, Audrey would have been shocked at Charlie marrying a woman like that. But she was the kind of woman men love to talk to.

'You look lovely tonight, my dear.' James complimented Audrey as she sailed into the room in a blue silk dress that revealed her honey-coloured shoulders and matched her eyes. He knew she needed a strong arm to lean on, and he offered his when they went into the dining room a little while later. Violet had seated her as far as possible from Charles, and she had even added a few more friends to the evening. She wanted to make the group as large as possible, so that Audrey and Charles would not be forced to be together. And the evening went surprisingly well. Only Audrey and her hosts knew how difficult it was for her. No one else would have suspected. Except Charlotte, who kept a sharp eye on Charles, and who had been especially charming and witty all night, as though to show Audrey whom he had married instead, as though to show her that she would never have measured up anyway.

'And what do you do?' she asked Audrey pointedly in a lull at dinner.

Audrey had looked at her and smiled, speaking very calmly, and no one saw her hands shake as she answered. 'I take care of my daughter.'

'How nice.' Charlotte smiled. Everyone knew that she was the future managing director of Beardsley's.

'Don't be so modest about your photographs, Audrey,' Violet piped up from the other end. 'She's very, very good.' She looked at Charlotte with barely concealed fury, and Charles stared at his plate. He and Audrey were both thinking of the portrait of Madame Sun Yat-sen that had run in the London *Times* with his article and given her so much pleasure.

And then the conversation had swept over them again, like a river running over rocks, and there were no further direct confrontations. Audrey thought it the most exhausting evening she had ever survived and she wandered out to the terrace for a breath of air, while some of the others were playing charades inside. James and Vi loved playing games with their guests, and even Charlotte had joined in, and was growing to be the life of the party. Everyone wanted to play with her, because she was so good at guessing the charade. She was smart as hell, it was just a shame she wasn't warmer.

Audrey sat down in one of the comfortable wicker chairs with a sigh and closed her eyes as she lay her head back in the moonlight. And she jumped a mile when she heard his voice, barely more than a whisper beside her.

'It's not easy, is it, Aud?' She opened her eyes, and at first said nothing, and then she sighed and nodded, offering him a small wintry smile.

'I suppose I shouldn't have come. They're your friends.' It was the first time she had spoken to him directly and their eyes told a long, sad tale. Neither of them pretended not to feel anything. It was obvious to anyone that they were both in pain.

'You belong here as much as I do.' He was faintly afraid that Charlotte would see him out there, talking to her, and make a scene later. She would have let him do anything in the world he wanted, except talk to Audrey. She was far too aware of the danger. 'I should have called Violet before we came . . . I never thought . . .' His eyes searched hers, wanting to feel the anger he had felt for her a year before, but it was gone suddenly, and all he felt now was sorrow.

'Grandfather died in June.'

'I'm sorry.' And he was. He knew how much she loved him. He knew better than anyone. But she only nodded. And then he asked her the question she had feared most. 'Why did you come here?'

She held her breath and then answered. 'To see . . . James and Vi.' The hesitation was only for a fraction of a second. And he turned his head away to look out at the water, silver dipped in the moonlight.

'I was half crazy when I came back from America last year. . . .'

She shook her head, not wanting to hear what he would say. It was too late. It didn't matter any more. It was much, much too late. 'You don't owe me any explanations.'

'Don't I?' He was a little drunk, but not enough to blur what he felt, not enough to make him think her less beautiful than she was . . . not enough to make him numb and not feel the same jolt as he looked into her blue eyes. . . . 'Maybe I need to say it. I never wanted to see you again when I came back. I think I even hated you for a while. And Charlotte was very kind to me. She put balm on the wounds . . . she helped me with my work, she sobered me up when I got drunk . . . she was there for me . . . constantly . . . in just the way you had refused to be . . . she came to India with me . . . and then she came to Egypt. I was there for six months, working on my next book.' She thought there were tears in his eyes, but she couldn't tell in the moonlight. 'She was marvellous. . . .' He sounded apologetic, but Audrey couldn't tell if he was apologising to her or to Charlotte. 'And I liked her. I like her very much in fact.' He turned back to face her squarely then and she could see that he was more than a little drunk. But it didn't matter. 'The trouble is, Audrey, I don't love her.' Audrey was shocked at his words, and she stiffened in her chair. She didn't want to hear what he was going to say . . . he had no right to have them both . . . but before she could say anything to stop him, he continued. 'I told her that before I married her. I'm not rotten enough to pretend to someone that I love them. . . .' His voice softened and Audrey felt a lump rise in her throat. '. . . or brave enough to pretend that I don't . . . she said it didn't matter. She didn't expect grand passion and high romance, only loyalty and friendship. And we are friends. Good friends. I like her. . . .' He was repeating himself and Audrey was shocked, at what he had said . . . at what he had done . . . it was madness. Why had he married her? But in the next breath, he answered her question. 'I wouldn't have married her, you know. It's not enough, no matter what she thinks. You and I know better, don't we?' He sounded bitter for a moment, and Audrey stood up. She didn't want to sit there and hear him tell her that he didn't love his wife, it made it all the more cruel that he had got married. 'The bitch is, she got pregnant when we were in Egypt. It must have been at the very end.' He looked at Audrey mournfully as she wondered if her heart would actually break, or just ache dully for the rest of her life. 'She's only two and a half months pregnant now . . . doesn't show yet . . . no one knows . . . she refused to have an abortion.' His eyes were so filled with pain as he looked at the woman he loved that Audrey couldn't restrain the tears any more. 'So we'll have a baby. And we'll be friends. And we'll be very loyal.' He sounded broken and empty as he turned away. 'And she'll make my books a great success, not that I give a damn. . . .' And then his voice faded again. 'I suppose it will be nice to have a child. . . .' He was thinking of Sean, and then suddenly he turned and took two steps to where Audrey stood and he touched her shoulder with his fingertips as her whole body trembled. 'I wanted you to know why. No matter how angry I was, Audrey, I wanted you to know that I loved you. Very, very much. . . .' The tears ran slowly down her cheeks, and he bent towards her and kissed her, and then without another word, he walked back into the party.

27

In the next few days, the house at Cap d'Antibes seemed to be shrinking moment by moment. Charles and his new bride made no move to leave the day after they arrived, and despite Violet's broad hints to Charlie, he went nowhere. Instead, he followed Audrey everywhere with his eyes, and Charlotte watched him watching Audrey. It was uncomfortable for everyone else, and Audrey valiantly tried to pretend she didn't notice. She went down to the beach with Molly as much as she could, and on drives along the coast with Karl and Ushi. She went shopping in town with Vi, and spent the rest of the time in her room, claiming that she was exhausted. But she knew she couldn't stay much longer, and she was anxious to leave almost from the moment they arrived. She just didn't want to hurt Violet's feelings.

She managed to avoid Charlie as much as she could, and he didn't approach her again after the first night. They were both nursing their wounds. Audrey had finally agreed to go with Ushi and Karl, and she was just waiting for them to leave Cap d'Antibes. She couldn't wait to go, and anywhere would have been a relief after the strain of being under the same roof with Charlie and Charlotte. Again and again Audrey tried to absorb the fact that Charlotte was pregnant . . . that Charlotte was having his baby . . . the one that she never had. She knew now that the only child she would ever have was Molly.

'I take it you brought her back from China.' Audrey was startled to find Charlotte standing just behind her as she watched Molly making sand pies with James. She turned to her, and it was almost hard to breathe with the woman so close to her. She had perfect, even features, and her makeup had been impeccably applied. Her dress was from Patou, with a beautiful hat to match. Everything about her overpowered Audrey. She was almost too perfect. And she had married Charlie.

'Yes . . . I did. . . .' She tried to remember what Charlotte had asked her. It was the first time they had spoken directly. 'I brought Mai Li back from Harbin . . . I lived there for eight months.'

'I know.' Her tone said she knew more than that, as Audrey fell silent. And then she plunged the knife in with one swift blow. 'You still love him, don't you?'

'I . . .' She was so shocked she didn't know what to answer. 'I . . . think we will always be friends. It's difficult to forget things like that, but times change.' It was all she could think of to say and as diplomatic as she could manage.

'Yes, that's right, times do change. I'm glad you understand that.' She said it pointedly. 'Charles has an enormous career ahead of him. He doesn't understand that yet. One day he will be the most important nonfiction writer in the world.' The trouble was that didn't mean anything to him, as Audrey knew only too well. He had always treated his success like a pleasant surprise, it was the discoveries he enjoyed so much, the travel, the adventure, the spirit of it all. But Charlotte knew nothing about that. 'He needs a woman who can help him.' Audrey nodded, fighting back tears, and then she looked at the woman who had won him.

'The baby will mean more to him than his career.'

For a moment, Charlotte looked stunned. 'He told you about that, did he?' She did not look pleased and Audrey nodded, her eyes vague.

'He just mentioned it . . . he's very happy,' she lied. 'I'm sure you'll both be very happy.' The tears stood out in her eyes as she looked at Charlotte, who nodded. She still looked disturbed that Charlie had told her about the baby, though maybe it was just as well. She smiled now at her opponent.

'You were never right for him anyway.' Saying that seemed an enormous presumption to Audrey. What did she know about who was right for him? She didn't even know the man. She had forced him to marry her by refusing to have

271

an abortion. And Audrey suspected that she hadn't done it out of love for him, or the baby. She couldn't even imagine this woman with a child, and at exactly that moment James returned to plop a fat, wet, sandy Molly into her arms, as the little girl let out a squeal of delight and she got sand and wet kisses all over her mother.

Audrey went on a drive later that afternoon with Karl and Ushi, and Ushi smiled at Audrey as they hung on to their hats and flying hair in the open car. 'We thought we would leave tomorrow. Will you come?' Audrey had been vacillating about not going with them, but she was desperate to leave Antibes now and she felt she needed an excuse to make a graceful exit. 'We go only to San Remo.' It wasn't far, but the atmosphere was very different, very Italian, and less chic, but very pretty.

Karl looked at her now. 'Will you come?'

Audrey smiled. It was her best way out, and she was crazy about Ushi and Karl. 'I'd love it. I'll only stay a few days, and then I'll let you two go on. I might go to Rome for a week or two before I go back to London.' And from there, she still had no idea where she was going. All her plans had gone awry, and she was in no hurry to go back to San Francisco.

'Why don't you come to Venice with us?' It was the most romantic place in the world, and the memory of her two days there with Charlie sprang instantly to mind.

'I don't think so.' She couldn't bear the pain of seeing it again. 'That's for honeymooners, not for old maids.' They hooted and yelled at the sound of her words, and she laughed and insisted that she was.

'You are the best-looking old maid I have ever seen!' Karl glanced at her appreciatively and she laughed and scolded him, but Ushi didn't care. The two of them were happy and well matched. They had been in love with each other for six years before they married. 'We will talk about Venice when we get to San Remo.'

'Never mind.' But she had at least agreed to go to San Remo with them and it would make it easier to leave the next day. She told Violet when they got back, and she was sorry to see them all go, and furious with Charlie. She complained bitterly to James that night that Charlie had driven everyone away, and ruined her party.

'He didn't drive everyone away, darling, just Audrey. Karl and Ushi were leaving anyway, and it'll be fun for her to go with them. She ought to visit them in Berlin sometime too. Ushi always gives such marvellous parties.' He smiled benevolently at his wife, kissed her tenderly on the lips and she was greatly cheered by his suggestion. A trip to Berlin was a wonderful idea, maybe they could all go. She brought it up the next day at breakfast, as they all, except Charlotte and Molly, sat around the breakfast table. Charlotte was still in bed, and Molly was being watched by James and Alexandra's nurse while Audrey had breakfast. She was very happy playing with them, and they treated her like a little dolly, especially Alexandra, who loved her.

'It was James's idea,' Violet chortled with glee, 'wouldn't it be fun if we all went to Berlin once the lovebirds get settled. We could stay at the Bayerischer Hotel and go to the opera.' Vi loved going to the opera in Berlin. She loved going to the opera anywhere, and more than that, she loved a party. But Ushi was enchanted with the idea too.

'We could give our first ball, Karl.' Her eyes danced as her mind whirled. And then she glanced at Violet, 'And you will not stay at the hotel. You will stay with us. And you, too,' she glanced at Audrey, and without thinking her glance took in Charlie. Suddenly they were all animatedly discussing their plans to go to Berlin and everyone was chatting and laughing, as Charlie began to tease them all, and told them funny stories of the last time he'd been in Berlin. He even teased Audrey and she laughed, and he regaled them all with a tale about her on the train in China, and everyone roared, especially Audrey. It was no secret to anyone in the group that they had been lovers, and their laughter was a nice note on which to end their vacation together, and no one even noticed Charlotte come into the room.

273

She never raised her voice, but when she spoke, it sent an electric jolt down Audrey's spine, and Charlie instantly fell silent.

'What's this about a trip to Berlin?' It was obvious she didn't approve, and then she smiled at Charles. 'Actually, I want you to meet a German publisher there.' She smiled at him. She wanted his books translated into seven languages before the year ended. It was part of what she referred to as her 'master plan'. It was only when discussing things like that that she really came alive. 'We could combine business with pleasure.' But the pleasure seemed to have died with her arrival.

To fill the uncomfortable silence, Violet chatted with Karl about their travel plans for the next week. He mentioned Venice, and Charlie's eyes instantly reached out to Audrey, but she looked away, and busied herself folding her napkin. They were going to be in Venice for the last week of their honeymoon, and after that, Karl had to be in Berlin by the end of September. He would begin teaching at the university again then, and Ushi was looking forward to the beginning of the social season. James gave them several suggestions about good restaurants, and a few side trips he loved, and a little while later the three travellers came downstairs, Audrey with Molly in her arms. For a woman who had never had children before, she had become extremely adept at taking her everywhere with her and Molly was happy and good-humoured wherever she went. She seemed to think it was all one big exciting adventure.

'Take care of yourself, Audrey,' Violet admonished. 'And call us to let us know when you're returning to London. We should be back ourselves fairly soon and you'll stay with us as soon as we get home. Before, if you like.' She always kept a housekeeper there, and she gave Audrey a firm hug and an extra squeeze. She was going to miss her. James kissed her as well, and everyone said goodbye to Karl and Ushi, and then suddenly Charlie was looking into Audrey's eyes, and there was such depth of sadness there that Violet had to turn away as she watched them. She knew Audrey had been avoiding him when it was time to go, but Charlie had come out of his room to say goodbye, and he was looking down at her with such tenderness that Audrey thought her heart would break.

'Goodbye, Charles.' At least she knew now that it was over. There were no more delusions that they might be together again someday. They both knew they wouldn't.

'Say hello to Venice for me.' His words said everything . . . that he still loved her and he remembered, but she only shook her head, holding Molly close to her.

'I won't be going. That's for Ushi and Karl.' He nodded. He understood perfectly. He never wanted to go back there again either. It would have been far too painful.

'Perhaps I'll see you in London sometime.' She didn't answer, she only looked at him and then turned away, and a few moments later she got in the car after kissing Vi and James again, and drove off with the Rosens.

28

'Are you feeling all right, Charlotte?' He looked at his wife solicitously after Audrey left, trying to feel some of the same things for her – but they just weren't there. He had to remind himself that the baby she was carrying was his, but even that didn't seem real yet. Nothing showed, and she was so brave about it that she hardly ever mentioned it. It was almost as though they both forgot it at times, but he smiled at her now, anxious to be kind to her, as though to remind himself that she was his wife and not Audrey.

But the house in Antibes was like a tomb without the Rosens and Audrey. He and James took a long walk on the beach, but he didn't share any of what was on his mind. Lady Vi made an effort to get to know Charlotte better, but she found that she disliked her as much as she had at first. There was nothing warm about the woman, nothing gentle, nothing soft, and Lady Vi wondered how Charlie stood her. It wasn't enough that she was intelligent.

'He might as well be married to a man for God's sake,' Vi complained to James in the privacy of their bedroom later that night. 'How on earth could he marry her?' Charlie had finally told him.

'She's pregnant.'

'Oh my God.' Violet stared at him in shock and then shook her head. 'How awful for Charlie. Is that why he married her?'

'I think so, although he didn't put it quite that bluntly. And I'm not quite as adept as you are with rude, pointed questions.' He smiled at his wife, grateful that their life was simpler than Charlie's. 'I think he would have preferred it if she'd had an abortion. But apparently she's Catholic.'

'She is?' Lady Vi was surprised. 'I didn't think she was. And she didn't go to church on Sunday.' They were all

Church of England, and Roman Catholics were rare among their friends.

'Maybe she didn't feel well. In any case, there it is, our Charles is going to be a daddy.'

'Is he pleased?'

'I'm not sure. I think he's still a bit numb, frankly. And actually, you know, I think he likes her. They've been having an affair for quite a while, and she went out to Cairo to be with him when he was there . . . I just don't think he thought of it as a permanent thing. I think he would have preferred Audrey in that case.'

'Thank God for that . . . poor Charlie . . . and poor Audrey. What a terrible mess.' She frowned at her husband then. 'You know, I'll bet she did it on purpose.'

James laughed at her suspicious nature. 'It's been done before, although I don't really think she's the type. She's too businesslike to resort to feminine wiles.'

'Don't be so sure. I think she's excited by the idea of building Charlie's career, and having him like a puppet on a string. Also, he's damn good-looking and I think she decided to get what she wanted. She'd never have got him otherwise.'

'Good Lord, you have an evil mind. Is that how you got me? Plotting and planning?'

'Of course,' she beamed happily, 'but at least I didn't use a cheap trick like getting pregnant.'

He rolled his eyes at the memory. 'I wish you had . . . you drove me mad for damn close to two years . . . bloody fanatical virgin. . . .' She blushed at the memory, and he ran a hand up the inside of her thigh and caressed her, and a moment later both of them forgot Audrey and Charlie.

29

The days Audrey and the Rosens spent in San Remo were easy and fun, and Audrey felt more relaxed than she had during the last few days in Antibes with Charlie and his wife around. It had been a terrible strain trying not to cause a scene, and dealing with her own feelings at the same time. She missed Violet and James but she was happy to have left, and San Remo was always fun, even now at the end of the summer.

Audrey had intended to leave Karl and Ushi there, and go on to Italy by train, but they were so insistent that she at least go as far as Milan with them, that she finally relented. She planned to go on to Rome after that, while they went to Venice, and in the meantime, they had a fabulous time in Milan staying with friends of Karl's in a palazzo the likes of which Audrey had never seen. There were frescoes on the walls, incredible tapestries that belonged in museums, and paintings by everyone from Renoir to Goya to da Vinci with an enormous collection by della Robbia. It was an extraordinary place, and a marvellous holiday. Their host was a *Principe*, a prince, and his wife, *Principessa*, and Audrey had a marvellous time staying up until dawn with them every night. They all drank too much wine, and went to every party in town. They even gave a 'little ball' for them, which was an impromptu affair for three hundred of their closest friends in Karl and Ushi's honour. Audrey wore one of the evening dresses she'd brought for the ship, and actually felt very plain next to the extravagantly dressed Italian women in their heavy emerald and ruby and sapphire necklaces and diamond tiaras.

They all hated to leave when the time came, Audrey most of all, and now her proposed trip to Rome seemed terribly dull as she sat eating breakfast one morning with Molly. She was thinking of going back to London earlier than planned, and secretly bemoaning the fact that she had nothing to do now. Maybe Violet would join her on a brief trip to Paris. But that morning Ushi and Karl brought up the trip to Venice again, and they absolutely insisted that she join them. They were certain that they didn't want time alone, and if they did they would let her know, they promised.

'We will be lonely without you now, Audrey.' And it was Molly they especially adored. Ushi scooped her up in her arms and wailed over the fact that she would never have a baby that looked like Molly, as Karl and Audrey laughed. 'I'm afraid not, my darling,' he teased her. Unfortunately, thus far, they had no reason to suspect she was pregnant yet, but they were having a good time trying. 'You must come with us. That's all!' He tried to look very Prussian as he said it and only succeeded in looking like a petulant child. He was a very handsome man, though different from Charlie or James. He had dark, exotic looks in a very Semitic way, and Audrey could easily see why Ushi thought he was handsome. She wondered then if she would ever find anyone for herself. Everyone seemed to have found the perfect mate, Violet in James, Ushi in Karl, and even their hosts in Milan seemed perfectly suited. She was beginning to feel the pain of being alone all the time, and couldn't imagine now what she had done with her life before Molly. 'So will you come?' They looked expectantly at her and she could no longer think of an excuse not to go with them.

'I won't so much as speak to you if I do, you know. Venice is the most romantic place in the world, and I won't spoil it for you.'

Ushi laughed mischievously and winked at Karl and he laughed and looked at Audrey, putting a finger to his lips, as though he were about to impart a deep, dark secret. 'We've already been there last year. . . .'

Ushi tittered naughtily and all three of them laughed. It was 1935, after all, not 1912, and all of them had had their little flings. Venice was where her love affair with Charlie had begun, and she was afraid to go to Venice with them. She was afraid that the memories would be too painful.

'You will come?' Ushi looked at her like a hopeful child and Audrey laughed and threw up her hands. They were impossible to resist, she had too much fun with them, and she hardly felt guilty any more for intruding on their honeymoon, although she knew she should have.

'All right. I'll come.' A cheer went up from the group, and they set out the next day in high spirits. They left their car at the station, and piled into a gondola like happy tourists as the *gondoliere* serenaded them all the way to the Gritti Palace. He asked them if they had been to Venice before and all three of them nodded, and as he took them beneath the Bridge of Sighs, he told them all to close their eyes and hold their breath and their wishes would come true. Ushi and Karl held hands as they did it. Audrey only smiled down at Molly in her arms, she had nothing left to make wishes for, and she was desperately fighting the memory of Charlie.

It was difficult just being there, and being so close to the love Ushi and Karl shared made it even harder. But on the other hand, she knew that if she could survive returning to Venice again, she could survive anything, and they were good sports about taking her everywhere with them. Eventually Audrey confided in Ushi. She had to share her feelings with someone. It was too painful being there, remembering it all, and knowing it was over forever. She told Ushi about their trip to China . . . her staying in Harbin . . . his coming to San Francisco . . . and her refusal to drop everything to marry him . . . and then his marriage to Charlotte.

'How terrible for you to meet him in Antibes.' She understood fully now how painful it must have been for her, and she was even sorry they had urged her to come to Venice. It seemed terribly unkind to have done it to her, now that she knew all the details. 'You know, I said to Karl, I don't think he loves her.' She was referring to Charlotte. 'She is a very smart woman, and Karl said he liked her. But she is not a woman with heart . . . you know, Audrey?' Audrey smiled at her English.

'He's married to her anyway, Ushi.'

'It must be very hard for him too.' Audrey nodded, but it didn't change anything. Now she had to forget him. 'You must meet someone else.' She was thinking of a friend of Karl's, a teacher at the university. He was forty years old, and a widower with two young children, and Ushi was very fond of him, much as Vi was of Charles. 'You will come to visit us.' She didn't say more for fear that Audrey would resist her.

For the rest of their stay, they did all the appropriate things, museums, churches, they visited the glass factories, and eventually Audrey stopped imagining that she saw Charlie at every corner. It had helped baring her soul to Ushi. And the night before they were due to leave, Karl turned to her with a gentle smile. He had grown very fond of their American friend, and they were both crazy about Molly.

'Why don't you come to Germany with us?'

Audrey laughed. 'Haven't you seen enough of me, Karl? It really is becoming a *ménage à trois*.' She smiled at his wife. 'I should think you'd be happy to get rid of me.' She was taking the train to London the next day, and they were going back to Berlin to the new home Ushi was so anxious to decorate, and Karl had to get back to the university.

'It would keep Ushi happy while I am working. James and Violet won't be back in London yet anyway.' He knew she would be staying with them. 'You will be too lonely there without them.' He was always concerned about her, and they had both been marvellous during the whole trip. And she had to admit, she was tempted to go with them.

'I really don't want to impose. . . .' She hesitated honestly, not to be coy, but they were so insistent that she return to Berlin with them for a week or two, that she relented. When they left the next morning, they were all in high spirits. Venice had been beautiful, but Audrey was happy to leave it.

The train they took followed the same route as the train she had taken with Charlie years before to join the Orient Express, but this time when the train reached Salzburg, instead of going east, they headed towards Munich, with a stop across the border in Rosenheim.

Ushi was sorry she hadn't had time to warn her family that they would be stopping in Munich for an hour. It wasn't enough time to go to her parents' house, but she thought she'd at least give them a call if it was a decent hour, or maybe even warn them from Rosenheim, if she could get a connection through the telegraph office there. The three of them laughed as Molly slept on one of the velvet banquettes as they finally left Italy, crossed Austria, and approached Germany. They felt the train slow down as they ordered another bottle of champagne and some caviar, and they all noticed soldiers and uniformed officers on the platform outside, conferring with the conductor and various officials from the train. The conductor finally shrugged and waved them inside. Ushi frowned and looked at Karl.

'What do you suppose that's all about?'

'Some of the *Führer*'s men.' He said it derisively but in a soft voice. He hadn't thought much of Hitler from the first, and he didn't like his strident speeches about Aryans, but he knew enough to keep his political views to himself. Others at the university had had trouble the year before, and the Nazis seemed to be quick to label intellectuals Communists if they didn't share their Nazi views. So he kept quiet usually except with Ushi of course, and he had been pretty outspoken with Charlie and James in the South of France. But now he seemed very relaxed about it as the porter arrived with the caviar, and a soldier standing directly behind him.

'Passports, please,' the soldier said, looking disapprovingly at the luxuriously appointed living room of the compartment where they sat. Karl handed over all three, and the soldier glanced at the American one first. '*Amerikanisch?*' he asked Audrey with a terse smile.

'Yes.' She was embarrassed to be caught slathering caviar on a piece of toast when he asked, or did all Americans do that? She smiled at him, and the soldier glanced over at the sleeping child.

'To whom belongs the little girl?'

'That's my daughter.' Audrey was quick to speak up. She always carried copies of Mai Li's adoption papers with her, but there seemed to be no trouble about that. He handed the passport back to her with a curt nod, and quickly turned to the passports the Rosens had given him.

'You do not have the same name. You are friends?' His eyes were warm, and Karl was quick to explain.

'We are just returning from our wedding trip. We didn't have time to change our passports before we left.' The soldier smiled as though pleased, but Audrey didn't like the way he looked at him.

He stared right into Karl's eyes. 'You are a Jew, aren't you?' Audrey was shocked at the blunt words and she watched her friend. The muscles tightened in Karl's jaw but his eyes gave away nothing.

'I am.' He didn't falter for an instant.

'And your wife is not. Jewish. Is that right?' He had seen the 'von' in her maiden name and knew that she wasn't. He took the passports and rapidly left the compartment without saying more. Audrey wanted to ask why he hadn't given the passports back, but she was afraid to say anything.

'They've got even more charming in the last two months apparently.' Karl looked annoyed and Ushi quickly touched his hand.

'Don't say anything, *Schatz*. They like to feel important. He probably got annoyed by the caviar and champagne.' Karl only shrugged with a smile.

'Jealous peasants, to hell with them.' The three of them laughed and at that moment the soldier returned accompanied by two officers. They did not mince words, but went directly to where Karl sat next to Ushi.

'Are you aware of the Nuremberg Laws?' The tallest of

the officers addressed Karl and Audrey saw that he had a razor-thin scar running lengthwise down his cheek and she wondered if he had won it in a duel. He wore the insignia of the SS on his lapels and his eyes were as cold as steel as he looked them over.

Karl seemed to remain very calm. 'I am not aware of the Nuremberg Laws.' He looked respectful but casual, and he gently held Ushi's hand. Her palm was damp with sweat, and his hand was trembling slightly.

'There was a congress meeting in Nuremberg one week ago, and the law of September fifteenth was enacted, making it punishable by death for a Jew to have intercourse with an Aryan.' He glanced rapidly at Ushi, back to Karl, and the threesome group was stunned into silence. Karl looked as though he were in shock. 'You can't be serious.'

The officer glared at him. 'The *Führer* is always serious, sir. This is an extremely serious offence.'

Karl's face had gone white. 'This woman is my wife.'

'That does not alter the crime.' He clicked both heels and stared at him. 'You will come with us now. You are under arrest, Herr Rosen.' He purposely omitted his title of *Doktor*.

For an instant they sat without moving, totally shocked, and then as two soldiers appeared and grabbed Karl by the arms, Ushi let out a horrible scream and grabbed at him. He told her to calm down but he looked desperately at her and then Audrey, begging her with his eyes to take care of Ushi. There was nothing he could do. He had to go with the soldiers. Audrey held tightly to her hand as they led Karl away and the two women stared at him in horror. Then as though rapidly coming to her senses, Audrey told the porter to unload their bags. They had to get off at once and find out where Karl had been taken.

Ushi was hysterical as Audrey tried to appear calm, and spoke to the porter in halting German to arrange for a taxi to drive them into town. This was utterly crazy. She kept urging Ushi to sit down on one of the bags, and she was trying to keep an eye on her as her mind raced and Ushi sobbed, and by then Mai Li was crying too, frightened by the tumult she sensed around her. Audrey's heart was pounding horribly as the train pulled away and they were left alone in the station. They had seen Karl driven away in an ominous black wagon and now Ushi wailed at her, sobbing uncontrollably.

'Where did they take him? . . . oh God . . . where did they take him?'

'We'll find out.' It was impossible. It was all a bad dream . . . 'intercourse with an Aryan' punishable by death? . . . they were crazy. Audrey spoke to the stationmaster as best she could and a car arrived to take them to a hotel, where Audrey dropped their bags in the lobby, demanded a room, any room, and immediately asked for a telephone connection to Ushi's father. It calmed Ushi down a little to have to go through the motions of calling him, but as soon as she had him on the line, she became hysterical again, and Audrey had to explain to him what had happened. It was a nightmare.

'My God . . . they did what? . . . oh my God, where is he?'

'We don't know. I was going to contact the police after we called you.'

'Don't do anything!' He sounded frightened, and he promised to make some calls and get back to her. And while they waited, Audrey urged Ushi to lie down on the room's narrow bed. She lay there, sobbing and Audrey brought her a glass of water which she sipped gratefully, looking at Audrey with huge, anguished eyes as Audrey tried to pacify both Mai Li and Ushi.

'Oh my God . . . what if they kill him? . . . oh my God. . . .' Ushi clung to her like a frightened child, and it seemed to take her father forever to call them back. But at last the phone rang and an operator announced a call from Munich. It was Audrey whom Manfred von Mann wanted to speak to, and not Ushi. He told Audrey what he was afraid to say to his daughter.

'They killed twelve men in Munich last week for precisely the same crime. We were thinking of calling them and telling

285

them not to come home. But the others were labourers, merchants, some indigents that the Communists made a fuss about. No one of Karl's stature, of course. We didn't think this would happen to him.' But it had and Audrey was terrified now that they might not get him out. It was hard to believe what Ushi's father was saying.

'Did they tell you where he is?'

'Not yet. But someone I know in the High Command is going to call me. How is Ushi?' He sounded like a nice man and Audrey glanced over her shoulder at her friend. She was trembling on the bed with a glazed look. She was in shock and Audrey was worried.

'Not very well, I'm afraid.' It was the only answer she could give.

'I will come to Rosenheim myself.'

'I think that's a very good idea.'

But when he arrived Ushi was hysterical because they had had no news all day. Ushi had insisted on calling the local police herself and then going there but they refused to let her see Karl all day despite all of her entreaties and the names she dropped on his behalf. They would have none of it and said that he was a condemned man and not to be spoken to. He had committed a crime against the Reich, and that she owed it to her people now to marry an Aryan, and produce children for the Reich. She got more and more hysterical as she talked to them, and she almost hit one of them, and would have, if Audrey had not physically pulled her away and forced her to go back to the hotel with her.

Audrey was aghast at what was happening to them, and once the Baron von Mann had arrived she had a moment alone to talk to him and ask him what he thought would happen to Karl. He looked grim as he answered her, thinking of the men who had been killed for the same reason the previous week. 'I don't know. They may send him to a camp. They are sending many people away now. Jews like Karl. I warned her of that.' He looked agonised by his own helplessness. 'They are capable of anything.'

And they were. The generals Baron von Mann knew insisted they couldn't do anything to help. According to the Nuremberg Law of September fifteenth of that year, Karl Rosen was guilty of a crime punishable by death. Audrey came to hate the words they heard again and again, and when the Baron returned to the two waiting women at midnight he did not have good news for them.

'They're taking him somewhere else tonight. I'm not sure where, but the officer in charge promised to tell us tomorrow. I'll go there first thing.'

'Taking him somewhere?' Ushi's eyes were wild, gone was the laughing girl of only hours before. She was barely recognisable now. Her hair was unkempt, her makeup was smeared, her face was tear-stained and there was even mascara on her dress from the tears that had fallen there, but she didn't care about any of it, only about Karl. 'Where are they taking him?'

'I promise you, darling. We will find out as soon as we can.' She wailed in her father's arms, and he cried at his own helplessness and the horror of his son-in-law's fate. He even regretted letting her marry him now, if this was the kind of grief she must bear. But he bore no malice to Karl, and he went directly to the police station again the next day, and was told that Karl had been taken to Unterhaching to a facility there. It was a long silent drive, and all that they heard were Ushi's sobs on the way. Even little Molly was silent as Audrey held her. When they arrived, they didn't even stop at a hotel, they went directly to the police station, fearing for Karl's life, and by miracle, they saw him being loaded into a truck, wearing chains, just as they arrived. Ushi let out a piteous scream and dashed to him as Molly began to cry, and by reflex Audrey held her close and hid her eyes, and Baron von Mann stood between them and the soldiers standing by. Ushi had almost reached Karl when her father caught up to her and pulled her back. She fought him ferociously and the soldiers leading Karl shoved him viciously with their sticks and he called out as they pushed him into the truck.

'I'm all right ... I'm all right ... *Ich bin* ...' They slammed the door as Ushi stared with wide, horrified eyes. He hardly looked like the same man. His clothes had been torn and his face and head were caked with blood, and she sobbed horribly as her father held her in his arms, and a moment later the truck was gone, and the only answer to their inquiries was that the problem had been 'resolved'.

The Baron insisted that the only thing left for them to do was to go home to Munich then. He could get more information there, and there was no point staying in Unterhaching now, so they all got back in the car and drove into Munich, not stopping until they reached his schloss. He confided his daughter into her mother's arms then, and Audrey fed Molly and put her to bed after a warm bath and sat alone in her room, waiting for news of Karl. They were all in shock. It had been like a nightmare for all of them, and there seemed to be nothing they could do to save him. Later that night, seeing the light under the door, the Baron invited her to come to the library to share a schnapps with him. They spoke of the insanity of the new laws, but even here the Baron didn't feel entirely free. They spoke in whispers next to a crackling fire, behind closed doors. No one trusted anyone in Germany any more, not even in their own house. He made several phone calls again that night, but to no avail, and it was two more days before the news finally came. With much regret, he had called Karl's parents to inform them and they were grateful for everything he was trying to do. But in the end, none of it helped. He set down the phone, and cried softly into his hands, before going upstairs to tell his wife and daughter. He told his wife first, and together they went in to see Ursula, locked in her room, almost mad by then. She stared at them as they came in, and sensed instantly what they were going to tell her. Audrey heard her piteous scream from her own room, and she ran out into the hall where she waited as though something would change, someone would come ... but it was over for Karl. He was dead, murdered by Hitler's men, and as Audrey stood in the long draughty hall she remembered the sound of his laughter, the warmth of his eyes, and she realised for the first time in her life what a rare gift love was . . . how ephemeral . . . how quickly gone . . . suddenly Ushi was no longer a bride . . . but a widow . . . Karl was gone . . . and it could have happened to anyone. She suddenly realised how lucky she and Charlie had been, and how foolish he was to waste his life now, with a woman he didn't love, and who had trapped him.

It was hours before Audrey was able to see Ushi that night, and when at last she did, there was nothing she could say to her. She only held her in her arms and let the girl cry. She sounded as though her heart would break, and when Audrey looked into her eyes again, she knew that Ursula von Mann Rosen would never again be the same woman.

30

The phone rang in Antibes just after six o'clock the next morning, James heard it first and groped over Violet's head to reach for it.

'What time is it?' she murmured at him, squinting at the clock she couldn't see. The sun had just come up, but it was only two hours after they had gone to bed, and they had all drunk far too much champagne. Charlie and Charlotte were still there and Violet didn't like her any more than she had before, and she really didn't give a damn any more. She couldn't imagine who was calling them now, as James sat up very straight on the edge of the bed next to her.

'Yes? . . . yes.' A long pause, a frown, and then, 'Audrey? What's wrong?' He had heard her crying on the other end and immediately suspected something terrible had happened to her. 'Did you have an accident?' Violet's heart stopped, thinking of the little girl, and she clutched James's arm instinctively. 'Oh my God . . . oh no . . .' He turned his eyes to Vi's and she looked panicky.

'What is it, James? . . . what happened to her?' He waved to her to be quiet, and carried on. The connection was far from excellent, and Audrey was much too upset for him to ask her to stop. She had had to talk to someone, and Vi and James were the only people she could call.

'My God, how terrible . . . oh the poor girl. How is she now?'

'Oh James . . .' Violet began to cry, certain that Molly had suffered a terrible accident, and James took hold of her hand and held it reassuringly, shaking his head and then mouthing to her.

'. . . it's . . . not . . . the . . . child. . . .'

'It's not?' She looked startled. Then who was it?

'Where are you now? Do you want to come back? We're

going home in a few days. It might do you good to come back here, Aud . . . all right . . . but for God's sake, get out. Wait for us in London at the house. And give me your number there. Try and get some sleep and Vi and I will call you in a few hours. Do you want to speak to her now?' He turned towards his wife hopefully, ready to hand her the phone. 'All right . . . I'll tell her that . . . and Audrey . . .' His eyes filled with tears and his voice went hoarse. 'Tell her how sorry we are.' They rang off and he sat staring at his wife. He didn't even know how to find the words, and then he sighed, and tried to remain calm. 'They've killed Karl.' It was blunt, but it told her what she had to know. She looked at him, horrified.

'Oh my God . . . James! Who killed Karl? And how is Ushi? . . . Oh no!' She began to cry, staring at him frantically, and he put an arm around her and brought her closer.

'The Nazis did it. They took him right off the train, put him in jail, and shot him. Apparently they've passed some totally insane law that makes it punishable by death for a Jew to have intercourse with an Aryan, married or not. Have you ever heard of such a thing? They're mad.' But worse than that they had killed Karl Rosen.

'Oh my God.' It was all she could say, and she cried in her husband's arms, and then they went downstairs hand in hand to have a cup of coffee. They were still sitting there at eight o'clock when Charlie came downstairs. He looked serious, and somewhat hung over, but as soon as he looked at them, he knew something was terribly wrong.

'Was that the phone I heard around six o'clock?' James nodded and Vi began to cry again. 'Oh my God . . . what is it, Vi?' He sat down next to her, and James told him what had happened to Karl, as Charlie sat staring at them.

'It can't be . . . they can't do a thing like that!' His voice was suddenly loud in the quiet room . . . they had been so happy . . . so carefree . . . so much fun . . . and so much in love. 'They're insane.'

'Yes, they are.'

'Is Ushi all right?' he asked James.

'I don't suppose she is. At least they didn't touch her anyway. They were on their way back to Berlin, but they're at her parents' in Munich now. Audrey's there with her.'

'What's she doing there?' He looked troubled at that. He didn't like to think of her anywhere near a horror like that, and it pained him to think that she had seen it happen.

'I didn't ask, but I imagine she was still travelling with them.'

'Is she all right?'

'She was terribly upset, understandably, and I told her we'd call her back in a few hours.' Charles nodded and poured a shot of whisky into his coffee cup, and offered the same to James. It was a bit early for it, but they both needed it, and Vi helped herself to some too, as Charlotte walked into the room wearing a beautiful white satin dressing gown.

'What's all this? We're all up before the dawn.' She smiled in her cool, businesslike way that always made one feel as though there should have been a desk in front of her, but this time no one smiled back.

Charlie looked at her dismally, sipping the powerful brew in his cup. 'The Nazis killed Karl Rosen.'

'How terrible!' She looked generally horrified and the four of them talked about it for the next two hours relentlessly. She had some very clear views about German politics, and thought Hitler far more dangerous than most people realised. The men were grateful for the views she shared with them, but in the end, none of it mattered anyway. Karl was dead, and would never come again.

James and Vi called Audrey again that afternoon, and she said she was leaving for London that night. The Nazis had refused to return Karl's remains for religious burial, so there would be no funeral, and Ushi was in such a state that she thought she ought to leave the family alone. There was nothing left that she could do for anyone, and it seemed kinder to just quietly disappear. She promised to call Vi and James the next day when she arrived at their home, and she sounded as shocked and dazed as they all did in Antibes. It was a quiet, mournful day for everyone, and Vi and James went for a long walk on the beach, as Charles sat quietly on the veranda and Charlotte took a nap in their room. It was dinnertime before they all met again, and when they did, Vi noticed that Charlotte didn't look well. She was almost green.

'Are you all right?' She knew how unpleasant early pregnancy could be, and in spite of herself she felt sorry for her. She looked terrible, and Charlotte shrugged with a game little smile that barely covered up the misery she had felt all day.

'I'm fine. I think I must have eaten something that didn't agree with me.' She had been throwing up all afternoon, and Charlie had felt genuinely sorry for her when he'd gone to their room to get something and found her on her knees in front of the toilet. He made a cup of weak tea for her but even that came back, and he hoped she wasn't going to feel that way for the entire pregnancy. It was the first time she had ever been ill since she'd told him.

Violet smiled at her sympathetically. 'I don't think it's anything you ate, Charlotte, my dear. That always happens to me for the first three or four months. Dry toast and tea is about the only remedy and even that doesn't help much sometimes.'

'I really don't think it's that.' She was embarrassed that Violet knew about the pregnancy. But Vi only looked at her knowingly and smiled.

She ate very little that night, and went to bed immediately. Violet was talking about going back to London with James to meet Audrey as soon as possible, although they invited the Parker-Scotts to stay on for as long as they wanted.

'We really should be going too. Charlotte has to get back and I have a book to do.' They were planning a safari in Africa as a delayed honeymoon, but it hadn't fit in with their work schedules so they had settled for a few weeks in the South of France, but now they both had serious work to do. And with the death of Karl, it marked an end to their summer revelry, and it was time for all of them to go home. The only thing that bothered him was that Charlotte was suddenly feeling so ill, and after having a last drink with James that night, and talking about Karl again, Charlie went back to their room, and found Charlotte moaning on the bathroom floor, her head resting on the toilet.

'Charlie . . .' She was so breathless she could barely speak by then. 'I'm having . . . a terrible . . . pain . . .' He thought instantly of a miscarriage and was about to run for Violet, but she waved him closer to her and pointed to the right side of her abdomen. 'There.'

'Shall I call a doctor?' He was terrified. Something terrible was happening to her, and without even waiting for her to answer him he bolted from the room and knocked on James and Violet's bedroom door.

'Yes?' Vi called out to come in and Charles looked dishevelled and worried as he strode into the room and found them talking quietly. They had been talking about Ushi and Karl again, the nightmare was haunting everyone. 'Charles, is something wrong?'

'Charlotte is deathly ill and she says she has an awful pain . . .' He looked helplessly at Violet. 'I'm afraid I don't know anything about all that, but she ought to have a doctor at once. I really think we ought to get her into hospital.' Without saying another word, Vi ran down the hall struggling into her dressing gown as she went, and Charles turned to his old friend. 'Maybe we shouldn't have talked. Sometimes I forget she's pregnant. . . .' He ran a nervous hand through his hair and waited for Violet to return, and when she did, she looked worried as she glanced at James.

'I think you'd better call Docteur Perrault.'

'Is she having a miscarriage?' Charlie was horrified, and consumed with guilt. They should never have spoken of such upsetting things in front of her, it was just that she seemed so strong all the time. 'Is she in terrible pain?'

Vi turned to him, sorry for him. 'She's all right, Charles.

Whatever happens, she'll be all right. Women's problems look more frightening than they are sometimes. We'll take her into hospital, and by tomorrow she'll be fine.' But he found that hard to believe as he carried her vomiting and gagging to the car, wrapped in a blanket and her ruined dressing gown. James drove, while Violet held her hand, and Charles stared into the backseat at her. She looked as though she were dying back there, and he felt even guiltier for all the things he didn't feel for her. It was like watching someone you didn't know.

James sped around the curves in the road as quickly as he dared as Charlie urged him on nervously, and the moment they got to the hospital in Cannes, Charlie sped inside and returned with two orderlies who summarily loaded Charlotte onto a gurney and disappeared with her. The threesome followed her rapidly, and Docteur Perrault was already there, waiting for them. He took a look at her as nurses checked her pulse and blood pressure, and Charles hovered nearby. It took him less than two minutes to assess the situation of 'Madame,' and he turned to Charles with a troubled frown.

'It is her appendix, monsieur. I believe it may have perforated, or it is very close. We must operate at once.' Charles nodded, somewhat relieved, although still worried for her.

'Will she lose the child?'

The doctor looked pained and frowned. 'She is pregnant as well?' Charlie nodded at him. 'I see . . . we will see what we can do, but there are very few chances she will keep the child.' Tears stung his eyes as he nodded at him. 'We will do what we can.' And almost as soon as he spoke, Charlotte was whisked away and Charles was left to sit in the waiting room with James and Vi.

The moments ticked by endlessly, and it was three hours before he saw the doctor again. He came in, removing his surgical cap, and with a sober look in his eyes that frightened them. For an instant, Charles thought she might be dead.

'Your wife is doing well, monsieur.' He looked directly into Charlie's eyes. 'Her appendix had indeed perforated, but I think we cleaned everything up in time. She will be here for three or four weeks and she will make a full recovery.' Charles was relieved for her, but the doctor hadn't told him what he really wanted to know. He took a deep breath and looked at him.

'And the child?'

The doctor stared at him, not wanting to say more in front of James and Vi. 'May I speak to you alone, monsieur?'

'Of course.' But he assumed that meant the worst for the baby she had been carrying, and he was shocked to realise how much that meant to him. It was almost as though that was all that he had left. He followed the doctor from the room, leaving Vi and James to wait for him, and the doctor led him into a small sitting room down the hall. He pulled out two chairs and indicated for Charles to sit in the other one, which he did.

'May I ask you some rather personal questions, sir?'

'Certainly.' But he still had told him nothing more of the child, and Charlie was afraid to press him. Perhaps there were complications . . . or the baby had been lost after all. He ran all the possibilities through his mind as he waited for the doctor to speak.

'How long have you been married to Madame?'

Charlie had no qualms about being honest with him, not for the sake of the well-being of their child. The baby meant a lot to him. He had sacrificed everything for the child. 'Almost four weeks. But she got pregnant three months ago, in Egypt. . . .' as though that mattered to anyone. But the doctor was shaking his head. 'She's more pregnant than that?' Then that was what he was worried about, but the doctor was looking at him sympathetically. So sympathetically it hurt.

'I'm afraid there is a misunderstanding here, and I do not wish to intrude on your personal life, monsieur. Madame is not pregnant. She has had a hysterectomy, five years ago, she said. I checked everything, everywhere, because of what you told me. There is no baby, monsieur. There is no pregnancy. There is no uterus. And there can never be. I am very sorry to have to tell you this.' He looked at Charles and Charles felt as though he had been hit.

'Are you sure?' His voice was a painful croak.

'Totally. Madame will tell you so herself, I'm sure, just as she told me. Perhaps she was afraid to admit to you that she can never bear children, but I'm sure that over the years you will adjust to this. There is adoption, of course. . . .' He reached out to touch Charles's arm. 'I'm very sorry, monsieur.' Charles only nodded his head, unable to speak as he stood up.

'Thank you . . . thank you for telling me . . .' was all he could finally say as he left the room . . . she had lied to him . . . lied to him . . . everything was a lie . . . about the baby she had conceived in Cairo, and he felt so guilty about it because he wanted to make love to her all the time and he wasn't careful enough . . . and the abortion she didn't want . . . how he had respected her for that . . . even though it meant marrying her . . . and the baby who would be like Sean . . . the baby that would never be born . . . that never was . . . she had *lied* to him . . . he was overwhelmed by blind rage as he walked into the other waiting room, and he could barely speak to Violet and James.

'Would you like to see your wife, monsieur?' A young nurse smiled sweetly at him and all he could do was shake his head. 'She is awake now . . . you can just see her for *une petite minute,*' but instead he pushed his way past the nurse, out of the door and stood waiting outside the hospital for Violet and James. He had to take big gulps of air, and Violet could see from his face that something terrible had happened to him, and she felt sure that Charlotte had lost the baby.

'Charles?'

'Don't speak to me . . . please.'

'. . . Charlie . . .' He wheeled on her then and grabbed her arm.

'Vi . . . don't . . . *please!*' She could see that he was crying then, but she didn't understand that they were not tears of grief but rage. 'Do you know what she did to me?' He railed at them, unable to control himself. 'She lied to me! There is no baby! There never was . . . she had a hysterectomy five years ago.' James stared at him and Vi caught her breath.

'You're not serious!' She was horrified. And poor Audrey . . .

'I am.'

'But that's hideous.' James clenched his teeth as he got in and started the car and gestured them both in beside him.

'Come on, you need a drink.' They gave him more than one when they took him home. He didn't wake up until noon the next day, and when he did, he showered and shaved and went directly to the hospital whereon he walked into Charlotte's room and looked grimly down at her. She knew why he had come and what his expression meant. She had taken a risk, and figured she could keep it from him, but she had lost the game. She was smart enough to know when it was time to lay her cards down.

'I'm sorry, Charles. I thought it was the only way you would marry me.' She was right of course but that didn't make it any better now, for either of them. 'I wanted to make something special of your career, and take care of you. . . .'

'I don't give a damn about my career. Don't you know that by now?'

'I didn't then. I understand it better now. But you're wrong, you know. You could be the biggest writer in the world, an internationally important man. . . .' She said it as though offering to make him king and he stared at her.

'And what would that make you? My publisher? Is that so terribly important to you?' She wanted him like a puppet on a string.

'Men like you have to be tended like special flowers.' She tried to smile but it was obvious that she was still uncomfortable from the surgery but she was completely alert. Her senses were not dulled, and her eyes focused on Charlie perfectly.

'Didn't you think I'd find out?'

'Are children so very important to you, Charles?' But she already knew the answer to that, she had learned it watching him play with Molly and Alexandra and little James. 'You don't need children to be fulfilled, you know. You have your work. And we have each other.'

'What an empty life that is.' He looked sadly at her. How little she knew of life, or of him. 'I suppose I should wait a week or two to tell you this . . . until you're on your feet again.' She suspected what was coming next, and she looked up at him sadly. She had wanted him for such a long time, like a rare, rare diamond she wanted to own. 'But I don't want to string you along with lies. I'm leaving you. The joke is over now. We can go back to our own lives. You have your own flat and I have mine, and everything will go back to the way it was before, except that I won't be seeing you again. Someone else can handle my work, perhaps your father would like to take it on again, but that's the least of our problems. I'll call my solicitor when I get back to town.'

'Why? . . . why are you doing this?' She struggled to reach for his hand but he eluded her and she was barely able to move after her surgery the night before. 'What difference does it make if there's no child?'

'I could live with that . . . but what I can't live with are lies. You trapped me into marrying you. You wanted to own me, like a piece of property. And I can't be bought, or trapped, or caged, or made to write on cue like a dancing dog. The only hope we had of something decent growing between us was that child. And that child was a lie.

'I called your father and told him what had happened to you, and he's on his way down from London now. I'll wait until he arrives and then I'm going back with Vi and James. Violet says you can stay at the house for as long as you like when you get out of hospital, and I'll let you explain it to your father if you like. I don't want to embarrass you. But

I don't want to be married to you either. I'm sure you'll thank me someday.' And with that, he turned and walked out of her room, and stood on the street outside, staring up at the sky. It was as though Charlotte had never entered his life at all, and all he could think of suddenly were Ushi and Karl, and the love they had shared, the love that was so like the one he had known with Audrey before, and suddenly all he wanted to do was to go back to her. He looked like a new man when he returned to Antibes and stormed into the house.

'What time do we leave?' he asked Vi and she stared at him.

'I thought you wanted to wait until Charlotte's father arrived.'

'He'll be here tonight and he's staying at the Carlton in Cannes anyway.'

'I suppose the four o'clock train tomorrow would do. I'll ask James,' and then cautiously, 'By the way, Audrey called again. She's back in London now.' He nodded, his eyes locked in hers. 'She said to say hello to you.' He nodded again, and then left the room with a worried frown.

He didn't see Charlotte again, and he spoke to her father at the Carlton on the phone. The conversation was terse and he seemed to be under the impression that Charlotte had had a miscarriage as well as appendicitis, but Charles refused to explain any of it to him. That was her problem. She had told the lies. Let her explain it to him.

His only problem was seeing Audrey again, and convincing her that he wasn't a total fool. There was always the possibility that she wanted nothing more to do with him. And that was what he had to find out now.

31

Charles rode back on the train to London with Vi and James, and the children, and their nurse, in three private compartments on the night train. Vi left most of the servants in Antibes. They were mostly French, and she only brought the butler and housekeeper down from London every year to oversee things. They had taken an earlier train that morning so as to be in London when Vi and James arrived. And as usual, when they did, everything was in perfect order there.

'Do you want to come in for a little while, Charles?' Lady Vi was holding Alexandra's hand, and James was helping to sort through the luggage, determining who belonged to what and what went to whose room. Most of it was Vi's, with second place going to Lady Alexandra, most of whose clothes Violet bought in Paris every year.

Charlie seemed to hesitate for a moment and she smiled. He looked very young suddenly and she felt sorry for him. He had had a terrible shock in the past two days, and she knew he had taken it very hard. They had talked about it quietly on the train while James slept, and he had admitted to Lady Vi how much he had wanted the baby. In some ways it surprised her. He had always seemed like such a free and easy person, she couldn't imagine him wanting to get tied down now. But it seemed to be the only consolation for him in marrying Charlotte.

'She'll agree to a divorce, of course, won't she?' She had assumed that Charlotte would be reasonable now that he knew the truth about the baby, but Charlie had shaken his head with a glum look as she stared at him.

'She's Catholic.'

Vi looked shocked. 'That was the excuse she used about the abortion . . . she can't be serious about refusing to let you go now. She married you on the basis of fraud, for heaven's sake.'

'I know. But she says she won't agree. She's still talking about the great things she can do for my career.' He had sighed and the conversation had gone nowhere. She wanted him to take some time to think it all out, while she recovered, and she was expecting to see him when she got back to London in a few weeks.

But his mind was far from Charlotte now as he hesitantly stepped into Vi and James's front hall and looked around as though expecting to see Audrey leap at him from a doorway.

'She might be out,' Vi whispered to him, knowing what he was thinking and he turned to smile at her, but the moment he did, he heard Audrey's voice, and turned to see her coming slowly down the stairs. Her face looked drawn despite her summer tan and her eyes were filled with grief. She had done nothing but think of Ushi and Karl since she got home, and it was easy to see how devastated she was by what had happened on the train.

She checked on the stairs for only an instant when she saw him and then came to kiss Vi, and then James, and the children. She turned to Charles with a look of sorrow in her eyes. 'Hello, Charles. How was the trip?'

'Fine.' He felt like a schoolboy. 'Are you all right?' He took a step towards her as she nodded and for a moment Violet thought he was going to kiss her. As though Audrey sensed it too, she stepped back and they stood awkwardly in the hall for a moment, as Vi took off her hat, and shooed the children upstairs with their nanny and then suggested that they all have a cup of tea. It had been an emotional week for all of them, although Audrey did not yet know of what had happened to Charlotte.

They all went into the library to sit down, and Violet disappeared to speak to the cook, and a moment later James went to discuss something with the butler, and suddenly Audrey found herself alone with Charles. The moment was extremely awkward. She assumed that Charlotte had gone directly to the office, or their flat, and she was suddenly wondering about the wisdom of staying with James and Vi if it meant seeing Charlie all the time. Antibes had been painful enough without repeating it now. She took refuge in talking about Karl, and she had to stop several times as she tried to explain to Charles what had happened.

'It was . . . the . . . most . . . terrible thing I've ever seen. . . .' She couldn't erase the memory of when they'd taken Karl off the train and Ushi had begun to scream . . . and then later, seeing him with blood caked around his head, and led off in chains. 'Oh Charlie,' as she said his name, it sounded like old times to him, 'what will happen to her now?' She sighed and closed her eyes for a moment, trying to regain her composure, and suddenly she felt him touch her hand.

'You have to try to forget it.' His voice was gentle but her eyes flew wide open.

'Forget it? How could I possibly ever forget it?'

'You won't. But there's nothing you can do now. And torturing yourself won't help. The memory will dim in time.' He looked at her very intently. 'Most things do.' She was inclined to disagree with him, and it was as though he read her mind, and knew exactly what she was thinking. 'But not all.' The words were barely more than a whisper as their eyes held. 'I know this isn't the right moment to tell you, but . . .' He took a breath and went on, '. . . I left Charlotte in Antibes.'

Audrey wasn't sure she understood him, but he said it so intensely. 'Will she be back soon?'

He shook his head. 'I mean I left her. I want a divorce.'

'Good God, Charlie! What happened?' She looked stunned, almost as stunned as he still felt.

'She lied to me about the baby.'

Audrey looked shocked. 'You mean it wasn't yours?'

'No, I mean it wasn't anyone's. She wasn't pregnant.'

'Are you sure?' Audrey couldn't begin to imagine telling a lie like that. 'Maybe she lost it.'

But he only shook his head again. 'She had appendicitis,

and we had to take her to the hospital. They operated, and I warned the doctor that she was pregnant.' He laughed bitterly and sat back in his chair, remembering the moment when the doctor had told him the truth. 'He must have thought me a damn fool anyway. He said she had a hysterectomy several years ago.' He sighed and tried to smile at the woman he still loved. 'She admitted it to me the next day. I think she felt the end justified the means. But I'm afraid I don't agree. The only thing I wanted out of that marriage was the baby.'

Audrey was not surprised, but the rest of the story shocked her profoundly. 'Will she agree to a divorce?'

'Not yet. But she will. There's really no other way. I'm not going to stay with her now. We agreed that it was just for the child, and I told her I didn't love her when we got married.'

Audrey was looking at him strangely, and the shock of Karl's death came instantly to mind again. She remembered how Ushi had loved him. What if she had known he would die only a few weeks later? Would she have done anything different in that case? Suddenly it cast a different light on everything and she didn't have the heart to be angry with Charlie. 'I'm sorry, Charlie.' She looked into his eyes, and he saw the same gentleness and compassion he had always found there, and for the first time in two days, he smiled.

'I'm not sure I am. . . .' And then, without further ado, he reached for her hand, and held it close to his heart. 'Can you ever forgive me?' He put her fingertips to his lips and she smiled at him. This time she did not pull her hand away, she only looked at him, trying to absorb all that had happened to them both in so few days.

'There's nothing to forgive, Charles. I couldn't come with you when you needed me.'

'I understand that better now. But I was so angry at the time. I wanted you to come with me so desperately.' Her staying in San Francisco didn't seem so unreasonable to him now, but at the time it had driven him mad. 'I wanted to come back and forget you . . . and I tried.' He smiled sheepishly and her eyes smiled in answer. 'And Charlotte helped certainly.' His eyes clouded as he said her name. 'I never realised how determined she was to get what she wanted. It's frightening really.' Audrey nodded, suspecting too that she wasn't going to give him up as easily as he thought.

'What did you tell her when you left?'

'That it was over. Permanently. I didn't want there to be any doubt in her mind.' And now he looked at Audrey and spoke directly to her. 'Or in yours . . . if it's of any interest to you.'

She grinned at him, looking suddenly girlish. 'It might be.' And then suddenly there was laughter in her eyes. Life was too short to waste a moment with someone one loved as much as she did Charlie. '. . . If you play your cards right. . . .'

'Aha! So that's it . . . you're going to make me dance, are you?' He was suddenly laughing too, and his heart felt lighter than it had in a year . . . in fact, since he had left her in China.

'I just might, Charles Parker-Scott. After all, you deserve it . . . running off and marrying someone else.' She looked at him with mock outrage and put a hand on her hip. 'What a rude thing to do!' He laughed harder and pulled her towards him so he could kiss her. And it was at exactly that moment that Vi walked back into the room.

'Ooops . . . sorry. . . .' She turned on her heel with a satisfied smile and was about to leave when Audrey called her back. 'I don't want to interrupt anything important.'

'Quite all right,' Charlie grinned. 'Audrey was just outlining a course of torture for me . . . to make me pay my dues, as it were.' His eyes sobered for only a moment. 'Not that I blame her.'

'Quite right,' Lady Vi agreed. 'You deserve to be horse-whipped, Charles, after what you put the poor girl through.'

'The poor girl? The poor girl! Think of me! I quite assure you I didn't have much of a good time with the old girl either!'

Lady Vi looked at him disapprovingly and Audrey smiled. It was odd how suddenly it was all so funny, when only a few hours before it was a stone in her heart from which she doubted she would ever recover. Audrey looked at him seriously for a moment. 'Are you sure it's over, Charles?'

'It should never have begun. I was terribly, terribly stupid.'

'And now?'

'I hope I'm a great deal smarter. I'll give up Beardsley as my publishers if I have to.'

'I don't think Mr Beardsley would be foolish enough to let you do that,' James added as he walked into the room, carrying a decanter. 'A bit of sherry anyone?'

The ladies agreed and Charles suggested something a trifle stronger. Suddenly he wanted to celebrate. He didn't know what would happen yet, but he felt freer than he had in a long, long time, and suddenly they all seemed so lucky to be alive. And in an odd way, what they had felt was like a gift from Karl and Ushi Rosen.

They tried calling Ushi to comfort her that night, but her father said that she wasn't speaking to anyone, and they could tell from his voice that they were still distraught about what had happened.

'It's difficult to believe, isn't it, Aud?' Charlie had his arm around her as they sat in front of the fire in the darkened library. James and Vi had already gone to bed and they had been talking for hours, about the past year, about Ushi and Karl, about her grandfather . . . and even Charlotte. 'Life is so much too short . . . you never know what a great gift you have, until you've lost it.'

'I think the secret of a successful life is enjoying each moment. It's just so impossible to believe that Karl is gone though. . . .' She looked pensively into the fire and felt Charlie pull her closer.

'Audrey . . .' She could feel him staring at her and she turned her eyes to his.

'Yes?'

'Will you marry me when I get this business with Charlotte settled?' He had thought about it all day, when to ask her, what would be proper, how long he should wait, and he had finally decided to throw caution to the winds and just ask her. And she was looking at him with a quiet smile. Being with Charlie was all she wanted.

'I should have done that a long time ago. It would have saved us both a lot of trouble.' But he was shaking his head. He understood better now.

'You couldn't have then. It's taken me a long time, but I do understand that.' And then he looked at her very intently. 'You didn't answer my question. Will you?'

'Yes.' It was a strong, quiet word, and as soon as she said it, he kissed her.

32

The matter of Charlotte did not resolve itself quite as easily as Charlie had hoped. She returned to London in early October, and as soon as he heard that she was back, he had his solicitor call her. But he ran into a brick wall when he did. Charlotte Parker-Scott, as she insisted on calling herself now, would not agree to a divorce, now or in the foreseeable future, ever as far as she was concerned. She put it down to religious reasons, but Charlie couldn't accept that explanation. In all the time they'd been together, she had never gone to church, except for their wedding.

'Then what do you suppose she wants?' The solicitor was puzzled. 'She's got all the money she wants, and she doesn't seem the sort of woman to cling.' She had dealt with him like a man. In fact, she had been rather brutal about it.

Charlie couldn't figure it out, but Audrey and James and Vi all agreed. They thought she wanted to be known as Charlie's wife. It gave her the dignity she had been lacking, an old aristocratic name, and the cachet of being married to one of England's biggest authors. She wanted to impress her friends.

'But she can't do that if I'm not there, can she?' Charlie still couldn't see the reasoning behind it. But the others insisted.

'Of course she can. All she needs is your name, and to give people the impression that you're married.'

'Fine. Then I'll let her keep the name.' He said as much to his solicitor and told him to call her, offering to let her keep his name, as long as she agreed to a divorce, but once again she declined their offer. He even offered to give her the rights to both of his films, since she had been so excited about them. But again she refused, and finally Charles went to see her father in desperation. He found him just as unbending as his daughter, possibly more so.

'But why? Why does she want a marriage in name only?'

'Perhaps she thinks you'll come back. And you might. . . .' The man sized him up with his eyes. 'She's good for your career, Charles. Charlotte will make you someone you will never be without her.' But that only mattered to them and not to Charlie.

'I'm quite content with the way things are. Professionally, I mean. And surely, she can't want a captive husband.'

Her father smiled, but his eyes were cold. Almost as cold as hers. 'Perhaps that's all right. I've suggested to her myself that she could do better, but she's quite satisfied to hang on to you, Charles. And I don't expect this to change our business arrangements.' Charles had another five years in his contract, and as he had said to Audrey only the day before, it could be damn awkward.

'I assume you'll have the good taste not to expect me to work with her.'

'If you insist.' But it was obvious that he would have preferred it, and then he narrowed his eyes as he looked at Charles. 'You know, she hasn't told me why you left her, but I suspect it's because of that woman you were in love with when you met her.'

'It had nothing to do with that, I can assure you. It has to do with a misunderstanding between Charlotte and myself.' A misunderstanding. Another word for a lie. Fraud. Deceit. He still wanted to kill her when he thought of it. 'She can explain it to you herself, if she likes. I will not, sir.'

'Nor will she. She's too much of a lady.' Like most fathers, he was blind to his daughter's flaws and Charles was half tempted to relieve him of his illusions on her behalf, but he would never have done that.

'So where does that leave you, my love?' Audrey asked him over dinner that night. They had been seeing each other almost every night, and frequently in the daytime, in the month that they'd been back in London. She was still staying with Vi and James, but she was talking about renting a flat for a while. She didn't want to impose more than she

309

already had, although it was wonderful for Molly to be with the other children, especially Alexandra who treated her like a big doll and loved to comb her hair and dress her. 'Do you suppose she'll come around?' Audrey was still asking about Charlotte.

'Eventually someone else will come along, someone much more important, and she'll be anxious to get rid of me. As fast as possible, I hope.'

'Maybe we could introduce her to someone.' She looked at Charles ruefully and he laughed as he pulled her into his arms to kiss her. And afterwards she told him of what she had done that afternoon, but he wasn't as excited as she had hoped he would be. She had spent the afternoon looking at flats, big enough for herself and Molly and one servant. 'You don't look very pleased.' There was disappointment in her eyes and he shrugged.

'I suppose I'm not. I want you here in London, of course.' He was glad that she had nothing to rush home for, but he had hoped to be rid of Charlotte by then, officially as well as physically. And for the moment, there was still no relief in sight. 'I have a better idea.' But he wondered what she would think of it. He was almost afraid to ask her. 'I never use my guest room. Fortunately, no one is stupid enough to want to stay with me.'

She laughed. 'And you're going to rent me a room?'

He smiled but shook his head. It was second best to what they wanted, but it would have to do for a while anyway, and he was tired of visiting her at Vi and James's. He wanted what they had once shared in China, waking up side by side every morning, falling asleep in each other's arms, feeling her silky mane cast over his arm, as he felt her soft breath on his chest. 'I'd like you to move in with me, Audrey. We could give the guest room to Molly, and put her nurse in the dressing room. And if that doesn't work, we could rent another flat. I wouldn't mind doing that actually. . . .' His face lit up as he looked at her and half an hour later they were talking animatedly about renting a house somewhere near Vi and James, and then suddenly he stopped and looked at her. 'You know I still want to marry you, don't you? This is just until I get the divorce, however long that takes. You do understand that?'

'Yes, my darling.' She smiled at him and melted into his arms. She had never been happier in her life, married or not. And she could hardly wait until they moved in together.

33

They went everywhere together socially. Charles introduced Audrey to all his friends, and she was welcomed
with open arms by everyone, all of whom were relieved to
see that he had dispensed with Charlotte Beardsley. They
went to parties, operas, balls, and she appeared everywhere
with Charles, including a costume ball where they ran into
Charlotte dressed as Der Rosenkavalier, all done up in
satin pantaloons, making a very handsome man, as Lady Vi
pointed out nastily. As they sailed past her Charles's eyes
had only met hers briefly and then she had turned away.
It was beginning to annoy him that she was clinging so
steadfastly to his name. He read about Charlotte Parker-
Scott in business columns everywhere, and he would have
much preferred sharing his name with Audrey. But thus far,
Charlotte had not agreed to the divorce, and by Christmas,
Audrey and Charles were settled in a new house, only five
blocks from Vi and James. They gave a housewarming party
on New Year's Eve, and the last guest didn't go home until
eight o'clock the next morning.

It was only three weeks later when King George died,
succeeded by Edward VIII, who was a handsome man of
forty-one. And it amazed Audrey to realise that she had met
him on the Riviera only a few months before, and now he
was the King of England. She wondered what would happen
to his romance with Wally Simpson now, the American
divorcée he had been so blatantly involved with. What was
tolerated in a prince would be forbidden a king, and she
suspected things weren't going to be easy for them. The
English were violently opposed to his being involved with a
divorced woman.

But the country's focus turned away from them as Hitler
marched into the Rhineland in the spring. It turned Charlie

and Audrey's thoughts to Europe again, and after sending a dozen letters to Ushi with no reply, Audrey finally called her parents, and was shocked at the explanation she got for their friend's silence.

'She is in a convent in Austria, my dear.' Her father sounded old and tired on the phone. Germany wasn't a pleasant place to live in any more. And when Audrey asked for her address, the Baron explained that it was useless. She had joined a cloistered order and could receive no mail from anyone, not even her parents. Even they were not allowed to contact her. She had renounced the world and all of them with it. Audrey was profoundly shocked. She couldn't get the memories out of her mind when she took Molly to the park that afternoon. She remembered how desperately Ushi had wanted to get pregnant. They had said they wanted six children . . . and now Ushi was a nun . . . a cloistered nun . . . they would never hear from her again. The thought brought tears to her eyes and she stopped in to see Vi that afternoon who was equally shocked. It seemed a terrible thing to both of them, and a terrible waste of her youth and charm and beauty. And it brought home to Audrey again how deeply Ushi had loved Karl, and how meaningless her life had become without him. It reminded her in some ways of what she felt for Charlie. Charles and Molly were her whole life now. It was frightening some-times, frightening to realise how much she loved them both and that they were her whole life. They meant more to her than anything. It was difficult to remember sometimes that technically Charlie was married to someone else. It seemed as though she and Charlie had been together forever. It was hard to remember now that someone had come between them, even briefly, and that someone had no importance to them.

'Does it bother you, Aud?' Violet had asked her once, and she had honestly told her it didn't.

'I suppose it should bother me more than it does. It's shocking of course, but no one we know seems to care, and we don't. The only thing that's difficult is that we can't have children. But Molly keeps us busy enough right now.' Vi smiled at her words. Molly was the sweetest child and she loved her almost as much as her own children.

Audrey took hundreds of pictures of her, as she did of Alexandra and little James. She loved taking photographs of the children. And Charles was working on a new book now. He had refused to go back to America to negotiate another film deal, hoping to discourage Charlotte's interest in him, but she had closed the deal for him anyway, and made him a small fortune, hoping to woo him back perhaps by impressing him. But if that was her intention, it didn't work. Charles was completely indifferent. He loved only Audrey, and little Molly who now called him Daddy, which was music to his ears.

The year rolled past them all too quickly, with Charlotte never relenting for a moment, and Audrey and Charles busy with their own lives. She was planning to do the photographs for his new book, and world events concerned them both. It was a year rife with ominous political events, as Hitler kept stretching out hungry fingers. Rome and Berlin made an agreement in the autumn. And in November, Hitler made an agreement with Japan as well, agreeing to join forces against Russia if need be.

But it was in December that they had the most shocking news of all. Its implications were far less important than the political intrigues of Adolf Hitler, yet like the rest of the country, Audrey was completely shocked as she stood in her kitchen on December tenth, listening to King Edward speak on the radio, as she watched Molly playing with her favourite dolly.

She stood riveted to the floor as she heard him speak, the man she'd seen in Antibes with Wally Simpson, and tears washed silently down her cheeks as she heard the words that would rock the entire nation, and then the world. 'I have found it impossible to discharge my duties as King . . . without the help and support of the woman I love. . . .'

Giving up a kingdom – what more could one ask of a man? She had a moment of thinking how lucky they were to love each other so much, and she found herself looking back at the memory of the woman she had met, wondering what in her had inspired so great a love. The poor man sounded anguished as he spoke, and after less than a year on the throne, he was abdicating to marry this twice-divorced American woman.

And even though he was not her king, her heart went out to him, for the agony that must have come before the decision . . . and in an odd, remote way, it reminded her of their situation with Charlotte . . . in the face of all odds, they had chosen to be together, legitimate or not . . . but their life was certainly simpler than King Edward and Mrs Simpson's.

Long after the radio went off, she stood in the kitchen, looking down at her child, and thinking of what he had done . . . giving up his kingdom for the woman he loved. . . . She knew she would never forget it, and she smiled through her tears as she thought of how much he must love her.

34

All of England cried over the abdication of King Edward VIII. He was succeeded by his brother, younger by only a year, George VI, but somehow he didn't present quite as dashing and romantic a figure as Edward, giving up all for the woman he loved. Audrey always defended him to her friends who were shocked by the abdication, and Charlie teased her that she just liked Wally because she was an American. But there was something deeply moving about what he had done that touched them both. He had been willing to give everything up for love, and that meant a great deal to both Charlie and Audrey.

Charlotte was still not making life easy for them, but after a year and a half they no longer really cared. They were beginning to accept their limitations as a fact of life, and Audrey was too busy with her photography to worry about it much anyway. Charlie encouraged her constantly, and she even had a show in a gallery, of some wonderful black and white shots she had taken over the years, some abstracts, some portraits, even her photograph of Madame Sun Yat-sen, and a number of marvellous shots of Molly.

Charlie was terribly proud of her, and their work seemed to combine very nicely. In fact, Charlotte was furious when he insisted that the only photographer he would work with now was Audrey. And there was nothing they could do to stop him. His contract was specific about his having the right to choose his own photographer, and the choice was obvious now.

'Still hanging on to her, eh Charles?' Charlotte sounded bitter when they spoke at the office one day. He had come in to see her father and she had cornered him.

'Rather like the way you're hanging on to me, you might say.' There was fury in his eyes now whenever he saw her.

He was far more resentful than Audrey over the fact that Charlotte wouldn't agree to divorce him. Audrey was relatively content as things were, but Charlie was anxious to have a baby and he refused even to consider it until he could marry Audrey. 'Aren't you ready to be sensible about this yet, Charlotte?' It was an argument they had had repeatedly, and he just couldn't understand why she was hanging on. It made no sense at all to him, and he always tormented himself trying to figure out what was behind it. No one's explanations or guesses ever satisfied him and only this woman had the answer.

'I'll never agree to a divorce, Charles.' She eyed him coolly and crossed the room to the door. 'You're wasting your time with her.'

'You're the one who's wasting time.' He stood up as though he would go to her and shake some sense into her, but she only shrugged and shut the door smartly behind her.

It infuriated him each time he thought about it, and even more so when Audrey's sister Annabelle wrote to her that she was getting married.

She got married in Reno over Easter, and the man she had married was a professional gambler. 'A bridge player,' as she put it, more genteelly. But he sounded like a worthless sort to Charles and it annoyed him to think that she was free to marry anyone she chose, while he and Audrey were stymied by Charlotte.

Annabelle and her new husband came to London that summer and Charles was shocked when he met her. He couldn't have imagined a woman more different from Audrey. She had grown even more spoiled in the time Audrey had been gone. She seemed to whine constantly wearing shockingly expensive gowns and large jewels, most of which Charles suspected were fake, although he didn't want to say so to Audrey. Audrey seemed uncomfortable enough with her, and he saw her staring at Annie more than once, as though trying to figure out who she was. They seemed more like strangers than sisters. It was a relief when she left again, although she managed to plant a few pointed barbs in Audrey's flesh before she did. She asked if she was planning to live with Charles forever, or was it just a passing fancy.

'He's waiting for his divorce to come through.' Audrey's eyes were calm, but they showed the pain she felt at the way her sister had said it.

'Haven't you heard that before?' She lazily blew smoke rings and looked at Audrey as though she were a common whore, and Annabelle a great lady.

'In this case, it's true.'

'Well, don't sit around for too long, sweetheart. You're not getting any younger.' Audrey looked at her with tired eyes. She was sad to see what Annabelle had become. There was something cheap about her now, as though she had hung out with the wrong people for too long, and it was obvious that she drank too much. She was always giddy, and she laughed too loud – when she wasn't complaining.

It was a relief when she left, although Charlie knew Audrey was depressed at first. It wasn't that she missed her, it was that she regretted what she had become.

'She's like someone I never knew ... a complete stranger. ...' She looked at Charlie with sorrow in her eyes. 'I brought her up, and look at her.' She looked like a cheap tart, and they both knew it, and the funny thing was that she had implied Audrey was a whore because she was living with Charlie. 'I don't suppose that marriage will last.' They had both thought he was awful. Audrey hadn't even introduced them to Vi and James. She would have been ashamed to. 'I don't even feel as though I have ties to San Francisco any more.' Charlie wasn't sure he minded that, and Audrey knew it. Nevertheless, it made her sick to think of them living in their grandfather's house. That man with his fat, smelly cigars, and his ugly diamond pinky ring. Her grandfather would have had apoplexy if he had seen him. The very thought made her laugh, and brought tears

318

to her eyes as she laughed harder and harder, thinking of what her grandfather would have said. Just thinking about it cheered her.

She had also thought of him when Franklin Roosevelt defeated Alfred Landon and was inaugurated again. It warmed her heart to think of the arguments they had had. Politics had been the greatest love they shared. And now she enjoyed discussing the same things with Charlie. They discussed it at length when Japan attacked China that summer, this time taking over most of the country in battles that stretched to year end and took thousands of civilian lives. Peking and Tientsin fell into Japanese hands, and two hundred thousand civilians were killed when they took Nanking. Audrey was instantly reminded of the days she and Charlie had spent there so peacefully. It was heartbreaking to think of all of that destroyed now. The Communists and Nationalists joined forces to fight the Japanese and she was suddenly relieved again to have taken Mai Li home with her. Supposedly Harbin was in no greater turmoil than it had been before, but the rest of the country was being devasted by the Japanese, and she couldn't imagine that life would have been easy for Molly. She hoped that Shin Yu and the others were all right, and wondered if the nuns would have taken them back to France, but somehow she doubted it. They were a staunch crew and would probably have stayed on, as they had before.

Also that summer, in July 1937, the Germans opened a camp called Buchenwald, a work camp of sorts for prisoners and 'undesirables'. At the same time, Jews were eliminated from trade and industry. They were now forbidden to go into parks, to attend public events, places of entertainment like theatres or museums or libraries. All public institutions were forbidden them then, even health resorts. And from July sixteenth on, all Jews had to wear yellow stars sewn onto their clothes so they could be identified on sight. It made them both think of Ushi and Karl again, and Audrey always wondered how she was, if she was even a little bit content in her convent. The death of Karl had brought Audrey and Charlie closer together at the time, and meant something special to them. They would never hear the word *Jew* in quite the same way again. They would always think of Karl, and each new edict they heard about in Germany seemed directed at his memory, and indirectly at them. It was hard to believe that he had been dead for two years now. Time had moved so fast, and the world was in the throes of difficult times that only seemed to get worse, and no one knew what it meant any more. In December, the Italians and the Germans withdrew from the League of Nations, which seemed ominous as well.

Audrey and Charlie were even more shocked when, in March of 1938, Hitler took over Austria, claiming that the Germans living there wanted annexation. It suddenly brought Ushi to mind again, and Audrey worried about what would happen to the nuns in her convent. She couldn't help but think of the nuns that had been killed in Harbin, and she already knew that the Germans were ruthless. It seemed as though everything was in turmoil these days, and the only stability they felt sure of was with each other.

It was amazing to realise that by the end of that year they had been living together for three years. Vi and James gave them a dinner party to celebrate their anniversary unofficially, and afterwards they all danced the samba and the conga, and listened to Benny Goodman's records. And when they went home that night, at four in the morning, Audrey said there was absolutely nothing more she wanted. She was thirty-one years old and she had never been more in love with Charlie.

The only thing missing was a child of their own, but that remained an impossibility, thanks to Charlotte, and they lavished all their love on little Molly.

But it was the following year that frightened everyone. After the Munich Accord, everyone had told themselves that nothing could go wrong and everyone in Europe pretended not to be worried. Suddenly, all of those who could were buying untold luxuries and fancy cars, giving gala balls and wearing incomparable jewels and furs, as though nothing would go wrong now, and as though their forced gaiety would ensure it. But the fears were still there, buried but alive, and the ugliness seemed to keep happening, like a monster no one could stop. And indeed they couldn't. Hitler continued to march forth with a vengeance. The Spanish Civil War ended, with untold loss of life. There were over a million dead in Spain, crippling the country almost beyond repair. If one listened, one could hear the drums of war warming up in the background.

Germany occupied Bohemia and Moravia, and signed a mutual nonaggression pact with Russia, which made Germany and Russia a doubly frightening force. And on September first, Hitler's forces attacked Poland, leaving the world stunned and breathless.

Two days later, on September third, Britain declared war on Germany, and Churchill became first lord of the Admiralty. It was to him that everyone would turn as the battles raged. And they were already off to a grim beginning. Within two weeks, German U-boats had sunk the *Athenia* and the *Courageous*. Audrey and Charles sat stunned in their kitchen as they heard the news. It was like watching a world gone mad around them. And Charlie was wondering if Audrey should go home. Europe no longer seemed like such a safe place to be. And most Americans were scurrying home as quickly as they could get there. The American Ambassador was attempting to book passages for everyone, and Charlie asked her if she wanted to join them.

She smiled at him and poured him another cup of tea before she answered and then she looked up at him with the quiet strength he had seen in her eyes before. 'I *am* home, Charlie.'

'I'm serious. I can send you back if you'd like. Molly and you. They're booking passages for all the Americans now, and this might be a good time to go. God knows what will happen next with that madman on the loose.' He was, of course, referring to Hitler.

'I'm staying here. With you.' She said it very quietly and he reached out and took her hand. They had loved each other for six years now . . . it had been almost exactly six years before that they had been crossing Asia by train. And they had come a long, long way side by side. She didn't even care any more if he married her, or if they had their own children. She was content with Molly and the man she loved. They were accepted by everyone in London society, and known by everyone as 'Mrs Driscoll' and Mr Parker-Scott. There was no pretence that they were anything other than they were, but it seemed to be good enough for everyone, and she wasn't going to leave him now, not after six years, because of a war. And if London went down in flames at Hitler's hand, then she'd stand beside Charles to the bitter end, and she told him so now in an impassioned speech that took him by surprise as he watched her. There was a depth and fire to the woman that he sometimes forgot, barred as it was by her quiet, competent exterior.

'I suppose that takes care of that, doesn't it?' But he was pleased that she wanted to stay with him, even though he'd already put his name on a list of volunteers, as had James. James wanted to be a pilot desperately, although Charles was far more interested in Intelligence and had told them so at the Home Office. He had the perfect cover as a journalist, and they told him they would be in touch. He suspected they were investigating him thoroughly and he would hear from them eventually, which he did. On the day Warsaw fell. It was a tragedy that touched them all, and spirits all over Europe were darkened.

Two days later Poland was divided up between Russia and Germany, like a carcass torn limb from limb by two wolves, and Audrey felt ill every time she heard snatches of news on the radio and terrible tales about the valiant people who had died in the ghetto. She talked to Charles about it endlessly, and he was relieved that he had heard from the Home Office at last. At least he could do something now, or so he thought. They had promised to be in touch with him shortly. But before they were, the British sent 158,000 men into France to defend their allies. Charlie was longing to be one of them. However it was another two months before Charlie heard from the Home Office and was appointed an Official War Correspondent and was free to enter any of the military theatres, waiting for assignment.

He was desperately jealous of James, already assigned to the RAF, and Violet had volunteered as a lorry driver for the Red Cross. She seemed to be enjoying it, and whenever Audrey saw her, she seemed terribly busy and preoccupied. She wasn't the old Lady Vi any more, going shopping with friends, playing with the children, and serving high tea in her library. Audrey was lonely at times, but she kept busy with her photography. There seemed to be a lot more to do now, and Charlie was anxious to be off. It was the following July before he got a call from the Home Office. Denmark and Norway had fallen three months before, the Lowlands the month after, Belgium as well. And Paris had fallen only two weeks before they called Charlie from the Home Office.

Until that time, he had been covering war news from London with occasional forays into the Lowlands and Belgium, and even Paris, all before they fell. But they had all been short trips, and he had been anxious to do something more exciting. He had complained to Audrey about it more than once, and she told him to be patient. He was writing for important newspapers around the world, feeding them the information that the British wished to share. He had met Churchill more than once, and was in awe of the man's great mind, and Audrey assured Charles that he was doing a splendid job, where he was, but she knew that he wouldn't be satisfied to sit there forever, particularly not with James in the RAF.

When Audrey saw Charlie's face the night he got the call, she knew that something had happened.

'What's up, love?' She eyed him suspiciously, as he walked in the front door.

'Nothing much. How was your day?'

'Okay.' She showed him the photographs she had developed that afternoon while Molly played outside with the neighbour's child, and then they made small talk for a while. Finally she looked at him with a small, sad, knowing smile. 'When are you going to tell me the news I won't like, Charles?'

'What makes you think that, Aud?' But he looked guilty as she asked. The trouble was she knew him too well. She had seen the troubled look in his eyes. In some ways he was excited with what they had offered him, and in other ways he hated leaving her behind now.

'What is it, Charles?' Her voice was soft, and her eyes so haunting as she looked at him that he couldn't hide it from her any more.

'Did you hear the news today?'

Slowly, she shook her head. For once, she hadn't played the radio in her darkroom while she worked, maybe because she was tired of all the ugly things she always heard. And now she had missed another one. 'What happened?' It was getting more depressing every day, and more depressing still, to her, was the fact that the United States refused to get involved, as though the war in Europe could still be ignored. They were playing ostrich and it infuriated her whenever she thought of it. She was ashamed to admit that she was an American now. She wanted the US to roll up its sleeves and come to the aid of all those so desperately in need of it. But she only looked up at Charles, with fear in her eyes. 'What's happened now?'

'We sank the French fleet in Oran today.'

'That's in Algeria, isn't it?' He nodded. 'Why?'

'Because they're not our allies any more. They're in German hands, Aud, and we didn't want the Germans to get their hands on their ships. It was a terrible waste. We didn't admit to it, of course. The news just said that the ships had been sunk. But we really had no choice.'

'Were many men killed?' She was so tired of hearing about it, thousands here and thousands there . . . and people like Karl . . . and the one who had died in Warsaw in '39. . . .

'About a thousand or so.' His eyes met hers for what seemed like a very long time. 'They want me to go over there, Aud.'

'To Algeria?' She felt something turn over in the pit of her stomach.

'To report on the sinking of the fleet in Oran, and then move on to Cairo for a little while, now that things are starting to happen there.' Actually nothing had yet, but Mussolini had threatened to invade Egypt only six days before, and the British wanted more of their correspondents over there, or at least they wanted him there anyway, but he suddenly felt terrible when he saw the look on Audrey's face. 'Don't look like that, Aud.'

Her eyes filled with tears and she turned her back to him. So this was what it was like to be involved, she thought to herself. Maybe the United States was right not to sink their men into it after all. But she could feel him standing right behind her, with his hands on her arms. He turned her slowly to face him again and took her face in his hands. 'I won't be gone for too long.'

'This is what you wanted, isn't it?' He had been chafing to do something like that for the last ten months since war had been declared, but now suddenly it all felt so different to her . . . now that it was Charles . . . she felt almost physically ill thinking of the danger he'd be in. 'When will you be back?'

'I don't know yet. It'll depend on what happens when I'm there. But being a war correspondent isn't like being a foot soldier after all, you come and go and it really isn't dangerous. . . .'

She was quick to cut him off, her eyes filled with pain, 'You can get killed just like everyone else. Damn you, why couldn't you do something sensible here at home?'

'Like what?' He raised his voice to her in spite of himself. 'Knit? Dammit, Audrey, I need to get out there and do this. Look at James. He's been bombing hell out of the Germans for the last six months for chrissake.'

'Well, good for him. But if he gets killed out there, showing off, it won't do Vi and the children any good will it?' She was crying now and he pulled her close to him. There were reasons why she felt that way, but she couldn't tell him. It wouldn't be fair to him. And she had only found out herself two days before that she was pregnant. She had been waiting for the right time to break the news to him.

'I'll be back, Audrey, I promise you . . . I'll be in Cairo perfectly safe. . . .'

And then suddenly she laughed through her tears and pulled away to look at him. 'That stupid place. Look what happened the last time you went there!'

He laughed too, knowing what she meant. 'I promise not to get married again. I give you my word.' He held up a hand in oath and she placed her own palm up against his.

'I love you so much. Swear to me that you'll take care of yourself, no matter what, or I'll come over and take care of you myself.'

'I believe you just might.' He looked amused, but she did not. She had a heavy burden to carry without him.

'I'm not afraid to come running after you. So don't forget that, kid.' And the look in her eyes said that she meant every word of it.

'I'll keep it in mind.' But neither of them thought of anything but each other's bodies later that night as they made love for the last time. He was leaving the next day. They hadn't given him much notice, but he thought it was just as well. He told her as he left that he didn't think he'd be gone for more than a month or two, if that. And she promised to take care of herself and Molly and write to him every day. He would be staying at Shepheard's Hotel and he had already heard that it offered every possible luxury, but he didn't tell her that as he gave her a last wave and disappeared in the jeep that came to pick him up at the crack of dawn. He had a military plane to catch in a little over an hour, and as he drove away he prayed that she and Molly would be all right. They had already spent more than one night in the bomb shelter nearest to their home, and everyone seemed fairly well used to it by now, but it was still an unpleasant way to live, and he worried about them whenever he was out. He would worry even more now, but at least he would be busy in Oran, and Cairo after that. Audrey was standing lost in thought in their living room after he left, with a vacant look in her eyes thinking of their baby.

She wondered if she should have told him before he left, but it wouldn't have been fair to him. She thought of the irony of Charlotte's lie to make him marry her . . . and now, when it was true, Audrey had said nothing to him. And then suddenly, panic filled her soul. What if he were killed . . . what if . . . she felt terror rise up in her throat and almost strangle her. It took her several hours to calm down, and she was still feeling shaken and bereft when she went to Violet's that night for dinner. She took Molly with her, because she didn't trust anyone to get her to the bomb shelter on time if need be. And the children were playing upstairs when Audrey looked at Lady Vi.

'How do you stand it?' Audrey's eyes looked different from before. Sleepier, and more worried now. She wasn't very far along yet, and she'd been so excited when she first heard, she had wanted to rush home and tell Charles, but she'd been waiting for just the right moment. She didn't want to worry him. And now . . .

'Stand what?' Lady Vi smiled at her. 'The air raids? I suppose one gets used to them.' The children certainly did. The children went right on playing in the shelter despite the bombs, as though they were used to them now. It always unnerved Audrey watching them. It seemed such a terrible way to grow up, worse still because they were all so used to it. But she shook her head at Vi.

'Not the air raids . . . the worry . . . doesn't it drive you mad worrying about him?'

This time Violet didn't smile. 'All the time. There isn't a moment I don't think about it, I'm afraid. But we haven't much choice, have we, my dear?' Their eyes met and

Audrey's eyes filled with tears, and suddenly she couldn't stand it any more. She had to tell someone, and as Vi came and put her arms around her, she looked mournfully up at her friend.

'Oh Vi . . . I'm having a baby . . . and Charlie doesn't know . . . I was going to tell him before he left but I didn't want to worry him . . .' She was sobbing now. 'And what if. . . .'

'Stop it!' Violet squeezed her shoulders hard, half happy for her, and half not. It was a terrible time to be pregnant, and alone. But she knew how badly Charlie had wanted a child, and she smiled down at her. 'That's wonderful news, Aud. Now, you must take very good care of yourself, eat as well as you can, despite the rationing, and get lots of rest!' They both thought of the air raids every night and Audrey smiled at her.

'Do you suppose I should have told him before he left?'

Lady Vi shook her head. 'You did the right thing. He'd be half mad worrying about you, and he wouldn't pay attention to what he's doing there. I do the same with James. I just tell him all is well with us, so when he's up in that plane, he can concentrate on what he's doing and come home as quickly as he can. They can't afford the distractions right now.' It could cost them their lives, but she didn't say that to her friend. The two women chatted for a long time, Audrey feeling relieved to have confided in her. Violet wasn't surprised at the pregnancy, she was only surprised that it hadn't happened long before this. She wondered if Charles would press Charlotte again now. Violet hadn't had a chance to say anything to him before he left, but she had heard some strange rumours about her. But she didn't want to upset Audrey now.

They were saying goodnight to each other, with Molly asleep in Audrey's arms, when the sirens began to wail, and Violet had to run and fetch Alexandra and James, and round her servants up, and they all went scurrying to the shelter together. Violet held Audrey's arm. She was afraid she would fall on the loose stones, and that was important now. Suddenly the child signified life to both of them, and it was important to protect this unborn child that only they knew about.

Once they were in the shelter, Audrey smiled at her.

'I'm glad I told you, Vi.'

'So am I.' She smiled, and the two women held hands as the bombs fell all around them.

35

Almost a week went by before she and Molly saw Violet again, and Vi looked worried this time. She confessed to Audrey as the children played that the RAF was engaged in night bombing raids on Germany. It was no secret she was doubly worried about James these days. He was flying almost all the time and although he had made an astonishing number of kills, she was worried sick about him. Audrey tried to cheer her, as she noticed how much weight Violet had lost recently. They all had, but Vi looked even thinner than most. She had always had such an easy, indolent life, and now suddenly she was daily battling reality and fear, with a sense of helplessness about it all. There was nothing she could do to keep James safe, except pray, and it was eating at her.

'He'll be fine, Vi.' Audrey had reassured her friend, hoping she was right and he'd be lucky. 'He's the best there is.' Their eyes met then, and Violet's eyes filled with tears. This time she needed Audrey to comfort her.

'I couldn't live without him, Aud.' Audrey put her arms around her and they held each other for a long time, deriving what comfort they could, and then Violet smiled at her.

'How do you feel?'

'All right.' She was nauseous much of the time, but it was for a good cause, and she didn't complain. She was excited about the baby now, and anxious to tell Charlie when he returned. It was due by March, and she was just two months pregnant. Nothing showed, of course, but she thought her stomach was rounder than it had been before. And she was tired most of the time, though it was difficult to say if that was from the pregnancy, or simply from lack of sleep. They were in the shelter almost every night, and the bombs seemed to fall on their neighbourhood constantly. Several houses had been destroyed, and things were constantly falling off shelves and shattering as the bombs hit. It was hard on everyone's nerves, but Audrey seemed to feel it more now, and Violet didn't like the looks of the circles she had under her eyes.

'You'd better take care of yourself. Charlie would be terribly upset if he saw you.'

'Do I look that bad?' She smiled. The nauseousness had been much worse in the last few days but the lack of sleep didn't help either.

'You look tired.' And Violet thought her unusually pale, but she didn't say anything. 'Do you rest in the afternoon?'

'When I can.' But Molly was an active girl, and Audrey liked working in her darkroom whenever she could. She hadn't told Molly about the baby yet, but she was planning to when it started to show. She loved the idea of it, and as she lay in bed at night, she would lay a hand on the tiny bulge she felt there and smile to herself, as though she had the sweetest secret in the world. She smiled at Lady Vi now, thinking of March. It seemed an eternity away. She kept wondering what it would be like. 'Is it as bad as they say? . . . having it, I mean?'

Lady Vi shrugged casually. She didn't want to frighten her. But it had been ghastly for her, and Alexandra had been delivered by Caesarean section, which was why there would be no more children for them. But they were satisfied with the two they had, and in all honesty, she wouldn't have wanted to go through it again in any case. 'It's not that bad. People make a great fuss about it of course. But actually you forget.' Audrey was watching her eyes, and she saw something there that frightened her. But it was too early to worry about it. And even if it was terrible, it was worth it to have his baby. Then in spite of herself she thought of Ling Hwei in Harbin, but she forced the memory from her mind. They had other things to think about now, and it was still more than six months away.

'I get scared sometimes when I think about it.'

'Don't.' Vi smiled kindly at her. 'It will happen so fast, it will be over before you know it, and then you'll have a fat beautiful baby in your arms.' The two women smiled at each other, sharing something very warm, the secret of giving life. Audrey was in better spirits when she went home, but that night was the worst air raid of the war. They all sat huddled in the shelter until dawn, and the next day Violet came to talk to her. 'I think we should send the children away, Aud. What do you think?' It was almost like being married to each other now. They had no one else to make decisions with, and now they consulted each other far more than they ever had before the war. They had talked about it before, but Audrey wasn't sure.

'Do you think it'll get much worse?'

'I don't see how it could. But . . .' She hated to say the words, but they were on her mind. 'We'd never forgive ourselves if something happened to them.' Too many houses had gone down, and people were getting hurt. A number in the neighbourhood had been killed. Audrey was trying to think of what Charles would have wanted.

She looked at Violet with unhappy resolve. 'I suppose we ought to do it now.'

Violet nodded. She hated to send them away, but she wanted them to be safe, and she had already spoken to her father-in-law about it, and to James the last time he came home. He wanted her to go too, and Audrey knew that. 'I don't really want to stay down there yet myself. I've got so much to do here.' Part of her volunteer work for the Red Cross meant driving a jeep for several generals whenever she could. Audrey had been planning to volunteer as well, but with the pregnancy she thought she would wait until she felt better. And she was deeply involved in taking photographs of the rubble one saw everywhere, and the faces etched with the sorrows of war. It would be a remarkable collection one day, but she wasn't thinking of her photographs either. She was thinking of Molly, and sending her away to the country with Alexandra and James. 'What do you say, Aud?'

'Let's take them down this week.'

'And stay ourselves?' Her father-in-law was going to keep an eye on them, and of course Vi would send the nurse with them.

'Not yet. I want to finish some of the work I started.' Audrey frowned. There were so many things she still wanted to photograph, and her darkroom was hung with hundreds of photographs she had taken.

'I'll call my father-in-law. We can drive them down this Saturday. Is that all right with you?'

'Fine.'

Violet nodded as she got ready to leave and frowned as she looked at Audrey again. She was losing weight instead of gaining it, and she still looked very tired. 'Try and get some rest before the trip.'

'Yes, ma'am.' They exchanged a smile and Lady Vi left, and on Saturday they set off in the family's touring car. Fortunately, James had bought a large Chevrolet station wagon before the war, and Audrey and Violet helped the older children and the nurse into the backseat, told Molly to get into the front seat beside them, and put all their baggage in the back, and four hours later they were driving through the countryside, where it seemed difficult to believe that there was a war going on. Everything was so pretty and peaceful here, and when they reached Lord Hawthorne's home. Audrey was enormously relieved that they had decided to bring the children there then, instead of waiting any longer. They would be safe and happy here, and he was enchanted to have all three of them, and looked forward to when the two young women would come down again to stay with them.

On the way home, Audrey told Violet that by November she wanted to come down to stay. She figured she'd be too pregnant to stay in London by then. It would be too difficult to run to the shelter every night, and Violet agreed with her.

'You might even think about coming down before that.'

'We'll see.' They were planning to come down again in

two weeks anyway, to spend a few days with the children and relax. But it was a relief for both of them not to have to worry about the children's safety in London any more. 'I feel better, don't you, Vi?'

Lady Vi smiled and nodded as she drove back to London in late afternoon. Everything went perfectly until they got a flat tyre, and the two women had to struggle changing it. Vi wouldn't let Audrey strain herself, for fear that it would do her some harm, so it was several hours before they were back on the road again. Just after they reached London, the air raid sirens began, and they had to abandon the car and go to the nearest shelter. The bombs seemed to be falling everywhere, and a flaming beam narrowly missed them as they dashed across the street, and Audrey heard someone scream. It was a harrowing night. It was midnight before they could come out again, and she and Vi hurried home, trying to avoid the debris in the streets so they wouldn't get another flat tyre. Audrey was exhausted when she got home, and half an hour later, the sirens shrieked again so she had to go back to the shelter. She looked for Vi as they often went to the same one, and she didn't see her for a long time. It was four o'clock in the morning when she realised that she was there as well, sleeping exhaustedly in a corner, wearing a scarf over her head, and an old coat of James's, which was the first thing that had come to hand in the dark cupboard. Audrey sat down quietly next to her, and she was startled when she suddenly felt a sharp pain in her back. She wondered if she had strained it earlier helping with the tyre, although Vi certainly did not let her do much. But the pain came again, and by the time they left the shelter shortly after dawn, she felt the same pain shooting down her legs, and she mentioned it to Vi as they walked home through the rubble.

'I think I've done something to my back.' She was so tired and she could barely move, and it took all the energy she had just to walk as far as Violet's house, as Violet looked at her with a frown.

'When did you do that?'

'God knows. Between the trip and spending the night running from one shelter to the next, I'm probably just tired.' She looked like hell but Violet didn't say anything about it.

'Why don't you come in for a minute before you go home? I'll make you a cup of tea.' Audrey smiled at her, it was the British solution for everything. A night filled with bombs followed by a cup of tea, but she was too tired to walk to her own house, and she went inside gratefully and she sat down in one of Violet's comfortable library chairs. Vi was back only moments later with a steaming cup of tea, and some scones. She always gave Audrey all of her treats. She knew how badly she needed them, and she still thought her too thin. 'How's your back?'

'All right.' But she was lying to her. It still hurt, and now there was a strange gnawing little pain way deep down in her abdomen. Violet saw something troubled in her eyes but she wasn't sure what it was. She sat down and lit a cigarette as Audrey drank her tea in silence.

'Maybe you should go to the doctor today. When are you seeing him again?'

'Not for another week.' She would be a good three months pregnant then, and she could hardly zip up her skirts any more. She didn't mind it. She felt proud of the little bulge, and she was excited thinking about when it would be really obvious. She could hardly wait to tell Charlie. He might even see it for himself when he came home from North Africa. 'I'm okay, Vi. Honestly.'

'Are you sure?'

'Quite.' But when she went to the bathroom before going home, she no longer was. There was a spot of blood on her underwear which gave her a shock, and more when she went to the bathroom. It wasn't a great deal, but enough to frighten her, and she mentioned it to Vi when she came out. 'Did that ever happen to you?'

Vi shook her head honestly, but she'd heard of it in

pregnancies that had gone on to produce sound children later on. 'I've heard of it though. It might not be anything. But I think you ought to have it checked.' They called the doctor immediately and he told Audrey to come in right then, if she could. Violet drove her to the hospital where he had to do rounds anyway, and he did not look pleased when he examined her. He asked if her breasts were still sensitive, and if she felt anything strange happening.

'Any cramps?'

'No.' She shook her head. She was deathly pale. And then she remembered the pains in her back, and she told him about them.

'I want you to rest, Mrs Driscoll.' He did not know that she and Charles weren't married. In fact, he didn't know Charles at all. 'I'm going to send you home with your friend, and you *must* stay in bed with your feet elevated, except in the case of an air raid, of course.' She promised to faithfully, and she went to Vi's house instead of her own. It was comforting not to be alone, and they talked endlessly about what it all meant, who they knew who had had what and it had turned out all right, but the bleeding didn't stop, even as Audrey lay in bed. It got heavier that night. Audrey prayed that she wouldn't have to get up for an air raid, and when the sirens began, she begged Violet tearfully to leave her there.

'Nothing's going to happen, Vi, and if I get up it will make the bleeding worse.'

'If you don't get up, you may be dead in an hour.' Violet was adamant with her, and helped her out of bed, putting her fur coat over Audrey's dressing gown. Lots of people went to the shelters half dressed. They were all used to it now, and the only thing one needed were stout shoes, and Violet saw that Audrey was wearing them.

They hurried to the safety of the shelter, and Vi hovered over her like a mother hen until they came home again. The bleeding had not got much worse. In fact, it lessened over the next two days, in spite of their nightly trips to the shelter, but on the third day, Audrey suddenly began having pains. They woke her up as she slept late one afternoon, and she felt a sharp slice of pain that went straight through her guts and she woke with a sharp 'oh' as Violet stood watching her.

'Are you all right?' Her voice was soft in the dim room.

'I don't know . . . I had a . . .' She couldn't even say the words as the pain shot through her again. She clutched the blankets and tried to catch her breath as she stared unseeingly at Vi, who was suddenly frightened for her. 'Oh God . . . Vi . . . call . . . the doctor. . . .'

'Are you bleeding very much?' She knew the doctor would ask, and they threw the covers back hurriedly to see a pool of blood on the sheets all around Audrey.

'Oh my God . . .'

'Never mind . . . it may still be all right . . . lie still . . . I'll be right back.' But she could hear Audrey's moans as she hurried to the phone. The doctor told Vi to bring her in at once, to carry her if she had to, which wouldn't be easy, but she rushed back to wrap her in blankets, as Audrey cried, and she rang for the butler to carry her to the car. He carried her ever so gently and Audrey bit her lip so as not to scream. The pain was the worst she had ever felt, and she kept thinking of Ling Hwei the night Molly was born. She knew now what agony the girl must have gone through, only that must have been even worse than this since the baby was full term. Audrey couldn't even imagine it. There were knife stabs of pain that cut straight through to her heart, and she felt like a freight train was pressing through her, tearing everything in its path. She was almost incoherent when they arrived at the hospital, and a nurse and an orderly put her on a trolley and hurried her inside.

Violet stood by as the doctor examined her, and Audrey screamed horribly. It was terrible to watch her writhe in pain, and as men had done for generations before, Violet found herself wondering if it was all worth it. It was so much worse to watch someone else going through the pain.

The doctor spoke to Lady Vi quietly before they took Audrey away and she was gasping with the pain as a nurse held her hands. 'She's going to lose the child, Lady Hawthorne. She almost has now.'

'Can't you make it easier for her?' It was exactly what James had said when Alexandra was born. But the doctor only shook his head.

'I'm afraid not. But it won't be long now.' It seemed an eternity to Violet as she stood holding her friend's hands. It was another five hours of unthinkable pain before the fetus finally came, already looking too much like a baby. It broke Violet's heart to see the dead baby as they wrapped it up and took it away, and she listened to Audrey sob in her arms. Both women cried, and Violet didn't leave her for two days. She developed a fever and she was still in pain, and it was days before she looked at Violet quietly with dead eyes.

'Thank you, Vi . . . I would have died if it weren't for you . . .'

'You'd have been fine . . . and you were so wonderfully brave.' Violet's eyes filled with tears, and she squeezed Audrey's hands. 'I'm sorry . . . I know how much you wanted it.' Audrey only nodded and turned her head away. She looked as though she had nearly died, which she had. It was the most frightening experience Violet had ever been through. She kept thinking of what she would tell Charles if something happened to Audrey, and the thought horrified her. By the time it had been all over, she had been silently begging Audrey not to die, and she was deeply grateful now. But it was so difficult to find the words to comfort her. She could only imagine how terrible she must feel. 'You'll have another one. Maybe ten of them.' She smiled through her own tears but it was obvious that Audrey didn't believe a word of it.

'It was so terrible, Vi. . . .' Instinctively, she had raised her head in pain, just in time to see the baby slide out of her. She would never forget what an awful sight it was. And she had wanted it so desperately. All she wanted now was to feel Charlie's arms around her and to cry in his arms, but she was grateful for Violet. Vi stayed with her every day until she was able to go home, and then nursed her like a child, keeping her in her own bed, until she finally seemed more herself again. Audrey was amazed at how long it took to get her strength back, and it was fully a month before she was up and dressed and looking herself, although there was something different about her now, something worried and sad. She thought of Charlie all the time and how desperately she missed him. He had written to her several times, but the letters were joking and light. He had no idea of what she was going through. And when Violet finally saw James she told him the whole ghastly tale. He was sorry for both of them, the woman who had suffered so much, and his wife who had stood by her so staunchly in the absence of Charlie.

'You're a damn fine girl, Vi.' He was proud of her. They were having a weekend together before he went back to his bombing raids. 'Poor Charles . . . what a blow. . . .' Vi never thought to tell him Charlie didn't know Audrey was pregnant when he left. 'He always wanted a child. That's why he married that dreadful girl.'

'By the way,' it brought something entirely different to mind. She still hadn't told Aud, and somehow it didn't seem appropriate just now, 'I heard the oddest thing about her, James.'

'Charlotte?' Violet nodded. 'Is she finally divorcing him? It's totally absurd the way she hangs on, and everyone knows the marriage was a farce. One would think she'd give up, the damn fool.' It always infuriated him to know that the woman was keeping Audrey from marrying Charles now, having lost the baby.

'I think I understand it now. I think she wanted to be married to Charles to cover up something else.' Lady Vi spoke hesitantly and James looked intrigued.

'Oh? What's the dirt?' He smiled.

'I hear . . .' She hated to say the word, but she wanted him to know. 'I was told she's a lesbian.'

'Charlotte?' For a moment he sounded amused, and then he looked at her pensively. 'Who told you that?'

'Elizabeth Williams-Strong.' She was the biggest gossip in town, but she usually got things right amazingly. 'And you know, I wasn't inclined to believe her at first, but . . . the oddest thing, I was driving the jeep for General Kildare several weeks ago, before Audrey got sick, and I saw her walking along the street with the most attractive young man . . . actually he looked more like a boy,' she blushed, 'and for some reason I was watching them. I was sitting there waiting for the General to come out of a shop. And do you know . . . it wasn't a boy at all. It was a girl. I'm quite sure it was,' she blushed beet red, 'and they kissed . . . I don't mean on the cheek . . . I mean a long passionate one. . . .'

James suddenly laughed and leapt at his wife. He had been hungry for her for too long. 'You mean like this?' He kissed her passionately, pretending to ravage her, and she pulled away laughing and looked at him.

'I'm serious, James!'

'So am I, by God. I haven't seen you in six bloody weeks!' They made love after that, but in the quiet aftermath as he smoked a cigarette, she looked at him and thought of Charlotte again.

'What do you make of that?'

'I think it explains everything.' And he had had another idea. 'You know, if Charles knew that, he might be able to blackmail her a bit into letting him go. I daresay. I'll tell him myself when I see him next week. Do you mind?'

'Are you serious? Of course not! It would be marvellous if he could ger rid of her.' And then she looked puzzled at what he had said. 'Where are you seeing him? Is he coming home?' He hadn't said anything about it to Audrey in the letter she'd received the day before.

'They're sending me to Cairo for two weeks.'

'Will it be dangerous?' She held her breath as she watched his eyes. She always knew the truth looking at him, but he shook his head and she could see that he was relieved.

'No, it won't. And to tell you the truth, it'll be a relief to stop bombing Hitler's boys. I'm getting damn tired of that.' And so was she.

'I'll ask Audrey if she has any messages for him.'

'Just give him my love,' was all she said and after James had gone, Audrey confessed to Lady Vi, 'How I envy him seeing Charles.' She longed for him now. She was still fighting the depression she had felt since she'd lost their baby. She felt empty and as though somehow she had failed, and the loss seemed overwhelming to her. It embarrassed her to admit it, even to Vi, with so many people losing people they loved, it seemed so shocking to be mourning a baby she didn't even know, but it didn't help reasoning it out. In her heart, it was a loss, and nothing dulled the pain, not even a visit to Molly in the peaceful countryside, although it helped a little bit, and she sat with the child on her lap, looking out over the green hills dotted with cows. She was glad that Molly was there and not in London.

'Is Daddy coming home soon?'

'I hope so, sweetheart. Uncle James went to see him this week, and I told him to give him a big kiss from you.' Molly looked satisfied as she hopped off her mother's lap, and ran back to play with Alexandra and James, but at that very moment James was not delivering a kiss to Charles, but news that rocked him to his very core.

'God, man . . . I'm so sorry . . . They never told me you didn't know.' There were tears in Charlie's eyes and James could have eaten his tongue. He had just told him that Audrey had lost the baby, he thought it was best if he knew, rather than deluding himself that the pregnancy was going on. It had never occurred to him that Audrey hadn't told him before he left that she was pregnant.

'Why didn't she tell me?' His eyes were wild, and James had never felt worse.

'She probably didn't want to worry you. But she's all right. . . .' He said the same thing as Vi. 'And she'll have another one. . . .' Charlie nodded, but he felt as though someone had set his heart on fire.

'Was it very bad?' He looked into James's eyes, and he didn't know what to say. He didn't know whether to lie to him now or not, but it was too late for that.

James nodded miserably. 'Violet said it was pretty awful for her, but she held up admirably. She's all right now though. I saw her myself last week. A bit pale and a trifle thin, but as pretty as ever.' He tried to smile, but Charlie looked desperately worried. He sighed and within an hour he had had seven drinks at Shepheard's bar. James didn't blame him a bit, and later that night, he helped him to his room. He hadn't even had time to tell him what he'd heard about Charlotte from Vi. But there was time for that. He would be in Cairo for two weeks. And they would have plenty of time for the London gossip.

36

James came back from Cairo with lavish messages of love for Audrey. He and Charles had decided not to tell her that he knew of the baby she had lost. It would be better to let her tell him herself when she thought the time was right. But James did tell him about Charlotte being a lesbian and Charlie could hardly wait to come back and put the screws to her. It was high time she stopped torturing him, and if she didn't agree to let him go this time, he was going to threaten to tell her father about her. It had cheered him no end. It was time the bitch got her hooks out of him, he told James, with seething fervour.

They reassigned James to the air raids on Germany, and Lady Vi was alone again. She and Audrey went down to visit the children several times, but during one of these trips, on their way back, Audrey startled her. She handed her a thick manilla envelope when they got back to town, and Lady Vi looked at it in surprise.

'More photographs?' She had taken some beautiful ones of the children and James, and Violet cherished them. But Audrey was shaking her head this time.

'No. My will.' She looked deep into her friend's eyes. 'I want you to promise me that if something happens to me, you'll keep Molly with you, at least until Charlie comes home. And if something should happen to both of us . . .' Her eyes held Vi's, as Violet stared at her. She was obviously still being morbid about the lost child, and Violet was sorry for her.

'Why would something happen to you?'

'You never know.' And then she decided to tell her all at once. 'I've registered with the Home Office as a photo-journalist. I did it a while ago actually, as soon as I lost . . . never mind. They seem to think they can use me as a photographer, and I'm leaving tomorrow night, Vi.' She was almost sorry now. She hated to leave her friend. But it meant being with Charlie again, and she couldn't give that up. For anyone. 'They're sending me to Cairo. I requested North Africa.'

'Does Charles know?' Vi was horrified as Audrey shook her head with a grin.

'Not yet. But he will. I'm hoping to hook up with him, and work on regular assignments with him. The man at the Home Office knows we've worked together before. He seemed to think it was a good idea.'

'Is he mad? You're a woman. My God, that's dangerous!'

Audrey sighed. 'No more than sitting here amidst the bombs every night.' James wanted Violet to go to the country now for a while, and without Audrey she probably would. 'I'm sorry, Vi.' She felt as though she were deserting her. 'I have to be with him.' Her huge blue eyes filled with tears and Violet held out her arms to her.

'You're a damn crazy girl, you know, Aud.' But most of all, she knew she was crazy about him. Audrey wanted to be with Charlie every hour of her life, and in a way, Violet couldn't really find fault with that. She loved James too, but Audrey and Charles shared something even more intense. It was as though they breathed the same air with one breath, and she knew how desperately Audrey had been missing him. 'Can I see you off?'

She shook her head. 'They're putting me on a military flight, and you know how they are about that.'

'Yes, I do.' Violet smiled. Suddenly, everything was changing. The war had affected all their lives, and she couldn't help wondering if it would ever be the same again.

They kissed each other goodbye the following afternoon, and Audrey finished packing her bags. She was leaving the house as it was, empty, locked up, like so many other homes in London.

As she left for the airport that night, she felt a thrill that she hadn't felt in years . . . not since the Orient Express or the trains climbing the mountains of Tibet . . . or the streets of Shanghai . . . or the wonders of Peking. . . . She was on the road again, to a place she had always dreamed of, to be with the man she loved. And she smiled happily to herself, as their plane took off for Cairo.

37

The Douglas DC-3 set down at Cairo Airport at six o'clock the next morning. They had stopped three times to pick up troops, mail, supplies, and to refuel on the way. Audrey was still surprised at how nice the Home Office had been to her.

She had a feeling that they already had a file on her and knew who she was from when they had checked out Charlie during their investigation before allowing him to become a war correspondent. And she also wondered if they weren't anxious to have the American press join them at every opportunity, hoping to sway the United States to enter the war, not that Roosevelt seemed inclined to help them. He had been sitting on his hands for almost a year, and there was no sign of American involvement in the near future. Audrey often wondered herself what it would take to convince them. But she wasn't thinking of her country as the plane set down sharply on the runway. The soldiers who had travelled with her chatted amiably among themselves, told a few more jokes, and collected their gear as they prepared to unload the plane.

'Where are you staying?' one of them asked. He had been admiring her since he boarded in London, and wondered what her legs looked like when she wasn't wearing trousers. She had worn sensible grey tweed trousers, a sweater, and one of Charlie's leather jackets. She had even bought boots that she thought she might be glad to have if they went into rugged areas to work, and she smiled at the young man, knowing how odd she looked in her costume.

'I'm going to try and get a room at Shepheard's.' It was where Charlie was staying, and she wasn't entirely sure if it was reserved for military use only. Charlie had raved about it to her in his letters, and she knew James had stayed there too when he went to Cairo.

'I'll look you up sometime.' The soldier smiled and Audrey looked at him pleasantly but offered him no encouragement. She had thought about buying herself a wedding band for the trip, but she had never hidden behind rules like that, and she didn't want to start now. She was thirty-three years old and independent. She didn't have to feel married to feel safe. After all, she had survived the ordeal of the miscarriage without the benefit of being married. She was still shaken by it and she wasn't sure what she would tell Charlie about it.

There were a thousand things she wanted to tell him when she arrived, but she had to find him first. A military jeep gave her a ride, and she found herself sandwiched between an Australian with a handlebar moustache and a belly laugh and a huge South African with bright red hair and a penchant for really filthy jokes. But she was in a war zone now, and she knew she had to get used to it quickly. It was better than sitting around in London, spending every night in the air raid shelters waiting for the all clear to sound and wondering if she still had a house to go home to.

'Whatcha doing here, luv?' The Aussie was the first to ask, and the driver told him to lay off in an accent that was pure Scots as he winked at Audrey. 'Came out here to see your boyfriend?' He was teasing her, he had seen the huge pack she carried and the twin cameras around her neck, one loaded with black and white film, the other with colour.

'Maybe so.' She smiled.

'Or to find a new one?' the South African suggested. They were all in desert uniforms, she noticed, in the yellows, browns, and greys that concealed them best here. 'I'll volunteer for that job.'

Audrey laughed. 'I have a friend here. He's a war correspondent.' They all booed and hissed as the jeep darted on, avoiding women and children and camels. There were sheep and goats everywhere, and here the women were veiled, as they had been in Turkey and Afghanistan years before when she'd travelled through those countries on the way to

China. She was faintly reminded of that trip now, although the atmosphere here was entirely different. But there was an aura of excitement travelling so far from London. The streets were crawling with European faces, most of them British, and there was an incredible assortment of military personnel here. One saw everything from Indians to New Zealanders, Australians, South Africans, Free French, Greek commandos, and even Yugoslavs and Poles, many of them having fled the Germans and come here to join the British. The Australians and New Zealanders were wearing leather sleeveless army jerkins to protect them from the cold desert nights. And everywhere around them was a cacophony of sounds and smells. It had all the wondrous excitement of her trip halfway around the world seven years before, and she suddenly wondered how she had been satisfied to stay in San Francisco and London for all these years. It was this that she loved so much, the distant and exotic, with all its magical visions and perfumes and promise.

'Want to take my picture, love?' Two men darted at her from the street as they stopped to allow two camels to enter a bazaar and Audrey laughed, and ducked as one of the men tried to kiss her.

'You're American, aren't you?' the South African asked as they got under way again.

'I am.'

'Ever been away from home before?' He smiled at her patronisingly and she laughed. This was no place for an amateur traveller and she wasn't.

'I lived in China for a year several years ago, and I've been living in London for five years now.'

He looked suddenly impressed and she noticed that the others were listening with fresh interest. 'Where in China?'

'Manchuria. Harbin. I ran an orphanage there for a while during the Japanese occupation.'

The Scottish driver whistled and the others looked intrigued as the Australian picked up the conversational ball with a deprecating look at his friend. 'That can't have

347

been easy.' She was obviously quite a woman. 'What did your husband say to all that?' It was a question they all wanted to be sure of, particularly if she was going to be staying in Cairo for a while. It was nice to know a woman's status, and she laughed at the question.

'Don't have one, I'm afraid.' And then she decided to shock them. These were the people she was going to live with from now on, men just like these, day in, day out . . . if Charlie let her stay . . . there was always that hurdle to cross . . . but she wasn't going home, no matter what he said. She had already decided that on the plane. And she was prepared to do battle with him. 'I have a lovely Chinese daughter though.'

They all hooted at once, but the Scotsman caught her eye in the mirror with a grin. 'One of your orphans from Harbin?' She nodded in answer. 'Good girl. How old is she now?'

'Six.' Audrey smiled, ready at the drop of a hat to show them her picture, and she showed a photograph she had taken herself as Molly grinned toothlessly at her. And the men quickly responded in kind. It turned out that despite their interest in her, two out of the three were married, and between them they had seven children. Photographs changed hands and were passed around, and all of them shook hands and introduced themselves, and by the time they arrived at Shepheard's Hotel, they were old friends. There was something amazingly friendly about comrades in wartime, and she was suddenly glad she had come. She wanted to do something useful here instead of merely marking time in London.

All of them got out at the hotel, and Audrey followed them to the desk and asked for Charlie. The desk clerk checked for his key, looked at his notes and informed her that Mr Parker-Scott was out.

'Is he away, or just out?' She wondered if he would even know. The man had a smooth olive skin and beautiful black eyes and she was surprised at how many Egyptians she saw were actually very handsome.

'I believe he's out for the afternoon, madam.' He spoke in impeccable clipped British tones and he sounded almost as though he had gone to Eton, as Audrey thanked him, and walked out onto the terrace to look around. The view was incredibly romantic as they looked out on the beauty of the city, and below them everything was teeming, as men in a dozen different uniforms raced by, calling to each other, and hurrying to their various tasks. Cairo was the centre of all activity, headquarters for the Middle East and African operations, and she sat fascinated on the terrace for hours as she waited for Charles and finally dozed off as she waited. When she awoke the sun was setting on the horizon and she came to with a start as someone grabbed her arm and shook her roughly. She couldn't remember where she was at first, and she looked into a face with familiar eyes, though the rest was not. And then suddenly she laughed as she realised who it was.

'My God, you've grown a beard!' But it was not the beard she noticed now. His eyes were dancing with fury.

'What the *hell* are you doing here?' The desk clerk had told him only that there was a lady waiting for him on the terrace, and he had found her in a corner, slumped over, her bag on the floor beside her, her camera pack on her lap, a hat pulled low over her eyes, and her cameras around her neck, wearing what he considered was a ridiculous outfit. For one second he had been pleased by the vision she presented, and then suddenly a wave of anger had swept over him. He didn't want her here. It was a war zone, and she didn't belong here. He wanted her back in London, in relative safety.

'I came to see you, Charlie.' She held out her arms as she stretched and smiled angelically at him. She had known he would be angry, and she knew she could handle it. He'd calm down eventually, and she knew she had done the right thing. She could never have continued to sit the war out in London while he trotted around the world, writing for assorted newspapers. 'Aren't you going to say hello?' She was fighting not to laugh he looked so enraged. 'I like the beard.'

He stood before her almost trembling with fury. 'Don't even bother to unpack your bags, Aud. You are leaving here on the first plane out tomorrow morning. How did you ever con them into letting you come?'

'I told them I was a freelance photographer,' and then she smiled at him for the clincher, 'and that we always work together.'

'What? And they believed you! The damn fools. . . .' He threw his own hat on the ground, and stalked across the terrace as the people closest to them smiled, and Audrey waited for him to return. He'd calm down sooner or later, and when he walked back towards her, she suggested that they have a drink. But there was something more in his eyes now.

'As long as I'm only staying one night, we might as well celebrate a little bit.' She eyed him in just the way that always melted his heart, but he only growled and slipped uneasily into a chair. He knew better than to trust her. She was far less docile than that, and if she had said she was leaving the next day, he wouldn't have believed her. 'Molly sends you her love.'

'How is she?' His eyes softened just a little bit, but he was not going to let down his guard, he told himself.

'She's fine. She's with Alexandra and James at James's father's place in the country and she seems to love it. He breeds Saint Bernards, and she's found one she loves. She wants to bring one home with her when she comes back to London.' Audrey and Charlie exchanged a smile, the first genuine one since he had discovered her sleeping on the terrace.

'We'll have to let a flat just for the dog.' He laughed softly, but his eyes were filled with worry. He couldn't keep it from her any more, and it was part of why he didn't want her in Cairo. He assumed that she should still be taking it easy. Though in fact, the trip to Cairo was the best thing that had happened to her since the miscarriage. 'There's something you didn't tell me about, Aud . . . before I left. . . .' Her heart pounded, wondering how he had heard, and then suddenly she knew . . . James. . . .

'Oh?' She tried to look nonchalant as she turned away and ordered another drink. 'Not really.'

'Yes, really.' He took a firm hold of her arm and waited till her eyes met his again. 'Why didn't you tell me?'

In spite of herself her eyes were filled with tears. 'I didn't want to worry you.' Her voice was barely more than a whisper. And without another word he took her in his arms and held her as she began to cry. 'I'm so sorry. It's all my fault. I keep thinking that if I hadn't done this or that . . . maybe . . .' She couldn't go on, but he understood.

'You can't do that to yourself, my love. It happened . . . and I'm so sorry . . . but there will be another time. I promise you that.' He smiled tenderly at her, his own eyes damp. 'Next time I hope you'll tell me.' She nodded and smiled as she blew her nose in the handkerchief he gave her. And then his brows knit again. In a way, it was a relief to see her. He had been so worried about her ever since he'd seen James. 'James said it was pretty awful. Are you all right?'

She didn't deny it. 'I'm fine. And Vi was wonderful.'

'I can imagine.' He touched her cheek with his long fingers, and gently kissed her lips, suddenly happier to see her than he would have cared to admit. 'I'm so sorry, Aud . . . I'm sorry I wasn't there.'

'You couldn't have done anything.' She took a deep breath and wiped her eyes again. 'It's been awfully hard . . . with you and Molly gone . . . that was all I could think of.' She turned sad eyes up to him, and he could see that it had taken its toll. 'I had to come.' He nodded. He understood, and perhaps she hadn't been wrong. He signed for their drinks after that and they went upstairs. He carried her bags, and when they reached his room, he carried her over the threshold and deposited her on the bed.

'Welcome home, to the future Mrs Parker-Scott.' He grinned, and she raised an eyebrow.

'Do you know something I don't? Have you heard from Charlotte?' She didn't even dare hope and he shook his head.

'No. But James had an interesting little tidbit. Did he tell you?' She shook her head. 'It appears that my charming wife has an interesting secret.'

'Oh?' Audrey was intrigued and he grinned more broadly. He had been in high spirits since James told him, except for his worry about Audrey. But it would be wonderful if they could get married as a result of his applying a little pressure on Charlotte.

'Apparently the dear lady has peculiar taste. She prefers women.'

'She's a lesbian?' Audrey was not as shy as Lady Vi and she looked at Charlie in amazement. 'Are you sure?'

'Fairly. Apparently Vi saw her kissing some woman on a back street. I'm surprised she didn't tell you.'

'It may have been at the wrong time,' which of course it had been. 'That's amazing. Now what?'

'I threaten to take an ad in the London *Times* if the bitch doesn't give me a divorce, what do you think?' They both laughed and Charles settled down on the bed next to her with a smile and a moment later they forgot everyone ... Charlotte and James ... and Lady Vi ... they remembered only each other and how happy they were to be together again.

38

The next morning, Charlie was more serious again, and he had qualms about letting Audrey stay. 'This is a war zone after all. And Mussolini has started to invade Egypt.'

She laughed gently at Charlie then and squeezed his hand on the table. 'You know how the Italians are, sweetheart. It could take them years to get this far.' And she had no intention of leaving. Day by day he got more used to having her there. A month later they were still waiting for the Italians to attack, and there was a kind of festive atmosphere everywhere. She had become friends with many of the men, and she and Charlie spent hours sitting on the terrace of Shepheard's Hotel, drinking with the other correspondents. The others had all got used to her, and Charlie had even stopped pushing her to go home. He loved having her there, and she really wasn't in any danger. The only unpleasant thing they ever had to deal with were the occasional sand storms they encountered when they were out in the desert. Others had got lost in the violent storms, and Charlie and Audrey had been severely warned by General Wavell, the commanding officer. They had no interest in losing war correspondents to dust storms in the desert. But most of their time was spent in Cairo proper, and the skirmishes with the Italians seemed halfhearted at best. Things were so much in control that Audrey even spoke of going home to Molly briefly for Christmas, but she was afraid that if she went, Charlie wouldn't let her come back, and Violet had written that she was spending Christmas with the children, and her father-in-law and James, and she assured Audrey that Molly was as happy as could be, so she decided to stay on with Charlie in Cairo.

In December, the British got serious about the Italians, and decided to run them out of Libya once and for all. On

January twenty-first, 1941, the British forces took Tobruk, and on February seventh, the Italians surrendered to the British.

But there was something much more interesting going on at that time, which Charlie and Audrey had been hearing about for weeks. Apparently, the Germans were more than a little displeased with the way the Italians had handled the Libyan campaign, and they were sending a German general and a German corps over to take command and give the British a run for their money. Rumours were flying everywhere by the time Tobruk fell, and when the Italians surrendered, everyone was talking about the mysterious German general due to arrive at any moment, and no one in the British High Command knew who he was. It was two days after the Italian surrender that Wavell invited Charlie to dinner, and he was vague with Audrey when he came back about what had been discussed.

'Did he say anything about the German general coming in? Have they heard who it is yet?' It was all anyone spoke of, and even among the other correspondents she'd dined with that night, that had been their main topic of conversation. Everyone wanted the scoop, especially the British.

'No, nothing yet.' But he avoided her eyes while he was undressing.

'Do you think Wavell's worried?' He thought he was very worried, but he didn't want to tell Audrey. What he had to tell her now was that he was going away for a few days and he couldn't tell her where. He was thinking about what to say when she suddenly stood before him. 'You're not listening to me, Charlie.' Her eyes searched his face. She knew him too well. It was exactly what he was afraid of. He could have faced a German general more easily than this woman.

'Yes, I am, Aud. I was just thinking about dinner. Good meal for once. They had some marvellous Egyptian thing for desert.'

'Don't give me that.' She sat on the edge of the bed and eyed him suspiciously. 'You've got something up your sleeve, Parker-Scott. What is it?'

'Oh for heaven's sake. Dammit, I'm tired, Aud, don't interrogate me tonight. If I knew something about the Germans, I'd tell you.' He turned his back on her, pretending to be annoyed, and he did the same once they were in bed, but she was in a playful mood that night and she kept running a hand between his thighs as he tried not to laugh, with his back turned to her in their bed. They had been living at Shepheard's for months now, and it was beginning to feel like home. But he was seriously worried now about what to tell Audrey.

'You're not very friendly tonight, Charlie,' she whispered to him and he rolled over and looked at her with a rueful smile.

'You know, you're a terrible pest sometimes. Has anyone ever told you that?'

She grinned at him, their noses almost touching on the pillow. 'No one's had this kind of opportunity before.' He smiled at her. He knew he was the only man she'd ever slept with.

'Don't you want to get some sleep tonight, Aud?' He had to get up early the next day, but he didn't want to tell her that now.

'I want to know what it is you're hiding from me. Did you fall in love with someone tonight? We already know what happens to you in Cairo. What's up, Charlie?' She propped herself up on her elbow and looked down at him. 'You know, you'd make a terrible spy. I can always tell when you're lying.'

'That's an awful thing to say, Aud.' Her words sent a chill down his spine, and he hoped she never said as much to the Home Office. 'I never lie to you.'

'Not about anything important. But your nose goes white when you tell lies. A little along the same principle as Pinocchio.'

He lay back against his pillows and closed his eyes in the comfortable bed. She was really hopeless. He opened his eyes again and stared at the ceiling. There was no point hiding from her any longer. She would hound him all night. His very own Mata Hari. 'I'm going away for a few days, and I can't tell you where, so don't ask me.'

'Charlie!' she exclaimed in surprise and sat up in bed. 'Then you are doing something you were lying to me about.' She was stunned at how accurate she had been, and he sounded tired and resigned now.

'I was not lying.'

'Yes, you were.' She looked delighted as she looked down at him. 'Now what was it?'

'I told you, Audrey. I can't tell you. It's top secret.' She hesitated at the words, only slightly stymied.

'Is it dangerous?'

'No.' He didn't want her to worry.

'Then why can't you tell me?'

'It's just a little trip with General Wavell. I promised him I wouldn't say anything.' He tried to make it sound like nothing at all that would interest her, and she suddenly wondered if General Wavell had a mistress.

'Is that it?'

'Well . . . Audrey . . . I can't say. It's a question of honour between men.' But he was doing everything he could to convince her, wishing he had thought of that before himself. And she took the bait, much to his relief. He let her attack him again after that, and she kissed him sleepily after they made love.

'How long will you and the General be gone?'

'Just a few days . . . now don't say anything to anyone.' He smiled to himself as she drifted off to sleep. He wasn't as bad a spy as she thought. He just prayed that he would be able to get the information for them.

39

While Charlie was dressing the next morning, Audrey loaded her cameras and sipped a cup of coffee. Their breakfast always came up on trays and Shepheard's served fabulous croissants that she complained were making her fat, but as she sang the same old refrain she glanced at Charlie's dresser with a look of surprise and he froze.

'What are you doing with my passport?' She always kept it in a closed compartment in her camera bag, in case someone asked her for it. She had a great deal more liberty everywhere as an American than she would have if she'd been British. Her American passport was a great advantage to her since America still hadn't entered the war. She was officially neutral as a result, unlike Charlie. She walked towards the dresser now to pick it up, still confused as to how it had got there, while he desperately thought of a reason to distract her as she advanced. He stopped her just before she reached for it and asked if she'd pour him a cup of tea, and as he said it, he scooped the passport up in his hand again and walked across the room as though to put it in her bag for her, but he found that as he fumbled with it, she was watching him and her eyes were very serious now. She set down the pot of tea and stared at him.

'That's not my passport, is it, Charlie?' She had caught on immediately, and he cursed the day he had let her stay in Cairo with him. She was just too damn smart for her own good, and his this time. And there was no avoiding her now.

He shook his head as he looked at her. 'No, Audrey, it's not.'

'Whose passport is it?'

They stood looking at each other from across the room, and she began to understand things for the first time. She suddenly knew now that he had been working for the Home

Office in Intelligence all along. He couldn't deny it to her now. He was going to trust her with his life, and he hoped he wasn't wrong. One careless word on her part could get him killed. 'It's my passport.'

She nodded. She understood perfectly. 'I had no idea before this.' Her voice was almost a whisper as she talked to him. 'Is it in a different name?' She wondered just how far they would go, and just how involved he was.

But he shook his head. 'My mother was American, they were able to get this for me fairly easily actually.' The only thing that had been forged were several entry and exit stamps from immigration offices around the world. He appeared to be fairly well travelled as an American, though not excessively so. Just enough for a journalist, and he had mastered a totally bland American accent that took her totally by surprise when he tried it on her. He had picked it up easily over the years, from his mother and from living with her. He had always been able to mimic his American friends anyway, this was just a little more of the same and she looked at him now with worried eyes.

'This is serious, isn't it?' He nodded. They both knew it was. 'Can I come?'

He shook his head. 'No, you can't.'

'Can I ask where you're going?'

And then he made his first big mistake. 'To Tripoli.' He was only going to tell her that much, but it was all he had to say. She instantly knew why.

'My God, you're going to find out, aren't you? . . .' He was going to find out who the German general was. He was going to pretend he was an American journalist . . . and then he would come back and report to Wavell. 'Charlie, you have to let me come!' She looked frantic now. 'You'll need my photographs.'

His face was harsh. 'I'll take them myself. Audrey, you're not going anywhere.'

'I'll follow you if you don't take me along.'

'You're insane.'

'Who's going to know we're not both for real? It'll look even better if you have a photographer along! And a girl! No one would suspect you of anything. Come on, Charlie . . . give me a break!'

'What is this dammit? A talent contest for *Life* magazine? You damn fool, you'd be risking your life if you came with me. I'm going to Port Said, and I'm taking a little fishing boat to Tripoli. We could get shot at, sunk. The Italians could decide I'm full of shit and kill me on the spot. Or the Germans more likely.' Her eyes filled with tears as she listened to him and she came and clung to him now.

'Don't leave me here. My whole life is with you, Charlie, it always has been . . . this is my destiny . . . you can't leave me now.' He stood there staring down at her, hardening his heart, not wanting to listen to her, but she was so convincing as she pleaded with him.

'I won't risk your neck.' He sounded harsh but only because he loved her so much, but now she sounded angry as she turned to him.

'That's my decision, not yours. And I made that choice myself when I decided to come here. I didn't know it would be like this.' It had been a picnic for them for these months, but the picnic was suddenly over. 'I made a decision to follow you anywhere last July, and I meant it, Charlie Parker-Scott. And you're missing a valuable chance to do this thing right if you don't take me along now. You'll have a lot more credibility if you have a dumb girl with you, with a bunch of cameras hanging around her neck.' What she said was true, but he would have taken anyone but her along.

'I won't take that chance!' He was shouting now, but so was she.

'I will! All right? And if you don't take me, dammit, then I'll meet you there. I'll get a damn jeep and drive there myself.' And suddenly he knew she would. He walked across the room and grabbed her by the arm, and shook her so hard her teeth rattled.

'Be sensible, damn you. I want you to stay here.'

Stubbornly she shook her head, and he sat down heavily in a chair and stared at her. 'I give up. But you're risking my life as well as your own, so you'd better watch your step every inch of the way.'

'I will . . . I swear. . . .' She looked gratefully at him, and he smiled tiredly at her.

'You drive a hell of a hard bargain, you know.'

'I try, sir.' She smiled at him. 'I try.'

40

It took them three hours to get from Cairo to Port Said by jeep, and the fishing boat that had been promised was waiting for them there. Charlie had torn the British labels out of all his clothes and he had told Audrey to bring anything that was either marked USA or was clearly American at first glance. She had worn an ancient pair of sneakers she'd brought along even though they weren't very comfortable, and she was glad that most of the clothes she had with her were old. She had a lot of sweaters she'd brought from San Francisco with her. They had all seen better days, but if someone went so far as to check, their story was more believable this way. He was an American journalist, supposedly, and she a freelance photographer, not that the owner of the fishing boat cared. He was only interested in the money he earned getting them as far as Tripoli. They stopped at Beida, Benghazi, Al-Agheila, and Sirte on the way, and the trip took two days in the smelly little boat. They had made good time, the captain said. Audrey had to fight valiantly not to be seasick, but she didn't dare be ill for fear that Charlie would never let her live it down. She took a few photographs when she felt up to it, and they were both quiet thinking of what lay ahead of them. The reality was brought home to them as they slid quietly into port, amidst the Italian and German warships all around, and the uniforms they saw everywhere. They were on enemy turf now, with one false passport, and if either of them made a slip, they'd both be dead. The owner of the fishing boat could have given them away, but he had been working for the British for the last year and had no desire to lose such a profitable source of income. He dropped them on the dock, and then steamed away again, back the way he had come to Port Said. They were going to have to find their own way back, and Audrey hoped it would be by land. She followed Charlie through the teeming port. They found a man who was willing to drive them to the Hotel Minerva, where Charlie walked her into the bar, and they both ordered drinks and then rented two rooms on the same floor. They chatted quietly for a little while, not sure whether or not to bother seeing the town's few sights.

'What are we supposed to do?' She looked quietly up at him, grateful to be on land again.

'We'll hear what we need to when it happens, I think. Everyone's going to be excited about it here.' She agreed with him, but neither of them expected to hear about it as soon as they did. The German general had arrived that night they learned the next day from two Italians talking excitedly at the bar, and he was staying at a hotel only a few blocks away. They didn't know his name, but he was one of the best, they grinned happily at Audrey and Charles. They were excited to know that they were members of the American press, and news would be released now to everyone.

'The English will shake in their shoes now!' they said, and Charlie smiled winningly at them, and when they left the bar after that, he glanced at Aud victoriously.

'I told you we'd hear.' But they still didn't know his name. They had to learn that now, as they went boldly to the hotel, and walked casually into the bar. Here everything was teeming with activity, and there were German uniforms as well as Italian ones, and an SS guard standing in the lobby talking animatedly. They noticed Audrey almost instantly when she and Charlie arrived, and two of the men smiled hungrily at her. Charlie propelled her straight to the bar with a disinterested look, and sipped sparingly at his drink. He didn't want to get drunk now, and he advised Audrey to be cautious too, while seeming to laugh and talk easily with her.

'Looks like this is where the action is, old girl.' He smiled at her. It was going to be easy now, as long as no one caught on to them, and both of them could feel the sweat roll down their backs and their arms as they fought to stay calm and pretended to be as relaxed as everyone else in the bar. An hour later as they talked about finding a place to eat, a dozen German officers suddenly walked in, and in the midst of them, a stocky, muscular, intensely blue-eyed man walked into the room, observing all of them. Everything about him seemed disciplined and military and neat as he seemed to take in everyone in the room, including Audrey and Charles, with his interested eyes. It was as though he were surveying them as part of his new command, and there was no doubt that this was the man they had come here to see. There was a symphony of clicking heels, endless salutes, and even the Italians looked impressed as his aides referred to him constantly as *Mein General*, but he did not look like a pretentious man, and Audrey said afterwards that he had intelligent eyes. One could almost hear his mind clicking as he looked at all of them, and she almost wanted to salute too. She felt breathless as they looked at him, and she could hear Charlie's breath catch and hoped no one else had. Then the General walked swiftly out of the bar, and her eyes met Charlie's for a long moment, wondering if he had recognised him.

'Do you know who he is?' Her voice was low and Charlie slowly shook his head. There was something familiar about the man and he thought he had seen photographs of him, but he wasn't sure.

'I want to ask around. I'm sure everyone knows.' But as they chatted at the bar for a little while afterwards no one did, except finally a young German officer who openly laughed at them.

'Americans! You must know the name of the greatest general in Germany!' He took them both for fools and shook his head. All of the Germans knew his name, even if the Italians did not. 'General Rommel of course!' Their mission was a success, and Audrey had to force herself not to squeal with delight and clap her hands as they sauntered out of the bar a little while after that. Even Charlie looked pleased with himself, and he squeezed her hand as they hailed a cab to go back to their hotel. They could eat dinner there. And they could go back to Cairo immediately. It had been as easy as that. But Audrey wasn't satisfied with merely knowing his name.

'Why don't we interview him?' she suggested over dinner and Charlie looked horrified.

'Are you crazy? What if they find us out?'

'Find out what? We're Americans. You're a journalist, I'm a photographer. All we can do is ask. . . .' Her eyes danced. 'And wouldn't that be something, Charlie?' She was enjoying herself now, and his dinner sank to the pit of his stomach like a rock as he thought of it. She was clearly out of her mind.

'Listen, you're getting carried away. . . .' But as he thought of it, he knew she was right. As long as they were there . . . and perhaps they could find out something more that way. . . . They talked about it over coffee, and planned it that night. They would go back to his hotel the next day, and leave a note requesting an interview with him. And then they'd wait. Audrey could feel her heart pound in her chest the next morning as they went to the hotel and dropped off the note she and Charlie had composed. They knew that the letter would go through the hands of several aides before reaching him, and it said nothing more than that they were two American journalists in Tripoli and would be honoured by an interview with General Rommel.

The man they handed the letter to asked them to come back at four o'clock that day for a response, and they were met by a pair of inquiring blue German eyes when they did, and they were summarily appraised by a young aide who asked them if they'd met the General before.

'No, we haven't.' Audrey smiled innocently at him. 'But we'd like to. We publish in several American newspapers and magazines, and I know the American public will be fascinated by the head of the new Afrika Korps.' She smiled sweetly at him, and it was obvious that he thought she was terribly stupid.

'We will give you an answer tomorrow at ten o'clock, fraulein.' And he gave Charlie a curt nod as the two walked away casually, chatting about nothing in particular until they got outside, when Audrey turned to him and said in a soft voice, 'You think they're on to us?'

He shook his head. 'I doubt it.' He kept the tone of his voice down, and they said little on the way back to their own hotel. They spent the rest of the afternoon wandering the streets of Tripoli, Audrey being whistled at by the Italians. It was exhausting just being there, feeling the strain of being there under false pretences, and Charlie was afraid they had been overly ambitious with her plot to interview Rommel. They knew all they needed now. They didn't have to go back with more, and he didn't want to delay too long, or the information would have diminished value to the British. 'What do you want to do tonight?' He glanced at her as they stood at the port and she smiled up at him.

'Pray.'

He smiled at her and they went back to their hotel and ate dinner there. They went to bed early and were back at the hotel at ten o'clock sharp the next morning. The same aide eyed them suspiciously as they stepped up to the desk, and Audrey felt her heart pound again as he handed Charlie a sealed note, which Charlie tore open halfway across the lobby. The note gave only the name of the hotel they had just come to and the inscription 13:00. He looked at Audrey in amazement.

'My God, we did it!' He didn't let his face show the excitement he felt and he whispered the words to her as he led the way to the bar; even though it was only shortly after ten in the morning. He ordered two beers, and passed her the single slip of paper. The words had been typed, and he wondered what they would do now. He had a notebook on him for the interview, and Audrey always carried all her cameras with her to be sure that she was prepared, and also to ensure that they weren't stolen.

'What'll we do until one?' She was as nervous as a bride on the morning of her wedding, but the next three hours flew by as they walked along and discussed what they wanted to ask General Rommel. Nothing had prepared them for the man when they finally met him. The rooms he had taken over as his headquarters were as lavish as the rest of the hotel, but he had had at least some of the frills removed and when he walked into the room where Charlie and Audrey waited, they were immediately struck by how important he looked. Even if he were standing stark naked anywhere in the world, one would have known that this was a man of importance, just from his bearing. He had intense, bright blue eyes, and a surprisingly warm smile, and he seemed extremely pleased to see them. He spoke highly of their president and said that he had been to America before the war, although he was too busy to go anywhere now. He looked faintly amused at the mild joke, and Audrey noticed a photograph of a plain woman on a desk nearby, and he instantly saw her eyes roam to the picture.

'This is my wife, Lucy.' And from the way he said it, it was clear that he adored her. It was amazing to think that they had actually got an audience with the man. Only by asking, they had been granted an interview with General Rommel, by pretending to be American journalists. Charlie still couldn't get over how easy it had been, and Audrey was shocked by how easy he was to talk to. He spoke of Germany before the war, of the *Führer* in loving tones that fell just short of the golden tones he had used to describe his wife. And as he spoke and Charlie took rapid notes, it was obvious how deeply entrenched he was in the military. He said that he loved to fly, and he was very interested in the little he had seen of Africa. He made a point of telling Charlie that the Afrika Korps was going to be an extraordinary arm of the army. And then, almost as he said the words he held a hand out for Audrey's camera. She was startled by the gesture and handed it to him, hoping that there was nothing on it to give her away, but they had checked each other over closely

366

before they left Cairo, and she thought they were okay. No telltale matchbooks or bits of paper with the name of their hotel, or room keys, or God forbid, Charlie's British passport, which he had hidden at the hotel in Cairo, taped to the underside of the rug beneath the bureau.

And now Audrey watched him as he meticulously went over her camera. 'Is something wrong?' That deafening heartbeat again, but his eyes met hers with a smile and a nod of approval.

'I have the same one. Only I use a different lens. Here,' he sprang to his feet, 'I show you.' And with two quick strides across the room, he pulled open a drawer and extracted three cameras identical to hers, each one with subtly different lenses, and she was interested in the way he used them. They chatted for several minutes about his lenses and her own, the reasons why he used each one, and why he had the different cameras. He was apparently extremely fond of taking pictures, and he was in no way disturbed when she took photographs of him as Charlie concluded the interview. In the end, they had spent almost two hours with him, and he shook their hands warmly as they thanked him and prepared to leave. 'You will hear great things of the Afrika Korps, my friends.'

'I'm sure we will.' Audrey smiled graciously at him, and it was not entirely insincere. She found that she had to remind herself on the way out of the hotel that these were the people who had murdered Karl Rosen. She looked at Charlie as they walked back to their hotel, still drunk on their own success. 'I hate to say it, but I like him.'

'So do I.' He was still startled by how direct the man was. He had of course not said anything factual about what his plans for the Afrika Korps were but he had been very chatty about everything else they asked him about and it would have been impossible, based on the interview, to hate him. The things that remained clearest about him were that he adored his wife, the army, and his cameras, and very probably in that order. He was the consummate military man

367

in every way, and Charlie found himself wondering if the British would be a match for him. He was beginning to fear that they wouldn't.

They went back to their hotel, packed a few things they had with them, paid, and left, catching a ride to the port. Charlie had decided that it was too dangerous to try and get back to Cairo by the inland route, and he wanted to see if there were any small boats for hire in the port. It took them hours of chatting with the captains of various small vessels but they finally discovered one who would take them as far as Alexandria for an enormous price, and they set out with the tide at sunset. Charlie looked down at her almost breathlessly and put an arm around her shoulders. He was praying that Rommel hadn't had them followed. But even if he had, there was nothing so shocking about their going on to Egypt from there. They were Americans, after all, in search of interesting war stories. He had even praised them for their courage, especially Audrey, 'so far from home', he had said, 'and in such a dangerous place for an attractive young woman'. There had been nothing lecherous in his face, and his eyes lit up every time he mentioned his beloved Lucy. He was a decent, straightforward man and Audrey was sorry they were on opposite sides of the war. She had also heard that his men respected him intensely. He was the kind of commanding officer who got right down and fought with his men. Everyone said he was bringing hundreds of tanks to North Africa.

It took them three days to make the trip this time, and in Alexandria they commandeered a jeep to take them back to Cairo, and when they saw Shepheard's Hotel again at last, it looked like a mirage in the desert. Audrey let out a squeal of glee as they arrived and she threw her arms around Charlie's neck with a gale of nervous laughter.

'We did it! *We did it!*' He told her to keep her voice down, but he was just as ecstatic as she, and he took her with him to see General Wavell an hour later. They only took long enough to shower and change their clothes and Charlie rescued his passport from its hiding place under the rug. It all seemed like a dream now. It was difficult to believe that they had actually interviewed General Rommel.

They drove to the Gezira, a sporting club where Wavell had played golf all afternoon, and he was obviously pleased to see Charles arrive, though a little startled to see Audrey, and Charlie was direct with him about her having gone to Tripoli with him. Wavell's face grew red as he listened, and he looked less than pleased with Charles, until she quietly handed him two rolls of film, and looked into his eyes.

'I think you'll be pleased with these, sir.' He looked at her and then back at Charles.

'I didn't realise you two worked as a team, Parker-Scott.' Charlie was about to say, 'Neither did I,' but didn't think the general would be amused by it. They had followed him into a private room where he locked the door and turned to face them. 'You are very fortunate to have come out alive.' He looked reproachfully at Charles. 'They could have held the girl hostage, you know, if they had reason to doubt your story.' Charlie would have gladly strangled her at that moment but he only nodded contritely at General Wavell.

'We got the information, sir.'

You could have cut the silence in the tiny room with a knife as he looked at them. 'Well?'

'General Rommel.'

A long slow smile dawned over the general's face as he looked at Charles. 'Well, I'll be damned.' And then his eyes narrowed. 'You saw him yourself? You're sure it was he?'

Audrey smiled and looked away. She could hardly wait until he saw the pictures. But Charlie was speaking to the General now. 'Yes, sir.' And then, barely able to repress his own smile, 'We interviewed him, sir.'

'You *what?*'

He took a quick breath and attempted to explain as quickly as he could. 'It was actually Miss Driscoll's idea. We posed as American journalists and interviewed him at his hotel.'

The general stared at them and then sat down in a chair, clutching the two rolls of film in his hand now, as though they might fly away. 'And these are photographs you took of Rommel during that interview?' He couldn't believe these two daredevils standing before him. They were obviously quite mad, but he was pleased that they were.

Charlie gave Audrey the credit she deserved. 'Actually, Miss Driscoll took the photographs, sir. I did the interview.'

'Did you take notes?'

'Yes, sir.' General Wavell beamed at them and pumped first Charles's and then Audrey's hand. 'You two are absolutely extraordinary.' He stared at them once more and then assured them that they would be hearing from him shortly. And in any case he wanted to see them both in his office at eight o'clock the next day. He wanted to see Charlie's notes, although Charlie warned him that Rommel had never shown his hand or said what his intentions were with his new Afrika Korps. But Wavell and his aides wanted all the details now, and they would develop the films that night. He shook their hands once more before he hurriedly left the club, and invited Audrey and Charles to stay on for drinks if they wanted to, but it was a little too sedate for them. They were happy to get back to Shepheard's and see their friends comfortably ensconced in the big wicker chairs on the terrace.

41

The British learned from other contacts in Tripoli in the next few weeks that exactly one month to the day after arriving in Tripoli, General Rommel reviewed his troops. He showed off his beloved new Afrika Korps to those standing by, in fact, much to the amusement of the British contacts, he showed it off several times. He used a canny trick to confuse anyone selling information to their enemies. He had many of the tanks go through the parade again and again, and it was only because of broken treads on two of the tanks that anyone had caught on to it. It was a brilliant trick for him to have used, and all observers were suitably impressed of course. He was a sly, brilliant man, and the British had a profound respect for him, and for Audrey and Charlie now that they had succeeded so well at their task of discovering his identity. The photographs Audrey had taken of him had been blown up and passed around and they were some of the finest that had ever been taken of any of the German High Command. General Wavell had teased her about them more than once.

'Pity you can't send them to his wife, you know. They're awfully nice ... she'd be very happy with them. . . .' But Audrey was too. They showed him as what he was, a thoughtful, intelligent, extremely skilled, perceptive, and probably decent man. She never thought she would say that about any of Hitler's men, and yet she had liked Rommel from the moment they'd met him.

Twelve days after he reviewed his troops in Tripoli, Rommel began moving them east and attacked Al-Agheila, on the coast, using tanks, and the British withdrew thirty miles to the northeast. It was Rommel's first victory, and he had used both his favourite tools on the enemy. He favoured both speed and surprise. He had also flown above the battle in its initial stages to get a better perspective of things, and by noon he was fighting with his troops in a tank of his own. The battle was won by the end of the afternoon. And by April tenth, the British had been forced back all the way to Tobruk, where they dug their heels in. They refused to give up Tobruk and said they wouldn't no matter what. And from Cairo, Charlie and Audrey listened to the tales they heard, and began to worry that Rommel would prevail there. He was a powerful soldier in many ways, and they had been deeply impressed by him. It was frightening to think of him advancing on them now. And the legends that surrounded him grew greater each day. He wore a British officer's desert goggles, 'spoils' he had plucked off the ground following a successful battle, and flew his own plane constantly to get a better feel of the land. He fought side by side with his men, in tanks and on foot, as well as in the air. He seemed to be everywhere from what the returning soldiers said, and it was obvious now that the Afrika Korps was a force to be reckoned with, and new or not, it was clearly made up of some of their very best soldiers.

The battles with Rommel seemed to rage on for months, while the British attempted to hold on to Tobruk and Rommel fought them for it, and Charles even went there once, snuck in by jeep late one night with a small force sent by General Wavell. Everyone was being extremely careful now. They covered any tracks they made in the desert sand, and even took their windshields out so there could be no reflection on the windscreen. They were learning some of their tricks from Rommel himself, who seemed to know them all. Charlie was shocked at how bitter the battle was, how many men were lost and how hopeless it seemed at times. But the British would not give in to Rommel.

Worse, the weather was no longer on their side. The gentle winter months had passed and now the rains made it difficult for tanks to manoeuvre, then the brutal dust storms of the dry months had sprung up, with walls of fine sand that got into everything, blinding everyone, British and German alike, until one choked with the misery of it. The sandstorms were so powerful that they pushed military trucks over on their sides. Helmets were abandoned and heads were wrapped instead, water became even more precious than before, and everywhere there were biting black flies. Once away from the luxuries of Cairo itself, the battlefield was a miserable place, with soldiers getting lost in the desert storms and dying as they wandered aimlessly, or starved to death in tanks. In fact, in early April, six British generals, staggering in the clouds of dust, had wandered inadvertently into a German camp and were taken prisoner.

Rommel and the Afrika Korps got to within sixty miles of Alexandria, and he was flying in spotter planes all the time now, but the British held fast in Tobruk, and Charlie was grateful to get back to Cairo at last to find Audrey waiting for him, relieved that he was all right. She flew into his arms as he came up the steps of the hotel. She had been sitting on the terrace, as usual, with friends, and passing the time while she waited for news of him, and suddenly there he was and she was laughing and crying and kissing his eyes and his cheeks and his beard as he spun her around in his arms.

'Crazy girl, what've you been up to since I've been gone?'

'Just waiting for you, my love.' She smiled into the eyes she loved so much. 'I was worried sick.'

'I'm invincible, my love, like the British fleet.' But there had been reports recently that that wasn't entirely true either. U-boats were taking a high toll of British ships and she looked worriedly at Charlie.

'I was worried about you every minute you were gone.'

'That's a terrible waste of time, Aud.' She followed him inside and they went upstairs to their room. 'We've survived everything else that's happened to us, we'll survive this. And think how lucky we are, we're here together, old girl, not like poor Vi who hardly ever sees James any more.'

'I know . . . but I like it better when the most dangerous thing you do all day is order a double whisky and soda at five o'clock on the terrace.' She smiled and he laughed at her, and with a sweep of his powerful arms he tossed her into bed, and they didn't go downstairs again that night. They lay together in the comfortable bed, and he told her what Tobruk had been like, and they talked and made love and dozed until the dawn when he got up and showered, and came back to the room to look down at her sleeping form. She looked like an angel who had fallen from the carved ceiling into his bed, and he thought about how lucky they were . . . and how lucky he was . . . and then he quietly got back into bed and ran a hand over her flesh again. It did something to him just being in the same room with her, and she smiled as she stirred and opened one eye to look sleepily at him.

'What a nice way to wake up, my love. . . .' She reached out and pulled him close to her, kissing his neck and his chest, and then his lips, her eyes closed, her body and her soul in his hands, ever hungry for him.

The British counter-attacked in June of 1941, hoping to push the Germans back, but General Wavell failed dismally and he was replaced by the man who was lovingly called 'The Auch'. General Auchinleck reorganised the Western Desert force and put General Cunningham in charge, and it took them fully four months to marshal their full strength to push Rommel back again. They met Rommel at Fort Maddalena on November eighteenth at last, and within a week it was clear that Cunningham would do no better where Wavell had failed. And on the twenty-sixth 'The Auch' removed Cunningham as well. On the thirteenth, Rommel lay siege to Tobruk again, determined to take it no matter what it cost him. And this time Charlie knew he had to go back to report on it. The battle was too important to be reported from the terrace of Shepheard's or the Gezira Sporting Club. In many ways, this had been an easy post for him, and he and Audrey went out to dinner every night, and often went to the nightclubs with their friends. But he couldn't do that now, and she was upset when she saw him pack the small duffel bag he took to the field with him.

'You're going to Tobruk again, aren't you?' Her eyes were wide with fear, and he nodded as he looked at her. One thousand men had been lost that day, and 'The Auch' had promised to get him there somehow. 'I don't want you to go.' Her voice was a whisper in the quiet room.

'I have to, Aud. That's why I'm over here.'

'But it's so stupid to get killed for a battle that has gone on for months anyway. They've been fighting over Tobruk since last spring for God's sake. And you've been there once before.'

He smiled gently at her. 'You know I have to, Aud.'

'Dammit, why can't someone else go? There are a million other correspondents here, and this isn't like a spy mission that no one else can do for chrissake. Any dummy can report a siege.'

'Then I guess this dummy will have to do.' He gently took her hand in his. 'Don't worry, Aud. I'll be perfectly fine, and I'll be back in a few days.'

'What if they take you prisoner?' She was suddenly terrified. Something told her that he shouldn't go to Tobruk this time.

'No one wants me except you, old girl.'

'I'm serious.' Her eyes were filled with tears now. And with good reason. It had happened this way once before.

He was gentle but firm with her, and he left late that night while she slept. It was going to be arduous getting there, and harder still sneaking in behind the lines, but he made it and reported on the battle diligently. He had been there for almost four days when he turned his back to hand a wounded man his canteen for a drink of the little water they had left, when he felt a sudden explosion that flattened him to the ground and an excruciating pain that radiated up his back, and the next thing he knew he was flat on his face and people were talking over him. Everything went black after that, and it got very hot and then very cold, and the pain was excruciating as he was bounced along for what felt like days, until he found himself in a tent somewhere behind the

375

lines. Someone had said that there were Bedouins nearby and he wondered if he'd been attacked by one of them, or kidnapped by them, or maybe he was in German hands . . . he didn't know anything any more . . . and it seemed years later when he heard someone call his name, and he thought he heard Audrey's voice though he couldn't be sure of it now. He couldn't be sure of anything except the terrible pain in his back and radiating all the way down his legs.

'Charlie? . . . Charlie . . . sweetheart. . . .' It seemed an eternity before he could open his eyes, but when he did she was looking at him and he was in the British Hospital in Cairo. There was a matron standing by in a starched uniform and there were men moaning everywhere and he found that he was one of them. 'It's all right, sweetheart. You're safe now. . . .' It was days before he was awake enough for her to explain it to him. He had been hit by shrapnel when he had turned to give the man a drink.

'Will I ever walk again?' he said to her mournfully as he lay on his face in the hospital bed, and she smiled at him.

'Yes . . . but you may not sit down. . . .' And then suddenly he understood where the pain was coming from, but it wasn't funny to him no matter how amusing everyone else seemed to think it was. He'd been hit in the buttocks. 'At least it won't show at dinner parties.' He smiled gamely at her, but he still felt like hell from the wound and the long trip back from the front lines.

'How are they doing up there?'

'Famously. We had a major victory. Rommel was pushed back yesterday.' But something even more important had happened in the meantime. 'Charlie . . .' She tried to rouse him from the stupor he fell into now and then from the fever and the drugs. 'The Japanese bombed Pearl Harbor yesterday.' Her voice sounded as though this was terribly important and he tried to concentrate and look at her at the same time.

'Where's that?'

'In Hawaii.' He still wasn't sure what it all meant but

she went on to explain rapidly. 'America's in the war now. Roosevelt declared war on the Japanese. He called it a "day of infamy", and he's right.' It was the place where she had been born, and somehow it hit close to home now just thinking of it, but Charlie was drifting back to sleep again. He was too sick to understand properly, and it was a full week before he was up to talking about it with her, as he lay on his side in his hospital bed.

'Well, you're in it with us now.'

She looked at him with a scowl. 'I've been in it all along.'

'You might have been, but your countrymen certainly were not. Remember that damn speech Lindbergh made in Des Moines in September, urging the United States not to get involved? And Roosevelt was certainly in no hurry to enter the war until they dropped a bomb on his back door. We could have used their help years ago.'

'At least you'll get it now. Or somebody will.' She smiled at him. They were going home in a few days when it was safe to catch a flight out and when Charlie was well enough to fly. There was something she still had to tell. They had already agreed to go down to the country to visit Vi and spend Christmas with Molly there, if there was room for them. It was the ideal place for Charlie to recuperate, but he complained bitterly when they left nonetheless. He wanted to stay in North Africa until the bitter end. He was adamant about it up until they boarded the plane, and then he seemed to relax. He suddenly began thinking of the pleasures of going home, and seeing Vi and James and Molly, and he turned to Audrey with a smile, and for the first time he noticed how pale she was. She didn't look well at all. She'd been indoors for weeks, tending to him, and her tan had faded, but more than that, he could see that she didn't feel well, and he was consumed with guilt for not noticing it sooner.

'How long have you looked like that?'

'Like what?' She feigned innocence, but she realised he was on to her. Finally. She had kept it from him for a long time. She was almost three months pregnant.

'You look pale. Do you feel all right?'

She smiled. She could tell him. They were going home, and there was no danger of his sending her home without him. 'I feel fine . . . considering. . . .' She was teasing him now, and he looked confused.

'Considering what?'

'Considering the fact that I'm almost three months pregnant.'

'You're *what?*' He was stunned as he stared at her. 'And you didn't tell me! God damn it, you should have been in bed all this time.' Neither of them had forgotten the miscarriage of the year before. But she'd gone to the doctor in Cairo, and he had just told her to take it fairly easy. And she had. She'd been careful, but of course she hadn't stayed in bed and she didn't intend to now. 'Are you crazy?' But the shock and anger in his voice faded to delight as he looked into her eyes tenderly. 'You rotten little secretive bitch. . . .' He kissed her. 'I love you.' He put a gentle hand on her tummy and looked at her with happy eyes. 'Can you feel him yet?'

'How do you know it's a boy?' The first one had been, but it was not something she liked to think of.

'Molly needs a brother.' They both smiled and held hands as the plane landed. That night they took the train down to Lord Hawthorne's house, and Vi was waiting for them with sandwiches and hot chocolate, and they peeked in at Molly. Audrey sat on the corner of the bed and stroked her hair, with tears rolling slowly down her cheeks. She looked up at Charles with a smile, and he bent down and kissed them both. It was good to be home . . . better still now that he knew about the baby.

42

The reunion with Molly and Vi and the children was too good to interrupt, but as soon as he was able to travel on his own, Charles insisted on taking the train to London.

'Why? You don't have anything to do there!' It was almost Christmas, and Audrey hated to be away from him, even for a minute, especially now. She seemed to want to cling to him all the time, and they both knew it was because of her condition. They hadn't told Molly yet. They felt it was too soon, and they wanted to be sure that Audrey wouldn't lose the baby, so she wouldn't be disappointed. 'Where are you going, Charles?'

'To do some business, that's all.' He didn't want to say anything to her until after he talked to Charlotte. In her delicate condition, he didn't want to get her hopes up. 'Sit on her today, Vi. Don't let her do anything.'

'I won't.' Violet had been through it once before, and she was going to do everything she could to prevent disaster from striking again. She wagged a finger at her friend and Audrey laughed, wondering where Charlie was going. They kept busy all afternoon, and Charlie sat on the train, thinking of what he would say to Charlotte. It was uncomfortable for him travelling on the train, but he would have walked over hot coals to get where he was going.

The train pulled into the station at exactly five minutes to four, and he hobbled outside on his crutches and hailed a taxi. He gave the driver his publisher's address and sat tensely in the back seat. He didn't even feel the pain of his wound, he was so intent on what he was doing, and he thanked the driver and gave him a handsome tip before hurrying inside, as fast as he could with his crutches. He went to the familiar office and stopped at the secretary's desk. He had decided that it would be best not to call ahead for an appointment, but to surprise her. The girl looked up at him now, she was new and although the face was familiar to her, she didn't know who he was, and she asked for his name when he asked for Charlotte.

'Please be so kind as to tell her it's her husband.' He smiled sweetly at the girl and she looked totally amazed. No one had ever told her that Mrs Parker-Scott had a husband. She just assumed she was widowed or divorced, but now she hurried into Charlotte's office to tell her that her handsome husband had returned from the war. She was thrilled to deliver the good news, much more so than Charlotte was to receive it. And the secretary emerged, red-faced, to explain that Mrs Parker-Scott was busy, and would he please be good enough to call for an appointment. 'Of course.' He smiled at her and walked to Charlotte's office door as the girl gasped.

'No . . . no . . . you can't!'

'It's all right.' He closed the door quietly behind him, and stood looking at Charlotte.

'Hello, Charles.' She sat coolly behind her desk, glancing at his crutches and then his face. 'Wounded?'

'Worse luck for you. Only slightly.'

'I never wished you any harm.' She looked as well coiffed and perfectly groomed as ever.

'I'm not quite sure I'd agree with you on that score.' He approached and sat down awkwardly across from her, never taking his eyes from hers. 'I've come to talk a little business with you.'

She looked briefly annoyed and shrugged. 'It won't do you any good, if you mean what I think you do. Or do you want to discuss your books?'

'Hardly. I handle that with your father, as you know. No, I thought we'd talk about our divorce.'

'Don't waste your breath, Charles. There won't be one.'

'No?' He smiled malevolently at her. 'Don't your friends object, Charlotte? I should think it would annoy them that you're married.'

Her eyes glittered with suspicion. 'What do my friends have to do with it?'

'I don't know. You tell me. Actually, I think it's rather interesting that you're so anxious to cover your homosexuality with the cloak of a respectably married woman.' If he had dared, he would have laughed. She looked as though she were going to choke as she sat there, and she half rose out of her chair, her face first white and then red, as she sat down hard again.

'How dare you suggest such a thing! How *dare* you! You and that dreadful woman you've been living with for all these years, how dare you try to smear me that way . . .' But she looked extremely nervous.

'Not at all.' He remained calm. 'I don't think it such a shocking thing. I'm surprised you're not more honest about it. Then again, you never have been terribly strong at that, my dear, have you?'

'Get out of my office!' She stood up and pointed at the door, but he wasn't moving.

'I'm afraid not, Charlotte dear. I'm not going anywhere until we settle this.'

'You have no proof. . . .' She was beginning to falter, and he moved in for the kill, with a lie even bigger than one of hers.

'I'm afraid I do. I've had you followed for the last year, and . . . well, you know the rest. . . .' He met her eyes and they were hard as steel, as she reached across the desk as though to grab him, but he avoided her easily and grabbed her arm hard.

'You pig!' She was crying, but he didn't feel sorry for her. She had tried to ruin his life, and he was not going to let her ruin Audrey's.

'Why don't we get to the point, Charlotte. I'm not enjoying this any more than you are. I want a divorce. *Now!*'

'Why?'

'That is absolutely none of your affair. But you have a great deal at risk here. And if you don't cooperate, I shall begin by telling your father, in fact I will be happy to show him whatever reports I have,' she paled at his words, 'and then I will smear it all over London.'

'That's slander!'

'Only if it's a lie . . . and it isn't!' Suddenly she deflated like a dying balloon and she stared across her desk at him with hatred.

'You're a rotten son of a bitch. . . .' Her voice trailed off and he shook his head.

'I think I've been a terrific sport about this for years actually, but the game is over now, Charlotte.' He stood up, pulled his crutches into place and looked down at her coldly. 'Are we quite clear? May I have my solicitors call you?'

'I'll think about it.' But she was bluffing and they both knew it.

'I will give you until tomorrow morning. After that, I will come in to see your father . . . with my reports. . . .'

'Get out of my office!' She was shaking from head to foot, and he inclined his head to her with a bitter smile.

'With pleasure.'

He smiled at the secretary when he left, and went back to his own empty house which he hadn't seen in a year and a half. He called Audrey that night and promised to be back the following afternoon. He slept well that night, until the sirens began. The air raids were particularly vicious just then, and he heard that several blocks of houses had been destroyed and the loss of life had been high. When he returned to his own house, he found several windows broken. He boarded them up, and then he bathed and dressed and went back to see Charlotte.

The same secretary was sitting there with a stupefied air, and she looked at him with dismay when she saw him coming. God only knew what Charlotte had told her to tell him. He knew all her ruses by now.

'Mrs Parker-Scott is expecting me.' It was only a half-truth, but the girl shook her head with a look of terror.

'She can't see you.'

'I'm sure.' He advanced on the door as he had the day before and she ran to where he stood, shaking her head.

'You can't go in there. Mr Beardsley is in there. . . .'

'It's all right. He's my father-in-law.' He beamed at her, and let himself in, hobbling in as quickly as he could with his crutches. He knew that her father's presence would unnerve Charlotte still further, and she would agree to what he wanted even more quickly. He had a briefcase under one arm, to convince her that he did have the reports he had mentioned.

But Charles wasn't prepared for the scene that met him in Charlotte's office. She was nowhere in sight, and Beardsley himself was sitting behind the desk with his head in his hands. Charles suddenly wondered if she had told him, for fear that he would do it for her. Beardsley looked up at him and his eyes were bottomless pools of despair and for an instant, Charlie felt sorry for him.

'Hello.' Charlie didn't know what else to say as their eyes met and the older man nodded.

'I didn't know she had an appointment with you.' He glanced at her calendar as though it made a difference. 'I had them call everyone else.'

'Is she ill?' Charlie looked surprised.

'You mean you didn't know?' He shook his head dumbly. 'She was killed last night, in the air raid. Her damn dog ran out of the house, and she went to find him, and a beam pinned her down.' He began to cry and Charlie pitied the man. However rotten she may have been to Charles, her father had adored her. 'They took her to the hospital as soon as they could, but . . .' He looked pitifully at Charlie. 'She died this morning.'

'I'm very sorry.'

Beardsley nodded. 'What did you want? I didn't think you two spoke to each other any more.'

'It's not important now.' He was suddenly embarrassed . . . it's nothing, I just came to blackmail your daughter,

383

sir . . . he felt slimy and anxious to get away. But he had been so anxious to sever his ties with her. It just seemed so ugly now, and so unimportant. He hadn't been fond of her, but he had liked her once, a long time ago, and it was that memory which came to him now. 'I'm sorry, sir. Is there anything I can do?'

Beardsley shook his head, and then looked at Charles pensively with the tears still on his cheeks. 'I never understood what happened between you two. I was very angry at you at first, but she always said it wasn't your fault. Decent of her, I thought.'

'Very,' Charles agreed, choking on the word, but saying it for his sake anyway. 'It was something just between us.' Her father nodded. 'Please let me know if there's anything I can do to help. I'll leave my number with the girl at the desk.' Beardsley nodded again, and Charles exited from the room, looking pale when he emerged and his eyes met those of the young secretary.

'I tried to tell you. . . .'

'It's all right.' He jotted his phone number at Lord Hawthorne's on a scrap of paper, and took a taxi back to the station, and by nightfall he was back in the country. He walked quietly into the large, baronial living room, wondering where everyone was. It had been a long, quiet ride for him on the train, thinking back to when he had married her, and why, and when she had lied to him about the baby. After so many years of hating her, suddenly he had no more malice. He only wanted to put it behind him and marry Audrey, and he was very sorry for old man Beardsley.

'Charles, is that you?' Lady Vi came out of the library wearing an apron, and holding a Christmas ornament in one hand. 'The children have been decorating the tree, it looks lovely.' And then she saw the tired look around his eyes. 'Something wrong?' She was always worried about James, always worried that someone would hear something before she did. But Charlie was quick to shake his head.

'It was just a long boring journey from London.'

She nodded, relieved, and offered him a cup of tea.

'She's fine. She actually took a nap this afternoon. After I threatened to tell you if she didn't.' He followed her into the kitchen and found Audrey there, and when she looked into his eyes, she knew that something had happened.

'What's up?'

'Nothing. Why?'

'You look tired.'

'I am tired.' He waved his crutches as he sat down. 'These don't make life easy.' And they both knew it would be months before he could give them up. His sciatic nerve had been affected by the shrapnel, not permanently they said, but it would take a long time to heal. In some ways, she was glad. She wanted him with her until she had the baby.

But she was still looking at him searchingly as he drank his tea. 'What aren't you telling me, Charles?' She was worried that it might be another spy mission, yet with his wound it didn't seem likely.

He laughed at her persistence. 'Mata Hari.' And then he decided to tell her. Vi was busy with the children again, and they could tell her later. 'Charlotte was killed last night.'

For an instant, Audrey looked stunned, not fully absorbing the implications. 'How do you know?'

'I went to see her yesterday.'

'What for?'

'What we talked about before. To be blunt about it, I went to blackmail her into giving me the divorce. I pretended to have had her followed for the last year.' He wasn't proud of it now, but had she lived, it would have been his only way out of their marriage.

'What did she say?' Audrey spoke quietly, still shocked at the news.

'She was livid, and she would have agreed to the divorce of course. She said she needed to think about it, which was a bluff, and when I went back today, I found her father in her office and he told me. . . .' Audrey reached out a hand and took his, she correctly guessed that he felt awful at what he'd done, and yet he'd had no choice. It was different only with hindsight. Who could have known she would have died last night? 'He was terribly upset and I felt like a complete bastard.'

She nodded. 'It's all right, Charles ... you couldn't help it. Is that why you went to London?'

'Yes.' He sighed. 'The end result is the same in any case, actually as awful as it sounds, this is better. It's quicker. I want to marry you right away.' He smiled and so did she.

'Is that proper?'

'Are you serious? Under the circumstances, it would be ridiculous if I pretended to be in mourning. I barely knew her, and she did everything possible to ruin my life. I hardly owe her a day of mourning.' Although he felt sorry for her anyway, or her father at least. He looked deep into Audrey's eyes. 'Will you marry me, Aud?'

'You know I will.'

'When?' He didn't want to wait a moment longer.

'Now ... tomorrow ... next week, whenever you want to.' She smiled.

They waited for James to come home, and got married the day after Christmas. Both Lord Hawthorne, and James stood up beside Charles, and Vi was the matron of honour. Molly was their flower girl, and Alexandra and James stood by as part of the wedding party. It was a lovely wedding on a crisp, cold sunny day, and Audrey borrowed a beautiful white challis dress from Vi, which was a trifle too big for her but covered the bulge of her growing tummy perfectly. That night Audrey and Charles lay side by side, thinking of how far they had come, and how much they loved each other.

They lay whispering in the dark and after they made love Charlie put an arm around her, and they lay looking at the moonlight, grateful to be far from the air raids in London.

'I want you to stay here until the baby comes.' She didn't like the way he spoke of the war, and she looked up at him worriedly.

'Aren't you staying too?'

'I will for as long as I can. But sooner or later they'll want to send me back, to Cairo or somewhere.'

'Just tell them to wait six months.'

'Just relax. No matter what, I'll be here.' It was a promise he hoped he could keep. He didn't want her to go through anything without him again, and with luck, the baby would come just at the end of his sick leave. He didn't want to be home for much longer. 'What'll we call him, by the way?'

'What about Edward, after my grandfather?'

He liked the sound of it, and pulled her closer to him. 'I like that. And what about Anthony after mine? Edward Anthony Parker-Scott.'

'Edward Anthony Charles . . .' she added with a smile, and drifted off to sleep in his arms. It felt so wonderful to be married.

43

After Christmas, the days seemed to drag, but Audrey felt healthier than she had in years. They went for long walks in the countryside, and Charles seemed to be getting stronger. He had to report to the nearest military hospital once a week, but they seemed to be pleased with his progress. And the baby seemed to be well established. She was getting larger every week and in the spring he teased her about how awkward she was becoming. She had hardly anything to wear, and he took her to London, to check on their house and Vi's and buy some clothes she could wear as she got larger. When they came back they always brought treats for Molly and the other children. Molly was a beautiful little girl, and she was excited about the baby that was coming that summer.

'How does she come, Mummy? Will a fairy drop her off in the garden? . . .'

'Well, no, not quite . . . Daddy and I have to go to the hospital to get the baby. And it might be a boy, you know.' She always referred to the baby as 'she', just as Charlie was certain it was a boy. 'A boy baby would be nice too.'

'Mmm . . .' She looked unimpressed. 'Maybe. Will Daddy have to go back to the war again, after the baby comes?' She looked worried and Audrey pulled her closer as she nodded.

'Yes, sweetheart, he will. Just like Uncle James.'

'And you too?'

Audrey shook her head. 'I'm going to stay here with you and the baby.' Molly looked relieved at her answer. She had survived their absence well, but she preferred having them home, understandably. Audrey was acutely aware of how much Alexandra and James missed their father. Charlie tried to make up for it by playing games with them, taking little James for drives, and even giving him driving lessons in the Chevrolet wagon, but nothing equalled their joy when James came home for an occasional weekend.

He came home at Eastertime, and Vi organised an egg hunt for everyone, writing funny sayings on the eggs, and hiding little prizes and goodies in obvious places. Audrey was more than six months pregnant by then, and Charles teased her about hiding her as the grand prize. She was the biggest egg of all, and he loved feeling the baby move when he put a hand on her stomach.

'Are you sure it's not twins?'

'Charlie, that's not funny!' But even Audrey had to admit she was enormous, and James teased them both about being on their honeymoon with Audrey in that 'shocking condition'. They were all relieved that Audrey and Charles had finally been able to get married.

It was a peaceful, happy time, a respite from the war, and Audrey was only sorry when she got a letter from Annabelle telling her that her husband had been killed in the Pacific. Audrey sat down to write a long serious letter to her, but only two weeks later, Annabelle wrote again. She had got married in San Diego to a naval officer. Audrey was shocked. Annabelle was truly a strange girl, and she could just imagine how badly she was behaving with all the military personnel in San Francisco. It troubled her deeply, but Charlie reminded her that there wasn't a damn thing she could do about it, and she had to admit that it had been years since she'd felt any closeness to her. Her life was here in England, now, and it almost seemed foolish to keep a half interest in the houses in Tahoe and San Francisco, except that she was content to leave them to Annabelle, who seemed to want to continue to live there. Her new husband had already shipped out, and she had returned to the house on California Street with her children, whom Audrey scarcely knew. Little Winston and Hannah.

'Strange, isn't it, how different people can be, even in the same family,' she mused to Charlie as they lay on the grass under a huge tree, her big stomach like a mountain under which she lay, while he gently stroked her coppery mane, and looked at her tenderly. He had never thought her more lovely. As they went back inside, hand in hand, the telephone rang. Charles was the first to pick it up, while Vi was out buying groceries, and Audrey sliced an apple for them to share. Lord Hawthorne had gone with Vi, and the children were all doing their homework with the nurse, even little Molly.

'Yes? . . . yes . . . no, this is Charles Parker-Scott, may I take a message for her?' There was a long silence, as he turned his back to his wife. 'Are they sure?' He spoke in an undertone. 'There's no mistake? . . . when will they know? . . . I see . . . please call us back.' He hung up and for an instant he didn't move as Audrey watched him. When he turned to face her again, his eyes were brimming with tears. He hadn't wanted to tell her, but he couldn't hide it.

'Oh Charlie . . . what is it? . . .' But she knew . . . in her heart of hearts she knew the moment Charlie began to speak on the phone. It was James. 'What happened?'

'James's plane went down after a raid on Cologne. He's missing in action. He may have been killed, or he may have been taken prisoner, they just don't know. They're going to call us back when they know more. Some of the planes aren't in yet.'

'Are they sure he's not one of those?'

He shook his head. 'They saw his plane go down.'

'Oh my God . . .' She sat down in a chair, holding her belly.

'Take it easy, Aud.' He went to get her a glass of water and she took a sip with a trembling hand, but they were both thinking of Vi. The second call came two hours later, just as she walked in the door, and she hurried for the phone as she always did, but Charles beat her to it. 'I've got it, Vi.' He turned his back to her as he had to Audrey with the first call. 'This is Parker-Scott here.' He suddenly sounded very British to Audrey's ears, and much too official. She didn't want this to be happening to them, and she didn't know what they'd say to Vi . . . and it could have been Charles instead of James . . . but she didn't want it to be either one . . . her eyes filled with tears and she had to turn away so Vi didn't see them. Charlie hung up the phone very quickly and his eyes were grim. He looked at Audrey and then at Vi. 'Let's go and sit down.' Violet instantly stiffened.

'What's wrong, Charles? Tell me now.' Her voice trembled as he guided her by the arm to a kitchen chair and sat her down before he spoke.

'I'll tell you as much as I know, Vi. James's plane went down on his way back from a bombing raid in Germany. They went over France, inside the Occupied lines. And no one knows for sure if he was killed. There is simply no way of knowing anything until we hear if he was taken prisoner or not. . . .' . . . or until the end of the war, but he didn't say it. 'The men who saw him go down think he may have made it.' Violet's gasp sounded like a physical pain, and her whole body shuddered.

'I see. When did this happen?'

'Early this morning.'

'Wouldn't they know by now?'

'Not necessarily. They may not know for weeks, or even months. You just have to wait . . . and pray. . . .' But it was terrible telling the children.

Vi told them herself, and little James tried to control himself manfully. He then went outside to sob in Charles's arms, as the women sat with Alexandra and Molly. Vi held her little girl on her lap, and Audrey held Molly. They talked about God, and how good He was, and how much He loved their Daddy. Molly sat watching them all with enormous eyes.

'Will Uncle James meet my other Mommy and Daddy now too?' She knew she had been born in China of other parents, and Audrey held her close to her with tears rolling down her cheeks.

'Maybe, sweetheart. But maybe he'll come home to us again.' And maybe not. Not knowing was the worst part.

After they got the children to bed, Violet sat staring into the fire with a look of complete despair. Telling the children that their father might be dead was the most difficult thing she had ever done, and now Audrey held out a hand to her, and the two women sat side by side, holding hands, talking about James.

'I still think he'll be home anyway. Does that sound very foolish?' She looked at both of them as tears flowed again, and Audrey told her that she wanted to believe the same thing. 'Perhaps the Free French will help him. He speaks French beautifully . . .' Her voice trailed off, and she insisted on going upstairs to bring Lord Hawthorne a brandy. He had retired to his study and was too proud to cry with the rest of them, but Charles knew how anguished he must be about James.

It was midnight before they all went to bed, and they kept waiting for the phone to ring, for news of James . . . that he had returned . . . that it was all a mistake . . . but the phone didn't ring again that evening.

44

The last days of her pregnancy were truly miserable for Audrey. Charles was almost well now, and he was getting restless being there. The disappearance of James had made him even more anxious to go back to the war and do something useful. Violet seemed much more high-strung than she had been before, although in quiet moments she insisted that she still felt as though James were alive somewhere, and she wouldn't give up hope until someone could tell her certainly that her husband had not survived his mission. But with each passing day, it seemed less likely that he had lived when his plane crashed.

The children were adjusting slowly to the reality, although perhaps less well than they might have if Violet had been able to admit that he was dead, or if they knew it for certain. It was difficult insisting that he was only temporarily absent from their lives. He was sorely missed by all, especially Vi and the children.

Audrey had got so enormous that she could barely move and, to make matters worse, in June they had a massive heat wave. She felt like a mountain on legs and she couldn't breathe at night. She could barely move as the baby kicked and shoved and pounded at her. It was like being beaten up inside, as she explained to Charlie, and two weeks after her due date in July, she was still waiting. The doctor said that that wasn't unusual, and he urged her to go for long healthy walks and to get lots of sleep, both of which seemed impossible to her, as encumbered as she was, but both Charles and Vi forced her to get out and walk frequently, and seventeen days after the baby was due, they had her walking over the rolling green hills, complaining at them as they egged her on, and all three of them laughed at her enormous bulk. The baby's arrival was the only thing that balanced the terrible grief they all felt over James.

'I am absolutely not going to walk one more step, you two. Do you understand? You're going to have to carry me back! First you make me eat an enormous lunch, then you drag me on a fifty-mile hike!' They were laughing, and she sat on a large rock, refusing to move an inch. 'This is *it*! You'll have to get a truck if you want to get me home.' She looked up at Charles and he laughed.

'It'll have to be an awfully big truck . . .' He said it pensively and she pretended to swat him. But she was genuinely tired when they got home and her back was killing her. Vi offered her a hot water bottle when she complained about it, and then Audrey mentioned something about feeling as though she had the flu.

'What makes you say that?' Vi looked at her suspiciously.

'I've had awful indigestion all day . . . and my back is killing me. . . .'

'Really?' Violet smiled victoriously and informed Charles a little while later that she suspected his son was going to make an appearance fairly soon.

'You mean now?' He looked panicky. 'Did she start?'

'No, no . . .' Violet smiled at him, but her eyes didn't smile any more as they once had . . . not without James. . . . 'I just recognise some of the warning signs. She's getting there.'

'It's about time.' He looked relieved, but he was startled when Audrey started reorganising the nursery that night instead of going to bed. She insisted that she didn't have everything she needed and she didn't get to bed until after one o'clock when he was already asleep. But she simply couldn't get comfortable and she had to get up and walk around. The backache was worse than it had been all day, and she had small nagging pains everywhere. She decided to take a warm bath, but even that didn't help, and then suddenly as she sat in the tub, a strong contraction gripped her, and it took her breath away. She had expected it to start gently, like the books said, but this was rough. And then when it was gone, she wondered if she had imagined how sharp the pain was. She felt better again, and lay lolling in the tub, and then just as she was about to get out, she was hit with another powerful pain, and she had to grip the taps so as not to scream or lose her balance. She got out as quickly as she could afterwards, wrapped herself in a towel, and was about to get Charles when her water broke all over the bathroom floor, and suddenly she felt panicstricken. Things weren't supposed to happen that way. It was all supposed to be orderly and calm, building up to a crescendo that would result in a baby in her arms. This suddenly jangled her, and she was trying not to think of the panic she had felt when she had the miscarriage.

As soon as she could she went to wake Charles. It was after four o'clock, and he stirred sleepily and then stared at her.

'I think this is it.' But she didn't look pleased. She looked frightened, and she held out a hand to him. 'Charlie . . . I'm scared. . . .'

'Don't be.' He sat up and smiled gently at her. 'It's going to be fine, darling. I'll get dressed. You just sit there, and then I'll help you get dressed too.' But before he could move, she had another pain again, and she clutched his arms, trying to catch her breath and fight the agony all at the same time, and he was shocked to see how much pain she was in. 'How long has this gone on?' He wondered why she hadn't wakened him sooner.

'I've only had a few pains like that . . . but they're . . . oh God . . . Charlie . . . oh . . .' She couldn't speak as she clung to him, and he helped her back onto the bed with a worried look.

'I'll call the doctor.'

'Don't leave me. . . .' She was already having another pain. It was incredible. She was already in hard labour and it had only started half an hour before.

'Just let me call the doctor, I'll be right back.' He tapped on Vi's door on the way and told her what was happening, as he hurried to the phone. The doctor answered sleepily and said he would meet them at the hospital right away. He sounded perfectly calm and Charlie envied him as he hurried back to their room, where Audrey was gripping Vi's hands, and sitting up in their bed with her legs bent and wide apart, fighting with the pains. Charlie looked at her and then at Vi, speaking to Violet first. 'We've got to get her to the hospital.' Vi wasn't so sure, but she didn't say anything, as Charlie hurried into the bathroom with his trousers and shirt and socks, and emerged again sufficiently dressed to get her to the hospital. He slipped into shoes and looked at Vi again. 'I'll start the car.' But Audrey was shaking her head and gesturing to him frantically, and he couldn't stand leaving her. He came back to the bed, and looked into her eyes. She looked so frightened and she was in so much pain. 'I'll hurry, I promise. . . .'

'No . . . don't go . . . I can't go. . . .'

Vi hated to frighten him. 'I think it may be too late. Call the doctor again and tell him what's happening. Maybe he can come here.'

'And have the baby at home?' Charles looked horrified. What if something went wrong? He wanted her in the hospital, but something in Vi's eyes told him he'd best listen to her – only an hour after labour had begun, Audrey had started to scream. The sound unnerved him horribly as he ran back to the phone and caught the doctor just before he left. The doctor agreed with Vi and said he would drive over to Hawthorne House at once. He was as good as his word, fifteen minutes later he was there. By then, Audrey's face was covered with sweat and she was clutching Charles's and Vi's hands, totally out of control, hysterical with the pain as the baby's head pushed down on her, and she suddenly began shaking.

The doctor came quietly into the room, looked at her, and then came closer to the bed, looking into Audrey's eyes with a stern air. He spoke loudly to her, but his voice was not unkind. 'Listen to me. Your baby will be here very soon. Listen to me! I want you to take a deep breath. . . .' He was watching her eyes as they grew wild with the oncoming contraction. 'Now! Breathe! . . .' He took her hands away from Vi and Charles. 'Breathe! Pant . . . pant . . . like a dog . . . that's it!' He was shouting at her and Charles was fascinated, but Audrey was doing what he said, and when the contraction ended this time, she looked pleased with herself. The doctor made her take another deep breath and then close her eyes, and then when he felt the contraction start beneath his hand resting lightly on her stomach, he gave her the same orders again. She was back in control, as Charles stood next to her, watching her. 'I'm going to examine you now, Audrey,' the doctor announced, and he told her to pant again, and asked Charles to hold her shoulders. But this time she lost control again from the pain of his examination. 'It won't be long,' he said quietly to Charles, and then began giving Audrey orders again. She lost her temper once, and for the last five minutes all she did was gasp, push, and scream, but suddenly the doctor moved even closer to her, and at the end of her most horrible scream, the doctor gave a satisfied grunt, and glanced only briefly at Charlie's face as the tears began to pour down his cheeks. The baby's head had appeared and he gave a loud wail as Audrey stared at Charles, who was looking at her and the baby between her legs in amazement.

'Oh, God . . . oh, darling . . . here he comes . . . he's beautiful!' Charlie was overwhelmed as the doctor turned the sturdy little shoulders and delivered the rest of him, and a moment later he lay on his mother's stomach looking up at her, as Charlie touched the son he had wanted for so long, and they both cried, and then looked at Vi, who was crying and laughing with them too. It was the most beautiful thing she'd ever seen. And she told the doctor so as he stood back, looking pleased.

'New methods all that . . . for a very old art.' He smiled at Audrey and her son. 'You did beautifully, Mrs Parker-Scott. Dr Dick-Read would be very proud of you.' He had been using his methods with enormous success, and Audrey had never looked more radiant as Charlie helped her put her son to her breast, and he suckled gently there. An hour later, she lay clean and combed and tidy in her bed, holding him, and Charlie sat next to her, staring at the miracle that had been born to them. He had soft reddish hair much like hers, and enormous eyes, but on the whole he looked rather like Charles, and the scene was so tender that Vi found that she had to leave them. She could almost not bear seeing them that way . . . not since James . . . she was ashamed of herself because she was so happy for them. It was six o'clock and the sun had just come up, and it was a beautiful blue and gold July day, as the birds began to sing in the trees outside.

Vi stepped outside the kitchen door and saw the doctor drive away, and then saw another car drive up, an old battered car she had never seen before, with a man at the wheel. She wondered who it was and couldn't imagine who, and then suddenly her heart stopped . . . it couldn't be . . . it couldn't be . . . she let out a scream that Charles and Audrey heard . . . and Charles left the room hurriedly to see what had happened to her. He saw the open kitchen door, and saw her standing outside, rooted to the spot, her hand over her mouth, as James got out of the car and stood there for just long enough to see the beauty of her . . . the woman he had dreamed of for three months as he crawled out of France, assisted by the Resistance . . . and suddenly there she was as he began to cry, and limped slowly towards her. He had lost an arm, but neither of them cared, he was alive . . . *alive!* . . . Charlie stood looking at them, and turned away. He went back to Audrey with tears running down his face and a look of astonishment, and she suddenly sensed that something more had happened. She sat up straight in bed and looked at him. 'Charlie, what is it?'

He couldn't find the words, and then began to sob . . . they had both come on the same day, only moments apart, his son, and his oldest, dearest friend. . . . 'It's James . . . he's here.' She lay her head back on the pillow, holding the baby, and began to cry. Their prayers had been answered after all. And Vi had been right all along. He had been alive . . . and now he was home.

'Thank God.' She reached out for Charlie's hand, and they sat there, grateful for the blessings bestowed on them.

It was a long time before James came in to see the three of them, and there were no words for what they felt. There were laughter and tears, and a little while later, the children where whooping and shouting and crying too, as James and Alexandra clung to him, and Molly danced around him and then peered at the little brother who had finally come. It was a day none of them would ever forget, and Charles and Audrey agreed easily to add yet another name to their firstborn. He was James Edward Anthony Charles Parker-Scott . . . and a beautiful baby.

45

It took Charlie another month to recover fully from his wounds and then he reported to the Home Office again. It still bothered him a bit from time to time, but not enough to keep him home any more. He had been home for long enough, nearly eight months, and he was anxious to get back into action. But they had new plans for him now. They wanted him to go back to North Africa again, though Casablanca this time. There was a great deal for him to do there, and Audrey was almost jealous when he left. Jealous of the excitement he would find . . . and desperately lonely without him. But he had important work to do. He had confided in her before he left. He was going over as a correspondent again, but he was secretly being assigned to something called Operation Torch. It was a combined British and American effort involving the landing of allied forces in North Africa in the autumn, to give them greater control over the Mediterranean. It was exactly what Charlie had been longing for, and his eyes had been filled with excitement as he explained it to her. He was even to be included in the meetings with General Eisenhower later on. He was shipped to Casablanca to help gather information prior to the landing of the allied troops later in the autumn: Casablanca was unlike Egypt in that it was not held by allied hands, but technically, Casablanca, Algiers, and Oran were all held by the Vichy French although there was constant intriguing going on. The Germans were there as well, though not in any organised form, the Free French, the British, the Americans, and everyone was selling information to everyone else, stealing mules and selling drugs. It was an extraordinary sort of place, and they were prepared for almost anything. The best part of it was that the Germans were too involved farther east to care about these cities now, and there was an excellent likelihood that the landing would be an enormous success as a result of that.

As she listened to him, Audrey had been truly envious, but she had to stay home with the baby now, and it was nice to be able to give Vi some time alone with James, after all she had done for her. Now they exchanged roles. Audrey took care of all four children most of the time, while James and Vi took drives and long walks, and cherished each moment now that he had returned from the dead. Audrey shared all of Charlie's letters with them. Casablanca sounded fascinating, and it was obvious that Charlie was happy there.

According to his letters, the city seemed to be seething with people and intrigue and confusion and decadence, and in an odd way, from what he said, Audrey was reminded of Shanghai. It was so totally different from the orderly life of Cairo, yet not so very far from there. It was filthy and fuming, according to Charles, and his description of his room at the hotel almost made Audrey's skin crawl. But the most important thing of all was that the landing of the allied troops in North Africa depended in great part on him. Of course he couldn't mention that in his letters to her and she was dying to know what was going on.

She knew that the Free French were heavily entrenched there, but officially the Vichy government was in power, although they didn't seem to bother anyone. The officials of the government seemed to be either drinking or with prostitutes most of the time, and it was remarkable what went on right beneath their noses all day long. No one seemed to care, as Italians and Germans and British and Americans wandered through the streets buying and selling whatever it was that had brought them there. Charlie wrote several interesting stories from there, and sent her photographs of children selling cigarettes and hookers standing on street corners, soldiers leering wickedly. It was a potpourri of humanity that sounded fascinating if one could overlook the seaminess of it. He also travelled to Oran and Rabat and Algiers. But Casablanca seemed to be the hub of it.

In September, October, and November the landing forces made their way across the Mediterranean. The Germans knew they were there but couldn't imagine what they were headed for. They were still busy farther east in Egypt and Libya and it took everyone by surprise when the Allies successfully landed simultaneously in Casablanca, Oran, and Algiers on November eighth of 1942. There was some brief skirmishing between the British and the Vichy garrisons, but the British subdued them quickly and Eisenhower's men rapidly settled in. And then the city was much as it had been before, only busier. It still teemed with activity and mystery, and intrigue between various factions shoved together there, and became a clearing house of sorts for the Free French passing people and information to and from the Resistance forces in Occupied France.

In January, Churchill, Roosevelt, and Generals Giraud and De Gaulle arrived in Casablanca for a much celebrated conference which left Eisenhower the Chief of the Allied Forces in North Africa, and shortly after that Tripoli fell into British hands. From that point on, Charlie reported directly to the Americans. He explained it at length to Audrey when he wrote and Audrey explained it to Vi and James. That was all she talked about any more: Charlie and his missions in North Africa, although she only mentioned it to James and Vi.

'Poor thing, she's so desperately lonely without him,' Vi said to James one night. She knew only too well how difficult it had been for her, but at least they knew Charlie was safe, for the moment at least. And he didn't seem to have any terrible missions he was embarking on, at least not from what he said in his letters.

At the time, James was waiting to be reassigned to a desk job, and Vi was thinking of going back to London with him, and leaving the children at Hawthorne House with her father-in-law and of course Audrey would stay on with Molly and Edward, as they called the baby. It was just too confusing to have three Jameses in the house.

'I mean, after all, someone might accuse me of dirtying my

nappies, and him of drinking a beer,' he had teased Audrey one day and she'd laughed. His sense of humour was as good as it ever had been, and Vi was her old self again, although there was still a razor's edge of pain buried in her eyes. She had been through a lot, waiting for news of James, when everyone else thought he had been killed. The tales of how he had made his way through France had been extraordinary. And the worst of them was when he had lost his arm. He had been delirious for eighteen days in a barn in Provence. Audrey shuddered just thinking of it. But now all was well.

In April, Charlie wrote to them that Rommel had returned to Germany, defeated and ill, and Audrey was reminded of the 'interview' they had done with him so long before. It made her hunger to be part of it again. In May, Vi and James moved back to town and opened their house again. He was able to live at home most of the time, and work in an office all day long, and Violet didn't want to be separated from him now. Not even for a day. Audrey understood perfectly, and she was waiting for Charlie to come home for a few days, but she got a telegram a few days before Edward's birthday that he was unable to get away as he had previously promised.

WILL DO MY BEST. SOON AS POSSIBLE. SORRY CAN'T COME HOME NOW. HOLD THE FORT. LOVE ALWAYS. CHARLIE. But she was getting tired of it. She had stopped nursing the baby a few months before, and she had taken photographs of everyone so many times that she couldn't imagine taking one more picture of any of them. And except for Edward, they all seemed to be fairly independent now. Molly had a busy life, and lots of friends, Alexandra and James were growing up, and baby Edward was just as happy with the nurse or Lord Hawthorne as he was with her. She was saying so much to Vi and James when she had dinner with them in London one night, and they had to repair to the shelter again. Nothing had changed.

'I sense that you're building up to something, Aud.' James looked at her. 'Am I correct?' He had read her mind before she knew it herself.

'I wasn't really thinking of that.' It had been a year and a half since she'd come home from North Africa and she was itching to go back, whether she admitted it or not, mostly because she wanted to be with Charlie again, and suddenly as she looked at them both, she knew James was right. That was exactly what she wanted to do. And she went back to the Home Office the next day, and explained her circumstances. She didn't have a hard time convincing them. She had done a good job for them before, and they had plenty of use for her in North Africa. They promised to contact her in a few days, and she hung around with James and Vi waiting to hear from them. When the call came she gave a whoop of joy, and took the train to the country that night. Now, as she thought of it, she wasn't so sure she had done the right thing. The baby still needed her, and Molly too . . . and yet she wanted so much to be with Charlie. The children were safe and content where they were, and she could come back when she wanted to. She was feeling terribly torn as she took the only cab to the house, and walked in the front door to find the baby in Lord Hawthorne's arms gurgling happily, and Molly wrestling with James good-naturedly. They looked up at her and she smiled at them, wondering how she could tell Molly she was leaving again. But Molly surprised her this time.

She sat down on the edge of her bed that night and began stroking the silky black hair that still reminded her at times of Ling Hwei, and told her that she was thinking of going again. 'I'll try not to stay away too long this time.'

'Has Daddy got hurt again?' She turned worried eyes up to Audrey's face. But Audrey shook her head with a reassuring smile.

'No, sweetheart, he's fine. I just feel like I need to be there with him, so he doesn't get too lonely.' It was something about her, and she wasn't proud of it. But it was part of her and it was real . . . the same genes that had led her father to the ends of the earth, and perhaps one day Edward would have the same thing and wonder where it came from.

'But I want to be here, too. Sometimes it's hard to know what is the right thing to do.'

Molly nodded. That made sense to her. She was nine years old, and although she hated seeing her mother go, she understood what she was saying to her. And Alexandra and James's Mummy was away too, although not as far. But they had each other, and Grampa, as they called him now. 'Will you write to me?' She turned her big eyes to her, and Audrey felt a catch at her heart. She felt even worse the next day when baby Edward started walking. It was almost impossible to tear herself away and she could feel herself floundering as she sat quietly in front of the fire with Lord Hawthorne late that night, drinking a glass of port. She was going to miss everyone and everything if she left. But this way, she missed Charlie.

'You have to go where your heart leads, Audrey,' Lord Hawthorne said. In some ways, he reminded her of her own grandfather, although he wasn't as severe or as difficult. But like her grandfather he was a wise man with a kind heart.

'Sometimes it's such a difficult decision to make. I want to be here with them, and there with him, and I don't know what to do.'

'I'll take good care of them for you.' He looked at her with a gentle smile and she knew he would.

'I know that or I wouldn't even consider it. . . .' And in her heart of hearts, she knew she had to go. But it was one of the most difficult things she had ever done, particularly when she held her baby in her arms and then handed him to Lord Hawthorne a few days later, and she hugged Molly for the last time also. She had asked them not to come to the station with her. She couldn't have stood that, and as the car drove away, she looked back and saw Molly running across the lawn after James, with her silky black hair flying in the breeze and little Edward toddling after them, squealing at the top of his lungs and laughing as he fell down. They only waved once and then they went back to their games and she knew they would be all right without her.

46

Audrey saw Vi for only a few moments before she left, and they talked hurriedly. She didn't have much time before her plane, and Violet drove her to the RAF base, and left her at the front gate. She knew it well, and she got out of the car and hugged Audrey.

'Take care of yourself, Aud. And come back safe and sound.'

'We both will. Take care of yourself and James.' The two women exchanged a tearful smile. 'I'm going to miss you terribly.' They had been through so much together, and like the children, she felt traitorous leaving her now. And yet it was so strong in her, to go, and to be with her man, wherever he was.

'You're a marvellous girl. I admire you enormously.'

'For what?' Audrey looked embarrassed and surprised.

'For having the courage to run off and be with him. It's the right thing to do, and the children will be just fine.' It was what she needed to hear and it freed her as she hugged Violet one last time and then watched her drive away as Audrey waved at her.

She reported in after that, and boarded the plane later that night, and a little while later they were on their way. She was suddenly reminded of the trip to Cairo again, when she had gone to find him without warning him. He wasn't expecting her this time either, but somehow she didn't think he'd mind.

It was a long uncomfortable flight in the draughty plane, and the plane came down hard on the runway, jarring her teeth and jangling her nerves. She hadn't seen him in almost a year, and her heart pounded now just thinking of him. She wondered what he would say when he saw her there. Perhaps he'd be furious at her for coming now that they were married and had a child. She clutched her camera as she got off the plane, and as she had done in Cairo, she hopped a jeep to his hotel, and the atmosphere was totally different here. It was more like Istanbul with its mosques and its bazaars and its filth and its smells, but there was a heady perfume in the air and she found her eyes darting everywhere, taking it all in, and instinctively she began focusing her camera and each time they stopped there were a dozen shots she had to take before they drove on, and suddenly she was glad she had come. It was where she belonged, and she took a deep breath and filled her lungs with the pungent odours in the air. She felt like a different person as she got outside his hotel and looked around, and walked slowly inside to ask for him. The man at the desk spoke to her in French and knew exactly who Charlie was.

'*Oui, mademoiselle, il est là.*' He was there. '*Dans le bar.*' She smiled. The bar. Where all business was transacted probably. She walked into the room, feeling her heart pound as it had for him for years, and it reminded her of a dozen other times . . . meeting him in Venice that time . . . and going to Istanbul . . . and Shanghai and Peking . . . watching him leave Harbin . . . meeting him in San Francisco . . . and Antibes and London again . . . Cairo when she'd come to him the first time. They had been around the world, circling it with their hearts and their hands, and now she stood directly behind where he sat, and ran a finger gently down the side of his neck.

'Buy you a drink?' He jumped a foot and turned around with an angry look, much to her delight, and then his eyes grew wide as he looked at her.

'Well, I'll be damned. . . .' He was stunned. 'What are you doing here?' But he did not look displeased. His eyes were warm, and all he wanted was to kiss her. He had missed her terribly, and he would never have dared asked her to come, now that she had the baby to take care of. But he was so glad she had come anyway.

'I just thought I'd see what you were up to . . . since you didn't come home . . .' He grinned in answer.

'Everything all right back there?' She nodded and he signalled to the waiter, and ordered a bottle of champagne.

'Everything at home is fine, and everyone sends you their love.' He pulled a chair out for her and she sat down next to him. She couldn't take her eyes off him, and as the waiter poured their champagne he leaned over and kissed her with the passion he had been saving for her for a year.

He smiled at her and lifted his glass. 'To the wanderlust that brought you back to me . . . and always has . . . and hopefully always will . . .' He looked at her tenderly as she lifted her glass and smiled at him.

'To us, Charlie.'

'Amen.' His eyes danced and he leaned over and kissed her.